KT-457-607

ROMAN BLOOD

A MYSTERY OF ANCIENT ROME

Steven Saylor

ROBINSON
London

Constable & Robinson Ltd
3 The Lanchesters
162 Fulham Palace Road
London W6 9ER
www.constablerobinson.com

First published in the UK by Robinson Publishing Ltd 1997

This paperback edition published by Robinson,
an imprint of Constable & Robinson Ltd 2005

Copyright © Steven Saylor 1997

The right of Steven Saylor to be identified as
the author of this work has been asserted by him in accordance
with the Copyright, Designs and Patents Act, 1988

All rights reserved. This book is sold subject to the condition
that it shall not, by way of trade or otherwise, be lent, re-sold,
hired out or otherwise circulated in any form of binding or cover
other than that in which it is published and without a similar
condition including this condition being imposed on
the subsequent purchaser.

A copy of the British Library Cataloguing in
Publication Data is available from the British Library

ISBN 1-84529-248-0
ISBN 978-1-84529-248-5

Printed and bound in the EU

3 5 7 9 10 8 6 4

DRS 55

Steven Saylor is best known as the author of the Roma sub Rosa series set in ancient Rome and featuring Gordianus the Finder. His work has been widely praised for its remarkable accuracy and vivid historical detail as well as for its passion, mystery and intrigue.

Steven divides his time between Berkeley, California, and Austin, Texas. His web address is www.stevensaylor.com.

Praise for the Roma sub Rosa series

'How wonderful to have a scholar write about ancient Rome; how comforting to feel instant confidence in the historical accuracy of the novel.'   *Sunday Times*

'Saylor has acquired the information of a historian but he enjoys the gifts of a born novelist.'   *Boston Globe*

'Saylor evokes the ancient world more convincingly than any other writer of his generation.' *Sunday Times*

'Saylor's scholoarship is breathtaking and his writing enthrals.'   *Ruth Rendell*

ROMA SUB ROSA

In ancient myth, the Egyptian god Horus (whom the Romans called Harpocrates) came upon Venus engaged in one of her many love affairs. Cupid, her son, gave a rose to Horus as a bribe to keep quiet; thus Horus became the god of silence, and the rose became the symbol of confidentiality. A rose hanging over a council table indicated that all present were sworn to secrecy. Sub Rosa ('under the rose') has come to mean 'that which is carried out in secret'. Thus 'Roma sub Rosa': the secret history of Rome, as seen through the eyes of Gordianus.

To Rick Solomon, this book:
auspicium melioris aevi

CONTENTS

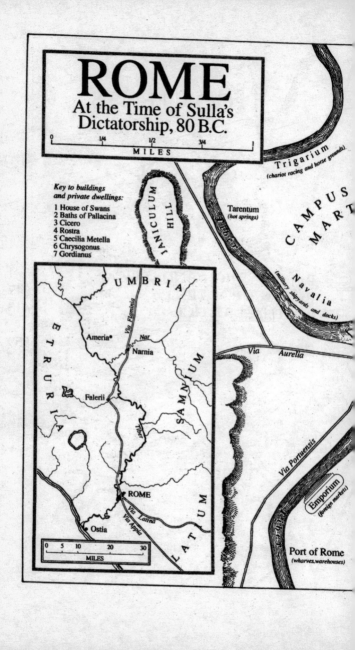

ROME
At the Time of Sulla's Dictatorship, 80 B.C.

0   1/4   1/2   3/4   1
MILES

*Key to buildings
and private dwellings:*

1 House of Swans
2 Baths of Pallacina
3 Cicero
4 Rostra
5 Caecilia Metella
6 Chrysogonus
7 Gordianus

JANICULUM HILL

Trigarium
(chariot racing and horse grounds)

Tarentum
(hot springs)

CAMPUS MARTI

Tiber

Navalia
(military shipyards and docks)

Via Aurelia

Via Portuensis

Emporium
(foreign markets)

Port of Rome
(wharves, warehouses)

UMBRIA

ETRURIA

Via Flaminia

Ameria

Nar

Narnia

SAMNIUM

Falerii

Tiber

ROME

Ostia

Via Latina

Via Appia

LATUM

0   5   10   20   30
MILES

Via Flaminia

Colline Gate

QUIRINAL HILL

VIMINAL HILL

CISPIAN SPUR

ESQUILINE HILL

Agger (defensive earthworks)

Necropolis (public cemeteries)

US

Villa Publica (voting stalls)
•1

•2

Circus Flaminius

Festival Gate

3•

•7

Subura

Forum Holitorium (vegetable markets)

CAPITOLINE

•4

Forum Romanum

OPPIAN SPUR

Tarpeian Rock

Via Sacra

Forum Boarium (cattle markets)

•5

PALATINE HILL

•6

CAELIAN HILL

Circus Maximus

AVENTINE HILL

Piscina Publica (public reservoir and pools)

SERVIAN WALL

Via Ostiensis

Via Appia

Via Latina

Saylor '81

Part One

High and Low

I

The slave who came to fetch me on that unseasonably warm spring morning was a young man, hardly more than twenty.

Usually, when a client sends for me, the messenger is a slave from the very lowest rung of the household – a grub, a cripple, a half-wit boy from the stables stinking of dung and sneezing from the bits of straw in his hair. It's a kind of formality; when one seeks out the services of Gordianus the Finder, one keeps a certain distance and restraint. It's as if I were a leper, or the priest of some unclean Oriental cult. I'm used to it. I take no offence – so long as my accounts are paid on time and in full.

The slave who stood at my door on this particular morning, however, was very clean and meticulously groomed. He had a quiet manner that was respectful but far from grovelling – the politeness one expects from any young man addressing another man ten years his elder. His Latin was impeccable (better than mine), and the voice that delivered it was as beautifully modulated as a flute. No grub from the stables, then, but clearly the educated and pampered servant of a fond master. The slave's name was Tiro.

'Of the household of the most esteemed Marcus Tullius Cicero,' he added, pausing with a slight inclination of his head to see if I recognized the name. I did not. 'Come to seek your services,' he added, 'on the recommendation of—'

I took his arm, placed my forefinger over his lips, and led him into the house. Brutal winter had been followed by sweltering spring; despite the early hour, it was already far too hot to be standing in an open doorway. It was also far too early to be listening to this young slave's chatter, no matter how melodious his voice. My temples rolled with thunder. Spidery traces of lightning flashed and vanished just beyond the corners of my eyes.

'Tell me,' I said, 'do you know the cure for a hangover?'

Young Tiro looked at me sidelong, puzzled by the change of subject, suspicious of my sudden familiarity. 'No, sir.'

I nodded. 'Perhaps you've never experienced a hangover?'

He blushed slightly. 'No, sir.'

'Your master allows you no wine?'

'Of course he does. But as my master says, moderation in all things—'

I nodded. I winced. The slightest movement set

4

off an excruciating pain. 'Moderation in all things, I suppose, except the hour at which he sends a slave to call at my door.'

'Oh. Forgive me, sir. Perhaps I should return at a later hour?'

'That would be a waste of your time and mine. Not to mention your master's. No, you'll stay, but you'll speak no business until I tell you to, and you'll join me for breakfast in the garden, where the air is sweeter.'

I took his arm again, led him through the atrium, down a darkened hallway, and into the peristyle at the centre of the house. I watched his eyebrows rise in surprise, whether at the extent of the place or its condition I couldn't be sure. I was used to the garden, of course, but to a stranger it must have appeared quite a shambles – the willow trees madly overgrown, their hanging tendrils touching tall weeds that sprouted from dusty ground; the fountain at the centre long ago run dry, its little marble statue of Pan pocked with age; the narrow pond that meandered through the garden opaque and stagnant, clogged with Egyptian rushes growing out of control. The garden had gone wild long before I inherited the house from my father, and I had done nothing to repair it. I preferred it as it was – an uncontrolled place of wild greenness hidden away in the midst of orderly Rome, a silent vote for chaos against mortared bricks and obedient shrubbery. Besides, I could never have afforded the labour and materials to have the garden put back into formal condition.

'I suppose this must be rather different from your master's house.' I sat in one chair, gingerly so as not to disturb my head, and indicated that Tiro should take the other. I clapped my hands and instantly regretted the noise. I bit back the pain and shouted, 'Bethesda! Where is that girl? She'll bring us food in a moment. That's why I answered the door myself – she's busy in the pantry. Bethesda!'

Tiro cleared his throat. 'Actually, sir, it's rather larger than my master's.'

I looked at him blankly, my stomach rumbling now in competition with my temples. 'What's that?'

'The house, sir. Bigger than my master's.'

'That surprises you?'

He looked down, fearing he had offended me.

'Do you know what I do for a living, young man?'

'Not exactly, sir.'

'But you know it's something not quite respect- able – at least insofar as anything is worthy of respect in Rome these days. But not illegal – at least insofar as legality has any meaning in a city ruled by a dictator. So you're surprised to find me living in such spacious quarters, as ramshackle as they may be. That's perfectly all right. I'm some- times surprised myself. And there you are, Bethes- da. Set the tray here, between me and my unexpected but perfectly welcome young guest.'

Bethesda obeyed, but not without a sidelong glance and a quiet snort of disdain. A slave herself, Bethesda did not approve of my keeping informal

6

company with slaves, much less feeding them from my own pantry. When she had finished unloading the tray, she stood before us as if awaiting further instructions. This was merely a pose. It was obvious to me, if not to Tiro, that what she chiefly wanted was a closer look at my guest.

Bethesda stared at Tiro, who seemed unable to meet her gaze. The corners of her mouth drew back. Her upper lip compressed and curled itself into a subtle arc. She sneered.

On most women, a sneer implies an unattractive gesture of disgust. With Bethesda one can never be so certain. A sneer does nothing to spoil her dark and voluptuous allure. In fact, it may increase it. And in Bethesda's limited but imaginative physical vocabulary, a sneer may mean anything from a threat to a brazen invitation. In this case, I suspect it was a response to Tiro's genteel lowering of the eyes, a reaction to his shy modesty – the sneer of the wily fox for the comely rabbit. I would have thought that all her appetites had been quenched the night before. Certainly mine had been.

'Does my master require anything more?' She stood with her hands at her sides, her breasts upraised, shoulders back. Her eyelids drooped, still heavy with paint from the night before. Her voice carried the sultry, slightly lisping accent of the East. More posing. Bethesda had made up her mind. Young Tiro, slave or not, was worth impressing.

'Nothing more, Bethesda. Run along.'

She bowed her head, turned, and made her way out of the garden and into the house, weaving sinuously between the hanging branches of willow. Once her back was turned, Tiro's shyness receded. I followed his gaze, from its origin at his wide-open eyes to its focal point, somewhere just above Bethesda's gently swaying buttocks. I envied him his modesty and shyness, his hunger, his handsome-ness, his youth.

'Your master won't allow you to drink, at least not to excess,' I said. 'Does he allow you to enjoy a woman now and again?'

I was unprepared for the full depth and ruddy richness of his blush, as blood-red as a sunset over the open sea. Only the young with their smooth, soft cheeks and foreheads can blush that way. Even Bethesda was too old ever to blush like that again, assuming she was still capable of blushing at all.

'Never mind,' I said. 'I have no right to ask you such a question. Here, have some bread. Bethesda makes it herself, and it's better than you might expect. A recipe passed down from her mother in Alexandria. Or so she says – I have my suspicions that Bethesda never had a mother. And though I bought her in Alexandria, her name is neither Greek nor Egyptian. The milk and the plums should be fresh, though I can't vouch for the cheese.'

We ate in silence. The garden was still in shadow, but I could feel the sun, palpable, almost menacing, edging along the scalloped tile roof like a burglar planning his descent. By midday the whole garden would be suffused with light, insufferably hot and brilliant, but for now it was cooler than the house,

8

which still retained yesterday's heat. The peacocks suddenly stirred in their corner; the largest of the males gave a shrill call and broke into a strut, displaying his plumage. Tiro glimpsed the bird and gave a start, unprepared for the spectacle. I chewed in silence, wincing at the occasional twinges of pain that flickered from my jaw to my temples. I glanced at Tiro, whose gaze had abandoned the peacock for the empty doorway where Bethesda had made her exit.

'Is that the cure for a hangover, sir?'

'What, Tiro?'

He turned to face me. The absolute innocence of his face was more blinding than the sun, which suddenly broke over the rooftop. His name might be Greek, but except for his eyes, all his features were classically Roman – the smooth moulding of the forehead, cheeks, and chin; the slight exaggeration of the lips and nose. It was his eyes that startled me, a pale lavender shade I had never seen before, certainly not native to Rome – the contribution of an enslaved mother or father brought to the empire's heart from gods-knew-where. Those eyes were far too innocent and trusting to belong to any Roman.

'Is that the cure for a hangover?' Tiro was saying. 'To take a woman in the morning?'

I laughed out loud. 'Hardly. More often it's part of the disease. Or the incentive to recover, for the next time.'

He looked at the food before him, picking at a bit of cheese politely but without enthusiasm.

9

Clearly he was used to better, even as a slave. 'Bread and cheese, then?'

'Food helps, if one can keep it down. But the true cure for a hangover was taught to me by a wise physician in Alexandria almost ten years ago – when I was about your age, I suspect, and no stranger to wine. It has served me well ever since. It was his theory, you see, that when one drank in excess, certain humours in the wine, instead of dissolving in the stomach, rose like foul vapours into the head, hardening the phlegm secreted by the brain, causing it to swell and become inflamed. These humours eventually disperse and the phlegm softens. This is why no one dies of a hangover, no matter how excruciating the pain.'

'Then time is the only cure, sir?'

'Except for a faster one: thought. The concentrated exercise of the mind. You see, thinking, according to my physician friend, takes place in the brain, lubricated by the secretion of phlegm. When the phlegm becomes polluted or hardened, the result is a headache. But the actual activity of thought produces fresh phlegm to soften and disperse the old; the more intently one thinks, the greater the production of phlegm. Therefore, intense concentration will speed along the natural recovery from a hangover by flushing the humours from the inflamed tissue and restoring the lubrication of the membranes.'

'I see.' Tiro looked dubious but impressed. 'The logic flows very naturally. Of course, one has to accept the starting premises, which cannot be proved.'

I sat back and crossed my arms, nibbling at a piece of crust. 'The proof is in the cure itself. Already I'm feeling better, you see, having been called upon to explain the mechanics of this cure. And I suspect I shall be entirely cured in a few minutes, after I've explained what you've come for.'

Tiro smiled cautiously. 'I fear the cure is failing, sir.'

'Oh?'

'You've mistaken your pronouns, sir. It's *I* who am to explain my coming to *you*.'

'On the contrary. It's true, as you could tell from the look on my face, that I've never heard of your master – what was the name, Marcus something-or-other Cicero? A total stranger. Nonetheless, I can tell you a few things about him.' I paused, long enough to make sure I had the boy's full attention. 'He comes from a very proud family, a trait of which he himself has a full share. He lives here in Rome, but his family originally comes from some-where else, perhaps to the south; they've been in the city for no more than a generation. They are something more than comfortably wealthy, though not fabulously so. Am I right so far?'

Tiro looked at me suspiciously. 'So far.'

'This Cicero is a young man, like yourself; I suppose a little older. He's an avid student of oratory and rhetoric, and a follower to some extent of the Greek philosophers. Not an Epicurean, I imagine; perhaps he's a Stoic, though not devoutly so. Correct?'

'Yes.' Tiro was beginning to look uncomfortable.

'As for your reason for coming, you are seeking out my services for a legal case which this Cicero will be bringing before the Rostra. Cicero is an advocate, just starting out in his career. Nevertheless, this is an important case, and a complicated one. As for who recommended my services, that would be the greatest of Roman lawyers. Hortensius, of course.'

'Of . . . course.' Tiro mouthed the words, barely whispering. His eyes were as narrow as his mouth was wide. 'But how could you—'

'And the specific case? A case of murder, I think. . . .'

Tiro looked at me sidelong, his astonishment frankly revealed.

'And not just murder. No, worse than that. Something much worse . . .'

'A trick,' Tiro whispered. He looked away, jerking his head, as if it took a great effort to tear his gaze from mine. 'You do it somehow by looking into my eyes. Magic . . .'

I pressed my fingertips to my temples, elbows akimbo – partly to soothe the pressure of my throbbing temples, but also to mimic a mystic's theatrical posing. 'An unholy crime,' I whispered. 'Vile. Unspeakable. The murder of a father by his own son. *Parricide!*'

I released my temples and sat back in the chair. I looked my young guest straight in the eye. 'You, Tiro of the household of Marcus Tullius Cicero,

12

have come to seek my services to assist your master in his defence of one Sextus Roscius of Ameria, who stands accused of killing the father whose name he bears. And – my hangover is completely gone.'

Tiro blinked. And blinked again. He sat back and ran his forefinger over his upper lip, his brows drawn pensively together. 'It *is* a trick, isn't it?'

I gave him the thinnest smile I could manage. 'Why? You don't believe I'm capable of reading your mind?'

'Cicero says there's no such thing as second sight or mind reading or foretelling the future. Cicero says that seers and portents and oracles are all charlatans at worst, actors at best, playing on the crowd's credulity.'

'And do you believe everything master Cicero says?' Tiro blushed. Before he could speak I raised my hand. 'Don't answer. I would never ask you to say anything against your master. But tell me this: has Marcus Tullius Cicero ever visited the oracle at Delphi? Has he seen the shrine to Magna Mater at Ephesus and tasted the milk that flows from her marble breasts? Or climbed the great pyramids in the dead of night and listened to the voice of the wind rushing through the ancient stones?'

'No, I suppose not.' Tiro lowered his eyes. 'Cicero has never been outside of Italy.'

'But I have, young man.' For a moment, I was lost in thought, unable to pull free from a flood of images, sights, sounds, smells of the past. I looked around the garden and suddenly saw just how

13

tawdry it was. I stared at the food before me and realized how dry and tasteless the bread was, how sour the cheese had gone. I looked at Tiro, and remembered who and what he was, and felt foolish for expending so much energy to impress a mere slave.

'I've done all those things, seen all those places. Even so, I suspect in many ways I'm an even greater doubter than your sceptical master. Yes, it's merely a trick. A game of logic.'

'But how can simple logic yield new knowledge? You told me you had never heard of Cicero before I came here. I've told you nothing at all about him, and yet you're able to tell me exactly why I've come. It's like producing coins out of thin air. How can you create something out of nothing? Or discover a truth without evidence?'

'You miss the point, Tiro. It's not your fault. I'm sure you're able to think as well as the next man. It's the sort of logic that's taught by Roman rhetors that's the problem. Retrying ancient cases, refighting ancient battles, learning grammar and law by rote, and all with the point of learning how to twist the law to the client's advantage, with no regard for right or wrong, or up or down for that matter. Certainly with no regard for the simple truth. Cleverness replaces wisdom. Victory justifies all. Even the Greeks have forgotten how to think.'

'If it's only a trick, tell me how it's done.'

I laughed and took a bite of cheese. 'If I explain, you'll have less respect for me than if I leave it a mystery.'

Tiro frowned. 'I think you should tell me, sir. Otherwise, how will I cure myself in the event that I'm ever lucky enough to be allowed to have a hangover?' A smile showed through the frown. Tiro was capable of striking poses no less than Bethesda. Or myself.

'Very well.' I stood up and stretched my arms over my head and was surprised to feel hot sunshine bathing my hands, as palpable as if I had immersed them in steaming water. Half the garden was filled with light. 'We'll take a walk around the garden, while it's still cool enough. Bethesda! I will explain my deductions, Bethesda will take away the food – Bethesda! – and order will be restored.'

We walked slowly, circling the pond. Across the water Bast the cat was stalking dragonflies, her black fur gleaming in the sunlight.

'Very well, how do I know what I know about Marcus Tullius Cicero? I said he comes from a proud family. That much is obvious from his name. Not the family name Tullius, which I've heard before, but the third name, *Cicero*. Now the third name of a Roman citizen generally identifies the family branch – in this case the Cicero branch of the Tullius family. Or, if no branch name exists, it may be unique to the individual himself, usually describing a physical feature. Naso for a man with a large nose, or Sulla, the name of our esteemed and worthy dictator, so-called for his florid complexion. In either case, Cicero is a most peculiar-sounding name. The word refers to the common chick-pea and can hardly be flattering. What exactly is the case with your master?'

'Cicero is an old family name. They say it comes from an ancestor who had an ugly bump on the tip of his nose, clefted down the middle, something like a chick-pea. You're right, it does sound odd, though I'm so used to it I hardly think of it. Some of my master's friends say he should drop the name if he means to go into politics or law, but he won't hear of it. Cicero says that if his family saw fit to adopt such a peculiar name, then the man who first bore that name must have been quite extraordinary, even if no one remembers why. He says he intends to make all Rome know the name of Cicero and respect it.'

'Proud, as I said. But of course that would apply to virtually any Roman family and certainly to any Roman lawyer. That he lives in Rome I took for granted. That his family roots are to the south I assumed from the name Tullius. I remember having encountered it more than once on the road to Pompeii – perhaps in Aquinum, Interamna, Arpinum—'

'Exactly,' Tiro nodded. 'Cicero has relatives all through that region. He himself was born in Arpinum.'

'But he did not live there past the age of, oh, nine or ten.'

'Yes – he was eight when his family moved to Rome. But how do you know that?'

Bast, having given up on catching dragonflies, was rubbing herself against my ankles. 'Think, Tiro.

16

Ten is the age for a citizen's formal education to begin, and I suspect, given his knowledge of philosophy and your own erudition, that your master was not educated in a sleepy little town off the road to Pompeii. As for the family not having been in Rome for more than a generation, I assumed that from the very fact that the name Cicero is unfamiliar to me. Had they been here from the time I was young, I would surely have at least heard of them – and I wouldn't forget a name like that. As for Cicero's age and wealth and his interest in oratory and philosophy, all that is evident simply from observing you, Tiro.'

'Me?'

'A slave is the mirror of his master. Your unfamiliarity with the dangers of wine, your modesty with Bethesda, these indicate that you serve in a household where restraint and decorum are of utmost concern. Such a tone can only be set by the master himself. Cicero is clearly a man of rigorous morals. This can be indicative of purely Roman virtues, but your comment about moderation in all things indicates an appreciation of Greek virtue and Greek philosophy. There is also a great emphasis on rhetoric, grammar, and oratory in the house of Cicero. I doubt that you yourself have ever received a single formal lesson in these fields, but a slave can absorb much from regular exposure to the arts. It shows in your speech and manner, in the polished tones of your voice. Clearly, Cicero has studied long and hard in the schools of language.

'All of which, taken together, can mean only one thing: that he wishes to be an advocate and present legal cases before the Rostra. I would have assumed so at any rate, from the very fact that you came to ask for my services. Most of my clients – at least the respectable ones – are either politicians or lawyers or both.'

Tiro nodded. 'But you also knew that Cicero was young and just beginning in his career.'

'Yes. Well, if he were an established advocate, I would have heard of him already. How many cases has he presented?'

'Only one,' Tiro acknowledged, 'and nothing you would have heard about – a simple partnership case.'

'Which further confirms his youth and inexperience. As does the fact that he sent you at all. Would it be fair to say that you're Cicero's most trusted slave? His favourite servant?'

'His personal secretary. I've been with him all my life.'

'Carried his books to classes, drilled him in grammar, prepared his notes for his first case before the Rostra?'

'Exactly.'

'Then you are not the sort of slave that most advocates send when they wish to call upon Gordianus the Finder. Only a fledgling advocate, embarrassingly ignorant of common custom, would bother to send his right hand to my door. I'm flattered, even though I know the flattery is unintentional. To show my gratitude, I promise not to

18

spread the word that Marcus Tullius Cicero made an ass of himself by sending his best slave to fetch that wretched Gordianus, explorer of dung heaps and infiltrator of hornet's nests. They'd get a bigger laugh out of that than they ever will out of Cicero's name.'

Tiro wrinkled his brow. The tip of my sandal caught on a willow root beside the stream. I stubbed my toe and stifled a curse.

'You're right,' Tiro said quietly, sounding very earnest. 'He's quite young, just as I am. He doesn't yet know all these little tricks of the legal profession, the silly gestures and empty formalities. But he does know what he believes in, which is more than you can say for most advocates.'

I gazed down at my toe, surprised to see that it wasn't bleeding. There are gods in my garden, rustic and wild and unkempt like the garden itself. They had punished me for teasing a naive young slave. I deserved it. 'Loyalty becomes you, Tiro. Just how old is your master?'

'Cicero is twenty-six.'

'And you?'

'Twenty-three.'

'A bit older than I would have guessed, both of you. Then I'm not ten years older than you, Tiro, but only seven. Still, seven years can make a great difference,' I said, contemplating the passion of young men out to change the world. A wave of nostalgia passed through me as gently as the faint breeze that rustled through the willow above our heads. I glanced down into the pond and saw the

two of us reflected in a patch of clear water sparkling in the sunlight. I was taller than Tiro, broader
in the shoulders and heavier in the middle; my jaw
was more prominent, my nose flatter and more
hooked, and my eyes, far from being lavender,
were a staid Roman brown. All we seemed to
have in common were the same unruly black curls;
mine were beginning to show strands of grey.

'You mentioned Quintus Hortensius,' Tiro said.
'How did you know that it was he who recommended you to Cicero?'

I laughed softly. 'I didn't know. Not for certain.
That was a guess, but a good one. The look of
amazement on your face immediately confirmed
that I was right. Once I knew for a fact that
Hortensius was involved, everything became clear
to me.

'Let me explain. One of Hortensius's men was
here, perhaps ten days ago, sounding me out about
a case. The one who always comes to me when
Hortensius needs my help – just thinking of the
creature makes me shudder. Where do men like
Hortensius find such abominable specimens? Why
do they all end up in Rome, cutting one another's
throats? But of course you wouldn't know about
that side of the legal profession. Not yet.

'At any rate, this man from Hortensius comes to
my door. Asks me all sorts of unrelated questions,
tells me nothing – lots of mystery, lots of posing, the
sort of wheedling these types engage in when they
want to know if the opposition has already approached you about a case. They always think the

enemy has got to you first, that you'll go along and pretend to help them anyway, then stab them in the back at the last moment. I suppose it's what they themselves would do in my place.

'Finally he goes his way, leaving a smell in the foyer that Bethesda can't eradicate with three days' scrubbing, along with only two clues as to what he was talking about: the name Roscius, and the town of Ameria – did I know the one, had I ever been to the other? Roscius is the name of a famous comedian, of course, one of Sulla's favourites, everybody knows that. But that's not whom he meant. Ameria is a little town up in the Umbrian hill country, fifty miles or so north of Rome. Not much reason to go there, unless you want to take up farming. So my answer was no, and no again.

'A day or two passed. Hortensius's handyman didn't come back. I was intrigued. A few questions here and there – it didn't take much checking to uncover what it was all about: the parricide case upcoming at the Rostra. Sextus Roscius of the town of Ameria stands accused of plotting the murder of his own father here in Rome. Odd – no one seems to know much about the matter, but everyone tells me I'm better off staying clear of it. An ugly crime, they say, certain to be an ugly trial. I kept expecting Hortensius to contact me again, but his creature never reappeared. Two days ago I heard that Hortensius had withdrawn from the defence.'

I gave Tiro a sidelong glance. He kept his eyes on the ground as we walked, hardly looking at me, yet I could almost feel the intensity of his concentration. He was an excellent listener. Had he been other than a slave, what a fine pupil he would have made, I thought; and perhaps, in another life, in another world, I might have made a fine teacher of young men.

I shook my head. 'Hortensius and his creature and this mysterious trial – I had put it out of my thoughts completely. Then you showed up at my door, telling me I'd been "recommended". By whom? Possibly, I thought, by Hortensius, who seems to have thought it wiser to pass along the parricide case to someone else. To a younger advocate, probably, someone less experienced. A beginning lawyer who would be excited at the prospect of a major case, or at least a case with such a harrowing penalty. An advocate who wouldn't know any better – who wouldn't be in a position to know whatever it is that Hortensius knows. Once you confirmed that it was Hortensius who'd recommended me, it was simple to proceed to the final pronouncement, steered along at every turn by the reactions on your face – which, by the way, is as clear and easy to read as Cato's Latin.' I shrugged. 'To some extent, logic. To some extent, a hunch. I've learned to use both in my line of work.'

We walked along in silence for a moment. Then Tiro smiled and laughed. 'So you do know why I've come. And you know what I was to ask you. I hardly have to say a word. You make it very easy.'

I shrugged and spread my hands in a typical Roman gesture of false modesty.

Tiro furrowed his brow. 'Now if only I could

read *your* thoughts – but I'm afraid that will take some practice. Or does the fact that you've treated me so well already mean that you agree – that you'll lend your services as Cicero needs them? He understands from Hortensius how you work, the fees you'll expect. Will you do it?'

'Do what? I'm afraid my mind reading stops here. You'll have to be more specific.'

'Will you come?'

'Where?'

'To Cicero's house.' Seeing the blank expression on my face, Tiro searched for a clearer explanation. 'To meet him. To discuss the case.'

This stopped me so abruptly that my scraping sandals actually raised a small cloud of dust. 'Your master truly is ignorant of decorum, isn't he? He asks me to his house. Asks *me*, Gordianus the Finder? As a guest? How strange. Yes, I think I very much want to meet this Marcus Tullius Cicero. Heaven knows he needs my help. What a strange one he must be. Yes, of course I'll come. Just allow me to change into something more appropriate. My toga, I suppose. And shoes, then, not sandals. It will only take a moment. Bethesda! *Bethesda!*'

II

The journey from my house on the Esquiline Hill to that of Cicero, close by the Capitoline, would take more than an hour of steady walking. It had probably taken Tiro half that time to reach my door, but Tiro had set out at dawn. We left at the busiest hour of the morning, when the streets of Rome are flooded with humanity, all stirred into wakefulness by the perpetual engines of hunger, obedience, and greed.

One sees more household slaves on the streets at that hour than at any other time of day. They scurry about the city on a million morning errands, conveying messages, carrying packages, fetching sundries, shopping from market to market. They carry with them the heavy scent of bread, baked fresh in a thousand stone ovens around the city, each oven sending up its slender tendril of smoke like a daily offering to the gods. They carry the scent of fish, freshwater varieties captured nearby in the Tiber, or else more exotic species transported overnight up-river from the port at Ostia – mud-caked molluscs and great fish of the sea, slithering octopi and squid. They carry the scent of blood that oozes from the severed limbs and breasts and carefully extracted organs of cattle, chicken, pigs, and sheep, wrapped in cloth and slung over their shoulders, destined for their masters' tables and their masters' already bloated bellies.

No other city I know can match the sheer vitality of Rome at the hour just before mid-morning. Rome wakes with a self-satisfied stretching of the limbs and a deep inhalation, stimulating the lungs, quickening the pulse. Rome wakes with a smile, roused from pleasant dreams, for every night Rome goes to sleep dreaming a dream of empire. In the morning Rome opens her eyes, ready to go about the business of making that dream come true in broad daylight. Other cities cling to sleep – Alexandria and Athens to warm dreams of the past, Pergamum and Antioch to a coverlet of Oriental splendour, little Pompeii and Herculaneum to the luxury of napping till noon. Rome is happy to shake off sleep and begin her agenda for the day. Rome has work to do. Rome is an early riser.

Rome is multiple cities in one. On any given hour's journey across it, one will see at least several of its guises. To the eyes of those who look at a city and see faces, it is first and foremost a city of slaves, for the slaves far outnumber citizens and freedmen. Slaves are everywhere, as ubiquitous and as vital to the life of the city as the waters of the Tiber or the light of the sun. Slaves are the lifeblood of Rome.

They are of every race and condition. Some spring from a stock indistinguishable from their masters. They walk the streets better dressed and more finely groomed than many a free man; they may lack the toga of a citizen, but their tunics are made of material just as fine. Others are unimaginably wretched, like the pockmarked, half-idiot labourers one sees winding through the streets in ragged files, naked except for a cloth to cover their sex, joined by chains at the ankles and bearing heavy weights, kept in line by bullies with long whips and further tormented by the clouds of flies that follow wherever they go. They hurry to the mines, or to galleys, or to dig the deep foundations of a rich man's house on their way to an early grave.

To those who look at a city and see not humanity but stone, Rome is overwhelmingly a city of worship. Rome has always been a pious place, sacrificing abundantly (if not always sincerely) to any and every god and hero who might become an ally in the dream of empire. Rome worships the gods; Rome gives adoration to the dead. Temples, altars, shrines, and statues abound. Incense may abruptly waft from any corner. One may step down a narrow winding street in a neighbourhood known since childhood and suddenly come upon a landmark never noticed before – a tiny, crude statue of some forgotten Etruscan god set in a niche and concealed behind a wild fennel bush, a secret known only to the children who play in the alley

26

and the inhabitants of the house, who worship the forsaken and impotent god as a household deity. Or one may come upon an entire temple, unimaginably ancient, so old it is made not of bricks and marble but of worm-eaten wood, its dim interior long ago stripped of all clues of the divinity that once resided there, but still held sacred for reasons no one living can remember.

Other sights are more specialized to their region. Consider my own neighbourhood, with its odd mixture of death and desire. My home sits partway up the Esquiline Hill. Above me is the quarter of the morgue workers, those who tend the flesh of the dead – embalmers, perfume rubbers, stokers of the flame. Day and night a massive column of smoke rises from the summit, thicker and blacker than any other in this city of smoke, and carrying that strangely appealing odour of seared flesh otherwise found only on battlefields. Below my house, at the foot of the hill, is the notorious Subura, the greatest concentration of taverns, gaming houses, and brothels west of Alexandria. The proximity of such disparate neighbours – purveyors of death on one hand and of life's basest pleasures on the other – can lead to strange juxtapositions.

Tiro and I descended the paved footpath that dropped steeply from my front door, passing the blank plaster walls of my neighbours. 'Be careful here,' I told him, pointing out the spot where I knew a fresh load of excrement would be waiting, slopped over the wall by the inhabitants of the house on the left. Tiro skipped to his right, barely avoiding the pile, and wrinkled his nose.

'That wasn't there when I came up the steps,' he laughed.

'No, it looks quite fresh. The mistress of the house,' I explained with a sigh, 'comes from some backward little town in Samnium. A million times I've explained to her how the public sewers work, but she only answers: "This is the way we did it in Pluto's Hole," or whatever her stinking little town is called. It never stays long; sometime during the day the man who lives behind the wall on the right has one of his slaves collect the stuff and cart it off. I don't know why; the path leads only to my door – I'm the only one who has to look at it, and the only one likely to step in it. Maybe the smell offends him. Maybe he steals it to fertilize his gardens. I only know it's one of life's predictable routines – the lady from Pluto's Hole will throw her family's shit over the wall every morning; the man across the way will carry it off before nightfall.' I gave Tiro my warmest smile. 'I explain this to anyone who's likely to visit me between sunrise and sunset. Otherwise you're likely to ruin a perfectly good pair of shoes.'

The pathway broadened. The houses became smaller and drew closer together. At last we reached the foot of the Esquiline and stepped into the wide avenue of the Subura Way. A group of gladiators, heads shaved except for barbaric topknots, came staggering out of the Lair of Venus. The Lair is notorious for cheating its customers, especially visitors to Rome, but natives as well, which is one of the reasons I've never patronized it, despite its convenient proximity to my house. Cheated or not, the gladiators seemed satisfied. They staggered into the street grasping one another's shoulders for support and bellowing out a song that had as many tunes as there were voices to sing it, still drunk after what must have been a very long night of debauchery.

At the edge of the street a group of young trigon players broke and scattered to get out of the gladiators' way, then reformed to begin a fresh round, each taking his turn at the points of a triangle drawn in the dust. They slapped the leather ball back and forth, laughing loudly. They were hardly more than boys, but I'd seen them going in and out of the side entrance to the Lair often enough to know that they were employed there. It was a testament to the energy of youth that they should be up and playing so early, after a long night's work in the brothel.

We turned right, proceeding westward along the Subura Way, following the drunken gladiators. Another road descending from the Esquiline emptied into a broad intersection ahead. A rule in Rome: the wider the street or the greater the square, the more crowded and impassable it will be. Tiro and I were forced to walk in single file, threading our way through the sudden congestion of carts and animals and makeshift markets. I quickened my pace and called back at him to keep up; soon we caught up with the gladiators.

Predictably, the crowd parted for them like mist before a heavy gust of wind. Tiro and I followed in their wake.

'Make way!' a loud voice suddenly called. 'Make way for the dead!' A cluster of white-robed embalmers pressed in upon our right, coming down from the Esquiline. They pushed a long, narrow cart bearing a body that was wrapped in gauze and seemed to float in a cocoon of fragrances – attar of roses, unguent of clove, unnameable Oriental spices. As always the smell of smoke clung to their clothing, mixed with the odour of burning flesh from the vast crematoria up on the hill.

'Make way!' their leader shouted, brandishing a slender wooden rod of the sort one might use to discipline mildly a dog or a slave. He struck nothing but empty air, but the gladiators took offence. One of them slapped the rod from the embalmer's hand. It flew spinning through the air and would have struck me in the face had I not ducked. I heard a squeal of painful surprise behind me, but didn't bother to look. I stayed low and reached for Tiro's sleeve.

The press of the crowd was too thick for escape. Instead of quietly turning back, as circumstances recommended, strangers were suddenly pushing in from all sides, smelling the prospect of violence and afraid they might miss seeing it. They were not disappointed.

The embalmer was a short man, pot-bellied, wrinkled, and balding. He rose to his full height and a little beyond, straining on tiptoes. He shoved his face, twisted with rage, against the gladiator's. He wrinkled his nose at the gladiator's breath – even from where I stood I caught a whiff of garlic and stale wine – and hissed at him like a snake. The sight was absurd, pathetic, alarming. The huge gladiator responded with a loud burp and another slap, this one knocking the embalmer backwards against the cart. There was a sharp crack of bone or wood, or both; the embalmer and the cart collapsed together.

I tightened my grasp on Tiro's sleeve. 'This way,' I hissed, indicating a sudden opening in the crowd. Before we could reach it the breach was filled with a crush of new spectators.

Tiro made a peculiar noise. I wheeled around. The noise was less peculiar than the expression on his face. He was looking downwards. There was a hard, heavy nudge against my ankles. The cart had spilled its contents onto the street. The body had rolled face-up against my feet, its gauzy shroud unwinding behind it.

The corpse was that of a woman, hardly more than a girl. She was blonde and pale, the way that all corpses are pale when drained of their blood. Despite the waxiness of her flesh, there was evidence of what had once been considerable beauty. The tumble had ripped her gown, baring a single breast as white and hard as alabaster, and a single nipple the colour of faded roses.

I glanced at Tiro's face, at his lips parted with spontaneous, unthinking lust, yet twisted at the corners with an equally spontaneous revulsion. I looked up and spotted another opening in the crowd. I stepped towards it, pulling on Tiro's sleeve, but he was rooted to the spot. I pulled harder. There was sure to be real trouble now.

At that instant I heard the unmistakable metallic slither of a dagger pulled from its sheath and glimpsed a flash of steel from the corner of my eye. It was not one of the gladiators who had drawn the weapon – the figure was on the opposite side of the cart, in the midst of the embalmers. A bodyguard? One of the dead girl's relatives? An instant later – so quickly there was no sense of motion at all, only of displacement – both figure and glint of steel were on the nearer side of the cart. There was a strange ripping noise, tiny but somehow final. The gladiator bent double, clutching his belly. He grunted, then moaned, but the noise was submerged in a loud collective shriek.

I never actually saw the assassin or the crime; I was too busy trying to push through the crowd, which scattered like kernels of grain from a ruptured sack the moment the first drop of blood fell to the paving stones.

'Come on!' I shouted, dragging Tiro behind me. He was still staring over his shoulder at the dead girl, unaware, I thought, of what had happened. But when we were safely away, well beyond the scuffling and confusion that continued around the upset cart; he drew up alongside me and said in a low voice, 'But we should stop and go back, sir. We were witnesses.'

'Witnesses to what?'

'To a murder!'

'I saw nothing. And neither did you. You were looking at the dead girl the whole time.'

'No, I saw the whole thing.' He swallowed hard. 'I saw a murder.'

'You don't know that. The gladiator may recover. Besides, he's probably just a slave.' I winced at the flash of pain in Tiro's eyes.

'We should go back, anyway,' Tiro snapped. 'The stabbing was just the beginning. It's still going on, see? Half the marketplace has been pulled into it now.' He raised his eyebrows, struck by an idea. 'Lawsuits! Perhaps one of the parties will be needing a good advocate.'

I stared at him, quietly amazed. 'Master Cicero is a lucky man, indeed. How practical you are, Tiro. A brutal stabbing takes place before your very eyes, and what do you see? A business prospect.'

Tiro was stung by my laughter. 'But some advocates make a great deal of money that way. Cicero says that Hortensius employs no fewer than three servants whose only job is to roam the streets, keeping an eye out for likely cases.'

I laughed again. 'I doubt that your Cicero would care to take on that gladiator for a client, or the gladiator's owner. More to the point, I doubt that *they* would care to deal with your master, or with any other advocate. The interested parties will seek justice in the usual way: blood for blood. If they don't care to take on the job themselves – though the stabbed man's friends hardly look cowardly or squeamish to me – they'll do what everyone else

33

does, and hire one of the gangs to do it for them. The gang will find the assailant, or the assailant's brother, and stab him in return; the new victim's family will hire a rival gang to return the violence, and so on. That, Tiro, is Roman justice.'

I managed to smile, giving Tiro permission to take it as a joke. Instead, his face became more clouded. 'Roman justice,' I said more sombrely, 'for those who can't afford an advocate, or perhaps don't even know what an advocate is. Or know, and don't trust them, believing all courts are a sham. It's just as likely that what we saw was the middle of such a blood feud, not its beginning. The man with the knife may have had nothing to do with the embalmers or the dead girl. Perhaps he was just waiting for the right moment to strike the blow, and who knows why or how far back the quarrel goes? Best to keep your nose out of it. There's no one you can call upon to stop it.'

This last was true, and a constant source of astonishment to visitors from foreign capitals, or to anyone unaccustomed to life in a republic: Rome has no police force. There is no armed municipal body to keep order within the city walls. Occasionally some violence-weary senator will propose that such a force be created. The response on all sides is immediate: '*But who will own these police*?' And they are right. In a country ruled by a king, the loyalty of the police runs in a clear, straight line to the monarch. Rome, on the other hand, is a republic (ruled at the time of which I write by a dictator, it is true, but a temporary and constitutionally legal dictator). In Rome, whoever plotted and schemed to get himself appointed chief of such a police force would simply use it for his own aggrandizement, while his minions' biggest problem would be deciding from whom to accept the largest bribe, and whether to serve that person or stab him in the back. Police would serve only as a tool for one faction to use against another. Police would merely become one more gang for the public to contend with. Rome chooses to live without police.

We left the square behind, and the Subura Way as well. I led Tiro into a narrow street I knew of, a shortcut. Like most streets in Rome, it has no name. I call it the Narrows.

The street was dim and musty, hardly more than a slit between two high walls. The bricks and paving stones were beaded with moisture, spotted with mould. The walls themselves seemed to sweat; the cobblestones exhaled the odour of dampness, an almost animal smell, rank and not entirely unpleasant. It was a street never touched by the sun, never dried by its heat, or purified by its light – filled with steam at high summer, coated with ice in winter, eternally damp. There are a thousand such streets in Rome, tiny worlds set apart from the greater world, secluded and self-contained.

The alley was too narrow for us to walk side by side. Tiro followed behind me. From the direction of his voice I could tell that he kept glancing back over his shoulder. From the timbre of his voice I knew he was nervous. 'Are there a lot of stabbings in this neighbourhood?'

'In the Subura? Constantly. In broad daylight.

That's the fourth I know of this month, though it's the first I've actually witnessed. The warmer weather brings it on. But it's really no worse in the Subura than anywhere else. You can have your throat slit just as easily on the Palatine, or in the middle of the Forum, for that matter.'

'Cicero says it's Sulla's fault.' The sentence began boldly but ended with an oddly stifled catch. I didn't have to see Tiro's face to know it had reddened. Rash words, for a citizen to criticize our beloved dictator. Rasher still for his slave to repeat it carelessly. I should have let the matter drop, but my curiosity was piqued.

'Your master is no admirer of Sulla, then?' I tried to sound casual, to set Tiro at ease. But Tiro did not answer.

'Cicero is wrong, you know, if that's what he thinks – that all the crime and chaos in Rome is Sulla's fault. Bloodshed in the streets hardly began with Sulla – though Sulla has certainly contributed his share of it.' There, I had put my foot onto thin ice myself. Still Tiro did not respond. Walking behind me, not having to meet my eyes, he could simply pretend not to hear. Slaves learn early to feign convenient deafness and a wandering mind. I could have stopped and turned around to face him, but that would have been making too much of the matter.

Yet I would not let it go. There is something about the mere mention of the name Sulla that fans a fire in every Roman, whether friend or foe, accomplice or victim.

'Most people credit Sulla with having restored order to Rome. At a very high price perhaps, and not without a blood-bath – but order is order, and there's nothing a Roman values more highly. But I take it Cicero has another view?'

Tiro said nothing. The narrow street wound to the left and right, making it impossible to see more than a few feet ahead. Occasionally we passed a doorway or a window, slightly recessed in the wall, always shut. We could hardly have been more alone.

'Of course Sulla is a *dictator*,' I said. 'That chafes the Roman spirit: We are all free men – at least those of us who aren't slaves. But after all, a dictator isn't a king; so the lawmakers tell us. A dictatorship is perfectly legal, so long as the Senate approves. For emergencies only, of course. And only for a set period of time. If Sulla has kept his powers for almost three years now instead of the legally prescribed one – well, then, perhaps that's what offends your master. The untidiness of it.'

'Please,' Tiro said in a strained whisper. 'You shouldn't go on about it. You never know who might be listening.'

'Ah, the walls themselves have ears – another bit of wisdom from Master Chick-pea's cautious lips?'

That finally stirred him up. 'No! Cicero always speaks his mind – he's as unafraid to say what he thinks as you are. And he knows a great deal more about politics than you seem to think. But he's not foolhardy. Cicero says: Unless a man is well versed in the arts of rhetoric, then the words he utters in a

37

public place will quickly fly out of his control, like leaves on the wind. An innocent truth can be twisted in a fatal lie. That's why he forbids me to speak of politics outside his household. Or with untrustworthy strangers.'

That put me in my place. Tiro's silence and anger both were justified; I had deliberately baited him. But I didn't apologize, not even in the roundabout and stuffy manner that free men sometimes use to apologize to slaves. Anything that might give me a clearer picture of Cicero before I met him was worth the trifling expense of offending his slave. Besides, one should know a slave very well before letting him know that his insolence pleases you.

We walked on. The Narrows widened just enough to let two walk abreast. Tiro caught up with me a bit, but not enough to walk side by side with me, keeping a formal distance behind and to my left. We reentered the Subura Way near the Forum. Tiro indicated that it would be quicker to walk directly through the Forum rather than around it. We passed through the heart of the city, the Rome that visitors think of, with its magnificent courts and fountains, temples and squares, where the law is made and the greatest gods are worshipped in their finest houses.

We passed by the Rostra itself, the high pedestal decorated with the beaks of captured ships, from which orators and advocates plead the greatest cases in Roman law. Nothing more was said of the dictator Sulla, yet I could not help but wonder if Tiro was thinking, as I was, of the scene at this very spot only a year before, when the heads of Sulla's enemies lined the Forum, hundreds every day, stricken from their bodies and mounted on stakes. The blood of his victims still showed as rusty stains against the otherwise white, unblemished stone.

III

As Tiro had said, Cicero's house was considerably
smaller than my own. Its exterior was almost self-
consciously modest and sedate, a single-storey
structure without a single ornament. The face it
presented to the street was utterly blank, nothing
more than a wall of saffron stucco pierced by a
narrow wooden door.

The apparent modesty of Cicero's home signi-
fied little. We were, of course, in one of the most
expensive neighbourhoods in Rome, where size
gives little indication of wealth. Even the smallest
house here might be worth the price of a block of
villas in the Subura. Besides that, the wealthier
classes of Rome have traditionally shunned any
display of ostentation in their homes, at least as
regards the exterior. They claim this is a matter of
good taste. I suspect it has more to do with their fear
that a vulgar show of wealth might kindle jealousy

among the mob. Consider also that a costly decoration on the outside of a house is far easier to carry off than the same decoration safely displayed somewhere inside.

Such austerity and restraint have never ceased to be regarded as ideal. Even so, in my own lifetime I have seen a definite veering towards public opulence. This is notably true among the young and ambitious, especially those whose fortunes flowered in the wake of the civil war and Sulla's triumph. They add a second storey; they build porticoes upon their roofs. They instal statuary imported from Greece.

Nothing of the sort appeared on the street where Cicero lived. Decorum reigned. The houses turned their backs upon the street, facing inward, having nothing to say to any stranger who might wander by, reserving their secret life for those privileged to enter within.

The street was short and quiet. There were no markets at either end, and wandering vendors apparently knew better than to disturb the silence. Grey paving stones underfoot, pale blue sky above, faded stucco stained by rain and cracked by heat on either side; no other colours were allowed, least of all green – not a single unruly weed could be seen sprouting through the cobbles or springing up beside a wall, much less a flower or a tree. The very air, rising odourless and hot from the paving stones, breathed the sterile purity of Roman virtue.

Even in the midst of such restraint, the house of Cicero was particularly austere. In an ironic way it was so unassuming that it actually drew attention to itself – *there*, one might say, *there* is the ideal dwelling for a wealthy Roman of the most rarefied Roman virtue. The little house looked so modest and so narrow that one might have assumed it to be the home of a once-wealthy Roman matron, now widowed and in reduced circumstances; or perhaps the town house of a rich country farmer who came to the city only for occasional business, never to entertain or enjoy a holiday; or perhaps (and so it was, in fact) such an austere house on such an unassuming street might belong to a young bachelor of substantial means and old-fashioned values, a citified son of country parents poised to seek his fortune among Rome's higher circles, a young man of stern Roman virtue so sure of himself that even youth and ambition could not lure him into the vulgar missteps of fashion.

Tiro rapped upon the door.

A few moments later a grey-bearded slave opened it. Afflicted by some palsy, the old man's head was in constant motion, nodding up and down and tilting from side to side. He took his time in recognizing Tiro, peering and squinting and extending his head on its slender neck in turtle fashion. The nodding never ceased. Finally he smiled a toothless smile and stepped aside, pulling the door wide open.

The foyer was in the shape of a semicircle with its straight wall to our backs. The curving wall before us was pierced by three doorways, each flanked by slender columns and capped with a pediment. The corridors beyond were concealed by curtains of rich red fabric, embroidered along the bottom with an acanthus motif in yellow. Standing Grecian lamps at either corner and a floor mosaic of no great distinction (Diana in pursuit of a boar) completed the decoration. It was as I had expected. The vestibule was adequately restrained and tasteful so as not to contradict the sternness of the stucco facade, yet so expensively appointed as to belie any impression of poverty.

The old doorkeeper indicated with a gesture that we should wait. Silent and smiling, he withdrew through the curtained doorway to our left, his wizened head bobbing above his narrow shoulders like a cork on gentle waves.

'An old family retainer?' I asked. I waited until he had passed from sight, and kept my voice low. Obviously the old man's ears were sharper than his eyes, for he had heard well enough to answer the door; and it would have been rude to talk about him in his presence, as if he were a slave, for he was not. I had noticed the ring of manumission upon his finger, marking him a freedman and citizen.

'My grandfather,' Tiro answered, with more than a little pride in his voice, 'Marcus Tullius Tiro.' He craned his neck and looked towards the doorway, as if he could see through the red curtain to watch the old man's shuffling progress down the corridor. The embroidered bottom edge of the curtain wavered slightly, lifted by a breeze. Thus I deduced that the hallway to the left led somehow to fresh air and sky, probably to the

43

atrium at the heart of the house, where presumably Master Cicero was taking comfort in the heat of the morning.

'Then your line has been serving the family for at least three generations?' I said.

'Yes, though my father died when I was very small, before I had the chance to know him. As did my mother. Old Tiro is the only family I have.'

'And how long ago did your master free him?' I asked, for it was Cicero's first and family names that the old man now bore in addition to his old slave name: Marcus Tullius Tiro, freed by Marcus Tullius Cicero. Such is the tradition, that an emancipated slave will take the first two names of the man who frees him, giving them precedence to his own.

'Going on five years now. Cicero's grandfather back in Arpinum owned him until that time. Owned me as well, though I've always been with Cicero, since we both were boys. The old master transferred ownership as a gift when Cicero completed his studies and set up his own household here in Rome. That was when Cicero freed him. Cicero's grandfather would never have bothered. He doesn't believe in manumission, no matter how old a slave becomes, no matter how long or how well he serves a master. The Tullius family may have come from Arpinum, but they're Roman to the core. They're a very stern and old-fashioned family.'

'And you?'

'Me?'

'Do you suppose Cicero will one day free you as well?'

44

Tiro coloured. 'You ask the strangest questions, sir.'

'Only because it's my nature. My profession, as well. You must have asked yourself the same question already, more than once.'

'Doesn't every slave?' There was no bitterness in Tiro's voice, only a pale and unassuming note of sadness, a particular melancholy I had met before. I knew then, in that instant, that young Tiro was one of those slaves, naturally intelligent and brought up amid wealth, who bears the curse of realizing how arbitrary and capricious are the whims of Fortune, which make one man a slave all his life and another a king, when at root there is no discernible difference between them. 'One of these days,' he said quietly, 'when my master is established, when I'm older. Anyway, what's the use of being free unless you want to start a family? It's the only advantage I can see. And that's something I don't think about. Not often, anyway.'

Tiro turned his face away, looking towards the doorway, staring at the spot where his grandfather had stepped through the curtain. He looked back at me and his face rearranged itself. It took me a moment to realize that he was smiling. 'Besides,' he said, 'better to wait until my grandfather dies. Otherwise there'll be two freedmen named Marcus Tullius Tiro, and how would men tell us apart?'

'How do they tell you apart now?'

'Tiro and Old Tiro, naturally.' He smiled a more genuine smile. 'Grandfather won't answer to the name Marcus. He thinks it's bad luck somehow if you call him that. Tempting the gods. Besides, he's too old to get used to a new name, even if he is proud of it. And it's no use calling him, anyway. These days he'll answer the door and that's about it. He can take a very long time. I think my master likes it that way. Cicero thinks it's good manners to keep guests waiting at the door, and even better manners to keep them pacing here in the anteroom, at least on a first visit, while Old Tiro announces them.'

'Is that what we're doing now? Waiting to be announced?'

Tiro crossed his arms and nodded. I looked around the room. There was not even a bench to sit upon. Very Roman, I thought.

At length Old Tiro returned, lifting the curtain for his master. How shall I describe Marcus Tullius Cicero? The beautiful all look alike, but a plain man is plain according to his own peculiarity. Cicero had a large forehead, a fleshy nose, and thinning hair. He was of medium height, with a thin chest, narrow shoulders, and a long neck with a prominent knob protruding from the gullet. He looked considerably older than his twenty-six years.

'Gordianus,' Tiro said, introducing me. 'The one they call the Finder.'

I nodded. Cicero smiled warmly. There was a restless, inquisitive sparkle in his eyes. I was immediately impressed, without quite knowing why.

And in the next instant dismayed when Cicero opened his mouth to speak. He said only two words, but that was enough. The voice that came from his throat was high and grating. Tiro, with his sweet modulations, should have been the orator. Cicero had a voice fit for an auctioneer or a comic actor, a voice as peculiar as his name. 'This way,' he said, indicating that we should follow him through the red curtain.

The hallway was quite short, hardly a hallway at all. We walked between unadorned walls for only a few paces, and then both walls ended. To the right was a broad curtain of pale yellow gauze, so fine I could see straight through it into the small but immaculately kept atrium beyond. Open to the sun and sky, the atrium was like a well carved out of the house, a reservoir spilling over with heat and light. At its centre a tiny fountain splashed. The gauzy curtain rippled and billowed gently, like a mist disturbed by a puff of air, like a living membrane sighing at the slightest breeze.

Facing the atrium was a large, airy room lit by narrow windows set high in the ceiling. The walls were of white plaster. The furniture was all of dark polished wood in rustic designs, embellished by subtle flourishes of woodwork, silver clasps, and inlays of mother-of-pearl, carnelian, and lapis.

The room was filled with an astonishing number of scrolls. This was Cicero's library and his study. Such rooms are often the most intimate in the homes of wealthy men, revealing more about their owners than do bedchambers or dining rooms, which are the domain of women and slaves. It was a private room, indelibly marked by its owner, but a public room as well – testifying to this were

the number of chairs scattered about, some of them
pulled close together, as if they had just been
vacated by a huddled group of visitors. Cicero
gestured to a group of three chairs, seated himself,
and indicated that we should do likewise. What
kind of man greets guests in his library rather than in
his dining room or veranda? A man with Greek
pretensions, I thought. A scholar. A lover of knowledge and wisdom. A man who would open a
conversation with a total stranger with a gambit
such as this:

'Tell me something, Gordianus the Finder –
have you ever considered murdering your father?'

IV

What must my face have looked like? I suppose I gave a start, winced, looked askance. Cicero saw all and smiled in that demure way that orators smile whenever they successfully manipulate an audience. Actors (I have known more than a few) feel much the same sort of satisfaction, the same thrill of power. The herdsman reveals the truth to Oedipus, and with a single word elicits gasps of shock and dismay from a thousand throats, all responding on cue. Behind his mask the herdsman smiles and makes his exit.

I pretended to gaze with an abstracted air at some nearby scrolls; I could see from the corner of my eye that Cicero still watched me, intent on gauging my every reaction. Orators think they can control everyone and everything with their words. I strained to bleed every hint of expression from my face.

'My father,' I began, and then had to pause to clear my throat, hating the interruption, for it seemed a sign of weakness. 'My father is already dead, esteemed Cicero. He died many years ago.' The mischief in his eyes receded. He frowned.

'My apologies,' he said quietly, with a slight bow of his head. 'I meant no offence.'

'None was taken.'

'Good.' After a suitable interval the frown vanished. The look of mischief returned. 'Then you won't mind if I pose the same question again – purely as a hypothetical matter, of course. Suppose then, only suppose, that you had a father you wished to be rid of. How would you go about it?'

I shrugged. 'How old is the old man?'

'Sixty, perhaps sixty-five.'

'And how old am I – hypothetically speaking?'

'Perhaps forty.'

'Time,' I said. 'Whatever the complaint, time will take care of it, as surely as any other remedy.'

Cicero nodded. 'Simply wait, you mean. Sit back. Relax. Allow nature to take its course. Yes, that would be the easiest way. And perhaps, though not necessarily, the safest. Certainly, it's what most people would do, confronted with another person whose existence they can hardly bear – especially if that person is older or weaker, especially if he happens to be a member of the family. Most especially if he happens to be one's father. Bear the discomfort and be patient. Let it be resolved by time. After all, no one lives forever, and the young usually outlive their elders.'

Cicero paused. The yellow gauze gently rose and fell as if the whole house exhaled. The room was flooded with heat. 'But time can be something of a luxury. Certainly, if one waits long enough, an old man of sixty-five will eventually expire on his own – though he may be an old man of eighty-five before that happens.'

He rose from his chair and began to pace. Cicero was not a man to orate while sitting still. I would later come to see his whole body as a sort of engine – the legs deliberately pacing, the arms in motion, the hands shaping ponderous gestures, the head tilting, the eyebrows oscillating up and down. None of these movements was an end in itself. Instead they were all connected together somehow, and all subservient to his voice, that strange, irritating, completely fascinating voice – as if his voice were an instrument and his body the machine that produced it; as if his limbs and digits were the gears and levers necessary to manufacture the voice that issued from his mouth. The body moved. The voice emerged.

'Consider,' he said – a tilt of the head, a subtle flourish of the hand – 'an old man of sixty-five, a widower living alone in Rome. Not at all the reclusive type. He's quite fond of going to dinners and parties. He loves the arena and the theatre. He frequents the baths. He even patronizes – I swear it, at sixty-five! – the neighbourhood brothel. Pleasure is his life. As for work, he's retired. Oh, there's money to spare. Valuable estates in the countryside, vineyards and farms – but he doesn't bother with

51

that any more. He's long left the work of running things to someone younger.'

'To me,' I said.

Cicero smiled slightly. Like all orators, he hated any interruption, but the question proved that I was at least listening. 'Yes,' he said, 'hypothetically speaking. To you. To his hypothetical son. As for the old man, his own life is now devoted solely to pleasure. In its pursuit he walks the streets of the city at all hours of the day and night, attended only by his slaves.'

'He has no bodyguard?' I said.

'None to speak of. Two slaves accompany him. More for convenience than protection.'

'Armed?'

'Probably not.'

'My hypothetical father is asking for trouble.'

Cicero nodded. 'Indeed. The streets of Rome are hardly the place for any decent citizen to go gadding about in the middle of the night. Especially an older man. Especially if he has the look of money about him, and no armed guard. Foolhardy! Taking his life into his hands, day by day – such an old fool. Sooner or later he'll come to no good end, or so you think. And yet, year after year he keeps up this outrageous behaviour, and it comes to nothing. You begin to think that some invisible demon or spirit must be looking after him, for he never comes to harm. Never once is he robbed. Not once is he even threatened. The worst that occurs is that he may be accosted by a beggar or a drunkard or some vagrant whore late at night, and these he can easily handle with a coin or a word to his slaves. No, time seems not to be cooperating. Left to his own devices, the old man may very well live forever.'

'And would that be so bad? I think I'm beginning to like him.'

Cicero raised an eyebrow. 'On the contrary, you hate him. Never mind why. Simply assume for the moment that, for whatever reason, you want him dead. Desperately.'

'Time would still be easiest. Sixty-five, you said – how is his health?'

'Excellent. Probably better than yours. And why not? Everyone is always saying how overworked you are, running the estates, raising your family, working yourself into an early grave – while the old man hasn't a care in the world. All he does is enjoy himself. In the morning he rests. In the afternoon he plans his evening. In the evening he stuffs himself with expensive food, drinks to excess, carouses with men half his age. The next morning he recovers at the baths and begins all over again. How is his health? I told you, he still patronizes the local whorehouse.'

'Food and drink have been known to kill a man,' I ventured. 'And they say that many a whore has stopped an old man's heart.'

Cicero shook his head. 'Not good enough, too unreliable. You hate him, don't you understand? Perhaps you fear him. You grow impatient for his death.'

'Politics?' I offered.

Cicero ceased his pacing for a moment, smiled,

and then resumed. 'Politics,' he said. 'Yes, in these days, in Rome – politics could certainly kill a man more quickly and surely than high living or a whore's embrace or even a midnight stroll through the Subura.' He spread his hands wide open in an orator's despair. 'Unfortunately, the old man is one of those remarkable creatures who manages to go through life without ever having any politics at all.'

'In Rome?' I said. 'A citizen and a landowner? Impossible.'

'Then say that he's one of those men like a rabbit – charming, vacuous, harmless. Never attracting attention to himself, never giving offence. Not worth the bother of hunting, so long as there's larger game afoot. Surrounded on every side by politics, like a thicket of nettles, yet able to slip through the maze without a scratch.'

'He sounds clever. I like this old man more and more.'

Cicero frowned. 'Cleverness has nothing to do with it. The old man has no strategy except to slip through life with the least possible inconvenience. He's lucky, that's all. Nothing reaches him. The Italian allies rise in revolt against Rome? He comes from Ameria, a village that waits until the last moment to join the revolt, then reaps the first fruits of the reconciliation; that's how he became a citizen. Civil war between Marius and Sulla, then between Sulla and Cinna? The old man wavers in his loyalty – a realist and an opportunist like most Romans these days – and emerges like the delicate maiden who traverses a raging stream by hopping from stone to stone without even getting her sandals wet. Those who have no opinions are the only people safe today. A rabbit, I tell you. If you leave it to politics to put him in danger, he'll live to be a hundred.'

'Surely he can't be as vapid as you describe. Every man takes risks these days just by being alive. You say he's a landowner, with interests in Rome. He must be a client to some influential family. Who are his patrons?'

Cicero laughed. 'Even there he chooses the blandest, safest possible family to ally himself with – the Metelli. Sulla's in-laws – or at least they were until Sulla divorced his fourth wife. And not just any of the Metelli, but the oldest, the most inert, and endlessly respectable of its many branches. Somehow or other he ingratiated himself to Caecilia Metella. Have you ever met her?'

I shook my head.

'You will,' he said mysteriously. 'No, politics will never kill this old man for you. Sulla may fill up the Forum with heads on sticks, the Field of Mars may become a bowl of blood tipping into the Tiber – you'll still find the old man traipsing about after dark in the worst parts of town, stuffed from a dinner party at Caecilia's, blithely on his way to the neighbourhood whorehouse.'

Cicero abruptly sat down. The machine, it seemed, needed an occasional rest, but the cracked instrument continued to play. 'So you see that fate will not cooperate in taking the odious old man off your hands. Besides, it may be that there's some urgent reason that you want him dead – not just hatred or a grudge, but some crisis immediately at hand. You have to take action yourself.'

'You suggest that I murder my own father?'

'Exactly.'

'Impossible.'

'You must.'

'Un-Roman!'

'Fate compels you.'

'Then – poison?'

He shrugged. 'Possibly, if you had the proper access. But you're not an ordinary father and son, coming and going in each other's household. There's been some bitterness between you. Consider: the old man has his own town house here in Rome, and seldom sleeps anywhere else. You live at the old family home in Ameria, and on the rare occasions when business brings you into the city, you never sleep in your father's house. You stay with a friend instead, or even at an inn – the quarrel between you runs that deep. So you don't have easy access to the old man's dinner before he eats it. Bribe one of his servants? Unlikely and highly uncertain – in a family divided, the slaves always choose sides. They'll be far more loyal to him than to you. Poison is an unworkable solution.'

The yellow curtain rippled. A gust of warm air slipped beneath its hem and entered the room like a mist clinging low to the ground. I felt it pool and eddy about my feet, heavy with the scent of jasmine. The morning was almost over. The true heat of the day was about to begin. I suddenly felt sleepy. So did Tiro; I saw him stifle a yawn. Perhaps he was simply bored. This was probably not the first time that he had heard his master run through the same string of arguments, refining his logic, worrying over the particular polish and gloss of each phrase.

I cleared my throat. 'Then the solution seems obvious, esteemed Cicero. If the father must be murdered – at the instigation of his own son, a crime almost too hideous to contemplate – then it should be done when the old man is most vulnerable and most accessible. Some moonless night, on his way home from a party, or on his way to a brothel. No witnesses at that hour, at least none who'd be eager to testify. Gangs roaming the streets. There would be nothing suspicious about such a death. It would be easy to blame it on some passing group of anonymous thugs.'

Cicero leaned forwards in his chair. The machine was reviving. 'So you wouldn't commit the act yourself, by your own hand?'

'Certainly not! I wouldn't even be in Rome. I'd be far to the north in my house in Ameria – having nightmares, probably.'

'You'd hire some assassins to do it for you?'

'Of course.'

'People you knew and trusted?'

'Would I be likely to know such people personally? A hardworking Amerian farmer?' I shrugged. 'More likely I'd be relying on strangers. A gang leader met in a tavern in the Subura. A nameless

57

acquaintance recommended by another acquaintance known to a casual friend . . .'

'Is that how it's done?' Cicero was genuinely curious. He spoke no longer to the hypothetical parricide, but to Gordianus the Finder. 'They told me that you would actually know a thing or two about this sort of business. They said: "Yes, if you want to get in touch with the kind of men who don't mind getting blood on their hands, Gordianus is one place to start." '

'*They*? Whom do you mean, Cicero? Who says that I drink from the same cup with killers?'

He bit his lip, not quite certain how much he wanted to tell me yet. I answered for him. 'I think you mean Hortensius, don't you? Since it was Hortensius who recommended me to you?'

Cicero shot a sharp glance at Tiro, who was suddenly quite awake.

'No, Master, I told him nothing. He guessed it –' For the first time that day, Tiro sounded to me like a slave.

'Guessed? What do you mean?'

'*Deduced* would be a better word. Tiro is telling the truth. I know, more or less anyway, what you've called me for. A murder case involving a father and son, both called Sextus Roscius.'

'You *guessed* that this was my reason for calling on you? But how? I only decided yesterday to take on Roscius as a client.'

I sighed. The curtain sighed. The heat crept up my feet and legs, like water slowly rising in a well. 'Perhaps you should have Tiro explain it to you later. I think it's too hot for me to go through it all again step by step. But I know that Hortensius had the case to begin with, and that you have it now. And I presume that all this talk about hypothetical conspiracies has something to do with the actual murder?'

Cicero looked glum. I think he felt foolish at finding that I had known the true circumstances all along. 'Yes,' he said, 'it's hot. Tiro, you'll bring some refreshment. Some wine, mixed with cool water. Perhaps some fruit. Do you like dried apples, Gordianus?'

Tiro rose from his chair. 'I'll tell Athalena.'

'No, Tiro, fetch it yourself. Take your time.' The order was demeaning, and intentionally so; I could tell by the look of hurt in Tiro's eyes, and by the look in Cicero's as well, heavy-lidded and drooping from something other than the heat. Tiro was unused to being given such menial tasks. And Cicero? One sees it all the time, a master taking out petty frustrations on the slaves around him. The habit becomes so commonplace that they do it without thinking; slaves come to accept it without humiliation or repining, as if it were a god-sent inconvenience, like rainfall on a market day.

Cicero and Tiro were not nearly so advanced along that path. Before Tiro had disappeared pouting from the room, Cicero relented, as much as he could without losing face. 'Tiro!' he called. He waited for the slave to turn. He looked him in the eye. 'Be sure to bring a portion for yourself as well.'

A crueller man would have smiled as he spoke. A

lesser man would have cast his eyes to the floor. Cicero did neither, and in that moment I discovered my first glimmering of respect for him.

Tiro departed. For a moment Cicero toyed with a ring on his finger, then turned his attention back to me.

'You were about to tell me something of how one goes about arranging a murder in the streets of Rome. Forgive me if the question is presumptuous. I don't mean to imply that you yourself have ever offended the gods by taking part in such crimes. But they say – Hortensius says – that you happen to know more than a little about these matters. Who, how, and how much . . .'

I shrugged. 'If a man wants another man murdered, there's nothing so difficult about that. As I said, a word to the right man, a bit of gold passed from hand to hand, and the job is done.'

'But where does one find the right man?'

I had been forgetting how young and inexperienced he was, despite his education and wit. 'It's easier than you might think. For years the gangs have been controlling the streets of Rome after dark, and sometimes even in broad daylight.'

'But the gangs fight each other.'

'The gangs fight anyone who gets in their way.'

'Their crimes are political. They ally themselves with a particular party—'

'They have no politics, except the politics of whatever man hires them. And no loyalty, except the loyalty that money buys. Think, Cicero. Where do the gangs come from? Some of them are spawned right here in Rome, like maggots under a rock – the poor, the children of the poor, their grandchildren and great-grandchildren. Whole dynasties of crime, generations of villains breeding pedigrees of vice. They negotiate with one another like little nations. They intermarry like noble families. And they hire themselves out like mercenaries to whatever politician or general offers the grandest promises.'

Cicero glanced away, peering into the translucent folds of the yellow curtain, as if he could see beyond it all the human refuse of Rome. 'Where do they all come from?' he muttered.

'They grow up through the pavement,' I said, 'like weeds. Or they drift in from the countryside, refugees from war after war. Think about it: Sulla wins his war against the rebellious Italian allies and pays his soldiers in land. But to acquire that land, the defeated allies must first be uprooted. Where do they end up, except as beggars and slaves in Rome? And all for what? The countryside is devastated by war. The soldiers know nothing of farming; in a month or a year they sell their holdings to the highest bidder and head back to the city. The countryside falls into the grip of vast landholders. Small farmers struggle to compete, are defeated and dispossessed – they find their way to Rome. More and more I've seen it in my own lifetime, the gulf between the rich and poor, the smallness of the one, the vastness of the other. Rome is like a woman of fabulous wealth and beauty, draped in gold and festooned with jewels, her belly big with a foetus named Empire – and infested from head to foot by a million scampering lice.'

Cicero frowned. 'Hortensius warned me that you would talk politics.'

'Only because politics is the air we breathe – I inhale a breath, and what else could come out? It may be otherwise in other cities, but not in the Republic, and not in our lifetimes. Call it politics, call it reality. The gangs exist for a reason. No one can get rid of them. Everyone fears them. A man bent on murder would find a way to use them. He'd only be following the example of a successful politician.'

'You mean—'

'I don't mean any particular politician. They all use the gangs, or try to.'

'But you *mean* Sulla.'

Cicero spoke the name first. I was surprised. I was impressed. At some point the conversation had slipped out of control. It was quickly turning seditious.

'Yes,' I said. 'If you insist: Sulla.' I looked away. My eyes fell on the yellow curtain. I found myself gazing at it and into it, as if in the vagueness of the shapes beyond I could make out the images of an old nightmare. 'Were you in Rome when the proscriptions began?'

Cicero nodded.

'So was I. Then you know what it was like. Each day the new list of the proscribed would be posted in the Forum. And who were always first in line to read the names? No, not anyone who might have been on the list, because they were all cowering at home, or wisely barricaded in the countryside. First in line were the gangs and their leaders – because Sulla didn't care who destroyed his enemies, or his imagined enemies, so long as they were destroyed. Show up with the head of a proscribed man slung over your shoulder, sign a receipt, and receive a bag of silver in exchange. To acquire that head, stop at nothing. Break down the doors of a citizen's house. Beat his children, rape his wife – but leave his valuables in place, for once head and body are parted, the property of a proscribed Roman becomes the property of Sulla.'

'Not exactly . . .'

'I misspoke, of course. I meant to say that when an enemy of the state is beheaded, his estate is confiscated and becomes property of the state – meaning that it will be auctioned at the earliest convenient date at insanely low prices to Sulla's friends.'

Even Cicero blanched at this. He concealed his agitation well, but I noticed his eyes shift for the briefest instant from side to side, as if he were wary of spies concealed among the scrolls. 'You're a man of strong opinions, Gordianus. The heat loosens your tongue. But what has any of this to do with the subject at hand?'

I had to laugh. 'And what is the subject? I think I've forgotten.'

'Arranging a murder,' Cicero snapped, sounding for all the world like a teacher of oratory attempting to steer an unruly pupil back to the prescribed topic. 'A murder of purely personal motive.'

'Well, then, I'm only trying to point out how easy it is these days to find a willing assassin. And not only in the Subura. Look on any street corner — yes, even this one. I'd gladly wager that I could leave your door, walk around the block exactly once, and return with a newfound friend more than willing to murder my pleasure-loving, whoremongering, hypothetical father.'

'You go too far, Gordianus. Had you been trained in rhetoric, you'd know the limits of hyperbole.'

'I don't exaggerate. The gangs have grown that bold. It's Sulla's fault and no one else's. He made them his personal bounty hunters. He unleashed them to run wild across Rome, like packs of wolves. Until the proscriptions officially ended last year, the gangs had almost unlimited power to hunt and kill. So they bring in the head of an innocent man, a man who's not on the list — so what? Accidents happen. Add his name to the list of the proscribed. The dead man becomes a retroactive enemy of the state. What matter if that means his family will be disinherited, his children ruined and reduced to paupers, fresh fodder for the gangs? It also means that some friend of Sulla's will acquire a new house in the city.'

Cicero looked as if a bad tooth were worrying him. He raised his hand to silence me. I raised my own hand to stave him off.

'I'm only now reaching my point. You see, it wasn't only the rich and powerful who suffered during the proscriptions, and still suffer. Once

Pandora's box is opened, no one can close it. Crime becomes habit. The unthinkable becomes commonplace. You don't see it from here, where you live. This street is too narrow, too quiet. No weeds grow through the paving stones that run by your door. Oh, no doubt, in the worst of it, you had a few neighbours dragged from their homes in the middle of the night. Perhaps you have a view of the Forum from the roof, and on a clear day you might have counted the new heads added to the pikes.

'But I see a different Rome, Cicero, that other Rome that Sulla has left to posterity. They say he plans to retire soon, leaving behind him a new constitution to strengthen the upper classes and put the people in their place. And what is that place, but the crime-ridden Rome that Sulla bequeaths to us? My Rome, Cicero. A Rome that breeds in shadow, that moves at night, that breathes the very air of vice without the disguises of politics or wealth. After all, that's why you've called me here, isn't it? To take you into that world, or to enter it myself and bring back to you whatever it is you're seeking. That's what I can offer you, if you're seeking the truth.'

At that moment Tiro returned, bearing a silver tray set with three cups, a round loaf of bread, dried apples, and white cheese. His presence instantly sobered me. We were no longer two men alone in a room discussing politics, but two citizens and a slave, or two men and a boy, considering Tiro's innocence. I would never have spoken so recklessly had he never left the room. I feared I had said too much already.

V

Tiro set the tray on a low table between us. Cicero glanced at it without interest. 'So much food, Tiro?'

'It's almost midday, Master. Gordianus will be hungry.'

'Very well, then. We must show him our hospitality.' He stared at the tray, hardly seeming to see it. He gently rubbed his temples, as if I had stuffed his head too full of seditious ideas.

The walk had made me hungry. The talk had left my mouth thick and dry. The heat had given me a deep thirst. Even so, I patiently waited for Cicero to initiate the meal – my politics may be radical but my manners have never been questioned – when Tiro gave me a start by leaning forwards eagerly in his chair, tearing a piece from a loaf, and reaching for a cup.

At just such moments one learns how deeply convention is bred into the soul. For all that life had taught me about the arbitrary nature of fate and the absurdities of slavery, for all that I had endeavoured from the moment I met him to treat Tiro as a man, I still let out a quiet gasp at seeing a slave take the first food from a table while his master sat back, not yet ready to begin.

They both heard it. Tiro looked up, puzzled. Cicero laughed softly.

'Gordianus is shocked. He's not used to our ways, Tiro, or to your manners. It's all right, Gordianus. Tiro knows that I never eat at midday. He's used to beginning without me. Please, eat something yourself. The cheese is quite good, all the way from the dairy at Arpinum, sent with my grandmother's love.

'As for me, I'll have a bit of the wine. Only a bit; in this heat it's likely to turn sour in the stomach. Is it only me who suffers from that particular malady? I can't eat at all in midsummer; I fast for days at a time. Meantime, while your mouth is busy with food instead of treason, perhaps I'll have a chance to say a bit more about my reasons for asking you here.'

Cicero swallowed and gave a slight wince, as if the wine had begun to sour the moment it passed his lips. 'We strayed from the subject some while ago, didn't we? What would Diodotus say to that, Tiro? What have I been paying that old Greek for all these years if I'm not even able to hold an orderly conversation in my own home? Disorderly speech is not only unseemly; in the wrong time and the wrong place it can be deadly.'

'I was never quite certain what the subject was, esteemed Cicero. I seem to recall that we were plotting to murder someone's father. My father, or was it Tiro's? No, they're both already dead. Perhaps it was yours?'

Cicero was not amused. 'I introduced a hypothetical model, Gordianus, simply to sound you out about some factors – methodology, practicality, plausibility – regarding a very real and very deadly crime. A crime already accomplished. The tragic fact is that a certain farmer from the hamlet of Ameria—'

'Much like the hypothetical old farmer you described?'

'*Exactly* like him. As I was saying, a certain farmer from Ameria was murdered in the streets of Rome on the Ides of September, the night of the full moon – almost eight months ago. His name you already seem to know: Sextus Roscius. Now, in exactly eight days – on the Ides of May – the son of Sextus Roscius will go on trial, accused of arranging the murder of his father. I'll be defending him.'

'With such a defence I should think there'd be no need for a prosecutor.'

'What do you mean?'

'From all you've said, it seems obvious that you think the son is guilty.'

'Nonsense! Was I that convincing? I suppose I should be pleased. I was only trying to paint the case as his accusers might describe it.'

'You're saying that you believe this Sextus Roscius is innocent?'

'Of course! Why else should I be defending him against these outrageous charges?'

'Cicero, I know enough about advocates and orators to know that they don't necessarily have to believe in a point to argue for it. Nor do they have to believe in a man's innocence to defend him.'

Tiro suddenly glowered at me across the table. 'You have no right,' he said, with a desperate little break in his voice. 'Marcus Tullius Cicero is a man of the highest principles, of unquestionable integrity, a man who speaks what he believes and believes every word he speaks, rare enough in Rome these days perhaps, but even so—'

'Enough!' Cicero's voice carried tremendous force, but little anger. He raised his hand in an orator's gesture of *desist*, and seemed unable to keep from smiling.

'You'll forgive young Tiro,' he said, leaning towards me with an air of confidentiality. 'He's a loyal servant, and for that I'm grateful. There are few enough to be found nowadays.' He gazed at Tiro with a look of pure affection, open, genuine, and unabashed. Tiro suddenly found it convenient to gaze elsewhere – at the table, the tray of food, the softly billowing curtain.

'But perhaps he is sometimes too loyal. What do you think, Gordianus? What do *you* think, Tiro – perhaps we should pose such a proposition to Diodotus the next time he calls and see what the master of rhetoric can make of it. A fit subject for debate: is it possible that a slave can be too loyal to his master? That is to say, too enthusiastic in his devotion, too ready to spring to his master's defence?'

Cicero glanced at the tray and reached for a bit of dried apple. He held it between his thumb and forefinger and studied it as if considering whether his delicate constitution could tolerate even such a tiny morsel in the full heat of the day. There was a pause and a silence, broken only by the trilling of a bird in the atrium outside. In the stillness the room around us seemed to breathe again, or rather to attempt to breathe, vainly struggling to catch a shallow breath and coming up short; the curtain billowed tentatively inward, then out, then in again, never quite enough to release a gust of air in either direction, as if the breeze were a warm and palpable thing trapped beneath its brocaded hem. Cicero frowned and replaced the morsel on the tray.

Suddenly the curtain gave an audible snap. A breath of warmth eddied across the tiles and over my feet. The room had finally released its pent-up sigh.

'You ask if I believe that Sextus Roscius is innocent of his father's murder.' Cicero spread his fingers and pressed the tips together. 'The answer is yes. When you meet him, you too will believe in his innocence.'

It seemed at last that we might be getting down to business. I had had enough of the games passing back and forth in Cicero's study, enough of the yellow curtain and the stifling heat.

'How exactly did he die, the old man?

Bludgeons, knives, stones? How many assailants? Were they seen? Can they be identified? Where was the son at the very moment the crime took place, and how did he learn the news? Who else had reason to kill the old man? What were the terms of his will? Who brings the charges against the son, and why?' I paused, but only to take a sip of wine. 'And tell me this—'

'Gordianus,' Cicero laughed, 'if I knew all this, I would hardly be needing your services, would I?'

'But you must know a little.'

'More than a little, but still not enough. Very well, I can at least answer your last question. The charges have been lodged by a prosecutor named Gaius Erucius. I see you've heard of him – or has the wine turned to vinegar in your mouth?'

'I've more than heard of him,' I said. 'From time to time I've actually worked for him, but only from hunger. Erucius was born a slave in Sicily; now he's a freedman with the shadiest law practice in Rome. He takes cases for money, not merit. He'd defend a man who raped his mother if there was gold in it, and then turn around and prosecute the old woman for slander if he saw a profit. Any idea who's hired him to take on the case?'

'No, but when you meet Sextus Roscius—'

'You keep saying that I'll soon be meeting someone – first Caecilia Metella, now Sextus Roscius. Will they be arriving soon?'

'Actually, it's best if we pay them a visit ourselves.'

'What makes you so certain that I'll be coming

along? I came here under the impression that you had work for me, but so far you haven't even explained what you want. Nor have you made any mention of payment.'

'I'm aware of your regular fees, at least as Hortensius explained them. I assume he would know.'

I nodded.

'As for the job, it's this: I want proof that Sextus Roscius is innocent of his father's murder. Better than that, I want to know who the real murderers were. Even better, I want to know who hired those murderers, and why. And all of this in eight days, before the Ides.'

'You talk as if I'd already accepted the job. Perhaps I'm not interested, Cicero.'

He shook his head and pressed his lips into a thin smile.

'You're not the only man who can deduce another man's character before you've met him, Gordianus. I do know a thing or two about you. Three things, in fact. Any one of them would persuade you to take this case. First, you need the money. A man of your means, living in a big house up on the Esquiline – there can never be enough money. Am I right?'

I shrugged.

'Secondly, Hortensius tells me that you love a mystery. Or rather that you hate a mystery. You're the type that can't abide the unknown, that feels compelled to wrest truth from falsehood, strike order from chaos. Who killed old Roscius, Gordianus? You're already hooked, like a fish on a line. Admit it.'

'Well . . .'

'Thirdly, you're a man who loves justice.'

'Did Hortensius tell you that, too? Hortensius wouldn't know a just man from—'

'No one told me. That I deduced for myself, in the last half hour. No man speaks his mind as candidly as you have who isn't a lover of justice. I'm offering you a chance to see it done.' He leaned forwards in his chair. 'Can you bear to see an innocent man put to death? Well, then – will you take the case, or won't you?'

'I will.'

Cicero clapped his hands and sprang to his feet. 'Good. Very good! We'll leave for Caecilia's house right away.'

'Now? In this heat? It's just past noon.'

'There's no time to waste. If the heat is too much for you, I could summon a litter – but no, that would take too long. It isn't far. Tiro, fetch us a pair of broad-brimmed hats.'

Tiro gave his master a plaintive look.

'Very well, then, fetch three.'

VI

'What makes you think she'll even be awake at this hour?'

The Forum was deserted. The paving stones shimmered with heat. Not a soul was afoot except for the three of us stealing like thieves across the flagstones. I quickened the pace. The heat burned through the thin soles of my shoes. Both my companions, I noticed, wore more expensive foot-wear than my own, with thick leather soles to protect their feet.

'Caecilia will be awake,' Cicero assured me. 'She's a hopeless insomniac – so far as I can tell, she never sleeps at all.'

We reached the foot of the Sacred Way. My heart sank as I gazed up the steep, narrow avenue that led to the imposing villas atop the Palatine. The world was all sun and stone, utterly without shade. The layers of shimmering heat made the summit of the Palatine seem hazy and indistinct, very high and far away.

We began the ascent. Tiro led the way, oblivious of the effort. There was something strange about his eagerness to come along, something beyond mere curiosity or the desire to follow his master. I was too hot to puzzle over it.

'One thing I must ask of you, Gordianus.' Cicero was beginning to show signs of exertion, but he talked through them, like a true stoic. 'I appreciated your candour when you spoke your mind in my study. No one can say you are less than an honest man. But hold your tongue in Caecilia's house. Her family has long been allied with Sulla – his late fourth wife was a Metella.'

'You mean the daughter of Delmaticus? The one he divorced while she lay dying?'

'Exactly. The Metelli were not happy about the divorce, despite Sulla's excuses.'

'The augurs looked in a bowl of sheep entrails and told him his wife's illness would pollute his household.'

'So Sulla claimed. Caecilia herself would probably take no offence at anything you might say, but you can never tell. She's an old woman, unmarried and child-less. Given to strange ways – such as happens when a woman is left to her own devices too long, without a husband and family to occupy her with wholesome pursuits. Her passion these days is for whatever Oriental cult happens to be new and fashionable in Rome, the more foreign and bizarre, the better. She's not much concerned with mere earthly matters.

'But it's likely there'll be another in the house with keener ears and sharper eyes. I'm thinking of my good young friend Marcus Messalla – we call him Rufus, on account of his red hair. He's no stranger to Caecilia Metella's house; he's known her since he was a child, and she's almost like an aunt to him. A fine young man – or not quite a man yet, only sixteen. Rufus comes to my house rather often, for gatherings and lectures and such, and he already knows his way around the law courts. He's quite eager to help in Sextus Roscius's behalf.'

'But?'

'But his family connections make him danger-ous. Hortensius is his half brother – when Horten-sius dropped the case, it was young Rufus he sent to my door to beg me to take it on. More to the point, the boy's older sister is that same young Valeria whom Sulla recently took to be his fifth wife. Poor Rufus has little affection for his new brother-in-law, but the marriage does put him in an awkward position. I would ask that you restrain yourself from slandering our esteemed dictator in his presence.'

'Of course, Cicero.' When I left the house that morning I had never expected to be circulating with high nobles like the Metelli and Messalli. I looked down at the garments I wore, a common citizen's toga over a plain tunic. The only touch of purple was a wine stain near the hem. Bethesda claimed to have spent hours trying to remove it without success.

By the time we reached the summit, even Tiro was showing signs of fatigue. His dark curls were pasted to his forehead with sweat. His face was flushed with exertion – or perhaps with something more like excitement. I wondered again about his eagerness to reach Caecilia Metella's house.

'This is it,' Cicero huffed, pausing to catch his breath. The house before us was a sprawling mass of rose stucco, ringed about by ancient oaks. The doorway was recessed beneath a portico and flanked by two helmeted soldiers in full battle gear with swords at their belts and spears in their fists. Grizzled veterans from Sulla's army, I thought, and gave a start.

'The guards,' Cicero said, making a vague gesture with his hand as he mounted the steps. 'Ignore them. They must be sweltering beneath all that leather. Tiro?'

Tiro, who had been staring in fascination at the soldiers' gear, sprang ahead of his master to rap at the heavy oak doors. A long moment passed in which we all caught our breaths and removed our hats beneath the shaded portico.

The door opened inward on silent hinges. Cool air and the scent of incense wafted out to greet us.

Tiro and the door slave exchanged the typical formalities – 'My master comes to see your mistress' – then we waited for another moment before the slave of the foyer came to usher us inside. He relieved us of our hats, then disappeared to fetch the announcer. I looked over my shoulder at the doorkeeper, who sat on a stool beside the portal busying himself with some sort of handicraft, his foot attached to the wall by a chain just long enough to allow him to reach the door.

The announcer arrived, obviously disappointed to find that it was Cicero and not some grovelling client from whom he might extort a few denarii before allowing further admission to the house. From small signs – his high voice, the visible enlargement of his breasts – I realized he was a eunuch. While in the East they are an indispensable and ancient part of the social fabric, the unsexed remain a rarity in Rome and are looked on with great distaste. Cicero had said that Caecilia was a follower of Oriental cults, but to keep a eunuch in her household struck me as a truly bizarre affectation.

We followed him around the central atrium and up a flight of marble steps. The announcer pulled back a hanging curtain, and I followed Cicero into a chamber that would not have looked too out of place in a high-priced Alexandrian brothel.

We seemed to have stepped into a large and overdecorated tent, plush and pillow-strewn, with carpets and hangings everywhere. Brass lamps hung from standing braziers in the corners and exhaled trickles of smoke. It was from this room that the smell of incense permeated the house. I could hardly breathe. The various spices were being burned without the least sensitivity to their individual proportions and properties. The crude concentrations of sandalwood and myrrh were nauseating. Any Egyptian housewife would have known better.

'Mistress,' the eunuch whispered in a high voice. 'The esteemed Marcus Tullius Cicero, advocate.' He quickly withdrew.

At the far end of the room was our hostess, sprawled face down amid cushions on the floor. Two female slaves attended her, kneeling on either side. The slaves were dark-skinned and dressed in Egyptian style, wearing diaphanous gowns and heavily made-up. Above them, dominating the room, was the object before which Caecilia prostrated herself.

I had never seen anything quite like it. It was clearly an incarnation of one of the Oriental earth goddesses, Cybele or Astarte or Isis, though I had never before seen this particular permutation. The statue stood eight feet tall, so tall that the top of its head grazed the ceiling. The thing had a stern, almost manly face and wore a crown made of serpents. At first glance I assumed that the pendulous objects adorning her torso were breasts, scores and scores of them. A closer look at the curious way in which the orbs were grouped made me realize they must be testicles. In one hand the goddess held a scythe, the blade of which had been painted bright red.

'What?' A muffled voice rose from the cushions. Caecilia floundered for a moment. The slave girls each took an arm and helped her up. She spun around and looked at us in alarm.

'No, no!' she shrieked. 'That stupid eunuch! Out, out of the room, Cicero! You weren't to come inside, you were to wait outside the curtain.

How could he have made such a stupid mistake? No men are allowed into the sanctum of the Goddess. Oh, dear, it's happened again. Well, by rights you should all three be sacrificed as a punishment, or at least flogged, but I suppose that's out of the question. Of course, one of you could take the place of the others – but no, I won't even ask it, I know how fond you are of young Tiro. Perhaps this other slave—' She glanced at my iron ring, the mark of a common citizen, and seeing I was no one's slave threw up her hands in disappointment. Her nails were unusually long and stained red with henna, in the Egyptian fashion.

'Oh, dear. I suppose this means I'll have to flog one of the poor slave girls in your place, just as I did when that eunuch made the same stupid mistake last week with Rufus. Oh, dear, and they're so delicate. The Goddess will be very angry. . . .'

'I don't see how he could make the same mistake twice. Do you think he does it on purpose?' We were seated in Caecilia's reception room, a high, long hall with skylights above and open doors at either end to admit the breeze. The walls were painted in the realist fashion to reproduce a garden – green grass, trees, peacocks, and flowers on the walls, blue sky above. The floor was green tile. The ceiling was draped with blue cloth.

'No, don't answer that. I know what you'd say, Cicero. But Ahausarus is far too valuable to be got rid of, and too delicate to punish. If only he weren't so scatterbrained.'

There were four of us seated around a small silver table set with cool water and pomegranates – Cicero, myself, Caecilia, and the young Rufus, who had arrived ahead of us but had known better than to enter Metella's sanctum, preferring to wait in the garden instead. Tiro stood a short distance behind his master's chair.

Metella was a large, florid woman. Despite her age she appeared quite robust. Whatever colour her hair might originally have been, it was now fiery red, and probably white beneath the henna. She wore it piled high on her head, wound in a tapering coil held in place by a long silver pin. The pointed tip poked through on one side; the needle's head was decorated with carnelian. She wore an expensive-looking stola and much jewellery. Her face was covered with paint and rouge. Her hair and clothing reeked of incense. In one hand she held a fan and beat the air with it, as if she were trying to disperse her scent about the table.

Rufus was also redheaded, with brown eyes, flushed cheeks, and a freckled nose. He was as young as Cicero had indicated. Indeed, he could have been no more than sixteen, for he still wore the gown that all minors wear, whether male or female – white wool fitted with long sleeves to deflect the eyes of the lustful. In a few months he would put on the toga of manhood, but for now he was still a boy by law. It was obvious that he idolized Cicero, and equally obvious that Cicero enjoyed being idolized.

Neither of the nobles showed any discomfort in

accepting me at their table. Of course, they were seeking my help in a problem with which neither of them had any experience. They showed me the same deference a senator may show to a bricklayer, if the senator happens to have an archway about to collapse in his bedroom. Tiro they ignored.

Cicero cleared his throat. 'Caecilia, the day is very hot. If we have dwelt long enough on our unfortunate intrusion into your sanctuary, perhaps we can move on to more earthly matters.'

'Of course, Cicero. You've come about poor young Sextus.'

'Yes. Gordianus here may be of some help to us in unravelling the circumstances as I prepare his defence.'

'The defence. Oh, yes. Oh, dear. I suppose they're still out there, aren't they, those awful guards. You must have noticed them.'

'I'm afraid so.'

'It's such an embarrassment. The day they arrived I told them flatly I wouldn't stand for it. Of course it didn't do any good. Orders from the court, they said. If Sextus Roscius was to abide here, it would have to be under house arrest, with soldiers at every door, day and night. "Arrest?" I said. "As if he were in a prison, like a captured soldier or a runaway slave? I know the law very well, and there is no law that allows you to hold a Roman citizen in his own home, or the home of his patroness." It's always been that way; a citizen accused of a crime always has the option to make his escape if he doesn't want to face trial and he's willing to leave his property behind.

82

'So they sent for a deputy from the court who explained it all very smoothly – it couldn't have been smoother if it had come from your own lips, Cicero. "Right you are," he says, "except in certain cases. Certain capital cases." And what did he mean by that, I wanted to know. "Capital," he said, "as in decapitation – cases involving the removal of the head, or other vital organs, resulting in death." '

Caecilia Metella sat back and fanned herself. Her eyes became narrow and misted. Rufus leaned forwards and tenderly laid his hand upon her elbow.

'Only then did I realize how terrible it all was. Poor young Sextus, my dear friend's only surviving son, having lost his father, might now have to lose his head as well. But even worse than that! This underling, this person, this deputy, went on to explain exactly what the word *capital* meant in a conviction for parricide. Oh! I would never have believed it if you hadn't confirmed it yourself, Cicero, word for word. Too terrible, too terrible for words!'

Caecilia fanned herself furiously. Her eyelids, heavy with Egyptian kohl, flickered like moth's wings. She seemed about to faint.

Rufus reached for a cup of water. She waved it away. 'I don't pretend to know the young man; it was his father whom I loved and cherished as a dear, dear friend. But he is the son of Sextus Roscius, and I have offered him sanctuary in my home. And surely, what that man, that deputy, that odious person described should never happen to any but the most wretched, the most foul and debased of murderers.'

She batted her eyes and reached out blindly. Rufus fumbled for a moment, then found the cup and put it in her hand. She took a sip and handed it back.

'So I asked this creature, this deputy, very reasonably, I thought, if it would be too much trouble to have these soldiers at least stand somewhere away from the house instead of hovering right by the door. It's humiliating! I have neighbours, and how they love to talk. I have dependents and clients arriving every morning looking for favours – the soldiers scare them off. I have nieces and nephews afraid to come to the house. Oh, those soldiers know how to hold their tongues, but you should see the looks they give a young girl! Can't you do something about it, Rufus?'

'Me?'

'Of course, you. You must carry some weight with . . . with Sulla. It's Sulla who set up the courts. And he *is* married to your sister Valeria.'

'Yes, but that doesn't mean . . .' Rufus blushed a deep red.

'Oh, come now.' Caecilia's voice became conspiratorial. 'You're a handsome enough young boy, as pretty as Valeria any day. And we all know that Sulla casts his net on both sides of the stream.'

'Caecilia!' Cicero's eyes flashed, but he kept his voice steady.

'I'm not suggesting anything improper. Charm, Cicero. A gesture, a look. Rufus needn't actually *do* anything, of course. Why, Sulla's old enough to be his grandfather. All the more reason he could condescend to do a small favour for a such a charming boy.'

'Sulla doesn't find me charming,' said Rufus.

'And why not? He married Valeria for her looks, didn't he? And you look enough like her to be her brother.'

There was an odd sputtering noise. It was Tiro, standing behind his master's chair, pressing his lips together to keep from laughing. Cicero covered the noise by loudly clearing his throat.

'If we could go back to something that was mentioned a moment ago,' I said. Three pairs of eyes converged on me. Cicero looked relieved, Tiro attentive, Caecilia confused. Rufus stared at the floor, still blushing.

'You mentioned the penalty for the crime of parricide. I'm not familiar with it. Perhaps you could explain it for my benefit, Cicero.'

The mood was suddenly sombre, as if a cloud had passed over the sun. Caecilia turned aside and hid behind her fan. Rufus exchanged an uncomfortable glance with Tiro.

Cicero filled his cup and took a long draught of water. 'It's not surprising that you shouldn't be familiar with the subject, Gordianus. Parricide is such a rare crime among the Romans. The last conviction, as well as I could ascertain, took place when my grandfather was a young man.

'Traditionally, of course, the penalty of death is carried out by decapitation, or for a slave, crucifixion.

In the case of parricide the penalty is very ancient and very severe, laid down long ago by priests, not lawmakers, to express the wrath of father Jupiter against any son who would dare to strike down the carrier of the seed that made him.'

'Please, Cicero.' Caecilia looked over her fan and batted her makeup-laden eyelashes. 'To have heard it once is enough. It gives me nightmares.'

'But Gordianus should know. To know that a man's life is at stake is one thing; to know the way in which he might die is something more. This is what the law decrees: that the condemned parricide, immediately following his conviction, shall be taken outside the city walls to the Field of Mars, close by the Tiber. Horns shall be blown and cymbals sounded, calling the populace to witness.

'When the people are assembled, the parricide shall be stripped naked, as on the day of his birth. Two pedestals, knee-high, shall be placed several feet apart. The parricide shall mount them, one foot on each pedestal, squatting down with his hands chained behind his back. In this fashion, every part of his naked body is made accessible to his tormentors, who are charged by the law to lash him with knotted whips until the blood pours like water from his flesh. If he falls from his perch, he is made to mount it again. The whips are to fall on every part of him, even to the bottoms of his feet and the nether regions between his legs. The blood that drips from his body is the same as the blood that ran through his father's veins and gave him life.

86

Watching it spill from his wounds, he may contemplate the waste.'

Cicero stared vaguely into the distance as he spoke. Caecilia stared at him, her eyes narrow and intense above her fan.

'A sack shall be prepared, large enough to hold a man, made of hides so tightly sewn as to be sealed against water and air. When the whipmasters have completed their work – that is, when every part of the parricide is so covered with blood that one can no longer tell where the blood ends and raw flesh begins – the condemned man shall be made to crawl into the sack. The sack shall be placed some distance from the pedestals, so that the assembled people may watch his progress and be given the opportunity to pelt him with dung and offal and to publicly curse him.

'When he reaches the sack, he shall be induced to crawl inside. If he resists, he shall be dragged back to the pedestals and the punishment begun again.

'Within the sack, the parricide is returned to the womb, unborn, unbirthed. To be born, the philosophers tell us, is an agony. To be unborn is greater agony. Into the sack, crammed against the parricide's torn, bleeding flesh, the tormentors shall push four living animals. First, a dog, the most slavish and contemptuous of beasts, and a rooster, with its beak and claws especially sharpened. These symbols are very ancient: the dog and the cock, the watcher and the waker, guardians of the hearth; having failed to protect father from son, they take their place with the murderer. Along with them goes a snake, the male principle which may kill even as it gives life; and a monkey, the gods' cruellest parody of mankind.'

'Imagine it!' Caecilia gasped behind her fan. 'Imagine the noise!'

'All five shall be sewn up together in the sack and carried to the river's edge. The sack must not be rolled or beaten with sticks – the animals must stay alive within the sack so that they may torment the parricide for as long as possible. While priests pronounce the final curses, the sack shall be thrown into the Tiber. Watchers shall be posted all the way to Ostia; if the sack runs aground it must be pushed back into the stream at once, until it reaches the sea and disappears from sight.

'The parricide destroys the very source of his own life. He ends that life deprived of contact with the very elements which give life to the world – earth, air, water, even sunlight are denied him in the last hours or days of his agony, until at last the sack should rupture at the seams and be devoured by the sea, its spoils passed from Jupiter to Neptune, and thence to Pluto, beyond the caring or the memory or even the disgust of mankind.'

The room was silent. Cicero at last took a long, deep breath. There was a thin smile on his lips, and I thought he looked rather proud of himself, as actors and orators tend to look after a successful recitation.

Caecilia lowered her fan. She was absolutely white beneath her makeup. 'You'll understand now, Gordianus, when you meet him. Poor young Sextus, you'll understand now why he's so distraught. Like a rabbit, petrified with terror. Poor boy. They'll do it to him, unless they're stopped. You must help him, young man. You must help Rufus and Cicero stop them.'

'Of course. I'll do whatever I can. If the truth can save Sextus Roscius – I suppose he's here, somewhere in the house?'

'Oh, yes, he isn't allowed to leave; you saw the guards. He would be here with us now, except . . .'

'Yes?'

Rufus cleared his throat. 'When you meet him, you'll see.'

'See what?'

'The man is a wreck,' said Cicero. 'Panic-stricken, incoherent, completely distraught. Almost mad with terror.'

'Is he so fearful of being convicted? The case against him must be very strong.'

'Of course he's frightened.' Caecilia batted her fan at a fly perched on her sleeve. 'Who wouldn't be, with such a terror over his head? And just because he's innocent, that hardly means . . . well, I mean to say, we all know of cases, especially since . . . that is, in the last year or so . . . to be innocent is hardly to be safe these days.' She darted a quick glance at Rufus, who studiously ignored her.

'The man is afraid of his shadow,' Cicero said. 'Afraid before he came here, but even more afraid now. Afraid of being convicted; afraid of acquittal. He says that whoever killed his father is determined to kill him as well; the trial itself is a plot to dispose of him. If the law fails them, they'll murder him in the streets.'

'He wakes me up in the middle of the night, screaming.' Caecilia swatted at the fly. 'I can hear him all the way from the western wing. Nightmares. I think the monkey is the worst part. Except for the snake . . .'

Rufus gave a shudder. 'Caecilia says he was actually relieved when they posted the guard outside – as if they were here to protect him, rather than to keep him from escaping. Escape! He won't even leave his rooms.'

'True,' Cicero said. 'Otherwise you would have met him in my study, Gordianus, with no need to come here disturbing our hostess.'

'That would have been a great loss and entirely to my detriment,' I said, 'never to have been welcomed into the home of Caecilia Metella.'

Caecilia smiled demurely to acknowledge the compliment. In the next instant her eyes darted to the table and her fan descended with a slap. That fly would never bother her again.

'But at any rate, I should have had to meet with her sooner or later in the course of my investigation.'

'But why?' Cicero objected. 'Caecilia knows nothing of the murder. She's only a friend of the family, not a witness.'

'Nevertheless, Caecilia Metella was one of the last to see the elder Roscius alive.'

'Yes, that's true.' She nodded. 'He ate his last meal here in this very room. Oh, how he loved this room. He once told me he had no use for the outdoors at all. Fields and meadows and country life in Ameria bored him without end. "This is all the garden I need," he once told me.' She gestured to the painted walls. 'You see that peacock over there, on the southern wall, with its wings in full array? There, it's lit up at this very moment by the skylight. How he loved that image, all the colours – I remember, he used to call it his Gaius, and wanted me to do the same. Gaius loved this room, too, you know.'

'Gaius?'

'Yes. His son.'

'I thought the dead man had only one son.'

'Oh, no. Well, yes, only one remaining son, after Gaius died.'

'And when was that?'

'Let me think. Three years ago? Yes, I remember, because it was the very night of Sulla's triumph. There were parties all over the Palatine. People made the rounds from one gathering to another. Everyone feasted – the civil wars were over at last. I hosted a party myself, in this room, with the doors to the garden thrown open. Such a warm night – weather exactly like what we're having now. Sulla himself was here for a while. I remember, he made a joke. "Tonight," he said, "everyone who's anyone in Rome is either partying – or packing." Of course, there were some who partied who should have packed. Who could have imagined things would go so far?' She raised her eyebrows and sighed.

'Then it was here that Gaius Roscius died?'

'Oh, no, that's the point. That's why I remember. Gaius and his father *should* have been here – oh, how that would have excited dear Sextus, to have rubbed elbows with Sulla in this very room, to have had the opportunity to introduce Gaius to him. And knowing the dictator's tastes in that direction' – she narrowed her eyes and looked askance at no one in particular – 'they might have hit it off rather well.'

'Sulla and the boy, you mean?'

'Of course.'

'Then Gaius was a comely youth?'

'Oh, yes. Fair-haired and handsome, intelligent, well-mannered. Everything dear Sextus wanted in a son.'

'How old was Gaius?'

'Let me think, he had taken his manly toga some time before. Nineteen, I imagine, perhaps twenty.'

'Considerably younger than his brother?'

'Oh, yes, I imagined poor young Sextus is – what, forty at the least? He has two daughters, you know. The elder is almost sixteen.'

'Were they close, the two brothers?'

'Gaius and young Sextus? I don't think so. I don't see how they could have been – they almost never saw each other. Gaius spent all his time with his father in the city, while Sextus ran the farms in Ameria.'

'I see. You were going to tell me how Gaius died.'

'Really, I don't see how any of this pertains to

the case at hand.' Cicero shifted uncomfortably in his chair. 'It's nothing more than gossip.'

I glanced at him, not without sympathy. Thus far Cicero had treated me with uncommon courtesy, partly because he was naive, partly because of his nature. But my talking so freely with a woman so far above me (a Metella!) irked even his liberal sensibility. He saw the dialogue for what it was, an interrogation, and he took offence.

'No, no, Cicero, let him ask.' Caecilia reproached him with her fan and indulged me with a smile. She was happy, even eager, to talk about her late friend. I had to wonder exactly what her own relationship had been once upon a time with party-going, fun-loving old Sextus Roscius.

'No, Gaius Roscius did not die in Rome.' Caecilia sighed. 'They were to have come here that night, to pass the early evening at my party; then we would all walk to sands were invited. Sulla's largesse was boundless. Sextus Roscius was quite anxious to make a good appearance; only a few days before, he had come by with young Gaius to ask my advice on his apparel. If things had gone as they should have, Gaius would never have died. . . .' Her voice died away. She raised her eyes to the sunlit peacock.

'The Fates intervened,' I prompted.

'As they have a nasty habit of doing. Two days before the triumph Sextus *pater* received a message from Sextus *filius* in Ameria, urging him to come home. Some emergency – a fire, a flood, I'm not sure. So urgent that Sextus rushed home to the

93

family estate and took Gaius with him. He hoped to be back in time for the festivities. Instead he stayed in Ameria for the funeral.'

'How did it happen?'

'Food poisoning. A bad jar of pickled mushrooms – one of Gaius's favourite delicacies. Sextus described the incident to me later in great detail, how his son collapsed on the floor and began vomiting clear bile. Sextus reached into his throat, thinking his son was choking. The boy's throat was burning hot. When he pulled out his fingers they were covered with blood. Gaius coughed up more bile, this time thick and black. He was dead within minutes. Senseless, tragic. Dear Sextus was never the same afterwards.'

'You say that Gaius was nineteen or twenty, yet I thought his father was a widower. When did the boy's mother die?'

'Oh – but of course, you wouldn't know. She died giving birth to Gaius. I think that was one of the reasons Sextus loved the boy so much. He resembled his mother a great deal. Sextus thought of Gaius as her final gift to him.'

'And the two sons – they must have been born almost twenty years apart. To the same mother?'

'No. Didn't I explain? Gaius and young Sextus were half brothers. The first wife died of some illness years ago.' Caecilia shrugged. 'Perhaps another reason the boys were never close.'

'I see. And when Gaius died, did that bring Sextus Roscius and his elder son closer together?'

Caecilia glanced away sadly. 'No. It was quite the

opposite, I'm afraid. Sometimes tragedy has that effect on a family, to deepen old wounds. Sometimes a father loves one son more than the other – who can change such a fact? When Gaius died, Sextus blamed the boy's brother. It was an accident, of course, but an old man in the throes of grief isn't always strong enough to blame the gods. He came back to Rome and frittered away his time – and his fortune. He once told me, now that Gaius was dead, he had no one to whom he cared to leave a legacy, so he was determined to spend it all before he died. Cruel words, I know. While Sextus *filius* ran the estates, Sextus *pater* blindly spent everything he could. You can imagine the bitterness on both sides.'

'Enough bitterness to lead to murder?'

Caecilia gave a weary shrug. Her vivaciousness had deserted her. The disguise of henna and make-up abruptly faded, revealing the wrinkled woman beneath. 'I don't know. It would be almost unbearable to think that Sextus Roscius was killed by his own son.'

'That night last September – on the Ides, wasn't it? – Sextus Roscius dined here . . . before his death?'

'Yes.'

'When did he leave your house?'

'He left early, I remember. It was his habit to stay on until well into the night, but that evening he left before the final course. It was the first hour after nightfall.'

'And do you know where he was headed?'

'Home, I suppose . . .' Her voice trailed off in an unnatural way. Caecilia Metella, having lived so many years alone, lacked at least one skill that all Roman wives possess. Caecilia Metella had no ability to lie.

I cleared my throat. 'Perhaps Sextus Roscius wasn't on his way home when he left you that night. Perhaps there was a reason he left early. An appointment? A message?'

'Well, yes, actually.' Caecilia furrowed her brow. 'It seems to me there was a messenger who came. Yes, a very common sort of messenger, the kind that anyone might hire off the street. He came to the servants' door. Ahausarus came looking for me, explaining there was a man outside the kitchens with a message for Sextus Roscius. I was hosting a small party that night; there were only six or eight of us in the room, not yet done with dinner. Sextus was relaxing, almost dozing. Ahausarus whispered in his ear. Sextus looked a bit startled, but he rose at once and left the room without even asking my leave.'

'I don't suppose, in some way or other, you happened to know what that message was?'

Cicero groaned, very faintly. Caecilia stiffened, and the natural colour rose in her cheeks. 'Young man, Sextus Roscius and I were very old, very dear friends.'

'I understand, Caecilia Metella.'

'Do you? An old man needs someone to look after his interests, and to show some curiosity when strange messengers arrive to disturb him in the night. Of course, I followed. And I listened.'

'Ah. Then could you tell me from whom this messenger came?'

'These were his exact words: "Elena asks that you come to the House of Swans at once. It's very important." And then he showed Sextus a token.'

'What sort of token?'

'A ring.'

'A ring?'

'A woman's ring – small, silver, very plain. The sort of ring a poor man might give to his lover, or the sort of petty token that a rich man might give to a . . .'

'I see.'

'Do you? After Gaius died, Sextus began spending a great deal of time and money in those sorts of places. I'm talking about brothels, of course. Do you think it pathetic, a man of his age? But don't you see, it was because of Gaius. As if there were a sudden, overwhelming desire in him to create another son. Absurd, of course, but sometimes a man must bow to nature. Healing takes place in mysterious ways.'

We sat in silence for a moment. 'I think you are a wise woman, Caecilia Metella. Do you know anything else about this Elena?'

'No.'

'Or the House of Swans?'

'Nothing, except that it's somewhere in the vicinity of the Baths of Pallacina, not very far from Sextus's house by the Circus Flaminius. Well, you don't think he would have patronized some tawdry establishment in the Subura, do you?'

Cicero cleared his throat. 'I think it may be time for Gordianus to meet young Sextus Roscius.'

'Only a few more questions,' I said. 'Sextus Roscius left the dinner party immediately?'

'Yes.'

'But not alone.'

'No, he left with the two slaves who had accompanied him. His favourites. Sextus always brought them.'

'You wouldn't happen to remember their names?'

'Of course I do, they were in and out of my house for years. Chrestus and Felix. Very loyal. Sextus trusted them completely.'

'Suitable slaves for a bodyguard?'

'I suppose they may have carried knives of some sort. But they weren't built like gladiators, if that's what you mean. No, they were there mainly to hold the lamps and to see their master to his bed. Against a gang of armed thugs I don't imagine they would have been much use.'

'And did their master need seeing to bed, or help walking through the streets?'

'You mean was he that drunk?' Caecilia smiled fondly. 'Sextus was not a man to stint himself of pleasure.'

'I suppose he was wearing a fine toga.'

'His finest.'

'And did he wear jewellery?'

'Sextus was not modest in appearance. I imagine there was gold showing on his person.'

I shook my head at the audacity of it: an old man

walking virtually unguarded through the streets of Rome after dark, drunk on wine and showing off his wealth, answering a mysterious summons from a whore. His luck had finally abandoned Sextus Roscius on the Ides of September, but who had been the instrument of Fate, and for what purpose?

VII

Sextus Roscius and his family had been installed in a
distant wing of the great house. The eunuch
Ahausarus led us there through a network of increasingly narrow and less resplendent hallways. At
last we entered a region where the paintings on the
walls badly needed restoration, then vanished altogether to be replaced by ordinary plaster, much of it
decayed and crumbling. The tile beneath our feet
became uneven and cracked, with holes the size of a
man's fist. We were far from the formal gardens and
the intimate dining room where Caecilia had received us, far beyond the kitchens and even the
servants' quarters. The odours here were less de-
lectable than those of roast duck and boiling fish.
We were somewhere near the indoor privies.

Like a true Roman patroness of the ancient
mould, Caecilia seemed willing to undergo embarrassment and even scandal to protect a family client,

but it was clear that she had no desire to have young Sextus Roscius anywhere near her within the house, or to spoil him with luxury. I began to wonder if Caecilia was herself convinced of the man's innocence, to have given him such begrudging shelter.

'How long has Roscius been living under Metella's roof?' I asked Cicero.

'I'm not sure. Rufus?'

'Not long. Twenty days, perhaps; he wasn't here any earlier than the Nones of April, I'm sure. I visit her often, but I didn't even know he was here until the guards were posted and Caecilia felt she had to explain. Before that she made no effort to introduce him. I don't think she cares for him very much, and of course his wife is so very common.'

'And what was he doing here in the city if he loves the countryside so much?'

Rufus shrugged. 'I'm not sure about that either, and I don't think Caecilia knows for certain. He and his family simply showed up on her doorstep one afternoon, pleading for admittance. I doubt she had ever met him before, but of course when she realized he was Sextus's son she opened her house immediately. It seems this trouble over the old man's death has been brewing for some time, beginning back in Ameria. I think they may have run him out of the village; he showed up in Rome with practically nothing, not even a household slave. Ask him who's caring for his farms back in Ameria and he'll tell you that most of them were sold, and some cousins are running the rest. Ask him to be specific and he throws one of his fits. Personally I think Hortensius dropped the case out of sheer frustration.'

Ahausarus made a show of admitting us with a flourish through a final curtain. 'Sextus Roscius, the son of Sextus Roscius,' he said, bowing his head towards the figure who sat in the centre of the room, 'a much-esteemed client of my mistress. I bring visitors,' he said, making a vaguely dismissive gesture in our direction. 'The young Messalla, and Cicero, the advocate, whom you have met before. And another, called Gordianus.' Tiro he ignored, of course, as he also ignored the woman who sat sewing cross-legged on the floor in one corner, and the two girls who knelt beneath the skylight playing some sort of game.

Ahausarus withdrew. Rufus stepped forward. 'You look better today, Sextus Roscius.'

The man gave a faint nod.

'Perhaps you'll have more to say this afternoon. Cicero needs to begin preparing his defence – your trial is only eight days away. That's why Gordianus has come with us. They call him the Finder. He is skilled at finding the truth.'

'A magician?' Two baleful eyes glared up at me.

'No,' said Rufus. 'An investigator. My brother Hortensius often makes use of his services.'

The baleful eyes turned on Rufus. 'Hortensius – the coward who turned tail and ran? What good can any friends of Hortensius do me?'

Rufus's pale, freckled face turned the colour of cherries. He opened his mouth, but I raised my hand to silence him. 'Tell me something,' I said in a loud voice. Cicero wrinkled his brow and shook his head, but I waved him back. 'Tell me now, before we go any further. Sextus Roscius of Ameria: did you murder or did you in any way cause the murder of your father?'

I stood over him, daring him by my very posture to look up at me, which he did. What I saw was a simple face, such as Roman politicians delight in extolling, a face darkened by sun, chapped by wind, weathered by time. Roscius might be a rich farmer, but he was a farmer nonetheless. No man can rule over peasants without acquiring the look of a peasant; no man can raise crops out of the earth, even if he uses slaves to do it, without acquiring a layer of dirt beneath his fingernails. There was an uncouthness about Sextus Roscius, a rough-hewn, unpolished state, a quality of inertness as blank and immovable as granite. This was the son left behind in the countryside, to whip the backs of stubborn slaves and see the oxen pulled from ditches, while pretty young Gaius grew up a pampered city boy with city ways in the house of their pleasure-loving father.

I searched his eyes for resentment, bitterness, jealousy, avarice. I saw none of these. Instead I saw the eyes of an animal with one foot caught in a trap who hears the noise of hunters approaching.

Roscius finally answered me in a low, hoarse whisper: 'No.' He looked into my eyes without blinking. Fear was all I could see, and though fear will make a man lie more quickly than anything else, I believed he was telling me the truth. Cicero must have seen the same thing; it was Cicero who had told me that Roscius was innocent, and that I would only have to meet him to know it for myself.

Sextus Roscius was of middle age. Given that he was a hardworking man of considerable wealth, I had to assume that his appearance on this day was not typical. The terrible burden of his uncertain future – or else the terrible guilt of his crime – lay heavy upon him. His hair and beard were longer than even country fashion might dictate, knotted and unkempt and streaked with grey. His body, slumped in the chair, looked stooped and frail, though a glance at Cicero or Rufus revealed that in comparison he was a much larger man with a fair amount of muscle. There were dark circles beneath his eyes. His skin was sallow. His lips were dry and cracked.

Caecilia Metella claimed he woke up screaming at night. No doubt she had taken one look at him and decided that his mind was unhinged. But Caecilia had never walked the endless, teeming streets of the poor in Rome or Alexandria. Desperation may verge into madness, but to the eye that has seen too much of both there is a clear difference. Sextus Roscius was not a madman. He was desperate.

I looked around for a place to sit. Roscius snapped his fingers at the woman. She was middle-aged, stout, and plain. From the way she dared to scowl back at him, she had to be his wife. The woman stood up and snapped her fingers in turn at the two girls, who scurried up off the floor. Roscia Majora and Roscia Minora, I assumed, given the unimaginative way that Romans ration the father's surname to all the daughters in a family, distinguishing them only by appending their rank.

Roscia the elder was perhaps Rufus's age or a bit younger, a child on the cusp of womanhood. Like Rufus she wore a plain white gown that kept her limbs concealed. Great masses of chestnut hair were braided into a knot at the base of her neck and cascaded to her waist; in country fashion, her hair had never been cut. Her face was strikingly pretty, but about her eyes I saw the same haunted look that marked her father.

The younger girl was only a child, a replica of her sister in miniature, with the same gown and the same long, braided hair. She followed the other women across the room but was too small to help them carry the chairs. Instead she grinned and pointed at Cicero.

'Funny-face,' she shouted, then clapped her hands to her mouth, laughing. Her mother scowled and chased her from the room. I glanced at Cicero, who bore the indignity with stoic grace. Rufus, who looked as handsome as Apollo next to Cicero, blushed and looked at the ceiling.

The older girl retreated after her mother, but before slipping through the curtain she turned and glanced back. Cicero and Rufus were taking their seats; they seemed not to notice her. I was struck again by her face – her wide mouth and smooth forehead, her deep brown eyes tinged with sadness.

She must have seen me staring; she stared back with a frankness not often found in girls of her age and class. Her lips drew back, her eyes narrowed, and the look on her face suddenly became an invitation – sensual, calculated, provocative. She smiled. She nodded. Her lips moved, mouthing words I couldn't make out.

Cicero and Rufus were across the room, their heads together, exchanging a hurried whisper. I glanced over my shoulder and saw only Tiro nervously shifting from foot to foot. She could only have been looking at me, I thought.

When I looked back, young Roscia Majora was gone, with only the swaying curtain and a faint scent of jasmine to mark her passing. The intimacy of her parting glance left me startled and confused. It was such a look as lovers exchange, yet I had never seen her before.

I stepped to the chair that had been set out for me. Tiro followed behind and slid it beneath me. I shook my head to clear it. Another look at the girl's father sobered me instantly.

'Where are your slaves, Sextus Roscius? Surely in your own home you would never think of asking your wife and daughters to fetch chairs for company.'

The baleful eyes glittered. 'Why not? Do you think they're too good for it? It does a woman good to be reminded every so often of her place. Especially women like mine, with a husband and father rich enough to let them sit about and do as they please all day long.'

'Pardon, Sextus Roscius. I meant no offence. You speak wisely. Perhaps next time we should ask Caecilia Metella to fetch the chairs.'

Rufus suppressed a laugh. Cicero winced at my impertinence.

'You're a real wise-mouth, aren't you?' snapped Sextus Roscius. 'A clever city man like these others. What is it you want?'

'Only the truth, Sextus Roscius. Because finding it is my job, and because the truth is the one thing that can save an innocent man – a man like you.'

Roscius sank lower in his seat. In a test of brawn he would have been a match for any two of us, even in his weakened state, but he was an easy man to beat down with words.

'What is it you want to know?'

'Where are your slaves?'

He shrugged. 'Back in Ameria, of course. On the estates.'

'All of them? You brought no servants with you, to clean and cook, to take care of your daughters? I don't understand.'

Tiro bent close to Cicero and whispered something in his ear. Cicero nodded and waved his hand. Tiro left the room.

'What a well-mannered little slave you've got.' Roscius curled his lip. 'Asking his master's permission to take a piss. Have you seen the plumbing here? Like nowhere else I've ever seen. Running water right in the house. My father used to talk about it – you know how an old man hates having to step outside to pass water in the night. Not here!

Too good a place for slaves to take a shit if you ask me. Usually doesn't smell this bad, except it's so damned hot.'

'We were talking about your slaves, Sextus Roscius. There are two in particular to whom I wish to speak. Your father's favourites, the ones who were with him the night he died. Felix and Chrestus. Are they in Ameria, too?'

'How would I know?' he snapped. 'Probably run off by now. Or had their throats slit.'

'And who would do that?'

'Slit their throats? The same men who murdered my father, of course.'

'And why?'

'Because the slaves saw it happen, you fool.'

'And how do you know that?'

'Because they told me.'

'Was that how you first learned of your father's death – from the slaves who were with him?'

Roscius paused. 'Yes. They sent a messenger from Rome.'

'You were in Ameria the night he was killed?'

'Of course. Twenty people could tell you that.'

'And when did you learn he had been killed?'

Roscius paused again. 'The messenger arrived two mornings after.'

'And what did you do then?'

'I came into the city that day. A hard ride. You can make it in eight hours if you have a good horse. Started at dawn, arrived at sundown – days are short in the autumn. The slaves showed me his body. The wounds . . .' His voice became a whisper.

'And did they show you the street where he was killed?'

Sextus Roscius stared at the floor. 'Yes.'

'The very spot?'

He shuddered. 'Yes.'

'I shall need to go there and see it for myself.'

He shook his head. 'I won't go there again.'

'I understand. The two slaves can take me there, Felix and Chrestus.' I watched his face. A light glimmered in his eyes, and I was suddenly suspicious, though of what I couldn't say. 'Ah,' I said, 'but the slaves are in Ameria, aren't they?'

'I already told you that.' Roscius seemed to shiver, despite the heat.

'But I need to visit the scene of the crime as soon as possible. I can't wait for these slaves to be brought to Rome. I understand your father was on his way to an establishment called the House of Swans. Perhaps the crime occurred nearby.'

'Never heard of the place.' Was he lying or not? I studied his face, but my instincts failed me.

'Even so, perhaps you could tell me how to find the spot?'

He could, and did. I was a bit surprised at this, given his ignorance of the city. There are a thousand streets in Rome; only a handful have names. But between Cicero and myself, and the landmarks Roscius could remember, I was able to piece together the route. It was complicated enough to need writing down. Cicero looked over his shoulder, muttering about Tiro's absence; fortunately Tiro had left his wax tablet and stylus on the floor behind Cicero's chair. Rufus volunteered to write out the notations.

'Now tell me, Sextus Roscius: do you know who murdered your father?'

He lowered his eyes and paused a very long time. Perhaps it was only the heat, making him groggy. 'No.'

'Yet you told Cicero that you fear the same fate – that the same men are determined to kill you as well. That this prosecution is itself an attempt on your life.'

Roscius shook his head and drew his arms around himself. The baleful light was extinguished. His eyes grew dark. 'No, no,' he muttered. 'I never said such a thing.' Cicero shot me a puzzled glance. Roscius's mutterings grew louder. 'Give it up, all of you! Give it up! I'm a doomed man. They'll throw me in the Tiber, sewn up in a sack, and for what? For nothing! What's to become of my little daughters, my pretty little daughters, my beautiful girls?' He began to weep.

Rufus stepped to his side and placed a hand on the man's shoulder. Roscius violently shook it off.

I rose and made a formal bow. 'Come, gentlemen, I believe we are finished here for the day.'

Cicero reluctantly stood. 'But surely you've only begun. Ask him—'

I placed a finger to my lips. I turned towards the doorway, calling after Rufus, for I saw that he was still trying to comfort Sextus Roscius. I held back the curtain and allowed Cicero and Rufus to pass through. I looked back at Roscius, who was biting his knuckles and shivering.

'There is some terrible shadow on you, Sextus Roscius of Ameria. Whether it's guilt or shame or dread, I can't make out. You obviously have no intention of explaining. But let this comfort you, or torment you, as the case may be: I promise you this, that I shall do everything I can to uncover your father's murderer, whoever he may be; and I shall succeed.'

Roscius slammed his fists against the arms of his chair. His eyes glistened, but he no longer wept. The fire returned. 'Do what you want!' he snapped. 'Another city-born fool. I never asked for your help. As if the truth by itself mattered, or meant anything at all. Go on, go gawk at his bloodstains in the street! Go see where the old man died on his way to visit his whore! What difference will it make? What difference? Even here I'm not safe!'

There was more. I did not hear it. I dropped my arm and let the heavy curtains absorb his abuse.

'It seems to me he must know much more than he's telling,' Rufus said as we walked through the corridors towards Caecilia's wing.

'Of course he does. But what?' Cicero made a face. 'I begin to see why Hortensius dropped the case.'

'Do you?' I asked.

'The man is impossible. How am I to defend him? You see why Caecilia has him stuck away in this smelly corner. I'm embarrassed to have wasted your time. I've half a mind to drop the case myself.'

'I would advise against that.'

'Why?'

'Because my investigation has only started, and we've already made a promising beginning.'

'But how can you say that? We've learned nothing, either from Caecilia or from Roscius himself: Caecilia knows nothing, and she's only involved because of her sentimental attachment to the dead man. Roscius knows something, but he won't tell. What could frighten him so badly that he won't help his own defenders? We don't even know enough to know what he's lying about.' Cicero grimaced. 'Even so, by Hercules, I still believe he's innocent. Don't you feel it?'

'Yes, perhaps. But you're mistaken if you believe we've discovered nothing of value. I stopped asking him questions only because I already have enough threads to unravel. I've learned enough this afternoon to keep me busy for at least the next two days.'

'Two days?' Cicero tripped over a loose tile. 'But the trial begins in eight days, and I still have no argument to build on.'

'I promise you, Marcus Tullius Cicero, in eight days we shall know not only where Sextus Roscius was killed – which is no small detail – but also why and by whom and for what reason. However, at this moment it would make me very happy to solve a far simpler but no less pressing mystery.'

'And what is that?'

'Where can I find these much-celebrated indoor privies?'

Rufus laughed. 'We've passed them already. You'll have to turn back. The second door on your left will lead you to it. You'll know it by the blue tile and a little relief of Triton above the door.'

Cicero wrinkled his nose. 'I suspect you'll know it from the smell. And while you're at it,' he called after me, 'see if you can find where Tiro has got to. The same thing happened the last time we came – claimed he got lost among the hallways. If he's still in the privy, I suppose he must be in some distress. Tell him it's what he deserves for refusing to follow my example of fasting at midday. So much food, it's an unnatural shock to the system, especially in this heat. . . .'

A turn to the left and a short walk down a narrow hallway brought me to the blue-tiled door. Small niches in the doorway contained tiny conical heaps of ash, the remnants of incense and sweet-burning woods to cover the fetid odours from within. On a day as stifling as this, the incense needed constant replenishing, but Caecilia's servants had been lax in their duties, or else all the incense had been claimed for the mistress's sanctum. I stepped through the heavy blue curtain.

There are no people on earth more adept at managing water and waste than the Romans. 'We are ruled,' as one Athenian wag once told me, 'by a nation of plumbers.' Yet here in one of the finest houses in the heart of the city something was badly amiss. The blue tiles needed scrubbing. The stone trough was clogged, and when I pressed the valve only a trickle of water emerged. A buzzing noise drew my eyes upward. Across the ventilating sky-light stretched an immense spider's web, filled with flies.

I did what I had come for and hurried from the room, sucking in a deep breath as I stepped through the blue curtain. The breath caught in my throat and I held it, listening to the sound of muffled voices from a doorway across the hall. One of the voices was Tiro's.

I crossed the hall and inclined my head towards the thin yellow curtain. The other voice was that of a young woman, a countrified voice but of some refinement. She spoke a few muffled words, then let out a gasp and a moan.

I understood at once.

I might have withdrawn. Instead I stepped closer to the curtain and pressed my face against the thin yellow cloth. I had thought it was to me that she had given that baffling, seductive glance, for my sake that she had lingered in the room. I had thought her silent message had been for me to decipher. But she had been looking through me all the while, as if I were transparent. It was Tiro, standing behind me, to whom she had given the look, the message, the invitation.

Their voices were low and hushed, no more than ten feet away. I could barely make out the words.

'I don't like it here,' she was saying. 'It smells.'

'But it's the only room close to the privy – it's the only excuse I could make – if my master comes looking for me I have to be close by . . .'

'All right, all right.' She let out a gasp. I heard

them grappling. I pushed back the edge of the curtain and peered into the room.

It was a small storage room lit by a single window near the ceiling. A white light eddied into the room but seemed incapable of filling it. Motes of dust spiralled through the dense, heavy air. Amid the stacks of boxes, crates, and sacks, I caught a glimpse of naked flesh: Tiro's thighs and buttocks. His thin cotton tunic was lifted up and pressed against his back by the girl's clutching fingers. His groin pressed into hers, retreated and bolted convulsively forwards in the ancient, unmistakable rhythm.

Their faces were joined together, concealed by a block of deep shadow. The girl was naked. The sexless gown, lying shapeless and abandoned on the floor, had given no hint of the voluptuous lines of her figure or the breathtaking purity of her white flesh, gleaming and hard like alabaster, moist with sweat in the hot airless room so that she shone as if she had been rubbed with oil. Her body responded to his, pressing against him, wriggling upright against the wall with a strange convulsive motion, like a snake writhing on a hot pavement.

'Soon,' Tiro whispered, in a husky, breathless voice I would never have recognized – a voice neither slave nor free, the voice of the animal, the beast, the body.

The girl wrapped her hands around his buttocks, holding him tight. Her head was thrown back, her breasts lifted high. 'A little longer,' she whispered.

'No, soon, they'll be waiting for me. . . .'

'Then remember, you promised, like last time – not inside me – my father would . . .'

'Now!' Tiro gave a long groan.

'Not inside me!' the girl hissed. Her fingers clawed into the tender flesh of his hips, pushing him away. Tiro staggered back, then forwards again, collapsing against her. He pressed his face to her cheek, then to her neck, then to her breasts as he slid downwards. He kissed her navel. He touched his tongue to the glistening strands of seed that clung to the smooth flesh of her belly. He embraced her hips and pressed his face between her legs.

I saw her naked, revealed in the soft, hazy light. Only her face was hidden in shadow. Her body was perfect, sleek and graceful, as pale and unblemished as heavy cream; neither a girl's body nor a woman's but the body of a girl awakening into womanhood, freed from innocence but unspoiled by time.

Without Tiro between us, I felt as naked as the girl. I drew back. The thin yellow curtain fell shut without a sound, gently rippling as if a stray breeze had wandered down the hallway.

VIII

'So they did it right there, in the rich woman's house, right under his master's nose. Good for them!'

'No, Bethesda. Right under *my* nose.' I pushed the bowl away and looked up at the sky. The glow of the city obscured the minor stars, but the greater constellations shone bright and glittering in the warm evening air. Far away to the west a band of thunderclouds loomed like the dusty wake of a mounted army. I lay back on the couch, closed my eyes, and listened to the stillness of the garden and all the little sounds inside it: the quiet sputtering of the torch, the chirr of a cricket beside the pond, the loud purring of Bast rubbing herself against the table leg. I heard the gentle clatter of dishes and Bethesda's light footfall as she retreated into the house. The cat followed after her; the purring grew louder for an instant and then diminished into silence.

Bethesda returned. I heard the rustle of her gown, then felt her presence as she joined me on the couch. My head dipped from her weight, then soft hands lifted me and cradled my face on her lap. Another weight dropped onto the foot of the couch. Warm fur stroked against my bare feet, and I felt the vibration as much as heard it – the loud contented purr of a cat grown fat on delicacies from its master's plate.

'Did the meal displease you, Master? You ate almost nothing.' Bethesda gently stroked my temple.

'The meal was delicious,' I lied. 'It was the heat that killed my appetite. And all the walking I did today.'

'You should not have walked so much in this heat. You should have made the rich woman hire you a litter.'

I shrugged. Bethesda stroked my neck and throat. I grasped her hand and ran her fingers against my lips. 'So soft and smooth. You work so hard, Bethesda – I tease you for being lazy, but I know better – yet you keep your hands as soft as a vestal's.'

'Something my mother taught me. Even the poorest girl in Egypt knows how to care for her body and to keep herself beautiful. Not like these Roman women.' Even with my eyes shut I could see the face she made, disdainful and haughty. 'Putting creams and makeup on their faces as if they were laying mortar for bricks.'

'The Romans have no style,' I agreed. 'No grace. Especially the women. The Romans became much too rich, much too quickly. They are a crude and vulgar people, and they own the world. Once upon a time they had manners, at least. A few of them still do, I suppose.'

'Like you?'

I laughed. 'Not me. I have no manners, and no money, either. All I own are a woman and a cat and a house I can't afford to keep up. I was thinking of Cicero.'

'From the way you describe him, he is a very homely man.'

'Yes, Bethesda, Cicero has nothing that would interest you.'

'But the boy . . .'

'No, Bethesda, Rufus Messalla is too young even for your tastes, and far too rich.'

'I meant the slave boy. The one who fetched you for his master. The one you saw with the girl. How did he look with his clothes off?'

I shrugged. 'I hardly saw him. Or at least not the parts of him that would interest you.'

'Perhaps you don't know the parts that would interest me.'

'Perhaps not.' With my eyes shut I saw them again, crushed against the wall, moving furiously together, shuddering to a rhythm from which all the rest of the world was excluded. Bethesda slid her hand inside my tunic and softly stroked my chest.

'What happened afterwards? Don't tell me they were caught, or I shall be very sad.'

'No, they weren't caught.'

'Did you let the boy know you had seen him?'

'No. I made my way down the corridor until I found Cicero and Rufus in the garden, sitting with Caecilia Metella, all three of them looking very grim. We spoke for a few moments. Tiro walked in a bit later, looking appropriately embarrassed. Cicero made no comment. No one suspected a thing.'

'Of course not. They think they know so much and he must know so little, being only a slave. You'd be surprised at the things a slave can do without getting caught.'

A tress of her hair fell against my cheek. I rubbed my face against it, breathing in the scents of henna and herbs. 'Would I be surprised, Bethesda?'

'No. Not you. Nothing surprises you.'

'Because I have a suspicious nature. Thank the gods for that.' Bast purred loudly against my feet. I settled my shoulders against Bethesda's thigh.

'So tired,' she said softly. 'Do you want me to sing?'

'Yes, Bethesda, sing something quiet and soothing. Sing something in a language I don't understand.'

Her voice was like still water, pure and deep. I had never heard the song before, and though I couldn't understand a word of it, I knew it must have been a lullaby. Perhaps it was a song her mother had sung. I lay half-dreaming in her lap, while images of the most horrendous violence passed harmlessly before my eyes. The images were unnaturally vivid, yet somehow remote, as if I watched them through a thick pane of coloured glass. I saw the drunken gladiators and the embalmers and the stabbing in the street that morning and Tiro's face flushed with excitement. I saw an old man set upon by thugs in an alley somewhere, stabbed over and over. I saw a naked man bound and whipped, pelted with excrement, sewn up in a bag with animals and cast alive into the Tiber.

At some point the lullaby ceased and changed into another song, a song I had often heard before, though I had never understood the words. It was one of the songs Bethesda sang to excite me, and while she sang it I sensed the movements of her body as she pulled off her robe, and I smelled the strong musk of her naked flesh. She rose up and over and beside me, until we lay close together upon the couch. She pulled my tunic above my hips, just as the daughter of Sextus Roscius had done for Tiro. I never opened my eyes, even as she bent down and swallowed me, even as I pulled her up and rolled atop her and pushed myself inside her. It was Bethesda's body I embraced, but it was the girl I saw behind my closed eyes, standing naked and defiled with the seed of a slave glistening on her flesh.

We lay together for a long time, unmoving, our bodies joined by heat and sweat, as if flesh could melt and fuse. Bast, who at some point had fled, returned and lay purring amid the tangle of our legs. I heard a peal of thunder and thought I only dreamed it, until a scattering of warm raindrops fell against my flesh, blown in from the garden. The torch sputtered and failed. More thunder, and

Bethesda huddled against me, murmuring in her secret language. The rain fell thick and straight, hissing on the roof tiles and paving stones, a long, steady rain, powerful enough to wash the foulest sewers and streets of Rome, the cleansing rain that poets and priests tell us comes from the gods to purify the sins of fathers and sons alike.

IX

The next morning I rose early and washed myself from the fountain in the garden. The parched earth had grown plump and moist from the night-long rain. The vegetation dripped with heavy dew. The sky above was milky pearl touched with coral, as opalescent as the inner surface of a shell. As I watched, the glaze of colour evaporated into mist; by imperceptible degrees the sky became a proper blue, suffused with light, cloudless, harbinger of the heat to come. I dressed in my lightest tunic and cleanest toga and ate a mouthful of bread. I left Bethesda sleeping on the couch. She lay clutching her robe as a coverlet against the still-cool morning, with Bast curled against her neck like a collar of black fur.

I made my way at a quick stride to Cicero's house. We had parted the day before with the understanding that I would pass by on my way to inspect the site of Sextus Roscius's murder. But when I arrived Cicero sent word by Tiro that he would not rise until noon. He suffered from a chronic malady of the bowels, and blamed the present relapse on having broken his regimen to eat a prune at Caecilia Metella's. He kindly offered the use of Tiro for the day.

The streets still gleamed with rain and the air had a clean, scrubbed smell when we set out. By the time we reached the foot of the Capitoline, passed through the Fontinal Gate, and entered the neighbourhood of the Circus Flaminius, the heat of the day had already begun to reassert its power over the city. The paving stones began to steam. Brick walls began to ooze and sweat. The freshness of morning turned humid and stifling.

I mopped my forehead with the edge of my toga and silently cursed the heat. I glanced at Tiro and saw that he was smiling, staring straight ahead with a stupid look in his eyes. I could imagine the reason for his high spirits, but I said nothing.

All about the Circus Flaminius is a network of mazelike streets. Those nearest the Circus, especially those that face the long structure itself and are thus most able to exploit the heavy traffic that surrounds it, are thick with shops, taverns, brothels, and inns. The outlying web of streets is crammed with tenements three and four storeys tall, many of which overhang the street and thus block out the sunlight. One street looks very much like another, and all are a hodgepodge of every age and quality of architecture. Given the frequency of fires and earthquakes,

Rome is constantly being rebuilt; as the population has grown and vast tracts of property have been amassed under the control of great landlords, the newer buildings tend to be of the poorest imaginable design and construction. Surrounding a venerable brick-and-mortar apartment building that has somehow withstood a century of catastrophes, one may see ramshackle tenements without the slightest ornament, looking to be made of nothing more than mud and sticks. Under Sulla, of course, these problems have only become worse.

We followed the route that Sextus Roscius had described, as copied down the day before by the young Messalla. Rufus's script was atrocious, almost unreadable. I remarked to Tiro that it was a pity he had been busy elsewhere and unable to take down the notes in his own firm, clean hand. 'Being a noble, Rufus has never bothered to learn how to make his letters, at least not so well that anyone else could read it. But you seem to have considerable skill in wielding your stylus.' I made the comment as offhandedly as I could, and smiled to see his ears turn red.

I had no doubt that the route was correct; it followed a natural path from the house of Caecilia Metella into the heart of the Circus district, taking the broadest streets, avoiding the more narrow and most dangerous shortcuts. We passed by several taverns, but old Sextus would not have stopped there, at least not on that night, not if he was so eager to reach the sender of the cryptic message.

We came into a broad sunlit square. Shops faced

inward towards the central cistern where the locals came to draw their daily water. A tall, broad-shouldered woman in dingy robes seemed to be the self-appointed mistress of the cistern, regulating the small line of slaves and housewives who stood about gossiping while they waited their turn. One of the slaves threw half a bucket of water on a group of ragged urchins loitering nearby. The children screamed with pleasure and shook themselves like dogs.

'Through there,' Tiro said. He studied the directions and bunched his eyebrows. 'At least I think so.'

'Yes, I remember from yesterday: a narrow passage between a wine shop and a tall red-stained tenement.' I looked about the irregular square, at the six streets that radiated outward. Of them all, the street that old Sextus had taken that night was the narrowest, and because it took a sharp turn early on, it afforded the least visibility. Perhaps it was the shortest way to the woman called Elena. Perhaps it was the only way.

I looked about and spotted a man crossing the square. I took him to be a minor merchant or a shopkeeper, a man of some means but not rich, to judge from his worn but well-made shoes. From the easy way he comported himself, looking idly about the square without seeming to notice a thing, I assumed he was a local who had crossed it many times, perhaps every day. He paused beside the public sundial mounted on a low pedestal, furrowing his brow and wrinkling his nose at it. I stepped up to him.

' "May the gods confound him," ' I quoted, ' "who first invented the hours, and who placed the first sundial in Rome!" '

'Ah!' He looked up, smiling broadly, and instantly picked up the refrain: ' "Pity me, pity me! They have segmented my day like the teeth of a comb!" '

'Ah, you know the play,' I began, but he was not to be interrupted.

' "When I was a boy my stomach was my clock, and it never steered me wrong; now even if the table overflows there's no eating till shadows are long. Rome is ruled by the sundial; Romans starve and thirst all the while!" '

We shared a quiet laugh. 'Citizen,' I said, 'do you know this neighbourhood?'

'Of course. I've lived here for years.'

'Then I'm sure you can help me. Starving and thirsty I'm not, but there is another craving I long to satisfy. I'm a lover of birds.'

'Birds? None around here but the pigeons. Too stringy for my taste.' He smiled, showing a wide gap between his teeth.

'I was thinking of a more elegant fowl. At home in water, on the earth, or heaven-bound. A friend of a friend told me there were swans hereabout.'

He understood at once. 'The House of Swans, you mean.'

I nodded.

'Right down that street.' He pointed to the space between the wine shop and the red tenement.

'Might one of these other streets take me there as easily?'

'Not unless you want to walk twice as far as you need to. No, this street is the only practical way. It's a single long block with only a few dead-end streets branching off. And the walk will be worth your while,' he added with a wink.

'I certainly hope so. Come, Tiro.' We turned and walked towards the narrow street. I could see only a little way down its length. The buildings on either side were high. Even in the bright morning light its walls seemed to close around us, dank and musty, a dim crevice of mortar and brick.

The buildings along its length were mostly long tenements, many with only a single door and no windows at street level, so that we walked for long stretches with blank walls on either side. Upper storeys overhung the lower; they would provide shelter when it rained, but they would also create deep pockets of shadow at night. All along the way, every fifty paces or so, brackets were mounted in the walls, filled with the still-smouldering stumps of last night's torches. Under each torch a small stone was set into the wall; each stone was engraved with the profile of a swan, the crude sort of work done by cheap artisans. The tiles were advertisements. The torches were there to guide the night-time clientele to the House of Swans.

'It should be soon,' Tiro said, looking up from the tablet.

'We've passed a side street to our left already, and now another to our right. According to Rufus's directions, Sextus Roscius found a large bloodstain in the middle of the street. But you don't think it could still be there, after all this time—'

Tiro's words never quite became a question. Instead his voice dropped on the final word as he looked down between his feet and came to a sudden stop. 'Here,' he whispered, and swallowed loudly.

Consider that a man's body contains a great deal of blood. Consider also the porous nature of paving stones, and the barely adequate drainage of many Roman streets, particularly those at the lower elevations. Consider that we had received a very light rainfall that winter. Even so, old Sextus Roscius must have lain for a very long time in the centre of the street, bleeding and bleeding, to have left such a large, indelible stain.

The stain was almost perfectly round and as far across as a tall man's arm. Towards the edges it became blurred and faded, blending imperceptibly with the general grime. But nearer the centre it was still quite concentrated, a very dark, blackened red. The day-to-day stamp of passing feet had worn the surface of the stones to their normal, oily smoothness, but when I knelt down to look more closely I could still detect tiny, desiccated crusts of red in the deeper fissures.

I looked up. Even from the centre of the street it was impossible to see into any of the second-storey windows except at a severely oblique angle. To see from the windows onto the street one would have to lean far over the sill.

The nearest door was several feet farther up the

street; this was the entrance to the long tenement on our left. The wall on our right was equally featureless, except for a food shop a little way behind us, at the corner where the street intersected with a narrow cul-de-sac. The shop was not yet open. A single square door, very tall and broad, covered the entire front. It was a wooden door, coloured with a pale yellow wash and marked along the top with various glyphs for grains, vegetables, and spices. Much lower down, in one corner, there was another marking on the door that made me suck in my breath when I saw it.

'Tiro! Here, come see this.' I hurried back and squatted down beside the door. From the level of a man's waist and below, the wood was covered with a film of soot and dust that thickened into a grimy band as it neared the street. Even so, at knee level, the handprint beneath the dirt was still quite clear to see. I placed my hand atop it and felt a strange shudder, knowing without a doubt that I was touching a bloody handprint left months before by Sextus Roscius.

Tiro looked at the handprint and back to the stain in the street. 'They're so far apart,' he whispered.

'Yes. But the handprint must have been made first.' I stood and walked past the door to the corner. The narrow little branch street was not a street at all, or if it ever had been, was now bricked in at the end with a solid two-storey wall. The space itself was perhaps twenty feet deep, and no more than five feet wide. At the far end someone had been burning refuse; bits of rubbish and bone peeked out of a waist-high pile of grey and white ash. No windows overlooked the space, either from the surrounding walls or from the tenement across the street. The nearest torches were mounted at least forty steps away. At night the little cul-de-sac would be utterly dark and unseen until one passed directly before it – the perfect place to lie in ambush.

'This was where they waited, Tiro, on this very spot, hidden in this recess, knowing he would come this way to answer the note from the woman Elena. They must have known what he looked like, well enough to recognize him from the light of the torches carried by his slaves, because they did not hesitate at all to spring out and begin stabbing him, here at the corner.'

I walked slowly towards the handprint. 'The first wound must have been somewhere in his chest or belly – I suppose they must have looked him in the face to be sure – because he had no trouble touching the wound, clutching it, smearing his whole hand with blood. Somehow he broke away. Perhaps he thought he could push this door open, but he must have fallen to his knees – you see how low the handprint is.' I glanced up the street. 'But the real slaughter took place there, in the middle of the street. Somehow he managed to scramble back to his feet and stagger that far before they overcame him.'

'Perhaps the slaves were trying to fight off the assassins,' Tiro said.

'Perhaps.' I nodded, though I could more easily imagine them bolting in a blind panic at the first glint of steel.

I bent down to examine the handprint again. The high, broad door gave a shudder and sprang outward, hitting me square in the nose.

'Here, what's that?' came a voice from inside. 'Another vagrant, sleeping in front of my shop? I'll have you beaten. Get on, let me open the door!'

The door shuddered again. I blocked it with my foot until I could stand and step safely aside.

A gnarled face peered from behind the door. 'I said, get on!' the man growled. The door swung outward in a wide arc, vibrating on its hinges, until it slammed against the wall beyond the cul-de-sac, completely covering over the narrow walkway where the assassins had hidden.

'Oh, not a vagrant,' the old man muttered, looking me up and down. I was still rubbing my nose. 'My apologies.' His voice carried not the least hint of friendliness or regret.

'This is your shop, sir?'

'Of course it's my shop. And has been since my father died, which was probably before you were born. His father's before that.' He squinted up at the sunlight, shook his head as if the brightness disgusted him, and shuffled back into the shop.

'You're only now opening the store?' I said, following him. 'It seems rather late.'

'It's my shop. I open when I'm ready.'

'When he's *ready*!' A voice shrieked from somewhere beyond the counter at the back of the shop.

The long room was steeped in shadow. After the burning light of the street I stared into the gloom like a blind man. 'When he's ready, he says! When I'm finally able to get him out of bed and dressed is when he's ready. When *I'm* ready, he could say. One of these days I won't bother to get out of bed, I'll just lie about like he does, and then where will we be?'

'Old woman, shut up!' The man tripped against a low table. A basket tipped over, and dried olives were scattered across the floor. Tiro stepped from behind me and began gathering them up.

'Who's this?' said the old man, stooping over and squinting. 'Your slave?'

'No.'

'Well, he acts like a slave. You wouldn't want to sell him?'

'I told you, he's not my slave.'

The old man shrugged. 'We used to have a slave. Until my stupid son freed the lazy bastard. That's who used to open the shop every morning. What's wrong if an old man likes to sleep late, if he's got a slave to open the shop for him? He didn't steal much, either, even if he was a lazy bastard. He should still be here, slave or not. A freedman has certain obligations to those who freed him, everybody knows that, legal obligations, slave or not, and right now is when we need him. But he's off in Apulia somewhere, got himself a wife. Give them their freedom and the first thing they want to do is go off and breed like decent folk. He used to open the shop. Didn't steal much, either.'

While he rambled on, my eyes grew accustomed to the gloom. The shop was in a dilapidated state, dusty and unswept. Half the shelves and counters were empty. The wrinkled black olives Tiro had scrambled to retrieve were covered with dust. I lifted the lid of a clay urn and pulled out a dried fig. The flesh was spotted with grey mould. The whole room was permeated with the musty odour of a house long unused, pierced by the sweet, sour stench of rotted fruit.

'How would you know?' piped a shrill voice from the back of the shop. I could see the woman more clearly now. She wore a dark shawl and seemed to be chopping something with a knife, punctuating each phrase with a sharp blow against the counter. 'You don't know anything, old man, or else you can't remember. Your head's like a sieve. That good-for-nothing Gallius stole from us all the time. I'd have had his hands cut off for stealing, only then what use would he have been to anyone? You can't sell a slave if he hasn't got hands, and nobody'll buy a known thief except the mines and the galleys, and there's no money in dead flesh, as the saying goes. He was no good. We're better off without his kind.'

The man turned towards me and made a face behind the woman's back. 'Well, then, are you here to buy something or to listen to the old woman talk nonsense?'

I glanced about, searching for something that looked reasonably edible. 'Actually, it was the signs on the door outside that drew my attention. The little symbols for fruits, grains . . .'

'Ah, Gallius did those, too. Just before my son freed him. He was a talented slave, even if he was lazy. He hardly ever stole from us.'

'There was one sign in particular I noticed. Unlike the others. Near the bottom of the door – the handprint.'

His face hardened. 'Gallius didn't paint that.'

'I didn't think so. It looks almost like blood.'

'It is.'

'Old man, you talk too much.' The woman scowled and banged her knife against the counter. 'Some things are to be seen but not spoken of.'

'Shut up, old woman! If it were up to me, I'd have washed it off a long time ago, but you wanted it left there, and as long as it's there you can't be surprised if people notice it.'

'How long has it been there?'

'Oh, months and months. Since last September, I suppose.'

I nodded. 'And how—'

'There was a man killed in the middle of the street, a rich man, from what I heard. Imagine, stabbed to death right in front of my shop.'

'After dark?'

'Of course – otherwise the door would have been open, wouldn't it? By Hercules – imagine if he'd come stumbling in here when the shop was open! There would never have been an end to the talk and the trouble.'

'Old man, you don't know anything about it, so why don't you just shut up? Ask the good man again if he came to buy something.' The woman kept her head bowed, like a bull's, staring at me from beneath her thick eyebrows.

'I know a man was killed, if you don't mind,' barked the old man.

'We saw nothing, heard nothing. Only the gossip the next morning.'

'Gossip?' I said. 'Then there was talk in the neighbourhood. Was he a local man?'

'Not that I knew of,' said the man. 'Only they say some of the regulars from the Swans were in the street when they turned him over next morning and recognized his face.'

'The Swans?'

'A house of entertainments, for men. I wouldn't know anything about it myself.' He rolled his eyes back in his head, indicating his wife, and lowered his voice. 'Though my boy used to tell some pretty wild stories about the place.'

The knife banged against the counter with a special ferocity.

'At any rate, it happened some time after we closed up the shop and went upstairs for the night.'

'Then you heard nothing? I'd think there might have been screams, some other noises.'

The man started to answer, but the woman interrupted.

'Our rooms are at the back of the building. We don't have a window on the street at the front. What's your interest in the matter, anyway?'

I shrugged. 'I only happened to be walking past and noticed the handprint. It seemed strange that no one should have covered it over.'

'My wife,' the old man said, with a pained expression. 'Superstitious, like most women.'

The knife came down. 'It stayed there for a very good reason. Have we had any thefts since it happened? Have we?'

The old man wrinkled his lips. 'She imagines that it keeps out thieves at night. I told her it was more likely to keep out customers.'

'But when the door's open, nobody can see it, it's hidden on the other side. It's only when the door's shut that you see it from the street, only when we're closed, and that's when we need the protection. You call me superstitious? A common criminal will think twice about robbing a shop after he's seen a bloody handprint on the entrance. They chop off a thief's hands, you know. It carries a power, I tell you. If we had contrived it ourselves, if it were anything less than blood, it would mean nothing, protect nothing. But the mark of a dying man, made with his own blood by his own hand, it carries a power. Ask the stranger here. He could feel it. Couldn't you?'

'I felt it!' It was Tiro, standing behind me. Three pairs of eyes turned to watch him blush apple-red.

'You're sure you won't sell him?' asked the old man, who suddenly started to wheeze.

'I told you already—'

'A power in it!' shrieked the old woman.

'Tell me: who saw the murder? There must have been gossip. People are in and out of your shop all day. If someone actually witnessed it, you would know.'

The old man abruptly stopped wheezing. He stared at me for a long moment, then looked at his wife. As far as I could see she only scowled back, but it may be that she made some sign imperceptible to my eyes, for when he turned back it seemed he had been given grudging permission to speak.

'There was one person . . . a woman. She lives in the tenement across the way. Her name is Polia. A young woman, a widow. Lives with her son, the little mute boy. It seems I recall another customer saying that Polia was talking to everyone about the murder right after it happened, how she had seen it with her own eyes, looking out of her window. Naturally, the next time they came into the shop I asked her about it. And do you know what? She wouldn't speak a word about it, turned as mute as the boy, except to say that I should never ask her again, and not to tell anyone anything that might . . .' He abruptly clamped his jaw shut with a guilty twitch.

'Tell me,' I said, picking through the dried figs to find a few worth eating, 'does the little mute boy like figs? Tiro, give the man a coin from my purse.'

Tiro, who had been carrying my bag across his shoulder, reached into it and pulled out a copper as. 'Oh, no, more than an as, Tiro. Give the man a sesterce, and let him keep the change. After all, I have an account for such expenses from your master.'

The old man accepted the coin and looked at it suspiciously. Beyond him I could see his wife, chopping away with an expression of grudging satisfaction.

'Such a quiet slave, and such fine manners. You're sure you wouldn't like to sell him?'

I only smiled and motioned to Tiro to follow. Before I stepped into the sunlight I turned back. 'If your son insisted on selling the only slave you had, why isn't he here to help you himself?'

As soon as the words were spoken, I knew the answer. I bit my lip, wishing that words once said could be unspoken.

The woman abruptly hurled the knife across the room, plunging it into the wall with a shudder. She threw her arms heavenward and flung herself face down across the counter. The old man bowed his head and wrung his hands. In the gloom of the dilapidated shop they seemed posed in an eerie tableau, frozen in a sudden eruption of grief that was almost terrifying, almost comic.

'The wars,' the old man muttered. 'Lost in the wars . . .'

I turned and put my arm around Tiro, who stood dumb-founded. Together we stole into the sunshine of the street.

X

The tenement house across the way was of fairly
recent construction. The windowless walls facing
the street had as yet been defaced with only a
modest amount of electioneering slogans (elections
having continued, though without much enthusiasm, under Sulla's dictatorship). More common
were some choice selections of ribald graffiti, probably left, to judge from the content, by satisfied
customers on their way home from the House of
Swans. I saw Tiro twisting his head to catch one of
the more obscene phrases, and clicked my tongue
like a disapproving schoolmaster. But with one eye
I scanned the litanies myself, curious to see if a
certain name appeared; but Elena – she who had
summoned Sextus Roscius – and whatever specific
talents Elena might possess were not mentioned.

A brief flight of steps led up to the tenement
door, which stood propped open in the morning

heat. From a small, bare anteroom, two passage-
ways led off to the left. One was a long, enclosed
stairway up to the second floor. The other was a
dark hallway that ran the length of the building,
flanked by numerous cubicles covered over with
ragged, unmatched draperies.

From the end of the hallway a tall, gaunt man
sprang up from where he had been sitting on the
floor and loped towards us, turning his head sidelong and rubbing his chin. He was the watchman.
Every tenement has at least one, and sometimes in
larger buildings one for every floor – an otherwise
unemployed resident who collects a small fee from
the others, or else from the landlord, to watch their
belongings while they're out during the day, and to
keep an eye on strangers and visitors. Sometimes a
slave may be used for the duty, but this tenement
hardly looked like the dwelling of slaveowners;
besides, I saw at a glance that he wore the iron
ring of a free Roman.

'Citizen,' he said, coming to an abrupt halt
before us. He was very tall and gaunt, with a
grizzled beard and a slightly wild look in his
eyes.

'Citizen,' I said, 'I'm looking for a woman.'

He smiled stupidly. 'Who isn't?'

'A woman named Polia.'

'Polia?'

'Yes. Upstairs, I think.'

'Polia?' he said again, rubbing his chin.

'A widow, with a young son. The boy is mute.'

The man shrugged, exaggerating the gesture. At

the same time he slowly turned his right hand palm-up.

'Tiro,' I began, but Tiro was already ahead of me, reaching into the leather bag across his shoulder. He drew out a couple of copper asses and showed them to me. I nodded, but made a gesture that he should wait. Meanwhile the gaunt giant loomed over us, staring at Tiro's closed fist with unabashed greed.

'There *is* a woman named Polia who still lives here?' I said.

The man pursed his lips, then nodded. I inclined my head to Tiro, who handed him a single as.

'And is she in her room now?'

'Can't say for certain. She's upper-storey. Has a room with a door and everything.'

'A door that locks?'

'Not well enough to bother with.'

'Then I suppose I'll have to deal with another watchman at the head of the stairs, won't I? Perhaps I should save the rest of my coins for him.' I turned towards the stairway.

The giant restrained me with a surprisingly gentle hand on my shoulder. 'Citizen, wait. You'd only be wasting your coins on him. He's good for nothing, starts drinking wine from the moment he wakes up. Probably asleep right now, in this heat. You'd only have to wake him up to ask him where Polia's room is. Here, I can show you myself, only walk quietly up the stairs.'

The giant led the way, easily taking two steps at a time, walking on exaggerated tiptoes; he seemed about to lose his balance with each step. As he had predicted, the upstairs watchman was fast asleep at the head of the stairs. The round little man sat against the wall with his pudgy legs spread out before him, a wineskin draped over one knee and a clay bottle propped lewdly between his thighs. The giant gingerly stepped over him, turning up his nose.

The narrow hallway was dimly lit by small windows at either end. The ceiling was so low that our guide had to stoop to avoid the lower beams. We followed him to a door midway down the hall, and waited while he quietly knocked. With each tap of his knuckles against the wood, he glanced nervously back at the sleeping watchman at the landing, and once when Tiro made the floorboards creak he pleaded for silence with both hands. I could only assume that the little drunkard had powers of retribution invisible to a stranger.

After a moment the thin, narrow door opened a finger's width. 'Oh, you,' said a woman's voice. 'I've told you a thousand times already, *no*. Why won't you just leave me alone? There must be fifty other women in this building.'

The giant glanced at me and actually blushed. 'I'm not alone. You have visitors,' he hissed.

'Visitors? Not – my mother?'

'No. A man. And his slave.'

She sucked in her breath. 'Not the ones who came before.'

'Of course not. They're standing here beside me.'

The door opened farther, just enough to reveal

143

the widow's face from cheek to cheek. There was not much to see in the dimness except two frightened eyes. 'Who are you?'

At the end of the hall the drunken watchman turned uneasily, upsetting the bottle between his legs. It spun about and rolled towards the steps.

'By Hercules!' The giant gasped and leaped on tiptoes towards the landing. Just as he arrived the bottle rolled over the edge and began descending the stairway, striking each step with a loud bang.

The little watchman was instantly awake. 'What's that? You!' He rolled forwards and staggered to his feet. The giant was already descending the stairs, hands over his head, but the little man was too quick for him. In an instant he had taken up a long wooden slat and was batting it about the giant's head and shoulders, screeching at him in a loud voice. 'Bringing strangers onto my floor again! Stealing my tips! Didn't think I'd catch you! Worthless pile of dung! Go on, go on, or do I beat you like a dog?'

The sight was absurd, pathetic, embarrassing. Tiro and I simultaneously laughed, and simultaneously ceased as we turned back to look at the young widow's ashen face.

'Who are you? What did you come here for?'

'Gordianus is my name. Employed by the most esteemed advocate, Marcus Tullius Cicero. This is his secretary, Tiro. I only want to ask a few questions, about certain events of last September.'

Her face grew even paler. 'I knew it. Don't ask me how, but I knew. I dreamed about it again last night . . . But you'll have to go away. I can't talk to anyone right now.'

Her face withdrew. She pushed at the door. I blocked it with my foot. The wooden panel was so thin and shoddy that it cracked from the pressure.

'Come now, won't you let me in? That's quite a watchdog you have at the head of the stairs, I hear him coming back now. I'm sure you'll be quite safe – you need only cry out if I should do something improper.'

The door abruptly swung open, but it was not the widow who stood before us. It was her son, and though he must have been no more than eight years old, he did not look particularly small, especially clutching an upright dagger in his right fist.

'No, Eco, no!' The woman grabbed the boy's arm and pulled him back. His eyes stayed fixed on mine, unblinking. Up and down the hall, doors rattled open. The little watchman, returning up the stairs, called out in a drunken voice, 'What's going on there?'

'Oh, for Cybele's sake, come in.' The woman succeeded in pulling the knife from her son's grasp and quickly latched the door behind us.

The boy kept his eyes on me, staring sullenly. 'Carve these instead,' I said, pulling out the figs and tossing them. He caught the lot with one hand.

The room was small and cramped, like most such apartments in most such buildings, but it had a window with shutters and space for two to sleep on the floor without even touching.

'You live here alone?' I asked. 'Just the two of

you?' I glanced about at the few personal items that littered the room: a change of clothing, a small basket of cosmetics, a few wooden toys. Her things, his things.

'What business is that of yours?' She stood in the corner of the room near the window, with the boy in front of her. She kept one arm around him, hugging and restraining him at the same time.

'None at all,' I said. 'Do you mind if I take a look from your window? You don't know how lucky you are, or I suppose you do, having a view onto the street.' The boy flinched as I stepped closer, but the woman held him tight. 'Of course it's not much of a view,' I said, 'but I imagine this street is quiet at night, and fresh air is a blessing.'

The sill came up to my thighs. The window was recessed a foot or more into the wall, forming a sort of seat; the woman had thrown a thin pillow over it. I had to lean far over to see out. Because we overhung the ground-floor apartments, I could see nothing of the outer wall below, but across the way and a bit to the right I could look down onto the entrance of the little food shop; the old woman was busy sweeping the street in front, attacking the job with the same aggressiveness she had shown on the chopping block. Directly below, standing out vividly at this distance against the surrounding paving stones, was the large stain left by the blood of Sextus Roscius.

I patted the cushion. 'It makes a nice seat, especially on a hot day like this, I imagine. It must be pleasant in the autumn as well, to sit here if the evening is warm enough. To watch the passersby. If you look up, you must be able to see the stars on a cloudless night.'

'I keep the shutters closed after dark,' she said, 'no matter what the weather's like. And I don't pay attention to people in the street. I mind my own business.'

'Your name is Polia, isn't it?'

She shrank against the wall, tightening her grip on the boy and clumsily fondling his hair. He made a face and reached up, pushing at her arms in agitation. 'I don't know you. How do you know my name?'

'Tell me, Polia, this wise policy of minding your own business – how far back does it go? Have you always followed it, or is it a recent resolution? Perhaps something you took up since, say, last September?'

'I don't have any idea what you're talking about.'

'When the watchman brought us up, you thought we might be someone else.'

'I only asked if it was my mother. She keeps coming to me for money, and I don't have any more to give her.'

'No, I heard the exchange quite distinctly. He told you it was a citizen and a slave, and you said, "Not the ones who came before." You sounded quite upset at the prospect of seeing them again.'

The boy's fidgeting escalated into an outright struggle. She clutched him hard and slapped the top of his head. 'Why don't you just go away? Why don't you leave us alone?'

'Because a man has been murdered, and another man stands to die for it.'

'What do I care?' she snapped. Bitterness spoiled what was left of her beauty. 'What crime had my husband committed when he died of the fever? What had he done to deserve death? Even the gods can't answer that. The gods don't care. Men die every day.'

'This dead man was stabbed directly below your window last September. I think you saw it happen.'

'No. How would I remember such a thing, anyway?' The woman and her child seemed to be performing a strange, wriggling dance, struggling together in the corner. Polia was beginning to breathe harder. The boy never took his eyes off me.

'It's not something I'd think you would forget. Here, you can see the bloodstain if you glance out of the window. But I don't need to tell you that, do I?'

Suddenly the boy broke free. I jerked back. Tiro moved to shield me, but there was no need. The boy burst into tears and ran headlong from the room.

'There, you see what you've done? You made me mention his father. Just because Eco can't speak, people forget he can hear as well as anyone. There was a time when he could speak, as well. But not since his father died. Not a word since then. The fever struck them both. . . . Now get out. I don't have anything to say to you. Get out!'

She fumbled with the knife while she spoke, then suddenly seemed to notice what she held. She pointed it towards us, clutching it clumsily, her hand shaking, looking more likely to cut herself than to stab with it.

'Come, Tiro,' I said. 'There's nothing more for us here.'

The little watchman had refilled his wineskin and sat at the head of the stairs, squirting the juice between his red-stained lips. He mumbled something and held out his hand as we walked past. I ignored him. The ground-floor watchman was where we had first seen him, huddled at the far end of the hallway. He ignored us.

The street was inhumanly hot.

Tiro hung back, walking slowly down the steps and looking perplexed.

'What's wrong?' I asked.

'Why didn't you offer her money? We know she saw the killing, the old man said so. Surely she could use the silver.'

'There's not enough money in my purse to make her talk. Couldn't you see that? She's a very frightened woman. I don't think she would have taken the money anyway. She's not accustomed to being poor, or at least poor enough to beg. Not yet, anyway. Who knows what her story is?' I tried to harden my voice. 'Who cares? Whatever it is, there are a thousand more widows in this city with the same stories, each one more pathetic than the last. All that matters to us is that someone silenced her long before we came. She's of no use to us now.'

I almost expected Tiro to take me to task, but of course that would never happen. He was a slave, and very young, and could not see how badly I had mishandled the woman. I had treated her as crudely as I had the shopkeeper and the watchmen. She might have spoken if I had touched in her some key other than fear. I walked quickly, oblivious of the bloodstain as it passed under my feet, too angry to notice where I was headed. The noonday sun beat down like a fist on my neck. I ran headlong into the boy.

We both started back, breathless from the collision. I cursed. Eco made a harsh, stifled noise in his throat.

I had enough wits to cast a wary glance at his hands. They were empty. I looked in his eyes for an instant, then stepped aside to walk on. He grabbed the sleeve of my tunic. He shook his head and pointed to the window.

'What do you want? We've left your mother in peace. You should go to her now.'

Eco shook his head and stamped his foot. He pointed again to the window. He gestured that we should wait, and ran inside.

'What do you think he wants?' said Tiro.

'I'm not sure,' I said, but even as I spoke I sensed the truth, and felt a prickling of dread.

A moment later the boy reappeared, carrying a black cloak over one arm and concealing something in the folds of his tunic. He pulled out his hand, and the long blade glinted in the sunlight. Tiro gasped and grabbed my arm. I held him gently back, knowing the knife was not for us.

The boy walked slowly towards me. There was no one else in the street; the hour was too hot.

'I think the boy wants to tell us something,' I said.

Eco nodded.

'About that night in September.'

He nodded again and pointed with his blade at the bloodstain.

'About the death of the old man in the street. The murder happened an hour or two after darkness fell. Am I right?'

He nodded.

'Then how could anyone have seen anything more than shadows?'

He pointed to the torch brackets fitted up and down the street, and then upward. His hands defined a sphere.

'Ah, yes, it was the Ides – the moon was high that night, and full,' I said. He nodded.

'The killers, where did they come from?'

Eco pointed to the recessed space now covered by the door to the food shop.

'Exactly as I thought. And how many of them were there?'

He held up three fingers.

'Only three? You're certain?'

He nodded vigorously. Then the pantomime began.

He ran a short way up the street, then turned around, prancing towards us with drooping eyes and a pompous stare. He gestured to either side with a flourish.

'Old Sextus Roscius,' I said. 'And he comes attended by his two slaves, one on either side.'

The boy clapped his hands and nodded. He ran to the shop door, wedged his shoulder behind it and swung it shut. Through the wood, from her counter at the back, I heard the old woman curse. The boy swung the dark cloak over his shoulders and crouched against the wall in the little cul-de-sac clutching the long knife. I followed him.

'Three assassins, you said. And who are you now, the leader?'

He nodded, then motioned that I should take the place of old Sextus, strolling down the moonlit street.

'Come, Tiro,' I said, 'You'll be Felix, or Chrestus, or whichever slave stood on his master's right hand, closest to the ambush.'

'Do you think this is wise, sir?'

'Be quiet, Tiro, and play along.'

We walked side by side down the street. Seeing it from the victim's angle, the narrow dead-end passage loomed up without warning; at night, even beneath a full moon, it must have been an invisible hole of darkness. Looking straight ahead as we passed by, I saw nothing but the slightest flicker of movement from the corner of my eye, and by that time it was too late. The mute boy was behind us without warning, seizing Tiro by the shoulder and shoving him aside. He did it twice, once to the left, once to the right: two assassins pushing aside two slaves. The second time, Tiro shoved him back.

I began to turn, but Eco pushed at my shoulders, telling me to stay as I was. From behind he threaded his arms through mine as if to hold me immobile.

With a pat on my arm he slipped away, into another role, and circled in front of me, pulling the cowl over his face, clutching the knife, walking with a limp. He reached up to seize my jaw with one hand and looked me square in the face. He raised the dagger and brought it down, slicing through empty air.

'Where?' I said. 'Where was the first wound?'

He tapped a spot between my collarbone and nipple, just above the heart. I reached up and touched it without thinking. Eco nodded, his face invisible beneath the shadow of the cowl. He pointed to the handprint on the shop door.

'Then Sextus must have struggled free—'

He shook his head and made a flinging motion.

'He was thrown to the ground?' A nod. 'And somehow had the strength to crawl to the door—'

Eco shook his head again and pointed to where the old man had struck the ground. He walked up to the imaginary body and began kicking at it viciously, making weird noises from the back of his throat. Sneering, barking, and – I suddenly realized with a feeling of sickness – mimicking a laugh.

'He was here then,' I said, taking my place at the boy's feet. 'Shocked, bewildered, bleeding. They drove him forwards, kicking at him, cursing and ridiculing him, laughing. He reached up and touched the door. . . .'

For the second time that morning I was struck square in the nose as the door swung outward with a creak and a shudder.

'What do you think you're doing?' It was the woman. 'You have no right—'

Eco saw her and froze. 'Go on,' I said, 'never mind her. Go on. Sextus Roscius had fallen, he leaned against the door. What then?'

The boy came towards me, limping again, and made a motion of seizing my toga with both hands and literally tossing me into the middle of the street. He limped quickly to the prostrate phantom and resumed kicking at it, moving forwards a little with each step until he stood directly over the massive bloodstain. He indicated his phantom companions at either side.

'Three,' I said, 'all three of the assassins surrounded him. But where were the two slaves, then? Dead?' No. 'Wounded?' No. The boy made an obscene gesture of disgust and dismissal. The slaves had run. I glanced at Tiro, who looked profoundly disappointed.

Eco squatted over the bloodstain, took out his knife and raised it high over his head, then brought it down within a finger's breadth of the street, over and over. He began to shake. He dropped forwards on his knees. He made a sound like a donkey quietly braying. He was weeping.

I knelt beside him and put my hand on his shoulder. 'It's all right,' I said. 'It's all right. I only want you to remember a little more.' He drew away from me and wiped his face, angry at himself for crying. 'Only a little more. Was there anyone else who saw? Someone else in the tenement, or across the street?'

154

He glared at the shopkeeper's wife, who stood staring at us from the entrance to her store. He raised his hand and pointed.

'Ha!' The woman crossed her arms and lowered her head, bull-like. 'The boy's a liar. Either that, or he's blind as well as dumb.'

The boy pointed again, as if by hurling his finger at her he could make her confess. Then he pointed at a little window above the shop, where the old man's face peered out at us for an instant before abruptly disappearing behind a pair of shutters closed from within.

'A liar,' the woman growled. 'He should be beaten.'

'You told me you lived at the back of the building, with no windows overlooking the street,' I said.

'Did I? Then it's only the truth.' She had no way of knowing I had seen her husband only an instant before, looming directly above her like the disembodied face of a *deus ex machina* in a play.

I turned back to Eco. 'Three of them, you said. Was there anything to distinguish them besides their cloaks? Tall, short, anything unusual? One of them limped, you say, the leader. Which was his crippled leg, the left or the right?'

The boy thought for a moment, then poked at his left leg. He scrambled up and limped about me in a circle.

'The left. You're certain?'

'Ridiculous!' the old woman screamed. 'The stupid boy knows nothing! It was his right leg that was bad, his right!' The words were out before she could stop them. She slapped a hand over her mouth. A smile of triumph crept over my face, then withered as she gave me a look such as Medusa might have given Perseus. For a moment she stood confused, then she took decisive action. She stormed into the street and seized the handle of the wide door, then stamped back into the shop, pulling it closed behind her in a great arc while Tiro scurried out of her way. 'We will reopen,' she shouted to no one in particular, 'when this rabble has cleared the streets!' The door closed behind her not with a great boom, but with an equivocal rattle and a thud.

'His left,' I said, turning back to the boy. He nodded. A tear ran down his cheek; he dabbed at it angrily with his sleeve. 'And his hand – which did he use for stabbing? Think!'

Eco seemed to stare into some great depth that loomed beneath the bloodstain at our feet. Slowly, trancelike, he transferred the blade from his right hand to his left. He narrowed his eyes. His left hand gave a jerk, making miniature stabbing motions in the air. He blinked and looked up at me, nodding.

'Left-handed! Good, left-handed with a game left leg – that should make him easy enough to spot. And his face – did you have a look at his face?'

He shuddered and seemed to be holding back tears. He nodded slowly, gravely, not quite looking me in the eye.

'A good look? Good enough so that you would recognize him if you were to see him again?'

He gave me a look of pure panic and began scrambling to his feet. I grabbed his arm and pulled him back, close to the bloodstain. 'But how could you have seen him so closely? Where were you, in the window of your room?'

He nodded. I glanced up.

'Too far to get a really good look at a man's face in the street even in broad daylight. And yet it was dark that night, even if there was a full moon.'

'Fool! Don't you understand?' The voice came from above me, from the window over the shop. The old man had pulled back the shutters and was peering down at us again, talking in a hoarse whisper. 'It wasn't that night that he got a good look at the man's face. They came back again, only a few days later.'

'And how do you know that?' I asked, craning my neck.

'They . . . they came into my shop.'

'And how did you recognize them? Did *you* see the crime?'

'Not me. Oh, no, not me.' The old man looked warily over his shoulder. 'But there's nothing that happens in this street day or night that my wife doesn't see. She saw them that night, standing where I am at this very window. And she knew them when they came back a few days later in broad daylight, the same three – she knew their leader by his limp, and one of the others by the size of him – a big blond giant with a red face. The third had a beard, I think, but I can't say more than that. The leader was asking questions around the neighbourhood, same as you. Only we didn't tell them a thing, not a thing, not one word about Polia claiming to have seen the stabbing herself from start to finish, I swear it. Didn't like the look of them. At least I didn't tell them anything; only it seems, now that I recall, I had to leave the shop, just for a moment, while the old woman got rid of them – you don't suppose she went off with her big mouth . . .'

Behind me I heard a strange animal cry. I turned, then ducked as Eco's knife went flying over my head. The old man's reflexes were amazingly quick. The knife went whistling towards the open window and struck against slammed shutters instead. The blade landed squarely in the wood, stuck for a long moment, then slipped free and fell to the street with a clatter. I turned and stared at Eco, amazed that a mere boy could have thrown the knife with such strength. He stood hiding his face in his hands, weeping.

'These people are mad,' whispered Tiro.

I grabbed Eco's wrists and pulled his hands from his face. He wrenched his head from side to side, trying to hide his tears. He pulled against my grip. I held him fast.

'The men came back,' I said. 'They came for you. Could they have seen you watching, the night of the murder?'

He wildly shook his head.

'No. Then they found out from the old woman in the shop. She led them to you. But according to the gossip it was your mother who saw the crime. Did she? Was she with you in the window?'

Again he shook his head. He wept.

'You were the only one who saw it, then. You and the old woman across the street. But the old woman had the sense to keep herself out of it – and to lead them elsewhere. You told your mother all the details, didn't you? Just as you've told us? And she started putting it out as if she'd seen the crime herself. Am I right?'

He shuddered and sobbed.

'Wretched,' I whispered. 'Wretched. So they came that day looking for her, not you. And they found her in your apartment. You were there?'

He managed to nod.

'And then what? Threats, bribes?' I asked, knowing it was something much worse.

The boy wrenched himself from my grip. Sobbing, whining, he began slapping his own face back and forth. Tiro huddled next to me, watching horrified. The boy finally stopped. He stamped his foot and looked me straight in the eye. Gritting his teeth, contorting his face into a mask of hate, he raised both arms. His hands moved slowly, stiffly, as if against his will. He made an obscene gesture, then crumpled his hands into fists as if they had been withered by fire.

They had raped his mother, Polia who had seen nothing, who would have known nothing of the crime if he had not told her, whose only crime was spreading second-hand gossip to an old lady across the street. They had raped her, and Eco had seen it happen.

159

I looked at Tiro to see if he understood. He covered his mouth and averted his eyes.

The boy suddenly pushed me aside and ran to the knife in the street. He snatched it up and ran back to me, taking my hand in his and pressing my fingers around the hilt. Before I could pay him, before I could make any gesture of comfort or understanding, he ran back into the tenement, pushing aside the gaunt watchman who was stepping out of the doorway for a breath of air.

I looked at the knife in my hand. I sighed and closed my eyes, suddenly dizzy from the heat. 'For his revenge,' I whispered. 'He thinks we bring justice, Tiro.'

XI

We sat out the worst of the afternoon's heat in a small tavern. I had meant to press on to find the whore Elena – the House of Swans could be only a short distance beyond the scene of the murder – but I lacked the heart. Instead we turned back, trudging up the narrow street until we reached the open square.

The concourse was almost deserted. Shopkeepers had closed their stalls. The heat was so intense that even the vendors with their carts had disappeared. Only a few vagrant children and a dog remained, playing in puddles about the public cistern. They had pushed back the iron cover, and one of the boys was standing dangerously close to the edge. Without even a glance over his shoulder, he hitched up his tunic and began urinating into the hole.

A mosaic of a bunch of red grapes inlaid above

the cornerstone of a small tenement advertised a nearby tavern. A sprinkling of purple and white tiles led around the corner and down a short flight of steps. The tavern was a small, musty room, dark and dank and deserted.

The heat had exhausted me beyond speech. After so much walking I should have eaten, but I had no appetite. I ordered water and wine instead, and cajoled Tiro into sharing. I ordered more, and by that time Tiro needed no persuasion. With his tongue loosened and his guard down, I felt an urge to ask him outright about his tryst with the daughter of Sextus Roscius. If only I had! But for once I stifled my curiosity.

Tiro was unused to the wine. For a while he became quite animated, talking about the events of the morning and the previous day, interrupting himself every now and again to say a word of praise for his wise master, while I sat bemused in my chair, only half-listening. Then he abruptly grew silent, staring at his cup with a melancholy look. He took a final sip, put down the cup, leaned back in his chair, and fell fast asleep.

After a while I closed my eyes, and while I never quite slept, I dozed fitfully for what seemed a very long time, opening my eyes occasionally to the unchanging sight of Tiro splayed slack-jawed in the chair across from me, sleeping the absolute sleep of the young and innocent.

The half dreams I dreamed, partly submerged in them, partly aware that I dreamed, were gnarled and uneasy, far from innocence. I sat in the house of

Caecilia Metella, interviewing Sextus Roscius; he babbled and muttered, and though he seemed to speak Latin I could hardly make out a word he said. When he rose from his chair I noticed that he wore a heavy cloak, and when he walked towards me it was with a terrible limp, dragging his left leg behind him. I turned away from him, horrified, and ran into the hallway. Corridors branched and merged like passages in a maze. I was lost. I parted a curtain and saw him from the back. Beyond him the young widow was pinned against the wall, naked and weeping as he violently raped her.

But as happens in dreams, what I first saw changed into something else, and I realized with a start that the woman was not the widow; it was Roscius's own daughter, and when she saw that I watched she was unashamed. Instead she kissed the empty air and flicked her tongue at me.

I opened my eyes and saw Tiro sleeping across the table. A part of me wanted to awaken, but was too weak. My eyes were too heavy, and I lacked the will to keep them open. Or perhaps this was only another part of the dream.

In the storeroom of Caecilia's house, the man and the woman continued to copulate. I watched them from the doorway, as timid as a boy. The man in the cloak looked over his shoulder. I smiled to myself, for now I expected to see Tiro's face, flushed with excitement, innocent, embarrassed. Instead I saw Sextus Roscius, leering and transfixed with an unspeakable passion.

I covered my mouth and started back, appalled.

Someone tugged at my sleeve. It was the mute boy, his eyes red from weeping, biting his lips to keep himself from simpering. He tried to hand me a knife, but I refused to take it. He shoved me aside angrily, then hurled himself at the copulating figures.

The boy stabbed at them brutally, indiscriminately. They refused to stop, as if the stabbing were a minor bother, not worth the pleasure it would cost them to pull apart and slap the boy aside. I knew somehow that they could not pull apart, that their flesh had in some way become merged and indistinct. Even as they heaved and writhed a pool of blood ran from their mingled bodies. It spread across the floor like a rich red carpet. It slithered beneath my feet. I tried to step forward but was frozen to the spot, unable to move or even to speak, as rigid as a corpse.

I opened my eyes, but it seemed to make no difference. I saw only an inundation of red. I realized that I had not opened my eyes at all and still dreamed against my will. I reached up to push my eyes open with my fingers, but the lids held fast together. I struggled, panting and out of breath, unable to will myself out of the dream.

Then, in an instant, I was awake. My eyes were open. My hands were on the table, trembling. Tiro sat across from me, peacefully napping.

My mouth was as dry as alum. My head felt stuffed with wool. My face and hands were numb. I tried to call for the taverner and found I could hardly speak. It made no difference; the man was dozing himself, sitting on a stool in the corner with his arms crossed and his chin on his chest.

I stood. My limbs were like dry wood. I staggered to the entrance and up the stairs to the alley, around the corner and into the square. The open concourse was blindingly bright and utterly deserted; even the urchins had abandoned it. I made my way to the cistern, knelt beside it and peered into the blackness. The water was too deep to give back any reflection, but I felt the rising coolness on my face. I pulled up the bucket, splashed my face, poured it over my head.

I began to feel remotely human, but still weak. I wanted only to be at rest in my own home, beneath the portico, gazing out at the sunshine in the garden, with Bast slinking against my feet and Bethesda bringing a cool cloth to soothe my forehead.

Instead I felt a tentative hand on my shoulder. It was Tiro.

'Are you all right, sir?'

I drew in a deep breath. 'Yes.'

'It's the heat. This terrible, unnatural heat. Like a punishment. It dulls the brain, Cicero says, and parches the spirit.'

'Here, Tiro, help me up.'

'You should lie down. Sleep.'

'No! Sleep is a man's worst enemy in this kind of heat. Terrible dreams . . .'

'Shall we go back to the tavern, then?'

'No. Or yes; I suppose I owe the man something for the wine.'

'No, I paid from your purse before I left. He was asleep, but I left the money on the counter.'

I shook my head. 'And woke him up before you left, so that no thieves could step in on him?'

'Of course.'

'Tiro, you are a paragon of virtue. You are a rose among thorns. You are the sweet berry in the midst of brambles.'

'I am merely the mirror of my master,' he said, sounding proud rather than humble.

XII

For a while the sun, though still high, was concealed behind a mantle of white clouds which
blossomed from nowhere. The worst of the heat
had passed, but what the city had absorbed
throughout the day it now gave back. The paving
stones and the bricks were like the walls of an oven,
radiating heat. Unless another thunderstorm came
to quench them, the stones would give off warmth
throughout the night, baking the city and all who
lived in it.

Tiro urged me to turn back, to hire a litter to take
me home or at least to return by foot to Cicero's
house on the Capitoline. But there was no point in
coming so near the House of Swans without
making a visit.

We walked down the narrow street again, past
the little cul-de-sac where the assassins had hidden,
now covered over by the open door of the food

shop. From its dim recess came the too-sweet smell of rotted fruit; I did not look inside. We stepped around the bloodstain and walked by the door that led to the widow's apartment. The gaunt watchman sat dozing on the steps. He opened his eyes as we passed and gave me a puzzled, disgruntled look, as if our interview had been so long ago he had forgotten our faces.

The House of Swans was even closer than I had thought. The street narrowed and veered to the left, closing off the view behind us. Abruptly, on our right, unmistakable in its gaudy attempt at opulence, was our destination.

How glamorous it must have appeared to men of modest means who made their way here by word of mouth, arriving by night, following the torches and the crude swan emblems that lined the street. How deliciously tawdry it must have appeared to a man of some refinement like old Sextus Roscius, how inviting to a man possessed of his overripe carnal appetites.

The facade stood out in sharp contrast to all around it. The surrounding buildings were plastered over and washed in quiet shades of saffron, rust, or mottled cream. The plastered front of the House of Swans was a bright, gaudy pink, embellished here and there, as about the window pediments, with red tiles. A semicircular portico intruded into the street. A statue of Venus was perched atop the half-dome, too small to match the space; the quality of the workmanship was truly painful to look at, almost blasphemous. Even Tiro snickered when he saw it. Within the portico a large lamp hung from the half-dome; one might charitably have said it was boat-shaped, though I suspect the gentle curvature and blunted tip were intended to suggest a human appendage rendered obscenely out of scale. How many nights had Sextus Roscius followed its light like a beacon, up the three marble steps to the black grille, where I now stood with Tiro, shamelessly knocking in broad daylight?

A slave answered the door, a tall, muscular young man who looked more like a bodyguard or gladiator than a doorkeeper. His manners were disgustingly servile. He never stopped smiling, bowing and nodding as he led us to a low divan in the gaudily appointed anteroom. We had to wait only a few moments before the proprietor himself arrived.

My host presented an appearance of roundness in all his aspects, from his belly to his nose to the balding crown of his head. What little hair remained had been industriously oiled and coiffed, and his jowls were grotesquely powdered and rouged. His taste in jewellery seemed as overwrought as his taste in furnishings. All in all he presented the spectacle of an Epicurean gone to seed, and his attempts to recreate the air of a Levantine brothel bordered on parody. When the Romans attempt to mimic the East, they seldom succeed. Grace and true luxury cannot be so easily copied, or purchased wholesale.

'Citizen,' he said, 'you come at an unusual time of the day. Most of our clients arrive closer to sundown. But all the better for you – you shall have your choice of the girls, with no waiting. Most of them are sleeping now, but I shall happily rouse them from their beds. That's how I find them most attractive myself, newly risen, still fresh and fragrant with sleep, like morning roses moist with dew.'

'Actually, I had a specific girl in mind.'

'Yes?'

'She was recommended to me. A girl called Elena.'

The man stared at me blankly and took his time answering. When he spoke I detected no guile, only the sincere forgetfulness of a man who has bought and sold so many bodies over the years that he cannot be expected to remember them all. 'Elena,' he said, as if it were a foreign word whose definition he could not quite recall. 'And was she recommended to you recently, sir?'

'Yes. But it's been some time since my friend last visited her. He's away from Rome, busy at his country estates. Business affairs keep him from visiting the city, but he writes to me with fond memories of this Elena, saying he wishes he could find a country woman whose caresses could satisfy him even a fraction as well.'

'Ah.' The man touched his fingertips together, pursed his lips, and seemed to count the rings on each hand. I found myself staring at the painting on the opposite wall, in which Priapus paid court to a band of naked courtesans, all of whom seemed appropriately awed by the overgrown stalk that rose rampant from between the god's legs.

'Perhaps you could describe this Elena.'

I thought for a moment, then shook my head. 'Alas, my friend makes no mention of her appearance, oddly enough. He only gives me her name, and a guarantee that I won't be disappointed.'

My host brightened. 'Ah, well, I assure you that I can make the same guarantee for any of my girls.'

'Then you're certain you have no Elena?'

'Actually, the name is familiar. Yes, I seem to remember the girl, dimly. But I'm sure there's been no Elena here for quite some time.'

'But what could have happened to her? Surely your girls are healthy.'

'Of course they are; I've never lost a girl to illness. She was sold, as I recall – to a private citizen, not to a rival house,' he added, as if to forestall me from searching for her elsewhere.

'A private citizen? My friend will be disappointed to hear it. I wonder if I know the buyer – perhaps there's some joke afoot behind my back. You couldn't tell me who the man was?'

'I'm afraid I couldn't possibly recall any details without consulting my accountant. And I should tell you that as a matter of policy I never discuss the sale of slaves except with a prospective buyer.'

'I understand.'

'Ah, here, Stabius is bringing a selection now. Four beautiful girls. Your only problem will be deciding which you want most. Or perhaps you'll insist on two at once. Or perhaps you'll want to try all four, one after the other. My girls turn even ordinary men into satyrs, and you, sir, look like no ordinary man to me.'

Compared to the brothels of Antioch or Alexandria, my host's initial offering was disappointingly humdrum. All four were brunettes. Two of them struck me as ordinary, almost homely, though for men who look only below the neck they possessed ample charms. The other two were attractive enough, though neither was as beautiful as the widow Polia, or at least as beautiful as the young widow must have been before her face was scarred by suffering. All four wore sleeveless coloured gowns of a fabric so clinging and sheer that only the finest details of their bodies remained a mystery. My host touched the youngest and prettiest on the shoulder and ushered her forward.

'Here, sir, I offer you the tenderest bud in my garden, my newest, my freshest blossom: Talia. As pretty and playful as a child. But already a woman, have no doubt.' He stood behind her and gently lifted the gown from her shoulders. It parted down the middle and for a brief moment she was displayed to me nude, her head bowed and her eyes averted. Behind me I heard Tiro gasp.

The brothel master gently fondled her breasts and ran his fingers down to her abdomen. I watched the gooseflesh rise from the downy skin below her navel. 'She blushes, you see – what a colour it gives her cheeks. Talia blushes in other places as well, too delicate to mention.' He covered her up. 'But despite her girlish modesty, I assure you she is shameless in bed.'

'How long has she been with you?'

'Oh, not long at all, sir. Only a month. Almost a virgin still, and yet astonishingly skilled with every orifice. Her mouth is especially talented—'

'I'm not interested.'

'No?'

'I had my heart set on Elena.'

My host clenched his teeth.

'Still, if she isn't here, then bring me your most experienced whore. I care nothing about looks. These girls are too young to know what they're doing; I've no interest in children. Bring me your most veteran whore. Show me a fullblown woman, a hot-blooded woman, no stranger to every imaginable scheme of love. And she must speak passable Latin. Exchanging words is half my pleasure. Is there such a woman in the House of Swans?'

My host clapped his hands. The slave called Stabius ushered the girls out of the room. Talia, the young blossom whom our host had unveiled for us, who had blushed and looked away with such conviction, covered her mouth with her hand as she left, yawning.

'Stabius!'

The slave turned back.

'Stabius, bring us Electra.'

The woman called Electra took her time. When my host at last announced her, I knew at once that she was the woman I wanted.

Her hair was her most striking feature, a great mass of black tresses accented with a spray of white at each temple. She wore her makeup with a skill

173

attainable only by years of practice; my host might have done well to take lessons from her. If her features were too bold to be called delicate, if her skin was no longer pristine, still, under the soft light of the atrium, one could say with complete conviction that she was beautiful. With age she had earned the dignity to wear a gown less revealing than those of the younger girls, a loose, long-sleeved white robe belted with a sash at the waist. The curves of her hips and breasts were alluring enough without being glimpsed through gossamer.

There is at least one such woman in every brothel, and in those cities dedicated to the specializations of pleasure one may find entire houses of them. Electra was the Great Mother. Not the mother of a grown man, but the mother one remembers from childhood; not old but wise, with a body neither lean and girlish nor old beyond beauty, but fulsome, primed, nourishing.

I glanced at Tiro and saw that he was quite astonished by her. She was not the type of woman he was likely to meet very often in the service of a master like Cicero.

I stepped aside with my host and negotiated. Naturally he wanted too much. I fretted again over the missing Elena. He grimaced and lowered his price. I demurred. He lowered his price again. I acquiesced. I instructed Tiro to pay him. He handed over the coins with a look of shock, whether because he thought the price extravagant (especially coming from his master's account), or because he realized what a bargain I had made, I couldn't tell.

Electra turned to lead the way to her room. I followed and gestured for Tiro to come along.

Tiro seemed startled. So did my host.

'Citizen, citizen, I had no idea you intended to take the boy along with you. Of course there must be a surcharge.'

'Nonsense. The slave goes where I go.'

'Sir—'

'The boy is a slave, mere property. You might as well charge me for taking along a pair of sandals. I was led to believe this was a comfortable establishment. Of course, I was also led to believe that I would find a certain girl here—'

My host turned the coins in his hand. Their jingling added to the clacking of the rings on his fingers. He raised an eyebrow, smacked his lips, and turned aside.

Electra's room was nothing like the vestibule and hallways. I suspected she had decorated it herself; it had the unerring simplicity of Greek taste and the comfortable feeling of a room long lived in. She reclined on a long, wide divan. There were two chairs. I motioned to Tiro to sit on one. I sat on the other.

She smiled and laughed quietly, perhaps thinking we were shy, or pretending to be. 'It's more comfortable here,' she said, smoothing her hand over the well-worn fabric of the divan. Her voice held only the trace of an accent.

'I'm sure it is. But I want to talk first.'

175

She shrugged knowingly. 'Of course. Would you like me to undress?'

I glanced at Tiro, who was already blushing. 'Yes,' I said. 'Take off your gown while we talk. Do it slowly.'

Electra stood. She brushed her hair back and reached behind her neck to undo the clasp. Behind her, on a small table beside the divan, I spotted a tiny hourglass. Its upper chamber was full; the sand flowed freely. She must have turned it when we came into the room, so smoothly I hadn't noticed. Electra was a true professional.

'Tell me about Elena,' I said.

She hesitated for only a heartbeat. 'You are a friend of hers? A client?'

'No.'

'How do you know her?'

'I don't.'

She seemed amused. 'Then why do you ask me about her?' The gown slipped easily from her shoulders and gathered in folds about her waist, trapped by the sash. Her flesh was surprisingly smooth and firm. Against her pale nakedness I noticed the jewellery she wore, silver bangles about her wrists and a slender necklace that defined a sumptuous curve above her breasts. Though she might not own them, obviously she had chosen the ornaments herself. Again her taste eclipsed her master's.

She seemed to make a point of ignoring Tiro, which left him free to stare at her. He watched with a kind of helpless intensity, his lips pursed and his eyebrows drawn together as if he might be in pain.

'Perhaps you should simply answer the question. I've already paid for you, after all. Displease me and I shall complain to your master, demand my money back. Perhaps he'll beat you.'

She laughed out loud. 'I don't think so,' she said. 'And neither do you.' She picked up a comb and a small mirror from the table and sat on the bed, gazing at her reflection and combing her hair. She was really quite extraordinary. My host should have demanded twice his starting price.

'You're right. I only said that to titillate the boy.'

She looked away from her mirror only long enough to arch an eyebrow at me. 'You have a wicked mind. I think we're wasting time, talking like this.'

I shook my head. 'Tell me about Elena. When did she leave?'

'Some time in the autumn. Before winter.'

'September, perhaps?'

'Yes, I think so. Yes, it was just after the Roman Festival. I remember because the holidays always bring in so much business. That would be late September.'

'How old is Elena?'

'A child.'

'As young as Talia?'

'I said a child, not a baby.'

'And what does she look like?'

'Very pretty. One of the prettiest girls in the house, I always said. Quite blonde, with skin like pale honey. I think her parents may have been Scythians. She had quite a beautiful body, very sumptuous for her age, full-breasted with wide hips and a tiny waist. How vain she was about her tiny waist!'

'Did she have a special client? A man who seemed to care for her in a special way?'

Electra looked at me uneasily. 'Is that why you're here?'

'Yes.'

'Are you a friend of that man? What is his name, Sextus?'

'Yes, that was his name. No, I was not his friend.'

'You speak as if he's dead.'

'He is.'

She put the comb and mirror in her lap. 'And Elena? Was she with him when he died? Do you know where she is now?'

'I know nothing at all about her, except what you can tell me.'

'She was a lovely girl. So delicate.' Electra looked suddenly very sad, and very beautiful. After a moment she took up the comb and the mirror again. 'She was not here for that long a time. A year, I think. The master bought her at auction at the temple of Castor, along with a half-dozen other girls, all the same age and colour. But she was the special one, even though he never saw it.'

'But Sextus saw it.'

'The old man? Oh, yes. After the first time, he came at least once every five or six days. Towards the end he sometimes came every other day.'

'The end?'

'After she became pregnant. Before she left.'

'Pregnant? Who was the father?'

Electra laughed. 'This is a brothel, in case you had forgotten. Not every client is satisfied simply to watch a woman comb her hair.' She shrugged. 'In a place like this a girl never really knows which man it might have been, though some girls like to have fantasies. It was Elena's first time. I told her how to get rid of it, but she wouldn't. By rights I should have told the master.'

'But you didn't. Why not?'

'I told you, Elena was so lovely, so delicate. She wanted the baby very much. I thought to myself, if she can hide it from the master long enough, he'll have to let her have it, even if he won't let her keep it.'

'But Elena told someone besides you. Some girls have fantasies, you say. What was her fantasy?'

Her eyes flashed with anger. 'You know already. I can tell by the way you ask.'

'I know only what you tell me.'

'All right. She told the old man, Sextus, that she was pregnant. She told him that the baby was his. And the fool believed her. Men that age sometimes want to make a child very badly. He had lost his son, you know; he talked to her about it constantly. Perhaps that's why she knew he would believe her. Who knows, perhaps it really was his child.'

'And how would this help Elena?'

'How do you think? It's what every girl in a house like this dreams of, at least until she learns better. A rich man falls in love with her, buys her from the master, takes her into his household. Or perhaps he even sets her free and settles her in her own apartment, where she can raise her baby as a citizen. In her wildest fantasies he might even recognize the bastard, make it an heir. One hears of such miracles. Elena was still young enough to dream like that.'

'And how did her dream end?'

'Sextus promised he would buy her and set her free. He even spoke of marrying her. So she told me. I don't think she imagined it.'

'And then?'

'He simply stopped coming. Elena put on a face for a while, but she was beginning to show the child, and the days kept passing. I held her in my arms when she wept at night. The cruelty of men . . .'

'Where is she now?'

'The master sold her.'

'To whom?'

'I don't know. I thought perhaps it was Sextus who bought her, after all. But you say he's dead – and you know nothing of Elena.'

I shook my head.

'They came for her, at the end of September. With no announcement, no preparation. Stabius came bursting in, saying she was to gather up her clothes. The master had sold her and she was to leave at once. She trembled like a kitten. She cried from happiness, and I cried with her. She didn't bother to take any of her things, she said that Sextus would buy her finer things. I followed her down the hall. They were waiting for her in the vestibule.

I knew when I saw them that something was wrong. I think she knew it too, but she tried to hide it. She gave me a kiss, and she smiled as she walked out of the door with them.'

'Not Sextus,' I said. 'Sextus Roscius was dead by then.'

'No, not the old man. Two men. I didn't like the look of them. Neither the big blond one nor the one with the limp.'

I must have made some noise or sign without realizing it. Electra stopped brushing her hair and stared at me. 'What's wrong? You know him – the man with the limp?'

'Not yet.'

She laid down her brush and stared at me with smouldering eyes. 'What sort of puzzle is this? Do you know where Elena is or don't you? Do you know who bought her?'

'I told you before. All I know of Elena is what you tell me.'

'That's a lie,' she said.

Tiro squirmed in his chair. I think he had never heard a slave talk in such a way to a citizen.

'Yes.' I nodded. 'It is a lie. There is one thing I know about Elena; it's why I'm here. I'll tell you. On the night that Sextus Roscius was killed – not far from here, Electra, only a few steps up the street – on that night he was at a dinner party in the house of a great noblewoman. Caecilia Metella: have you ever heard the name? Did Elena ever mention it?'

'No.'

'It was after dark when a messenger came. He

brought a written message for Sextus. It was from Elena, urging him to come at once to the House of Swans.'

'Impossible.'

'Why?'

'Elena couldn't write.'

'But perhaps someone else in the house could.'

'Stabius can, a little. And the clerks, but we never see them. It doesn't matter. Sending a message to a wealthy man, fetching him like a dog from a great matron's house – Elena was a dreamer, but she wasn't mad. She would never have done such a thing, certainly not without asking my advice.'

'You're certain?'

'Absolutely.'

I nodded. I looked at the hourglass. There was a considerable amount of sand remaining. 'I think we've talked enough,' I said.

It was Electra's turn to check the hourglass. She closed her eyes for a moment. The agitation and anxiety slowly vanished from her face. She stood and unbelted the sash at her waist. 'Only one other thing,' she said softly. 'If you should hear news of Elena and the baby, would you let me know? Even if the news is bad. You wouldn't need to see me again if you didn't want to. You could simply have a slave leave word with Stabius. He would see that I received the message.'

'If I discover anything, I'll make sure that you know.'

She nodded in gratitude, and let the gown fall from her hips.

I gazed at her for a long time. She stood motionless, her head bowed, with one foot slightly before the other and her hands at her sides, allowing me to study the lines of her body, to breathe in the alluring odour of her flesh.

'You are a beautiful woman, Electra.'

'Some men have thought so.'

'But I didn't come here because I needed a woman. I came looking for Elena.'

'I understand.'

'And though I paid your master, it wasn't your body I wanted.'

'I know.' She looked up at me. 'But there is plenty of time remaining.'

'No. Not for me. Not today. But there is a gift you can give me. A favour.'

'Yes.'

'The boy.' I gestured to Tiro, who stared back at me with a look of mingled lust and stupefaction. His face was quite red.

'Of course,' Electra said. 'You want to watch us?'

'No.'

'You want to take us both together?' She inclined her head and gave me a wry smile. 'I suppose I could share you.'

'You misunderstand. I'll wait in the vestibule. This would be strictly for the boy's pleasure, not for mine. And perhaps for your pleasure, as well.'

She raised a sceptical eyebrow. What sort of man, after all, would pay good money to have his slave entertained by a whore?

I turned to leave. Tiro started up from his chair. 'But, sir—'

'Quiet, Tiro. Stay. A gift. Accept it graciously.'

I left, closing the door behind me. I lingered in the hall for a long moment, half-expecting Tiro to follow me. He didn't.

In the vestibule, business had begun to pick up. The proprietor greeted new guests; Stabius and another slave paraded the merchandise. All the seats were taken and some of the clients had to stand. I stood among them, out of the way and out of sight. It was not long before Tiro came walking rapidly down the hall, awkwardly adjusting his tunic about his shoulders. His face was damp with sweat, his hair tousled. He had not even bothered to straighten his clothes before fleeing the room.

'Finished?' I said.

I expected a grin, but he barely glanced at me before he plunged into the small crowd and headed relentlessly for the door. I followed after him, glancing over my shoulder at the latest selection of girls. Young Talia was among them. Her owner had pulled the robe back from her shoulder and was gently fondling her breasts. 'See how she blushes?' I heard him say. 'What a colour it gives her cheeks. She blushes in other places as well, too delicate to mention. . . .'

In the street Tiro walked so fast I had to run to catch up. 'I shouldn't have done it,' he said, shaking his head and staring straight ahead.

I laid my hand on his shoulder. Though he

shrank away, he obeyed as a horse obeys, slowing his pace. 'You didn't find her desirable, Tiro?'

'Of course I did. She's . . .' He searched for a word, and finding none adequate gave a despairing shrug.

'You didn't enjoy yourself?'

'Of course I did.'

'Then you might at least thank me.'

'But I shouldn't have done it.' He scowled. 'It was Cicero paying, not you. You'll charge him the expense. What do you think he would say if he knew? Using his money to buy a woman for me . . .'

'Then he needn't know. Anyway, I had paid for the whore already; it was a legitimate expense, you must admit that. It only made sense that one of us should use her.'

'Yes, when you put it that way. Even so . . .' He looked me straight in the eye, only for an instant, but long enough for me to see inside him. The guilt he felt was not for abusing Cicero's trust, but for betraying another.

That was when I first knew just how badly Tiro had been smitten by the daughter of Sextus Roscius.

XIII

We walked again past the widow Polia's tenement, past the bloodstain, past the old shopkeeper and his wife. Tiro was in a mood to walk fast; I matched him and then set a faster pace. I had had enough for one day of strangers and their tragedies. I longed to be home again.

We entered the square. The shops had reopened; the street vendors had returned. The sun was still high enough to reach over the rooftops and strike the public sundial. An hour of daylight remained.

Children were playing about the cistern; housewives and slaves stood waiting to fetch water for the evening meal. The square was alive with noise and movement, but something was amiss. Only gradually I realized that half of the crowd or more had their faces turned in the same direction. A number of them were pointing.

Rome is a city of fire and smoke. The people are

sustained by bread, bread is baked in ovens, ovens release plumes of smoke. But the smoke of a tenement fire has an altogether different appearance. The smoke rises thick and black; on a clear and windless day it thrusts upward in a great column. Currents of ash roil and thrash against the sky, only to be sucked inward to the core, thrown higher and higher against the sky.

The fire lay directly in our path, somewhere between us and the Capitoline. Tiro, seeing it, seemed suddenly relieved of all anxieties. His face took on a smooth, healthy lustre of excitement as he quickened his pace. Man's instinct is to flee from fire, but city life obliterates the animal urges; indeed, we passed not a single person going in the opposite direction as we neared the fire, but instead found ourselves drawn into an ever-growing congestion of pedestrians and wagons as people from all about rushed to see the catastrophe at its peak.

The fire was near the foot of the Capitoline, just outside the Servian wall, in a block of fashionable apartments south of the Circus Flaminius. A four-storey tenement was almost completely engulfed. Flames belched from the windows and danced about the roof. If there had been a drama of the type the crowd so adores, we had missed it; there were no helpless victims screaming from the upper windows, no babies being thrown to the street. The inhabitants had already escaped or else were dead inside.

Here and there in the crowd I saw women tearing their hair, men weeping, families huddle together. The mourners and the destitute were swallowed up in the general mass of the crowd, who watched the flames with various expressions of awe and delight.

'They say it started in mid-afternoon,' said a man nearby, 'and took all this time to swallow the whole building.' His friend nodded gravely. 'Even so, I hear there were several families trapped on the upper floors, burned alive. You could hear them screaming. They say a flaming man came hurtling out of an upper window not more than an hour ago, landing in the midst of the crowd. If we move over that way, we might be able to see the spot where he landed. . . .'

In the open corridor between the crowd and the flames a grey-bearded man was running hectically to and fro, hiring strangers off the street to help contain the conflagration. The wage he offered was hardly more than a volunteer's honorarium, and not many took him up. On the northward side, looking up the hill, the fire seemed to pose little danger of spreading; there was no wind to carry the flames, and the wide space between the buildings was adequate protection. But on the southward side, towards the Circus, another, shorter tenement nearly adjoined the burning building, with only the width of a tall man's reach between them. Already the facing wall was scorched, and as the burning building began to crumble, heaps of ash and debris tumbled into the gap between them, with some of the flaming material landing on the roof of the lower structure, where a team of slaves hastily shovelled it off.

A noble, finely dressed and attended by a large retinue of slaves, secretaries, and gladiators, stepped out of the crowd and approached the distressed greybeard. 'Citizen,' he called out, 'are you the owner of these buildings?'

'Not the burning building,' the man snapped. 'That would be my stupid neighbour Varius, the kind of fool who lets his tenants build fires on the hottest day of the year. You don't see him here, fighting the fire. Probably on holiday down at Baiae. This is mine, the one that's still standing.'

'But not, perhaps, for long.' The noble spoke in a fine voice that would not have been out of place in the Forum. I had not yet seen his face, but I knew who he must be.

'Crassus,' I whispered.

'Yes,' Tiro said, 'Crassus. My master knows him.' There was a trace of pride in his voice, the pride of those who appreciate a brush with celebrity no matter what its nature. 'You know the song: "Crassus, Crassus, rich as Croesus." Already they say he's the richest man in Rome, not counting Sulla, of course, which makes him richer than most kings, and growing richer every day. So Cicero says.'

'And what else does your master say about Crassus?' The object of our conversation had wrapped one arm around the greybeard's shoulder. Together they walked to a spot with a better view of the breach between the two buildings. I followed behind, and stared beyond them into the blinding cleft, impassable for the constant rain of ash and smouldering bricks.

'Men say that Crassus has many virtues and only one overwhelming vice, and that is avarice. But Cicero says that his greed is only the symptom of a deeper vice: envy. Wealth is the only thing Crassus has. He keeps hoarding it up because he's so jealous of other men's qualities, as if his envy were a deep pit, and if he could fill it full enough of gold and cattle and buildings and slaves, then he could finally stand level with his rivals.'

'Then we should feel pity for Marcus Crassus? Your master is very compassionate.'

We moved beyond the mass of the crowd and drew near enough to hear Crassus and the tenement owner shouting above the roar of the flames. The fire was like hot breath against my face, and I had to blink my eyes against flying cinders.

We stood at the heart of the crisis. It seemed a strange place to transact business, unless you considered the advantage it gave Crassus. The poor greybeard looked in no condition to strike a hard bargain. Above the roar of the flames I could hear Crassus's trained oratorical voice like chiming bells.

'Ten thousand denarii,' he shouted. I couldn't hear the landlord's answer, but his face and his gestures indicated outrage. 'Very well.' Crassus shrugged. He seemed about to offer a higher price when a sheet of flame abruptly shot up about the base of the endangered building. A group of workers immediately ran to the spot, beating against the flames with rugs and passing a chain of buckets. Their efforts seemed to douse the flames; then the fire leaped up in another spot.

'Eight thousand, five hundred,' said Crassus. 'My final offer. Better than the value of the raw land, which is all that may be left. Consider the expense of having the rubble carted off.' He stared into the conflagration and shook his head. 'Eight thousand denarii, no more. Take it now if you're interested. Once the flames start in earnest I won't offer you an as.'

The greybeard wore an expression of agony. A few thousand denarii was hardly adequate compensation. But if the building was gutted it would be utterly worthless.

Crassus called to his secretary. 'Gather up my retinue. Tell them to be ready to move on. I came here to buy, not to watch a building go up in flames.'

The greybeard broke down. He clutched at Crassus's sleeve and nodded. Crassus made a sign to his secretary, who instantly produced a fat purse and paid the man on the spot.

Crassus raised his hand and snapped his fingers. Immediately his entire retinue went into action. Gladiators and slaves scurried about the building like ants, seizing buckets from the hands of exhausted volunteers, tearing up paving stones and throwing rocks, dirt, and anything else that would not burn into the breach between the buildings.

Crassus turned on his heel and walked straight towards us. I had seen him many times in the Forum, but never so close. He was not a bad-looking man, slightly older than myself, with thinning hair, a strong nose, and prominent jaw. 'Citizen!' he called to me. 'Join the battle. I'll pay you ten times a workman's daily wage, half now and half later, and the same for your slave.'

I was too stunned to answer. Crassus walked on, unperturbed, making the same offer to every able-bodied man in the crowd. His secretary followed behind, disbursing payments.

'They must have seen the smoke and come straight over the hill from the Forum,' Tiro said.

'A chance to buy property at the foot of the Capitoline for next to nothing – why not? I hear he keeps slaves posted on the hilltops to watch for fires such as this, so that he can be first on the spot to buy up the spoils.'

'It's not the worst stories they tell about Crassus.' Tiro's face turned livid, either from my sudden scrutiny or from the heat of the flames.

'What do you mean?'

'Well, only that he made his fortune by profiting from the proscriptions. When Sulla had his enemies beheaded, their property was confiscated by the state. Whole estates went up on the auction blocks. Sulla's friends were able to buy them for scandalous prices. Everyone else was afraid to bid.'

'Everyone knows that, Tiro.'

'But Crassus finally went too far. Even for Sulla.'

'How?'

Tiro lowered his voice, though no one could possibly have heard us amid the rumble of the flames and the sudden din of Crassus's hirelings. 'I overhead Rufus telling my master one day. Rufus is connected to Sulla by marriage, you know,

192

through his sister Valeria; he hears all sorts of things that otherwise would never leave Sulla's house.'

'Yes, go on.'

'The story goes that Crassus had an innocent man's name added to the proscription lists, just so he could get his hands on the man's property. This was an old patrician who had no one to protect his interests; his sons had been killed in the wars – fighting for Sulla! The poor man was rounded up by thugs and his head was chopped off that very day. His estates were auctioned off a few days later, and Crassus saw to it that no one else was allowed to bid. The proscriptions were strictly for political enemies, and terrible enough, but Crassus used them to satisfy his own greed. Sulla was furious, or pretended to be, and hasn't let him run for a public office since, for fear that the scandal will come out.'

I searched the busy crowd for Crassus. He stood amid the swirling mass of slaves and gladiators, heedless of the confusion, staring wide-eyed and smiling like a proud parent at his latest acquisition. I turned around and followed his gaze. As we watched, the wall of the flaming tenement gave way and fell in on itself with a great shudder and a shower of sparks. The fire was contained. The smaller building would not be lost.

I looked again at Crassus. His face was flushed with an almost religious joy – the ecstasy of a bargain well and truly struck. In the reddish glow of the bonfire his face looked smooth and younger than its age, flushed with victory, set about eyes that glittered with an unquenchable greed. I stared into the face of Marcus Licinius Crassus, and I saw the future of Rome.

XIV

Cicero was still in seclusion when I returned with Tiro to the house on the Capitoline. The old manservant solemnly informed us that his master had stirred before midday and managed to descend to the Forum to conduct some business, but had returned after only a short while, weakened by the disquiet in his bowels and exhausted from the heat. Cicero had retired to his bed with word that not even Tiro should disturb him. It was just as well. I had no stomach for reciting the day's events and parading the players before Cicero's caustic eye.

Tiro assumed authority to offer me food and drink, and even a bed if I felt too weary to make my way home. I declined. He asked at what hour he should expect me the next day. I told him he would not be seeing me at all until the day after, at the earliest. I had decided to pay a visit to the town of Ameria and the country estates of Sextus Roscius.

The stroll down the hill and through the Forum refreshed my mind. The dining hour approached, and an evening breeze carried scents of cooking from every corner. The Forum had reached the end of another long day of business. The lowering sun cast long shadows across the open squares. Here and there business continued in an informal vein. Bankers gathered in small groups at the foot of the temple steps to exchange the final gossip of the day; passing friends exchanged last-minute invitations to dinner; a few stray beggars sat in tucked-away corners counting the day's revenue.

Rome is perhaps most appealing at this hour. The mad trafficking of the day is done, the languor of the warm night still lies ahead. Dusk in Rome is a meditation on victories accomplished and pleasures yet to come. Never mind that the victories may have been trivial and impermanent, or that the pleasures may fail to satisfy. At this hour Rome is at peace with herself. Are the monuments to the gods and heroes of her past pitted with corrosion and weathered by neglect? In this light they appear newly hewn, their crumbling edges made smooth and their fissures erased by gentle twilight. Is her future uncertain, unforeseen, a feverish leap into darkness? At this hour the darkness looms but does not yet descend, and Rome may well imagine it will bring her only sweet dreams, dispensing its nightmares to her subjects.

I left the Forum for more common streets. I found myself wishing that the sun could stand still on the horizon, like a ball come to rest on a windowsill, so that twilight might linger indefinitely. What a mysterious city Rome would become then, perpetually bathed in blue shadow, her weed-ruptured alleyways as cool and fragrant as mossy riverbanks, her great avenues pocked with deep shadows where the narrower tributaries lead off to those places where the masses of Rome are constantly getting and begetting themselves.

I came to that long, serpentine, unrelieved passageway through which I had taken Tiro the day before, the Narrows. Here the sense of peace and serene expectation wavered and abandoned me. To traverse the Narrows while the sun is still rising is one thing; to pass through while the light fails is another. Within a few steps I was already plunged into premature night, with black walls on either side, an uncertain greyness ahead and behind, and a thin ribbon of twilight-blue sky above.

In such a place it is easy to imagine not only all manner of sounds and shapes, but a whole catalogue of other phenomena detected by a nameless sense more rarefied than hearing or sight. If I thought I heard footsteps following me, it was not for the first time in the Narrows. If it seemed that those footsteps halted whenever I stopped to listen, and resumed when I decided to press on, this was not my first encounter with such an experience. But on this night I began to feel an unaccustomed sense of dread, almost of panic. I found myself walking more and more quickly, and glancing over my shoulder to make sure that the nothing I had seen only moments before was the same nothing that still doggedly pursued me. When at last I stepped out of the Narrows and into the broader street, the last traces of twilight seemed as open and inviting as the noonday sun.

I had one last bit of business to transact before I made my way up the Esquiline. There are stables on the Subura Way, not far from the pathway that leads up to my house, where farmers visiting from the country find stalls and straw for their nags, and riders relay their steeds. The proprietor is an old acquaintance. I told him I would be needing a mount the next day for a very quick journey north to Ameria and back again.

'Ameria?' He sat hunched over a bench, squinting at his tallies for the day beneath a newly lit lamp. 'A hard eight hours of riding, at the least.'

'The least is the most I can manage. Once I'm there I'll need to attend to my business with what's left of the day, and head back to Rome early the next morning. Unless I have to make a very fast escape before that.'

The stablemaster scowled at me. He has never been quite sure what I do for a living, though he must suspect it has some criminal element, given the oddities of my comings and goings. Even so, he has never given me less than the finest service.

'I suppose you're going alone, like a damned fool?'

'Yes.'

He hawked up a mass of mucus and spat onto the straw-littered floor. 'You'll be needing a quick, strong horse.'

'Your quickest and strongest,' I agreed. 'Vespa.'

'And if Vespa's not available?'

'I can see her tail from here, hanging over the gate to her stall.'

'So you can. One of these days I suppose you'll come back to me with the stories of her sad end, and how you did your best to keep her out of harm's way. "Very fast escape" indeed. From what? But of course you're not telling me. She's my best mare. I shouldn't loan her to a man who'll ride her too hard and put her in danger besides.'

'It's more likely that one of these days I shall take Vespa and she'll return to you unscathed and without a rider, though I don't suppose you'll shed a tear over that. I'll be here before dawn. Have her ready for me.'

'The usual fee?'

'No,' I said, and watched his jowls droop. 'The usual — and a special gratuity besides.' In the combination of blue twilight and soft lamplight, I could make out the lines of a grudging smile on his ugly face. I would pass on the extra fee to Cicero.

Day lingers longest on the summits of the seven hills of Rome. The sun had departed for good, but the hillside of the Esquiline was still brighter than the narrow, deep-shadowed artery at her feet. As I hurried up the rough pathway to my house, I entered a latitude of lingering, pale blue twilight. Above the hilltop the stars were already shining faintly in a sky of deepest blue.

My nose told me the news first. The smell of

excrement baked for long hours in the sun wafted down the dry cobblestones. Some time during the day my countrified neighbour had thrown a gift over her wall onto my walkway, and my other neighbour had not yet claimed it. From long habit I held my breath, hitched up my toga and stepped a little to the left as I approached the dark mass brooding like a toad on the walkway. By chance I happened to glance down, remembering with a smile the warning I had given Tiro about soiling his shoes.

I stopped short. Despite the dying light and the softening shadows, the footprints embedded in the excrement had an almost preternatural clarity. Two men, at least, had paid a visit in my absence. They had both managed to step in the excrement on their way out.

For no rational reason I quickened my pace. The beating of my heart was suddenly loud in my ears. Above its pounding I imagined I heard a woman calling my name from somewhere below, at the foot of the hill.

The door to my house stood wide open. On the outer frame someone had smeared a dark, glistening handprint. I did not have to touch it to know; even in the colourless twilight I could see that the handprint had been made with blood.

Within the house all was still. No lamps, no candlelight; the only illumination came from the lingering twilight in the central garden, a great lozenge of ghostly blue that seeped between the columns and into the open rooms. The floor spread beneath me dim and uncertain, like the surface of a pool, but directly before my feet I could make out quite clearly a spattering of blood – great drops of blood, some whole, some smeared as if they had been stepped upon. The droplets formed a trail that ended against the wall of Bethesda's room.

At the very centre of the wall there was a great explosion of blood, black as pitch against the white plaster, with tiny filaments fanning towards the ceiling and a broad smear trailing down to the floor. Beside this was a message scrawled in blood. The letters were small, irregular, and clumsy. In the darkness I could make nothing of them.

'Bethesda?' I whispered. The word sounded stupid and useless in my ears. I said it louder, and again louder, frightened by the shrillness in my voice. There was no answer.

I stood very still. The silence was absolute. Darkness seemed to gather in the corners and seep outward, filling the room. The garden turned ashen grey beneath starlight and moonlight. Twilight was over. True night had begun.

I stepped away from the wall, trying to think of where I might find a lamp and tinder. Bethesda had always tended to fires in the house. At the thought of her a great pit of dread opened inside me. At that moment I tripped against something on the floor.

The thing was small, soft, motionless. I stepped back and slipped on blood. The shape at my feet was almost lost in darkness and mutilated beyond recognition, but I knew in an instant what it was, or had been.

There was a flickering light at the door. I started back, cursing myself for having no weapon. Then I remembered the knife the mute boy had given me, still hidden in the folds of my tunic. I reached for it, searching blindly until I felt the hilt against my palm. I drew out the knife and walked quickly, steadily to the doorway, meeting the lamplight as it emerged from the darkness, slipping behind and seizing its bearer with an arm around her throat.

She shrieked and bit at my forearm. I tried to break free, but her teeth were clamped against the flesh. 'Bethesda,' I pleaded, 'let me go!'

She broke away and spun around, her back to the wall. She reached up to wipe the taste of blood from her mouth. Somehow she had managed to hold the lamp aloft and burning without losing a drop of oil.

'Why did you do that?' she screamed. She beat her fist against the wall behind her. There was a kind of madness in her eyes. By the lamplight I saw the bruises on her face and throat. The neck of her gown had been badly torn.

'Bethesda, are you hurt? Are you bleeding?'

She closed her eyes and took a breath. 'Only a little hurt.' She held up her lamp and looked into the room, then made a face so wretched that I thought some new menace had entered the house. But when I followed her gaze to the floor I saw only the broken and blood-matted corpse of her beloved Bast.

I tried to hold her, but Bethesda would not be held. She pulled away with a shiver and hurriedly went from room to room, using the flame from her lamp to light every lamp and candle. When the whole house was alight and she had satisfied herself that no intruders lurked in the darker corners, she bolted the door and went about the house again, closing all the windows.

I watched her in silence. In the wavering light I saw the shambles that had been made of the house: furniture overturned, hangings ripped from the walls, objects smashed and broken. I lowered my eyes, numb from looking at chaos, and found myself studying the trail of blood on the floor, the mangled body of Bast, the writing on the wall. I stepped closer. The letters were of different sizes, many of them misshapen and inverted, but the spelling was correct. It had obviously been made by someone unused to writing, perhaps a complete illiterate reproducing the symbols from a copy. It hurt my eyes to read it:

BE SILENT OR DIE.
LET ROMAN JUSTICE
WORK ITS WILL.

Bethesda walked past me, cutting a wide swathe around the corpse of the cat and averting her eyes from the wall. 'You must be quite hungry,' she said. Her voice was strangely calm and matter-of-fact.

'Very hungry,' I admitted. I followed her to the back of the house, into the pantry.

She lifted the lid from a pot and pulled out a whole fish, flipping it onto the table where it gave off a strong smell in the warm, still air. Beside it lay a handful of fresh herbs, an onion, some grape leaves. 'You see,' Bethesda said, 'I had just come back from the market.'

'When did they come? How many of them?'

'Two men.' She reached for a knife and brought it down on the fish, chopping the head off with a single, clean stroke. 'They came twice. First they came late this morning. I did as you've always said, I kept the door locked and bolted and talked to them through the little window. I told them you were gone and probably would not be back until very late. They wouldn't say who they were. They said they would come back.'

I watched as she cleaned the fish, using her fingernails and the sharp tip of the knife. Her hands were extraordinarily nimble.

'Later I went to the market. I was able to get the fish very cheap. The day was so hot, the market was dusty, the man was afraid it would spoil before he could sell it. Fresh fish from the river. I finished my shopping and came up the hill. The door was closed, the latch was in place. I checked for that, as you always say to.'

She began to chop the herbs, bringing the blade down hard and fast. I thought of the old shopkeeper's wife.

'But the day was so very hot, and so still. No wind from the garden at all. I could barely stay awake. I left the door open. Only for a little while, I thought, but I guess I forgot. I was so sleepy I went to my room to lie down. I don't know if I slept or not, but after a while I heard them in the vestibule. Somehow I knew it was the same men. I heard them talking low; then there was a loud noise, like a table overturned. They started shouting, calling your name, yelling obscenities. I hid in my room. I could hear them tramping through the house, turning over furniture, throwing things against the walls. They came into my room. You always imagine you can hide if you have to, but of course they found me right away.'

'And then what?' My heart raced in my chest.

'Not what you think.' She reached up to wipe a tear from her eye. 'The onion,' she said. I saw the bruise that circled her wrist like a bracelet, left by a strong man's grip.

'But they hurt you.'

'They pushed me. They hit me a few times. One of them held me from the back. They made me watch.' She stared down at the table. Her voice became grim. 'I had been squabbling with Bast all day. She was crazy from the smell of the fish. One of them found her in the kitchen and brought her to the vestibule. She bit him and scratched his face. He threw her against the wall. Then he pulled out a knife.' She looked up from her work. 'They wrote something. With the blood. They said it was for you, and that you shouldn't forget it. What does it say? Is it a curse?'

'No. A threat. It doesn't make sense.'

'It has to do with the young slave who came yesterday, doesn't it? The new client, the parricide?'

'Perhaps, though I can't see how. Cicero sent for

me only yesterday. It wasn't until today that I started stirring up trouble – yet they must already have been on their way here, even before I spoke with the shopkeeper and his wife. . . . How did you escape from them?'

'The same way I got away from you just now. With my teeth. The big one holding me was quite a coward. He squealed like a pig.'

'What did they look like?'

She shrugged. 'Bodyguards, gladiators. Fighters. Big men. Ugly.'

'And one of them had a limp.' I spoke the words as a certainty, but Bethesda shook her head.

'No. No limp. I watched them both walk away the first time.'

'You're sure. No limp?'

'The one who held me I didn't really see. But the one who wrote was very big, and blond, a giant. His face was bleeding from where Bast had scratched him. I hope he carries a scar.' She flipped the fish back into the pot, sprinkled it with the herbs and covered it all with grape leaves. She poured in water from an urn, put the pot over the fire, and stooped to tend the flame. I noticed that her hands had begun to shake.

'Men like that,' she said, 'would not be satisfied with killing a cat, do you think?'

'No. I think they might not.'

She nodded. 'The door was still open. I knew I had to get away while the blond giant was still busy smearing letters on the wall, so I bit the man holding me as hard as I could, here.' She indicated the thickest part of her forearm. 'I slipped from his arms and ran out the door. They followed me. But they stopped suddenly as they were passing between the neighbours' walls. I could hear them behind me, making disgusted noises, snorting like pigs.'

'That would be when they stepped in the pile of excrement.'

'Yes. Imagine men who could smear their hands in cat's blood, turned into squeamish matrons from a bit of shit on their sandals? Romans!' The word came out of her mouth like venom. Only a native Alexandrian can pronounce the name of the world's capital with such withering disgust.

'I lost myself in the street, until I thought they must be gone. But when I came back to the foot of the pathway I was afraid to come up. I went into the tavern across the street instead. I know a woman who cooks there, from seeing her in the market. She let me hide in one of the empty rooms upstairs, until I saw you coming home. She lent me a lamp. I called out from below, to warn you before you reached the house, but you didn't hear.' She gazed into the fire. 'Will they come back?'

'Not tonight,' I assured her, having no idea whether they would or not.

Having eaten, I longed for sleep, but Bethesda would not let me rest until the corpse had been disposed of.

Romans have never worshipped animals as gods. Nor are they sentimental about household creatures. How could it be otherwise with a race that esteems human life so very little? Beneath the numbing apathy of their masters, the slaves of Rome, imported from all over the earth, but especially from the East, often lose whatever notions of sacred life they may have acquired as children in faraway lands. But Bethesda retained a sense of decorum and awe in the face of an animal's death, and in her way she grieved for Bast.

She insisted that I build a pyre in the centre of the garden. She took a dress from her wardrobe, a fine gown of white linen which I had given her only a year before. I winced as I watched her rip the seams to form a single winding sheet. She wrapped the broken body in thickness after thickness, until no more blood would soak through to stain the outermost cloth. She laid the bundle onto the pyre and muttered something to herself as she watched the flames leap up. In the still air the smoke rose straight upwards, blotting out the stars.

I longed for sleep. I ordered her to join me, but she refused to come until the floor had been washed clean of blood. She knelt beside a pail of heated water and scrubbed far into the night. I convinced her to leave the message on the wall untouched, though she clearly thought that leaving it was an invitation to all manner of magical disaster.

She would not allow me to extinguish a single lamp or candle. I fell asleep in a house with every room alight. At some point Bethesda finished her scrubbing and joined me, but her presence brought me no comfort. All through the night she kept rising to check the bolts on the doors and windows, to refill the lamps and replenish the candles.

I slept in fits and starts. I dreamed. Over endless miles of barren waste I rode a white steed, unable to remember when or how I had departed, unable to reach any destination. In the middle of the night I woke, feeling already weary from a long, unpleasant journey.

XV

It would never do for Bethesda to stay alone in the house while I was gone. A year before, the problem would never have arisen; then I had kept two strong young male slaves. Except on those rare occasions when I needed an entourage or a body-guard and took them with me, they had stayed with Bethesda — one to accompany her on errands, the other to watch the household in her absence, both to assist and protect her in the home. Best of all, they had given her someone to boss; at night I tried not to smile as she recounted her grievances against them and fumed at the gossip she imagined they passed behind her back.

But slaves are a constant expense and a valuable commodity, especially to those barely able to afford them. A chance offer from a client at a moment of need had weakened me into selling them both. For the last year Bethesda had managed on her own without incident, until now. My foolishness had almost brought us to complete disaster.

I could not leave her alone. Yet, if I hired a bodyguard for the day, would she be any safer? The assassins might very well return; would a single bodyguard, or two, or three be enough if they were bent on murder? If I found somewhere for her to stay, I would be leaving the house deserted. Such men, foiled of capturing any prey, might very well set fire to everything I owned.

Long before the first cock's crow of the morning I was awake, turning the dilemma over in my head. The only advice that came to me from staring at the candlelit ceiling was to drop the case entirely. There would be no trip to Ameria. At first light I could descend to the Subura and dispatch a messenger to Cicero, telling him I withdrew from his employ and asking him to settle my account. Then I could board myself up in the house with Bethesda all day, making love and strolling in the garden and complaining about the heat; and to any intruder who beat on the door I could simply say: 'Yes, yes, I choose silence over death! Let Roman justice work its will! Now go away!'

There is a cock on the hillside which crows long before all the rest; I suspect he belongs to my country neighbour who throws her offal over the wall — a country cock with country habits, unlike the lazier and more luxurious birds of Rome. When he crowed, there would be two hours until dawn. I decided I would rise then and make my choice.

The nature of time changes while the world sleeps. Moments congeal, moments attenuate, like lumps in thin cheese. Time becomes uneven, elusive, uncertain. To the sleepless the night seems eternal and yet still too short. I lay for a long time watching the flickering shadows above my head, unable to sleep but unable to follow any of the thoughts that flitted through my head, waiting for the cock's crow until I began to think the bird had overslept. Then it came at last, distinct and shrill in the warm, still air.

I sprang up, realizing with a start that I had actually been asleep, or somewhere on sleep's border. For a confused moment I wondered if I had dreamed the cock's crow. Then I heard it again.

Amid the light of many candles I changed my tunic and splashed my face. Bethesda had finally come to rest; I saw her curled on a straw mat beneath the colonnade at the far corner of the garden, surrounded by a ring of candles, asleep at last. She had chosen a spot as far as possible from the wall where Bast had died.

I crossed the garden, walking quietly so as not to wake her. She lay curled on her side, hugging herself. The muscles of her face were soft and relaxed. A lustrous strand of blue-black hair lay in disarray across her cheek. In the glow of the candles she looked more like a child than I had ever seen her. A part of me longed to gather her up in my arms and carry her to the bed, to hold her there warm and safe, touching and dreaming until the morning sun on our faces made us wake. To forget about whatever sordid mess Cicero had swept me into, to turn my back upon it. Looking at Bethesda, I felt a wave of such tenderness that my eyes were veiled with tears. The image of her face dissolved; the candlelight melted into glistening mist. It is one thing, so I am told, to join fortunes in marriage to a free woman. It is something else to own a woman as a slave, and I have often wondered which is more bitter and which more sweet.

The cock crowed again, joined this time by another from far away. In that instant I decided.

I knelt beside Bethesda and woke her as gently as I could. Even so she gave a start and stared at me for a moment as if I were a stranger. I felt a pang of doubt and turned away, knowing that if she saw my hesitation it would feed her own fear, and there would be no end to it. I told her to dress and comb her hair and grab a handful of bread if she was hungry; as soon as she was ready we would take a short walk.

I quickly turned aside and busied myself extinguishing candles. The house fell dark. After a short time Bethesda emerged from her room and announced that she was ready. Her voice had an anxious edge but no note of distrust or reproach. I uttered a silent prayer that I was making the right choice, and wondered to whom I was praying.

The pathway down the hill was lined with shadows, black within black. Beneath the glow of my torch the stones underfoot took on the properties of illusion, casting confused, jumbled shadows while their edges loomed up treacherous and sharp. It would almost have been safer to proceed without a light. Bethesda tripped and clutched my arm. She peered from side to side, unable to watch her feet for fear of something lurking in the darkness.

Halfway down we entered a long trough of fog that flowed and eddied like a river in the notch of the valley, so thick that the torchlight reflected back upon itself, wrapping us in a cocoon of milky white. Like the uncanny heat that had gripped Rome, there was something freakish about the fog. It brought no refreshment or relief; the great mass was warm and clammy with abrupt pockets of chilled air. It devoured light. It swallowed sound. The grinding of the loose stones beneath our feet was muffled and distant. Even the crickets stopped their chirring, and for the moment the cocks were silent.

Bethesda shuddered beside me, but I was secretly glad of the fog. If it would last until sunrise, I might be able to make my exit from the city unobserved even by eyes hired to watch me.

The stablemaster was asleep when we arrived, but a slave agreed to wake him. He was disgruntled at first; I was an hour earlier than expected, and at any rate the slave could have handled the departure without his master being disturbed. But when I explained what I wanted and offered terms, he was suddenly wide-awake and genial.

For the next two days at least he would take Bethesda into his household. I warned him not to work her too hard as she was accustomed to her own rhythms and unused to heavy work. (This last was a lie, but I had no intention of letting him work her to her limit.) If he could set her to some steady task, sewing perhaps, she would more than earn her keep.

In the meantime I wanted to hire two sturdy slaves from him to watch my house. He insisted he could spare only one. I was sceptical until he roused the boy from bed. An uglier youth I had never seen, nor a larger one. Where he came from I could not imagine. He had the uncouth name of Scaldus. His face was raw and red, blistered by the intense sun of the past week; his hair stuck out in stiff bunches from his head, the same texture and colour as the bits of straw that clung to his scalp. If his sheer size failed to intimidate any caller, his face might do the job. He was to take up a post outside my door and not to leave it until I returned; a woman from the stables would bring him food and water through the day. Even if he proved weaker than he looked or a coward, he could at least raise an alarm if intruders came to the house. As for the expense, the stablemaster agreed to extend my credit. The added fee I would pass on to Cicero.

There was no need to return to the house. Everything I needed for the journey I had brought with me. A slave fetched Vespa from the stable. I mounted her, turned around, and saw Bethesda staring up at me with her arms crossed. She was not happy with the arrangement, as I could see from the tightness of her lips and the glimmer of anger in her dark eyes. I smiled, relieved. She was already recovering from the shock of the night before.

I had an impulse to bend down and kiss her, even in front of the stablemaster and his slaves; instead I turned my attention to Vespa, calming her early-morning friskiness, guiding her into the street and easing her into a gentle trot. Long ago I learned that whenever a master shows affection for a slave in public the gesture must go awry. No matter how sincere, the act becomes patronizing, embarrassing, a parody. Even so, a sudden fear gripped me, a premonition that I might regret forever having denied myself that parting kiss.

The fog was so thick I would have been lost had I not known the route by heart. The mist swirled around us, swallowing the clatter of Vespa's hooves and hiding us from the twice-million eyes of Rome. Around me the city seemed to stir, but that was an illusion; the city had never quite slept. All night long men and horses and wagons come and go in the deep-shadowed streets. I passed through the Fontinal Gate. I broke into a trot as I passed the voting stalls on the Field of Mars, taking the northward route of the great Flaminian Way.

Rome receded, invisible, behind me. The muted stench of the city was replaced by the smells of tilled earth and dew. Hidden by mist, the world seemed open and boundless, a place without walls or even men. Then the sun rose over the black and green fields, dispelling every vapour before it. By the time I reached the great northward curving arm of the Tiber, the sky was hard as crystal, utterly cloudless, and pregnant with heat.

Part Two

Portents

Part Two

Poems

XVI

The rich on their way from city to villa and back again travel in retinues with gladiators and bodyguards. The wandering poor travel in bands. Actors go in troupes. Any farmer driving his sheep to market will surround himself with shepherds. But the man who travels alone – so runs that proverb as old as the Etruscans – has a fool for a companion.

Everywhere I have lived there is a belief among city folk that life in the countryside must be safer, quieter, less fraught with crime and menace. The Romans especially are blindly sentimental about country life, imbuing it with a tranquil, lofty character beyond the reach of crime or base passion. This fantasy is believed only by those who have never spent much time in the countryside, and especially by those who have never travelled for day after day across the roads that Rome has laid like spokes radiating through the world. Crime is everywhere, and nowhere is a man in more danger at any given moment than when he is on the open road, especially if he travels alone.

If he must travel alone he should at least travel very fast, stopping for no one. The old woman who appears to lie hurt and abandoned beside the road may in fact be neither hurt nor abandoned nor even a woman, but a young bandit among a troupe of bandits, murderers, and kidnappers. A man can die on the open road or disappear forever. For the unwary a journey of ten miles may take an unexpected turn that ends in a slave market a thousand miles from home. The traveller must be prepared to flee at a moment's warning, to scream for help without embarrassment, and to kill if he must.

In spite of these thoughts, or perhaps because of them, I passed the long day without incident. The distance I needed to cover required long, unbroken hours of hard riding. I steeled myself to it early on and fell into the rhythm of constant speed. Not a single rider overtook me during the day. I passed traveller after traveller as if they were tortoises beside the road.

The Flaminian Way travels north from Rome, crossing the Tiber twice as it passes through southeastern Etruria. At length it reaches the river Nar, which runs into the Tiber from the east. The road crosses a bridge at the town of Narnia and enters southernmost Umbria. A few miles north of Narnia a minor road branches west, back towards the Tiber. It ascends a series of steep hills and then drops into a shallow valley of fertile vineyards and pastures. Here, nestled in a V of land between the Tiber and the Nar, lies the sleepy hill town of Ameria.

I had not travelled north of Rome in many years. When I had to leave the city, my business usually took me west to the seaport at Ostia or else south along the Appian Way through that region of lush villas and estates that ends at the resorts of Baiae and Pompeii, where the rich vent their boredom in manufacturing new scandals and plotting new crimes, and where the powerful had chosen sides in the civil wars. Occasionally I ventured east, into the rebellious territories that had vented their rage against Rome in the Social War. Southward and eastward I had seen first-hand the devastations of ten years of warfare – farms in ruin, roads and bridges destroyed, piles of corpses left uncovered and rotting until they turned to mountains of bones.

I had expected the same in the north, but here the land was largely untouched; here the people had exercised caution to the extent of cowardice, always hedging their bets, sniffing out the neutral path until the clear victor emerged and then rushing to his side. In the Social War they had declined to join the other client states in pressing Rome for their rights, waiting instead until Rome called on them for help and so securing those same rights without revolt. In the civil wars they had danced the dagger's edge between Marius and Sulla, between Sulla and Cinna until the dictator emerged triumphant. Sextus Roscius the elder had himself been a declared supporter of Sulla even before it became convenient.

Warfare had not spoiled the rolling pastures and dense woodlands that carpeted the southern reaches of Etruria and Umbria. Where in other regions one could sense in a thousand ways the disruptions brought by war and resettlement, here there was a feeling of timelessness, changelessness, almost of stagnation. People showed neither friendliness nor curiosity at a passing stranger; faces turned towards me from the fields, stared blankly, and turned back to their work with a disinterested scowl. The dry spring had so far yielded little colour to refresh the earth. Meagre trickles ran through stony creek beds; a fine dust covered and obscured everything. Heat lay heavy on the land, but there was something else that seemed to blanket the earth: a suffocating and dispiriting gloom beneath the blinding sunlight.

The monotony of the journey gave me time to think; the ever-changing countryside freed my mind from the cobwebs and cul-de-sacs of Rome. Yet the mystery of who had mounted the attack on my house defied solution. Once I began the investigation in earnest, I was open to danger from any quarter – the shopkeeper and his wife, the widow, the whore, any of them might have passed an alert to the enemy. But my visitors had come on the very morning after I first met with Cicero, even as I was on my way to the scene of the crime, before I had interviewed anyone. I counted the names of those who knew from the day before that I had been engaged in the case: Cicero himself, and Tiro;

Caecilia Metella; Sextus Roscius; Rufus Messalla; Bethesda. Unless the plot against Sextus Roscius was more convoluted and madly illogical than I could imagine, none of these people had any reason for driving me from the case. There was always the possibility of an eavesdropping servant in either Cicero's or Caecilia's house, a spy passing information to the enemies of Sextus Roscius; but given the loyalty inspired by Cicero and the kind of punishments to be incurred under Caecilia, the likelihood seemed absurdly small. Yet someone had known of my involvement early enough to see that hired enforcers were on my doorstep the very next morning, someone willing to kill me if I refused to turn aside.

The more I turned it over in my head the more tangled the problem became, and the more the danger seemed to grow, until I began to wonder if Bethesda was safe where I had left her. Having no idea where the threat came from, how could I protect her against it? I pushed the doubt from my mind and stared at the road ahead. Fear was useless. Only the truth could bring me safety.

At the second crossing of the Tiber I stopped for a while beneath the shade of a massive oak beside the riverbank. While I rested, a grey-haired farmer and three overseers came riding down from the north with a train of thirty slaves in tow. The farmer and two of his men dismounted and sat cross-legged in the shade, while the third led the slaves, who were chained neck to neck, down to the river to drink. The farmer and his men kept to themselves.

After a few suspicious glances they ignored me completely. From overhearing bits of his conversation I gathered he was a Narnian who had recently come into a property near Falerii; the slaves were being led to reinforce the workers there.

I took a bite of bread and sipped at my wineskin and gently waved aside a bee that circled my head. The slaves lined up at the riverbank and dropped to their knees, splashing the dust from their faces and bending down to drink like animals. Most were middle-aged; a few were older, some much younger. All of them wore a sort of sandal for protection, a scrap of leather strapped to each foot. Otherwise they were naked, except for two or three who wore a thin rag tied about the waist. Many had fresh scars and welts across their buttocks and backs. Even the sturdiest among them looked haggard and unhealthy. The youngest, or at least the smallest, was a thin, naked boy at the end of the train. He sobbed continually and kept muttering incoherently about his hand, which he held in the air at a crooked angle. The overseer shouted at him, stamped his foot, and finally snapped his whip, but the boy would not stop complaining.

I finished my bread, drank a mouthful of wine, and leaned back against the tree. I tried to rest, but the constant whimpering of the slave punctuated by the slashing of the whip set my nerves on edge. To a rich farmer, slaves are cheaper than cattle. When they die they are effortlessly replaced; the influx of slaves into Rome is endless, like crashing waves upon a beach. I mounted Vespa and rode on.

The day grew hotter and hotter. Throughout the afternoon I saw hardly another person. The fields had been abandoned until a cooler hour, and the road was empty; I might have been the only traveller in the world. By the time I reached Narnia the fields began to stir again and the traffic slowly increased. Narnia itself is a busy market town. Gravestones and small temples line its outer streets. At the centre I came upon a wide square shaded by trees and ringed by shops and animal pens. The sweet smell of straw and the strong odours of oxen, cows, and sheep were heavy in the heated air.

There was a small tavern at one corner of the square. Set into the open wooden door was a clay tile that showed a young shepherd with a lamb slung over his shoulders; a wooden sign above the lintel bade welcome to the Bleating Lamb. The place was dim and gloomy within, but cool. The only other customer was an emaciated old man who sat at a table in the corner, staring rigidly at nothing. My host was an enormously fat Etruscan with dark yellow teeth; he was so huge he almost filled the tiny room. He was happy to bring me a cup of the local wine.

'How far to Ameria?' I asked him.

He shrugged. 'How fresh is your horse?'

I looked about and caught my reflection in a plated ewer on the counter. My face was red and sweaty, my hair tangled and powdered with dust. 'No fresher than I am.'

He shrugged again. 'An hour if you pressed it.

Longer if you care to keep the animal's heart from bursting. Where have you come from?'

'Rome.' The word was out before I could call it back. All day I had been reminding myself of the dangers of the countryside, yet a few moments inside a quaint tavern had already loosened my lips.

'Rome? All this way in a single day? You must have had an early start. Have another cup. Don't worry, I'll cut it with plenty of water. Rome, you say. I have a son there, or used to. Fought for Sulla in the wars. Supposed to get a piece of land out of it. Maybe he did. I haven't had a word from him in months. All this way since this morning? You have family in Ameria?'

It is easier to trust a fat face than a gaunt one. Treachery shows itself like a scar on a haggard face but hides well behind a plump, infantile blandness. But the eyes do not lie, and his were completely without guile. My host was merely curious, talkative, bored.

'No,' I said. 'Not family. Business.'

'Ah. It must be important for you to ride so long and so hard.'

Guileless or not, I decided to trust him with no more of the truth than I had to. 'My patron is an impatient man,' I said. 'As impatient as he is rich. There's a parcel of farmland up near Ameria in which he's taken an interest. I've come to check it out for him.'

'Ah, happens all the time these days. When I was a boy it was all small farmers hereabout, local people who passed their land from father to son. Now

226

strangers come up from Rome, buying it all up. Nobody knows who owns half the land any more. Never your neighbours; instead it's some rich man down in Rome who comes up twice a year to play farmer.' He laughed, then his face darkened. 'And the larger the farms the more slaves they bring in. They used to march them right through the square here, or cart them through in wagons, until we put a stop to that and routed them off the main way. It doesn't do for men in chains to come through here and get a sniff of freedom. Too many unhappy slaves about make a man like me uneasy.'

Still staring at nothing, the old man in the corner banged his cup against the table. The taverner waddled across the room. The least exertion made him wheeze and gasp for air.

'So you worry about runaway slaves?' I said.

'Things happen. Oh, not so much in the town, but I have a sister who married a farmer up north. Lives in the middle of nowhere. Of course they have their own household slaves and a few freed-men for protection. Even so, only a fool would leave his doors unlocked at night. I tell you, one of these days it's going to be more than just two or three runaway slaves. Imagine if it were twenty – or a hundred, and some of them professional killers. There's an estate not thirty miles up the way where they send slaves to be trained as gladiators. Imagine a hundred of those beasts escaped from their cages with nothing to lose.'

'Ah, you're a fool!' barked the old man. He raised his cup and emptied it in a single draught.

The red wine spilled from the corners of his grey mouth and dribbled down his grizzled neck. He slammed the cup down and stared rigidly ahead. 'Fool!' he said again. 'Nothing to lose, you say? They'd be crucified and disembowelled! Do you think Sulla and the Senate would let a hundred gladiators go about killing landholders and raping their wives? Even a slave doesn't want to have his hands nailed to a tree. Don't worry, misery won't object so long as there's plenty of fear to keep it in line.'

The old man thrust out his chin and made a ghastly smile. I finally realized he was blind.

'Of course, Father.' The fat Etruscan simpered and made a bow that the old man could not possibly have seen.

I leaned forwards and turned the cup in my hand. 'Afraid of the slaves or not, sometimes it seems a man is not safe even in his own household. A father may not be safe even from his son. Only water this time.' I held up my cup. The taverner bustled over.

'Whatever do you mean?' His hands were unsteady as he poured from the jug. He glanced uneasily over his shoulder at the old man.

'I was only thinking of some gossip I heard yesterday in Rome. I mentioned my trip to some of my associates in the Forum and asked if they happened to know anything about Ameria. Well, most of them had never heard of it.'

I took a long sip and fell silent. The taverner pinched his brow, marshalling a host of plump wrinkles in the furrow of his forehead. The old man moved at last, inclining his head in my direction. The little room was suddenly as quiet as a tomb.

The Etruscan wheezed. 'And?'

'And what?' I said.

'The gossip!' It was the old man. He sneered and turned away, suddenly disinterested or pretending to be. 'The little pig lives for it. Worse than his mother ever was.'

My host glanced at me and made a helpless grimace.

I shrugged wearily, as if it were hardly worth the effort of telling. 'Only something about a trial about to take place in Rome, involving a man from Ameria. The name is Roscius, I think; yes, like the famous actor. Accused of – well, I'm almost ashamed to say it – accused of killing his own father.'

My host nodded slightly and stepped back. He pulled a rag from the belt of his tunic, rubbed the beads of sweat from his forehead, then began wiping the counter, wheezing from the effort. 'Is that right?' he finally said. 'Yes, I'd heard something about it.'

'Only something? A crime like that, in such a small place, so nearby, I'd have thought it would have been on everyone's lips.'

'Well, it didn't exactly happen here.'

'No?'

'No. The crime actually occurred in Rome. That's where Old Man Roscius was murdered, so they say.'

'You knew him, did you?' I tried to keep my voice light, as if I were only half-listening. My host might not be suspicious, but the old man certainly was. I could tell from the way he pursed his lips and slowly moved his jaw from side to side, listening to every word.

'Old Sextus Roscius? No. Well, hardly. We used to see him in here occasionally when I was a boy, isn't that right, Father? But not much lately. Not for years and years. A citified Roman with worldly ways, that's what he became. Must've come home occasionally, but he never stopped in here. Am I right, Father?'

'Fool,' the old man growled. 'Fat, clumsy fool . . .'

My host wiped his forehead again, glanced at his father and gave me an embarrassed smile. I looked at the old man with as much feigned affection as I could muster and shrugged as if to say, *I understand these things. Old and impossible to put up with, but what is a good son to do?*

'Actually, when I asked if you knew this Roscius, I meant the son. If it's true, what he's charged with – well, you have to wonder what sort of man could commit such a crime.'

'Sextus Roscius? Yes, I know him. Not well, but well enough to greet him on the street. A man about my own age. He'd come to market here on holidays. It wasn't rare for him to pay a visit to the Bleating Lamb.'

'And what do you think? Could you tell by looking at him?'

'Oh, he was bitter against his old man, no doubt about that. Not that he'd go on and on, he wasn't the ranting sort, even after he'd had a few. But he'd let out something every now and then. Probably other people would hardly notice, but I listen. I hear.'

'Then you think he might actually have done it?'

'Oh, no. I know for a fact that he *didn't*.'

'And how is that?'

'Because he was nowhere near Rome when it happened. Oh, there was plenty of talk when the news came about the old man's death, and there were plenty of people who could tell you that Sextus hadn't left his main farm in Ameria for days.'

'But no one accuses the son of actually wielding the knife. They say he hired assassins.'

My host had no answer for that, but was clearly unimpressed. He furrowed his brow in thought. 'Strange that you should mention the murder. I was practically the first to hear about it.'

'The first in Narnia, you mean?'

'The first anywhere. In happened last September.' He stared at the opposite wall, remembering. 'The murder happened at night; yes, I suppose it must have. It was cold weather hereabouts, blustery winds and grey skies. If I was superstitious, I suppose I'd tell you I had a grim dream that night, or woken up with a ghost in the room.'

'Impious!' the old man snapped, shaking his head in disgust. 'No respect for the gods.'

My host seemed not to hear him, still staring into the depths of the mottled clay wall. 'But something

231

must have woken me, because I was up very early the next morning. Earlier than my usual habit.'

'Always was the lazy one,' the old man muttered.

'There's no reason for a taverner to be up early; customers seldom come before mid-morning. But that morning I was up before daylight. Perhaps it was something I ate.'

The old man snorted and scowled. 'Something he ate! Can you *believe* that?'

'I washed and dressed. I left my wife sleeping and came down the stairs, into this room. I stepped into the street. It was a bit chilly, but very still. Over the hills I could see the first streaks of dawn. The sky had cleared overnight; there was only a single cloud on the eastern horizon, lit up all red and yellow from below. And up the road there was a man coming from the south. I heard him first – you know how sound carries when the air is still and cold. Then I saw him, in a light chariot drawn by two horses, racing so fast that I almost stepped inside to hide myself. Instead I stood my ground, and as he drew by he slowed and stopped. He pulled off the leather cap he was wearing, and then I saw it was Mallius Glaucia.'

'A friend?'

My host wrinkled his nose. 'Some man's friend, but not mine. Used to be a slave, and even then he was insolent and arrogant. Slaves take after their masters, they say, and that was never truer than with Mallius Glaucia.

'You'll find two branches of the Roscius family over the hill in Ameria,' he went on. 'Sextus

Roscius, father and son, the respectable ones who built up their farms and their fortunes; and those two cousins, Magnus and Capito, and their clan. Foul types I'd call them, though I can't say that I've ever had personal dealings with them more than to serve them a cup of wine. But you can tell that some people are dangerous just by looking at them. That's Magnus and old Capito. Mallius Glaucia, the man who came thundering up from the south that morning, was Magnus's slave from birth, until Magnus freed him. A reward for some unspeakable crime, I have no doubt. Glaucia went on serving Magnus, and still does. As soon as I saw it was him in the chariot, how I wished I'd stepped back into the doorway before he'd had a chance to see me.'

'A big man, this Mallius Glaucia?'

'The gods themselves don't come any bigger.'

'Fair of face?'

'Fair-haired, maybe, but as ugly as a baby. Red-faced like a baby, too. Anyway, he comes thundering up in his chariot. "You're open early," he says. I told him I wasn't open at all yet, and made to step back inside. I was just closing the door when he blocked it with his foot. I told him again I wasn't open for business and tried to close the door, but he held his foot fast. Then he pushed a dagger through the breach. As if that weren't bad enough, the dagger wasn't clean and shiny – oh, no. The blade was covered with blood.'

'Red or black?'

'Not too fresh, but not too old either. It was mostly dry on the blade, but in places where it was

233

thickest it was still a little moist and red in the centre. Try as I might I couldn't close the door. I thought of crying out, but my wife is a timid woman and my son is gone, my slaves would be no match against Glaucia and what help could I expect . . .' He glanced guiltily at the old man in the corner. 'So I let him in. He wanted wine, straight, without water. I brought him a cup; he downed it in a single swallow and then threw it against the floor and told me to bring him a bottle. He sat right where you're sitting now and drank down the whole thing. I tried to leave the room several times, but whenever I moved away he'd begin talking to me in a loud voice, in such a way and such a tone that I knew he meant me to stay and listen.

'He said he'd come from Rome, starting well after dark. He said he came with terrible news. That was when he told me Sextus Roscius was dead. I didn't think much of it. "An old man," I said to him. "Was it his heart?" And Glaucia laughed. "Something like that," he said. "A knife in his heart, if you want to know." And he stabbed the bloody blade into the table.'

My host pointed with his short, stubby arm. I looked down and saw beside my cup a deep gouge in the rough-hewn wood.

'Well, I suppose he saw the look on my face. He laughed again – it must have been the wine. "Don't get all frightened, taverner," he says. "It wasn't me that did it. Do I look like the type who'd kill a man? But this is the very blade, pulled straight from the dead man's heart." Then he turned angry. "Don't look at me that way!" he says. "I told you I didn't do it. I'm just a messenger bringing bad news to the relatives back home." And then he staggered out of the door and got into his chariot and disappeared. Can you blame me if I say I'll never make a point of rising early again?'

I stared at the table, into the scar left by the blade. By a trick of light and concentration it seemed to grow deeper and darker the longer I stared into it. 'So this man came to tell Sextus Roscius that his father had been murdered?'

'Not exactly. That is, it wasn't Sextus Roscius he came to tell. The tale goes that Sextus didn't hear the news until later that day, after the gossip had already started making the rounds. A neighbour met him on the road and offered his condolences, never imagining that he hadn't yet heard. The next day a messenger sent by the old man's household arrived from Rome – he stopped in this very tavern – but by then it was stale news.'

'Then whom did this Glaucia come to tell? His old master, Magnus?'

'If Magnus was in Ameria. But that young scoundrel spends most of his time in Rome these days, mixing with the gangs, they say, and doing business for his elder cousin; I mean old Capito. That was probably the man Glaucia came to tell. Though you wouldn't expect Capito to weep for old Sextus; the two branches of the Roscius line are hardly fond of each other. The feud goes back for years.'

The bloody knife, the messenger sent in the middle of the night, the old family feud; the conclusion seemed obvious. I waited for my host to spell it out, but he only sighed and shook his head, as if he had reached the end of the tale.

'But surely,' I said, 'given what you've told me, no one believes that Sextus Roscius killed his father.'

'Ah, that's the part I can't figure out. Can't figure it out at all. Because what everyone knows, hereabouts anyway, is that old Sextus Roscius was killed by Sulla's men, or at least by some gang acting in Sulla's name.'

'What?'

'The old man was proscribed. Named an enemy of the state. Put on the lists.'

'No. You must be mistaken. You've confused the stories with another.'

'Well, there were a few others from these parts who had regular business and houses in Rome who got put on the lists, and either lost their heads or fled the country. But I wouldn't be confusing them with Sextus Roscius. It's common knowledge hereabouts that the man was proscribed.'

But he was a supporter of Sulla, I started to say, then caught myself.

'It's like this,' the taverner said. 'A band of soldiers arrived from Rome a few days later and made a public announcement, declaring that Sextus Roscius *pater* was an enemy of the state and as such had been killed in Rome, and his property was to be confiscated by force and put up for auction.'

'But this was last September. The proscriptions were already over; they'd been over for months.'

'Do you suppose that was the end of Sulla's enemies? What was to keep him from tracking down one more?'

I rolled the empty cup between my palms and stared into it. 'Did you actually hear this announcement yourself?'

'Yes, as a matter of fact. They announced it first in Ameria, I'm told, but they did the same thing here, seeing as the towns have families in common. We were shocked, of course, but the wars have left so much bitterness, so much loss, I can't say that anyone shed a tear for the old man.'

'But if what you say is true, then the younger Sextus Roscius was disinherited.'

'I suppose he was. We haven't seen him around here for quite some time. The latest gossip says that he's down in Rome, staying with his old man's patroness. Well, there's obviously more to the stories than meets the eye.'

'Obviously. Then who bought up the old man's estates?'

'Thirteen farms, that's what they say he had. Well, old Capito must have been first in line, as he came away with three of the best, including the old family homestead. They say he tossed out young Sextus himself, kicked him right out the door. But it's his property now, fair and square; he bid on it at the state auction down in Rome.'

'And the other farms?'

'All bought up by some rich fellow in Rome; I

can't recall that I ever heard his name. Probably never even set foot in Ameria, just another absentee landlord buying up the countryside. Like your employer, no doubt. Is that your problem, Citizen, jealousy? Well, this is one plum that's already been picked. If you're looking for good land in Ameria you'll have to look farther.'

I looked out of the open door. From where she was tied, Vespa's tail cast a weirdly elongated shadow that flicked nervously across the dusty floor of the doorway. Shadows were long; the day was rapidly dying, and I had no plan for the night. I pulled some coins from my purse and laid them on the table. My host gathered them up and disappeared through a narrow doorway at the back of the shop, turning sideways to squeeze himself through.

The old man turned his head, pricking up his ears at the rustling noise. 'Greedy,' he muttered. 'Every coin he gets, he runs to put it into his little box. Has to keep a running tally hour by hour, can't wait until he closes the tavern. Always the fat one, always the greedy pig. It comes from his mother, not from me, you can tell by looking.'

I stepped quietly towards the door, but not quietly enough. The old man shot to his feet and stepped into the doorway. He seemed to stare into my face through the milky egg-white membranes that covered his eyes. 'You,' he said, 'stranger. You're not here to buy land. You're here about this murder, aren't you?'

I tried to make my face a mask, then realized there was no need. 'No,' I said.

'Whose side are you on? Sextus Roscius, or the men who accuse him?'

'I told you, old man—'

'It is a mystery, how an old man could be proscribed by the state, and then his own son should be accused of the crime. And isn't it odd that wretched old Capito should be the one to profit? And odder still that Capito should be the first man in Ameria to get wind of the murder, and the message should be borne in the middle of the night by Glaucia – who could only have been sent by one man, that wicked Magnus. How did Magnus know of the incident so swiftly, and why did he dispatch a messenger, and how did he happen to possess the bloody dagger? It's all clear to you, isn't it? Or so you think.

'My son tells you young Sextus is innocent, but my son is a fool, and you would be a fool to listen to him. He says he hears everything that's said in this room, but he hears nothing; he's always much too busy talking. I'm the one who hears. For ten years, since I lost my eyes, I've been learning how to hear. Before that, I never heard anything – I thought I heard, but I was deaf, just as you are, just as every man with eyes is deaf. You would never believe the things I hear. I hear every word spoken in this room, and some that are not. I hear the words men whisper to themselves, not even realizing that their lips move or the breath still sighs between their lips.'

I touched his shoulder, thinking to gently push him aside, but he stood his ground like an iron rod.

'Sextus Roscius, young and old, I've known

them both for years. And let me tell you, however impossible it may seem, whatever else the evidence may tell you, the son was behind the murder of his father. What a hatred they had for each other! It started when Roscius took his second wife and had a son by her, Gaius, the son he spoiled and petted until the day of the boy's death. I remember the day he brought the infant into this tavern and forced the pretty gold-haired thing on every man in the room, because what fellow isn't proud of a new son, and young Sextus meanwhile stood in the doorway, forgotten, ignored, puffed up like a toad with hatred. I still had eyes then. I can't remember what a flower looks like, but I can still see that young man's face and the look of pure murder in his eyes.'

I thought I heard my host returning, and looked over my shoulder.

'Look towards me!' the old man shrieked. 'Don't think I can't tell when you turn away from me – I can tell from the sound of your breathing. Look at me when I talk to you! And listen to the truth: the son hated the father, and the father hated the son. I felt the hatred grow and fester in this very room, year after year. I heard the words that were never spoken – the words of anger, resentment, revenge. And who could blame either one of them, but most of all the father – to have had such a son, such a failure, such a disappointment. A greedy little pig, that's what he's turned out to be. Greedy and fat and disrespectful. Imagine the heartbreak, the bitterness! Is it any wonder my grandson never visits, and won't speak to his father? They say Jupiter demands that a son should obey his father, and a father his own father, but what kind of order can there be in a world where men go blind or else grow fat as pigs? The world is a ruin, lost, with no redemption. The world is dark. . . .'

I stepped back, appalled. In the next instant the fat taverner jostled me aside, seized the old man by his shoulders and pulled him out of the doorway. I stepped through and glanced back. The old man's milky eyes were fixed on me. He babbled on. The son averted his face.

I untied Vespa, mounted her, and rode through what remained of the town of Narnia and across the bridge as quickly as I could.

XVII

Vespa seemed as eager as I to leave the village of Narnia behind. She made no complaint as I rode her doggedly down the final leg of the day's journey. When we came to a fork in the road just north of the village, she seemed reluctant to stop.

A public trough stood at the junction. I made her drink slowly, reining her back after every few swallows. A crude signpost stood behind the trough, a goat's skull mounted on a stick. Across the bleached brow someone had painted an arrow pointing to the left and the word AMERIA. I turned from the broad Flaminian Way onto the Amerian side road, a narrow path that meandered up to the saddle of a steep ridge.

We began the ascent. Vespa at last began to weary, and the jolts against my backside made me grit my teeth. I leaned forwards, stroking her neck. At least the heat of the day had begun to dissipate, and the ridge cast us into cool shadow.

Near the summit I came to a band of slaves who clustered about an ox cart, helping to push it onto the ridge. The vehicle lurched and swayed and finally attained the level ground. The slaves leaned against one another, some of them smiling with relief, others too weary to show any expression. I rode up beside the driver and waved.

'Do you make this trip often?' I asked.

The boy gave a start when he heard me, then smiled. 'Only when there's something to take to market at Narnia. The dangerous part is going *down* that hill.'

'I can imagine.'

'We lost a slave last year. He was helping to brake the cart on its way down and fell under the wheel. It isn't nearly as steep on the other side going down into Ameria.'

'But downhill all the same. That should please my horse.'

'She's a beautiful animal.' He looked at Vespa with a farm boy's admiration.

'So,' I said, 'you come from Ameria?'

'Nearby. Just outside the town, at the foot of the hill.'

'Perhaps you could tell me how to find the home of Sextus Roscius.'

'Well, yes. Except that Sextus Roscius doesn't live there any more.'

'You mean the old man?'

'Oh, the one who was murdered? If that's who

you're looking for, you'll find what's left of him in the family cemetery. He never lived in Ameria that I knew of, not since I was born.'

'No, not the old man; the son.'

'He used to live near my father's place, if you mean the one with the two daughters.'

'Yes, he has a daughter about your age; a very pretty girl.'

The lad grinned. 'Very pretty. And very friendly.' He arched his eyebrows in an effort to look worldly. The image of Roscia's naked body flashed through my mind. I saw her pressed against the wall, wilted with satisfaction, with Tiro on his knees before her. Perhaps Tiro had not been the first.

'Tell me how to find his house,' I said.

He shrugged. 'I can tell you how to find it, but as I said, it's not his any more. They drove Sextus Roscius out.'

'When?'

'About two months ago.'

'And why was that?'

'The law, laid down from Rome. His father had been proscribed. Do you know what that means?'

'Only too well.'

He drew a finger across his throat. 'And then they take all your land and all your money. They don't leave the family a thing. There was some auction held down in Rome. My father said he wouldn't mind bidding on some of the land, especially the parcels next to ours. But he said it wouldn't serve any use. The auctions are always rigged. You have to be a friend of a friend of Sulla's, or else know the right man to bribe.'

Twice now I had been told the proscription story. It made no sense, but if it was true it would surely be a simple matter to prove Sextus Roscius innocent of his father's death.

'Tell me then, who lives there now?'

'Old Man Capito. Bought up the family house and some of the best farmland. My father spat on the ground when he heard he was going to be our new neighbour. All through the winter Capito allowed Sextus and his family to stay on. People thought that was only right, that Capito should take pity on him. Then he kicked them out for good.'

'And did no one take them in? Surely Sextus Roscius had friends who owed him some obligation.'

'You'd be surprised how fast a man can lose his friends when there's trouble from Rome; that's what my father says. Besides, Roscius was always a loner; I can't say that he seemed to have many friends. I suppose my father was the closest to a friend he had, us being neighbours and all. After Capito kicked him out, he spent a few nights under our roof. He and his wife and daughters.' The boy's voice trailed off, and I saw from his eyes that he was thinking of Roscia. 'But he didn't stay in Ameria for long. He headed straight for Rome. They say the old man had a powerful patroness, and Sextus was going to ask her for help.'

We rode on for a moment in silence. The wheels

of the ox cart creaked and banged against the rutted road. The slaves trudged alongside. 'You told me the old man was proscribed,' I said.

'Yes.'

'And when that was announced, did no one protest?'

'Oh, yes. There was a delegation sent to Sulla and everything. But if you really want to know about that, you'd have to talk to my father.'

'What is your father's name?'

'Titus Megarus. I'm Lucius Megarus.'

'And my name is Gordianus. Yes, I'd like very much to speak with your father. Tell me, how do you think he would take it if you were to bring a well-met stranger home to dinner?'

The boy was suddenly wary. 'I think it might all depend.'

'On what?'

'From the way you talk, you've got some sort of interest in Capito and his land.'

'I do.'

'And whose side are you on?'

'I am for Sextus and against Capito.'

'Then I believe my father would be happy to see you.'

'Good. How much farther is your house?'

'Do you see that plume of smoke on the right, just over those trees? That's it.'

'Very close. And where is Capito's place?'

'A bit farther on, on the other side of the main road, to your left. We'll be able to glimpse the roof for a moment when we come around this corner.'

'Very well. Do this for me: when you get home, tell your father that a man from Rome would like to speak with him tonight. Tell him I'm a friend of Sextus Roscius. I would wait until morning, but I haven't the time. If he could invite me to his table, I would be most grateful. If I could sleep under your roof I would be doubly so; a stall in the barn would suffice. Would he be insulted if I were to offer money?'

'Probably.'

'Then I won't. This is where we part for a while.' As we rounded the bend I caught a glimpse through the trees of lowering sunlight on a distant red tile roof.

'Where are you going?'

'I'm going to drop in briefly on your new neighbour. There's probably no point in it, but I want at least to have a look at the place, and maybe at the man himself.' I gave the boy a wave, then coaxed Vespa to a steady trot.

The house in which Sextus Roscius the younger had been born and raised and over which he had ruled in his father's absence was a grand example of the ideal country villa, an imposing mansion of two storeys with a red clay roof, surrounded by a rust assemblage of sheds and barns. In the dwindling light I heard the ringing of cowbells and the bleating of sheep as the herds were led homeward. Workers were tramping in from the fields through the grape arbours; a long row of scythes seemed to float above a sea of leaves and tendrils. The sharp blades caught the last rays of the setting sun and gave off a cold sparkle the colour of blood.

The main house was in the midst of extensive renovations. A network of catwalks and netting obscured the facade, and symmetrical wings were being built onto each side. The new wings stood hollow and gaping in a state of half-completion. Peering through the skeleton of the left wing, I could see the beginnings of a formal garden behind the house, where a red-faced fighting cock of a man strode impatiently amid the earthworks and trellises, barking commands at a group of slaves. The slaves leaned upon their shovels and fingered their spades, wearing on their dirt-streaked faces the bored, humiliated expression of men who have been yelled at for a very long time.

The master continued to rant with no sign of stopping. He paced back and forth, waving his arms and strangling fistfuls of air. He was a man on the brink of old age, with white hair and a bent back. I could see his face only in glimpses as he turned back and forth. His skin was very weathered, pitted and scarred. Nose, cheeks, and chin all seemed to merge without distinction. Only his eyes were notable, glinting sharply in the fading light like the blades of the faraway scythes.

I dismounted and held Vespa's rein while I rapped at the door. The tall, thin slave who answered stared meekly at my feet and told me in a cowed whisper that his master was busy outside the house.

'I know,' I said. 'I saw him putting on a parade in the garden. But it's not your master I want.'

248

'No? I'm afraid my mistress is also indisposed.' The slave looked up, but not quite high enough to meet my eyes.

'Tell me, how long have you been Capito's slave?'

He frowned, as if debating whether the question was dangerous. 'Only for a short time.'

'Only since the estate changed hands – is that what you mean? In other words, you came with the house.'

'That's correct. But please, perhaps I should tell my master—'

'No, tell me this: there were two slaves who served your old master's father in Rome, named Felix and Chrestus. Do you know the ones I mean?'

'Yes.' He nodded doubtfully and seemed to find great fascination in my feet.

'They were with him in Rome when the old man was killed. Where are they now?'

'They are . . .'

'Yes?'

'They were here for a while, in this house. They served my former master Sextus Roscius while he was still here as a guest of my new master Capito.'

'And after Sextus Roscius left? Did he take the slaves with him?'

'Oh, no. They remained here, for a while.'

'And then?'

'I believe – of course I don't really know—'

'What's that? Speak up.'

'Perhaps you should talk to my master Capito.'

'I don't think your master would care speak to me, at least not for long. What is your name?'

'Carus.' He gave a small start and pricked up his ears, as if he heard something within the house, but the sound came from outside. In the quiet twilight I could distinctly hear Capito's ranting from the back of the house, joined now by a coarse female voice. It could only be the mistress of the house. They seemed to be shouting at each other in front of the slaves.

'Tell me, Carus. Was Sextus Roscius a better master than Capito?'

He looked uncomfortable, like a man with a full bladder. He made an almost imperceptible nod.

'Then perhaps you will help me when I tell you that I am Sextus Roscius's friend. The best friend he has left in the world. I need to know this very badly: where are Felix and Chrestus?'

His expression became more pained, until I thought he would tell me that they were dead. Instead he glanced over his shoulder, then back at my feet. 'In Rome,' he said. 'My master traded them to his partner in the city, that other one who came into all of Sextus Roscius's wealth.'

'You mean Magnus.'

'No, the other one.' He lowered his voice. 'The golden one. Felix and Chrestus are in Rome, in the household of a man called Chrysogonus.'

Chrysogonus, a Greek word: golden-born. For an instant the name floated shapeless in my mind, then all at once it seemed to explode in my ears like a thunderclap. In my mind the word became a key, pressed into my hand by the unwitting slave, a shiny golden key to unlock the mystery of Sextus Roscius's murder.

From the garden I could still hear Capito ranting and his wife screaming in response. 'Say nothing to your master,' I hissed at the slave. 'Do you understand? Nothing.' I turned to the post and mounted Vespa. Thinking we had finally come to our destination, she snorted in rebellion and shook her head; I coaxed her on. I rode with one eye over my shoulder, careful now that I should not be seen by Capito. No one must know I had been here; no one must know where I slept. *Chrysogonus*, I thought, shaking my head at the magnitude of it. I shuddered at the danger. Of course it had always been there, but now I had eyes to see it.

I came to the main road and headed back towards the branch that would lead me to the house of Titus Megarus. Above the trees, in the fading light, I saw the rising plume of smoke with its promise of comfort and rest. I mounted a small rise and abruptly saw two riders approaching from the Flaminian Way. Their mounts proceeded at a slow pace, as weary as Vespa. The men seemed almost to be dozing, as if tired from a long day of riding, then one after the other they looked up and I saw their faces.

They were both big, broad-shouldered men, dressed in light summer tunics that left their muscular arms bare. Both were clean-shaven. The man on the right had shaggy black hair, glowering eyes, and a cruel mouth, and held the rein in his left hand. His friend had coarse, straw-coloured hair and the look of a brute, ugly and slow; he was so big that his horse looked like an overburdened pony, and across one cheek were three slender, parallel red scabs, the unmistakable mark of a cat's claw.

My heart pounded so fiercely that I thought they must surely hear it. They stared at me coldly as I passed. I managed a nod and a feeble greeting. They said nothing and turned their eyes to the road. I quickened Vespa's pace and after a moment dared to look over my shoulder. Above the shallow rise I saw them turn onto the road that led to Capito's house.

XVIII

'The dark-haired one,' said my host, 'yes, that would be Magnus. Yes, he limps on the left, and has for years; no one knows exactly why. He tells different stories. Sometimes says it was done to him by a crazy whore in Rome, sometimes claims it was a jealous husband, or then again, a gladiator on a drunken rampage. Always claims he killed the one who did it to him, and he probably did.'

'And the other, the big ugly blond?'

'Mallius Glaucia, I have no doubt. Magnus's ex-slave and now his right-hand man. Magnus spends a lot of time in Rome these days, while his cousin Capito is busy remaking the Roscius villa; Glaucia runs back and forth between them like a dog fetching bones.'

The world was dark and full of stars. Moonlight played over the low, rolling hills, turning them to silver. I sat with Titus Megarus on the rooftop of his house, situated so that we had a wide view to the south and west. On the horizon ran a line of high hills that marked the farther edge of the valley; somewhere beyond lay the course of the Tiber. Close by, a few scattered lights and moonlit roofs marked the sleeping town of Ameria, and to the left, obscured by the intervening trees, I could just make out the upper storey, no bigger than my thumbnail, of the house where Capito and Magnus and Mallius Glaucia were all gathered for the night. A single window was lit, sending out a pale ochre light.

Titus Megarus was not a worldly man, but he was an excellent host. He met me himself at his door and immediately saw that Vespa was given a place in his stables. He declined to converse about anything controversial at his dinner table, saying it caused indigestion. Instead, over the course of the meal, each of his five children took turns singing a song. The food was plentiful and fresh; the wine was excellent. Slowly I relaxed and shed my fear until I found myself half-reclining on a divan on the roof garden of his house. In the open peristyle below, the women and children of the house were gathered. One of Titus's daughters sang while another played the lyre. The sound rose sweet and low on the warm evening air with a vague echo, as if it came from a well. At his father's invitation the boy Lucius sat near us, listening but not speaking.

I was so weary and saddle sore I could hardly move, and so comfortable I didn't want to. I lay on the divan with a cup of warm wine in one hand, struggling against sleep, gazing out over the utter peacefulness of the valley and wondering at the murderous secrets hidden there.

'It was this Mallius Glaucia who came to my house last night,' I said, 'along with some other assassin. I'm sure of it – the claw marks leave no doubt. The same man who rode like a demon all night to get the news of Sextus Roscius's murder to Capito here in Ameria. Surely he was sent on both errands by the same master.'

'Glaucia does nothing without a command from Magnus; he's like one of those shadow puppets at carnivals.'

Titus stared up at the stars. I closed my eyes and imagined Bethesda beside me on the divan, warmer than the evening breeze, softer than the pale, translucent clouds that scudded across the waxing moon. There was a burst of feminine laughter from the peristyle below, and I thought how naturally she would fit in with the simple manners of the countryside.

Titus sipped his wine. 'So Sextus has gone and got himself charged with the old man's murder. That's news to me; I suppose I should go to trade gossip at the tavern in Narnia more often. And you're here to sniff out the truth. Good luck. You'll need it.' He shook his head and leaned forwards, scrutinizing the lights from his new neighbour's villa. 'Capito and Magnus want him out of the way for good. They won't rest until the man is dead.'

I glanced towards Capito's villa, then upward at

the stars. All I wanted was sleep. But who could say if my host would be in such a talkative mood in the morning?

'Tell me, Titus Megarus . . .' Between the wine and weariness my voice deserted me.

'Tell you what, Gordianus of Rome?' His speech was slurred. He seemed such a naturally sober man, so moderate in all other things, that I thought he must be the sort that indulged in wine only when there was company to entertain.

'Tell me everything. All you know about the death of old Sextus Roscius, and his feud with Capito and Magnus, and all that came after.'

'All a rotten scandal,' he scowled. 'Everyone knows there's something smelly about the whole business, but no one does anything about it. I tried, but it got me nowhere.'

'Begin at the beginning. This feud between the late Sextus Roscius and his cousins Magnus and Capito – how far back does it go?'

'It was a feud they inherited at birth. All three had the same grandfather; Sextus's father was the oldest of three sons, Capito and Magnus were sons of the younger sons. When the grandfather died, virtually all the estate went to the oldest son, naturally – to the father of old Sextus Roscius. Well, you know how that goes, sometimes there's a gracious settlement with the rest of the family, sometimes there's an ugly break. Who knows all the petty details? All I know is that it carried into the cousins of the second generation, with Capito and Magnus always against old Sextus, always conniving for some way to get a bigger share of the family fortune. Somehow or other they've succeeded. A few gullible souls in Ameria think they were simply blessed by Fortune. Anyone with a brain in his head can see they must have got blood on their hands, though they've been clever enough to wash it off.'

'Very well; the father of the elder Sextus Roscius inherits the family estates, leaving the rest with a pittance. The elder Sextus is his prime heir – I assume he was the oldest son in the family?'

'The only male child; the Roscii are not prolific breeders.'

'Very well, the elder Sextus inherits, much to the ongoing chagrin of his impoverished cousins Capito and Magnus. How impoverished were they?'

'Capito's father always held on to one of the farms down by the Nar, enough for a modest living. It was Magnus who had the worst of it. His father lost the one farm he inherited and finally killed himself. That's why Magnus left for the city, to make his way there.'

'Bitter men. And if Magnus went to Rome to learn about life, murder is a lesson easily picked up. Now correct me if my memory fails: old Sextus marries twice. The first union produces Sextus *filius*. The wife dies, and Sextus *pater* remarries. A second son is born, Gaius, and the beloved young wife dies in childbirth. Young Sextus gets the run of the farms, while his father and Gaius go off to Rome. But then, three years ago, on the eve of Sulla's triumph, young Sextus summons his father and brother home to Ameria, and while they're here Gaius dies from something he ate. Tell me, Titus, what did the gossips in Ameria say about that?'

He shrugged and sipped more wine. 'Gaius wasn't known much hereabouts, though you'd find everyone agreed he was certainly a handsome young man. Personally, I found him too airy and cultivated; I suppose that was the way his father raised him, with tutors and fancy dinner parties. Not the boy's fault.'

'But his death – it was accepted as accidental?'

'There was never any question.'

'Suppose it wasn't an accident. Might Capito and Magnus have had something to do with it?'

'It seems far-fetched. What would they have gained, except to spite his father? If they wanted to kill someone, why not the old man, or the whole family? Certainly, Capito is a violent man. He's stabbed and beaten more than one slave to death, and they say once down in Rome he threw a total stranger into the Tiber, just because the man wouldn't step aside on the bridge, and then dived in after him, trying to make certain he drowned. I suppose he and Magnus might have murdered Gaius from pure cruelty, but I don't think it's likely.'

'Nor do I. It's merely an incidental detail.' Perhaps it was the wine warming my blood, or the fresh breeze off the hillside; suddenly I felt fully awake and alert. I stared at the light from Capito's house. It wavered on the rising ripples of warm air and seemed to stare back at me like a baleful eye.

'Let's go to last September, then. Sextus Roscius is murdered in Rome. Witnesses see the chief perpetrator, a strong man in black robes with a lame left leg.'

'Magnus, without a doubt!'

'He appears to know his victim. He is also left-handed, and quite strong.'

'Magnus, again.'

'The assassin is accompanied by two other thugs. One is a blond giant.'

'Mallius Glaucia.'

'Yes. The other – who knows? The shopkeeper says he had a beard. The widow Polia could identify them all, but she'll never be persuaded to testify. At any rate, it's Glaucia who arrives very early the next morning to give the news to Capito, carrying with him a bloody knife.'

'What? That's a detail I haven't heard before.'

'It comes from the taverner in Narnia.'

'Ah, the one with the blind father. They're both completely daft. Weak blood.'

'Perhaps. Perhaps not. The taverner tells me that Glaucia took the news straight to Capito. Who was the first to tell Sextus Roscius of his father's death?' I looked at him and raised an eyebrow.

Titus nodded. 'Yes, that was me. I heard it early that morning at the common well in Ameria. When I saw Sextus that afternoon, I felt sure he knew already. But when I offered him my grief, the look on his face – well, it was a strange look. I couldn't call it grief; you must know there was little love between them. Dread, that's what I saw in his eyes.'

'And surprise? Shock?'

'Not exactly. Confusion and fear.'

'So. The next day a more official messenger arrives, sent by the old man's household in Rome.'

Titus nodded. 'And the day after that the remains of the dead man arrived. The Roscii are buried on a little hill beyond the villa; you can see the stelae from here on a clear day. Sextus buried his father on the eighth day and then began the seven days of mourning. Sextus never finished them.'

'Why?'

'Because within that time the soldiers arrived. They must have come from Volaterrae, up north, where Sulla was campaigning against the last Marian remnants in Etruria. Anyway, the soldiers arrived and made a public announcement in the town square that Sextus Roscius the elder had been declared an enemy of the state and that his death in Rome had been a legal execution at the behest of our esteemed Sulla. His entire estate was forfeit. Everything was to be auctioned – lands, houses, jewellery, slaves. The date and the place were announced, somewhere in Rome.'

'And how did young Sextus react?'

'No one knows. He went into seclusion at his villa, refusing to leave the house and seeing no visitors. All this might be quite proper for a man in mourning, but Sextus stood to lose everything. People began saying that perhaps it was true that his father had been proscribed. Who knows what the old man had been doing down in Rome?

Perhaps he was a Marian spy, perhaps he had been found out in some plot to assassinate Sulla.'

'But the proscriptions legally ended on the first of June. Roscius was killed in September.'

Titus shrugged. 'You talk like an advocate. If Sulla wanted the man dead, why shouldn't it be legal, so long as the dictator declared it so?'

'Was there much interest in the auction?'

'Everyone knows they're fixed. Why bother? Some friend of Sulla's would end up paying a pittance for it all, and anyone else who cared to bid would be escorted from the hall. Believe me, we were all surprised when Magnus and a band of thugs from Rome showed up at Sextus's door with some sort of official writ, telling him to surrender all his property and vacate at once.'

'So he was pushed aside as easily as that?'

'There was no one to see what actually happened, except the slaves, of course. People love to embellish. Some say that Magnus came upon him burning myrrh at his father's grave, slapped the censer from his hands, and bullied him from the shrine at spear point. Others say he ripped the clothes from Sextus's back and chased him into the road naked, setting hounds after him. I never heard either tale from Sextus; he refused to speak of it, and I wouldn't press his shame.

'In any case, Sextus and his family spent one night in the home of a merchant friend in Ameria, and the next morning Capito moved into the villa. You can imagine the eyebrows that were lifted at that. Not everyone was displeased; Sextus has his enemies and Capito his friends in this valley. Sextus goes directly to Capito; again, no one was there to witness it. In the end, Capito allows Sextus back onto the property, making him stay in a little house at one corner of the estate where they usually put up seasonal labourers at harvest time.'

'And that was the end of it?'

'Not quite. I called a meeting of the Amerian town council and told them we had to do something. It took considerable persuasion, believe me, to get some of those old bones to make a decision. And all the while Capito was glaring at me from across the table – oh, yes, Capito sits on our esteemed town council. Finally it was decided that we should protest against the proscription of Sextus Roscius, to attempt to clear his name and see that his property was restored to his son. Capito went along with everything. Sulla was still encamped at Volaterrae; a delegation of ten men was sent to plead our case – myself, Capito, and eight others.'

'And what did Sulla say?'

'We never saw him. First we were made to wait. Five days they kept us waiting, as if we were barbarians asking for favours, and not Roman citizens petitioning the state. Everyone was impatient and grumbling; they would have dropped it all and come home right then if I hadn't shamed them into seeing it through. At last we were allowed to see not Sulla, but Sulla's deputy, an Egyptian called Chrysogonus. You've heard of him?' Titus asked, seeing the look that crossed my face.

'Oh, yes. A young man, they say, of natural

charm and great handsomeness, and the intelligence and ambition to turn them to his utmost advantage. He started as a slave in Sulla's household, toiling in the gardens. But Sulla has an eye for beauty and doesn't like to see it wasted on drudgery. Chrysogonus became the old man's favourite. This was some years ago, when Sulla's first wife was still alive. Sulla eventually sated himself with the slave's body and rewarded him with freedom, riches, and a high place in his retinue.'

Titus snorted: 'I wondered what the story was. All we were told was that this Chrysogonus was a powerful man who had access to Sulla's ear. I told them we wanted to see the dictator himself, but all the secretaries and adjutants shook their heads as if I were a child and said we'd be much better off to win the sympathy of this Chrysogonus first, who would then put the case before Sulla on our behalf.'

'And did he?'

Titus looked at me ruefully. 'It went like this: we finally won our audience and were ushered standing into the presence of his Goldenness, who sat staring at the ceiling as if someone had struck him in the forehead with a hammer. Finally he condescended to blink his blue eyes and favour us with a fleeting glance. And then he smiled. I swear, you've never seen such a smile; as if Apollo himself had come down to earth. There was something aloof in it, but not cold. It was more like he was sorry for us, and sad, the way you might imagine a god would be sad to look at mere mortals.

'He nodded. He inclined his head. He fixed his

blue eyes on you and you had the feeling that a superior being was doing you a very great favour simply to acknowledge your existence. He listened to our petition and after that every man said his piece, except Capito, who kept in the back as stiff and silent as a stone. And then Chrysogonus stood up from his chair and threw back his shoulders, and he pushed a lock of golden hair from his forehead and put a finger to his lips, as if he were thinking hard; and it was almost embarrassing to be a mere grubby mortal presuming to share the same room with such a perfect specimen of manhood.

'He told us we were fine Romans to have gone to such pains in pursuit of justice. He said that such occurrences as the one we described were very, very rare, but that indeed, lamentably, regrettably, there had been a handful of instances of men falsely proscribed. At the very earliest opportunity he would present our petition to the great Sulla himself. In the meantime, we should be patient; surely we could see that the dictator of the Republic had a thousand concerns pressing on him from all sides, not least of which was a final effort to eradicate the vestiges of the Marian conspiracy where it was festering in the Etruscan hills. Ten heads bobbed up and down like corks on a wave, and mine was one of them. And I remember thinking, though I'm ashamed to say it now, that I was glad we hadn't been allowed to see Sulla, for if being in the presence of his deputy was this intimidating, what bigger fools would we have made of ourselves dealing with the great man himself?

'But then I cleared my throat, and somehow I found the nerve to say that if we couldn't see Sulla, at least we insisted on having some sort of clear answer before we returned to Ameria. Chrysogonus turned his blue eyes on me and raised his eyebrows ever so slightly, the way you might look at a slave who has the impertinence to interrupt a conversation with some trifle he thinks is important. And finally he nodded, and said, "Of course, of course," and then he told us that when he returned to Rome he himself would take a stylus and mark the name of Sextus Roscius from the proscription lists with his own hand, and see to it that the dead man's property was reconstituted and the deed restored to his son. We would have to be patient, of course, for the wheels of justice turn slowly in Rome, but never against the will of the people.

'Then he looked straight at Capito, understanding that he had come into at least some of the confiscated property, and asked him if he would agree to such justice, even at his own expense. And Capito nodded and smiled as innocently as a child, and declared he had only the spirit of Roman law at heart, and if it could be proved that his late cousin had in fact not been an enemy of the state and of the beloved Sulla, he would gladly restore his share of the estate to the rightful heir, not even charging for the improvements he had made. And that night we celebrated with wine and a roast lamb at our tavern at Volaterrae and slept well, and in the morning we returned to Ameria and went our separate ways.'

'What happened then?'

'Nothing. Sulla and his army finished their business at Volaterrae and returned to Rome.'

'There was no word from Chrysogonus?'

'None.' Titus shrugged guiltily. 'You know how it is, how you let such things languish – I'm a farmer, not a politician. I finally drafted a letter in December, and another in February. No answer. Perhaps something would have been done if Sextus Roscius himself had kept after it, but he was more secluded than ever. He and his family stayed in their little house on the estate and no one heard a word from them, as if they were prisoners, or as if Capito had made them his slaves. Well, if a man won't stand up for himself, he can't expect his neighbours to drag him to his feet.'

'How long did this go on?'

'Until April. That was when something must have happened between Capito and Sextus. In the middle of the night Sextus showed up at my doorstep with his wife and his two daughters. They were riding in a common ox cart, carrying their goods in their arms with not even a slave to drive. He asked me to take him in for the night, and of course I did. They stayed for four or five nights, I can't remember—'

'Three,' said a quiet voice. It was the boy Lucius, whose presence I had almost forgotten. He sat against the corner of the low wall with his knees pulled to his chest. He was faintly smiling, the same way he had smiled at the mention of Roscius's daughter when I met him earlier that day.

'Well, then, three,' said Titus. 'I suppose it

seemed longer. Sextus Roscius brought his gloom with him. My wife kept complaining he would bring ill luck. And of course, that young Roscia . . .' he began, lowering his voice. 'His elder daughter. Not exactly the best moral influence to bring into a home with young men.' He glanced at Lucius, who looked up at the moon with a convincing imitation of deafness.

'Then he left for Rome, telling me his father had had a patroness there who might have some influence with Sulla. No mention of a trial for murder. I assumed he'd got desperate enough to go and petition this Chrysogonus for himself.'

'I don't suppose it would surprise you to learn that Chrysogonus himself benefited from the carving up of Sextus Roscius's estates.'

'Well, isn't that a dirty piece of business. And how do you know that?'

'A slave named Carus told me this afternoon. He answers the door at Capito's villa.'

'Then the three of them were in it from the beginning – Capito, Magnus, and Chrysogonus.'

'So it appears. Who but Chrysogonus could have illegally entered Sextus *pater* into the already closed proscription lists? Who wanted the old man dead, except Capito and Magnus?'

'Well, there you have it. It was those three who plotted the murder of old Sextus Roscius, conspiring all along to have him added to the proscription lists and then buy up the land after the state confiscated it. And any outsider who might try to clear the matter up comes face to face with

Chrysogonus, which is like having your nose to a brick wall. What a business, even dirtier than I thought. But now this, to blame Sextus Roscius for his father's murder — surely they've gone too far even for a close friend of Sulla. It's absurd, unspeakably cruel!'

I looked up at the moon. It was already fat and white; in six days it would be full for the Ides, and Sextus Roscius would meet his fate. I lazily turned my head and peered through heavy lids at the yellow window shining from Capito's villa. Why were they still awake? Surely Magnus and Glaucia were as tired from their day of riding as I was. What were they plotting now?

'Even so,' I said, losing the words in a yawn, 'even so, there's still some part that's missing from the puzzle. Something that keeps it all from making sense. Even dirtier than you thought. . . .'

I looked at the yellow window. I shut my eyes for just an instant, and didn't open them again for many hours.

XIX

I woke with a blink to find myself alone in a dark room choked with heat. My mouth was dry, but I felt amazingly refreshed. I had slept without dreams. I lay on my back, and for a long moment was content simply to be still and sense the flow of life in my arms, legs, fingers, toes. Then I stirred, and realized there was a stiff penalty to pay for having ridden so hard the day before. I managed to sit up and swing my aching legs onto the floor. I was amazed again at how refreshed I felt, considering that I was waking while the world was still dark, until I glimpsed an odd flickering at the edge of the drapery that hung over the window, like a glint of white steel lit from nowhere amid the blackness. I pushed myself up from the divan and staggered stiffly to the window. I pushed the curtain aside and was consumed by hot, blinding light.

At the same instant the door to the tiny room

creaked open and Lucius stuck his head inside. 'Finally,' he said, using the exasperated tone with which children mimic their parents. 'I tried to wake you twice before, but I couldn't even make you groan. Everyone else has been up for hours.'

'How late is it?'

'Exactly noon. That's why I came to see if you were up yet, because I just got back from town and noticed the sundial in the garden, and I wondered if you could still be asleep.'

I looked about the room. 'But how did I get here? And who undressed me?' I stooped, groaning, to pick up my tunic, which had slid from the arm of a chair onto the floor.

'Father and I carried you down here from the roof last night. You don't remember? You were like a sack of bricks, and we couldn't make you stop snoring.'

'I never snore.' Bethesda had told me so. Or did she lie to soothe my vanity?

Lucius laughed. 'They could hear you all over the house! My sister Tertia made a game of it. She said—'

'Never mind.' I started to slip the tunic over my head. The thing became twisted and tangled as if it had a life of its own. My arms were as stiff as my legs.

'Anyway, Father said we should undress you, because your clothes were so sweaty and soiled from the trip. He made old Naia wash them for you before she went to bed last night. It's so hot today, they're already dry.'

I finally managed to cover myself, none too graciously. I looked out of the window again. Not a breeze stirred the treetops. Slaves were busy in the fields, but the court below was empty except for a little girl playing with a kitten. The light on the paving stones was blinding. 'This is impossible. I'll never make it back to Rome today.'

'And a good thing.' This came from Titus Megarus, looming now behind his son with a stern look on his face. 'I looked in this morning on that mare you rode from the city yesterday. Are you in the habit of driving a horse till it drops?'

'I'm not much in the habit of using horses at all.'

'That doesn't surprise me. No true horseman would have exhausted a fine animal in that fashion. You weren't seriously thinking of riding her back today?'

'Yes, I was.'

'I can't allow it.'

'Then how am I to leave?'

'You'll take one of my horses.'

'Vespa's owner will not be pleased.'

'I've thought about that. Last night you told me that the trial of Sextus Roscius is scheduled for the Ides.'

'Yes.'

'Then I'll come into the city the day before and bring Vespa with me. I'll return her to the stables on the Subura Way myself, and if it might help I'll find my way to the house of this advocate Cicero and tell him what I know. If he wants to call me as a witness at the trial – well, I suppose I'd be willing to show my face, even if Sulla himself is there. And here, before I forget, take this.' He pulled a rolled parchment from his tunic.

'What is it?'

'The petition the Amerian town council presented to Sulla – to Chrysogonus, actually – protesting against the proscription of Sextus Roscius. This is the copy the council kept for itself. The original should be kept somewhere in the Forum, but these kinds of documents have a way of disappearing when they might embarrass someone, don't they? But this is a valid copy; it bears all our names, even Capito's. It's doing no good sitting in my house. Maybe Cicero can use it.

'Meanwhile I'll lend you one of my horses. He won't be able to match your white beauty for strength, but you'll only be riding him half as hard. I have a cousin with a farm midway between here and Rome. You can stay with him tonight and ride into the city tomorrow. He owes me some favours, so don't be afraid to eat your fill from his table. Or if you can't wait to reach Rome, you can try to talk him into trading one of his horses for mine and then keep riding like a crazy man until you get to the city.'

I raised an eyebrow, then acquiesced with a nod. The stern look softened. Titus was very much a Roman father, used to giving lectures and imposing his will on everyone in his house. His duty to Vespa done, he smiled and mussed his son's hair. 'And now you'll go wash your face and hands by the well and then join us for the meal. While city folk may have just risen, some of us have been up since cock's crow working up an appetite.'

The whole family gathered in the shade of a massive fig tree to take their midday meal. Titus Megarus had another son besides Lucius, an infant boy, as well as three daughters, all with the same family name plus another to mark their order, in the traditional Roman style: Megara Majora, Megara Minora, Megara Tertia. Though I couldn't quite discern who was a resident and who might only be visiting, joining the meal that day were also two brothers-in-law, one of them married with young children, two grandmothers, and one grandfather. The children ran about, the women sat on the grass, the men sat on chairs, and two slave women moved among us making sure that no one went hungry.

Titus's wife leaned against the tree trunk, nursing the infant; her eldest daughter sat nearby and cooed a lullaby that seemed to follow the meandering tune of the stream that rippled nearby. One was never far from music in the home of Titus Megarus.

Titus introduced me to his father and brother-in-law, who already seemed to know something about my visit. Together they derided Capito and Magnus and their henchman Glaucia, then drew away from the topic with nods and pursed lips as if to let me know I could rely upon their discretion. Soon the conversation turned to crops and the weather, and Titus pulled his chair closer to mine.

'If you were planning on another look at Capito

273

and company before you leave, you may be disappointed.'

'How's that?'

'I sent Lucius on an errand into town this morning, and on his way back he passed the three of them on the road. Magnus muttered something faintly insulting, so Lucius politely asked them where they were headed. Capito told him they were on their way to one of his new estates on the Tiber to do some hunting. Which means, of course, that they can't possibly be back before sundown, if they come back today at all.'

'Which leaves the house to Capito's wife.'

'Ah, there's the gossip. While Lucius was in town he heard they'd had a terrible row yesterday and the old woman stormed out of the house after nightfall to go to stay with her daughter in Narnia. Meaning there's no one in charge of the estate now except a grizzled old steward Capito inherited from Sextus Roscius. They say the man drinks wine all day and hates his new master. I only tell you this in case you had any unfinished business at Capito's house. The master and his wife and friends all being gone, I suppose that might be an inconvenience to you. Or perhaps not.'

He turned back to the general conversation wearing the subtle smile of a conspirator quite pleased with himself.

In fact, I left Titus Megarus with no intention of stopping again at Capito's house. I had already learned what I needed in coming to Ameria; I even carried in my pouch a copy of the petition Titus and his fellow citizens had submitted to Chrysogonus to protest against the proscription of Sextus Roscius. I hardly bothered to look back on the serenity of the Amerian valley as I left it. My thoughts as I guided my undistinguished mount up the hillside were all of Rome, of Bethesda and Cicero and Tiro; of the people on the street of the House of Swans. I frowned, remembering the widow Polia, then smiled, remembering the whore Electra; and I abruptly swung my mount around and headed back towards Capito's house.

The slave Carus was not pleased to see me. He recognized me with a plaintive look, as if I were a demon come especially to torment him.

'Why so glum?' I said, stepping past him into the vestibule. The walls had been freshly coloured with a pink wash. The tiled floor, checkered black and white, was obscured by drifts of sawdust, and the whole room rang with the unnatural echoes of a house under renovation. 'I should think this would be a holiday for you, with your master and mistress away.'

He screwed up his face as if he were about to tell a lie and then thought better of it. 'What do you want?'

'What used to go here?' I asked, stepping closer to a niche containing a very bad copy of a Greek bust of Alexander. It was absurdly pretentious, certainly not the sort of thing the countrified young Sextus Roscius would have kept in his house; more like something you'd find in the home of a high-wayman who loots the villas of the tasteless rich.

'A spray of flowers,' Carus said, staring bleakly at the copy with its vapid expression and wild tendrils of hair, almost more a Medusa than an Alexander. 'In the days before the change, my mistress kept a silver vase in that niche, with fresh flowers from the garden. Or sometimes in spring the girls would bring wildflowers down from the hillsides. . . .'

'Is the steward drunk yet?'

He looked at me suspiciously. 'Analaeus is hardly ever sober.'

'Then perhaps I should ask: is he indisposed?'

'If you mean unconscious, probably so. There's a little house at the far corner of the estate where he likes to slip away when he's able.'

'The house where Sextus and the family stayed after Capito evicted him?'

Carus looked at me darkly. 'Exactly. I saw Analaeus headed that way this morning after the master left, taking the new slave girl from the kitchens with him. That and a bottle of wine should keep him busy all day.'

'Good, then we won't be disturbed.' I strolled into the next room. This was where they did their living. The place was scattered with the debris of a party from the night before, the kind of party three rough-natured men might hold in the absence of their wives. A timid young slave girl was busy trying to straighten the mess, moving from disaster to disaster with a look of total helplessness on her face. She wouldn't meet my eyes. Carus clapped his hands at her and shooed her from the room.

Mounted prominently on one wall was a large

family portrait done in encaustic on wood. I recognized Capito from my glimpse of him the day before: a white-haired, waspish-looking man. His wife was a stern matron with a large nose. They were flanked by various grown children and their spouses. The entire family seemed to be glaring at the artist as if already suspicious of being overcharged.

'How I detest them,' Carus whispered. I looked at him in surprise. He kept his eyes fixed on the painting. 'The whole lot of them, rotten to the core. Look at them all, so smug and self-satisfied. This portrait was the first thing they did after they moved into the house, brought an artist all the way from Rome to do it. So eager to capture for all posterity that gloating look of triumph on their faces.' He seemed unable to go on speaking; his lips trembled as if he were nauseated with loathing. 'How can I tell you what I've seen in this house since they came? The meanness, the vulgarity, the deliberate cruelty? Sextus Roscius may not have been the best of masters, and the mistress may have had her moments of anger, but they never spat in my face. And if Sextus Roscius was a terrible father to his daughters, what business was that of mine? Ah, the girls were always so sweet. How I pitied them.'

'A terrible father?' I said. 'What do you mean?'

Carus ignored me. He closed his eyes and turned away from the portrait. 'What is it you want? Who sent you to Ameria? Sextus Roscius? Or that rich woman he spoke of in Rome? What have you come for, to kill them in their sleep?'

'I'm not a killer,' I told him.

'Then why are you here?' Suddenly he was fearful again.

'I came because there was a question I forgot to ask you yesterday.'

'Yes?'

'Sextus Roscius – *pater*, not *filius* – saw a prostitute in Rome. I mean to say there were many prostitutes, but this one was special to him. A young girl with honeyed hair, very sweet. Her name—'

'Elena,' he said.

'Yes.'

'They brought her here not very long after the old man was murdered.'

'Who brought her?'

'It's hard to remember exactly who or when. Everything was confusion, all this nonsense about lists and the law. I suppose it was Magnus and Mallius Glaucia who brought her here.'

'And what did they do with her?'

He snorted. 'What didn't they do?'

'You mean they raped her?'

'While Capito watched. And laughed. He made the kitchen girls bring him food and wine while it was going on, scaring them out of their wits. I told them to stay in the kitchen, that I'd do the serving – and Capito struck me with a whip and swore he'd have my balls chopped off. Sextus Roscius was furious when I told him. This was when he was still allowed in the house, even though the soldiers had thrown him out. He argued with Capito constantly, and when he wasn't arguing he sulked, stuck in the little house across the way. I know they argued a lot about Elena.'

'And when they brought her here, was she already showing her pregnancy?'

He gave me an angry, frightened look, and I could see that he was wondering how I could know so much and not be one of them. 'Of course,' he snapped, 'at least when she was naked. Don't you understand, that was the point. Magnus and Glaucia claimed they could make her abort the child, especially if they both took her at once.'

'And did they?'

'No. After that they left her alone. Perhaps Sextus managed to soften Capito, I don't know. Her belly grew larger and larger. She was put with the kitchen slaves and did her share of work. But right after she had the baby she disappeared.'

'When was this?'

'Three months ago? I can't remember exactly.'

'So they took her back to Rome?'

'Maybe. Or maybe they killed her. It was either her they killed, or the baby, or both of them.'

'What do you mean?'

'Here, I'll show you.'

Without a word he led me out of the house and into the fields behind. He threaded a path through the grape arbours, wending past slaves who skulked and slept in the leafy shade. A winding pathway led up a hillside to the family gravesite whose stelae I had glimpsed the day before.

'Here,' he said. 'You can tell from the earth which are the newer ones. The old man was buried here, beside Gaius.' He pointed to two gravesites. The older one was decorated with a finely carved stele picturing a handsome young Roman in the guise of a shepherd surrounded by satyrs and nymphs; there was a great deal of engraving below, in which I glimpsed the words GAIUS, BELOVED SON, GIFT FROM THE GODS. The newer mound was marked only with a simple uninscribed slab that had the look of being merely temporary.

'You can tell how much his father doted on Gaius,' said Carus. 'A beautiful piece of work, isn't it? Done specially by an artisan in the city who knew the boy; it looks just like him. He was very handsome, as you can see; the stone even captures that look in his eyes. Of course the old man so far has nothing better than a beggar's stele, not even marked with his name. Sextus intended to have it there only until he could commission a special one done up from portraits of his father. You can wager Capito won't be wasting any of his new fortune on a stone.'

He touched his fingers to his lips and then to the top of each slab, in the old Etruscan manner of showing respect for the dead, then led me to a weedy patch nearby. 'And this was the grave that appeared after Elena vanished.'

There was nothing but a small mound of earth and a broken stone at the head to mark the spot.

'We heard her giving birth the night before. Screaming loud enough to wake the whole house. Maybe Magnus and Glaucia had done something terrible to her insides, after all. The next day Sextus showed up at the house, though Capito had long since stopped allowing him inside. But Sextus forced his way in and cornered Capito in his study. They slammed the door, and I heard them arguing for a long time, first yelling and then very quiet. Later Elena was gone, but I didn't know where. And then some of the other slaves told me about the new gravesite. It's a small grave, isn't it? But rather large for just a baby. Elena was small herself, hardly more than a girl. What do you think, could it hold both a girl and her baby?'

'I don't know,' I said.

'Neither do I. And no one ever told me. But this is what I think: the baby was born dead, or else they killed it.'

'And Elena?'

'They took her to Chrysogonus, in Rome. That was the rumour among the slaves, anyway. Perhaps it's only what we wish might be the truth.'

'Or perhaps it's Elena who's buried here, and the child lives on.'

Carus only shrugged and turned back towards the house.

Thus I departed from Ameria even later than I had hoped. I took the advice of Titus Megarus and spent the night with his cousin. All that day on the road and that night under a strange roof I pondered what Carus had told me, and for some reason the words that lingered in my thoughts were not about Elena or her child, or about Capito and his family, but something he had said about his former master: 'And if Sextus Roscius was a terrible father to his daughters, what business was that of mine?' There was something disturbing in those words, and I puzzled over them until at last sleep captured me again.

XX

I reached Rome shortly after midday. The weather was sweltering, but the climate in Cicero's study was quite chilly.

'And where have you been?' he snapped, pacing with crossed arms about the room, staring at me and then into the atrium, where a household slave sat pulling weeds. Tiro stood at a table before a bunch of scrolls unrolled and held down by weights. Rufus was there as well, sitting in the corner and tapping at his lower lip. The two of them gave me sympathetic glances that told me I was not the first to receive Cicero's wrath that day. The trial was only four days away. The first-time advocate was not bearing up well.

'But surely you knew I was in Ameria,' I said. 'I told Tiro before I left.'

'Yes, good for you, running off to Ameria to let us handle the case here alone. You told Tiro you'd be back yesterday.' He gave a small burp and made a face, clutching his belly.

'I told Tiro I'd be gone for one day at the least, possibly more. I don't suppose it would interest you to know that since I last saw you my home was invaded by armed thugs – and may have been attacked again – I can't say because I haven't yet returned there, having come straight here instead. They threatened my slave, who luckily escaped, and they butchered my cat, which may seem a small thing to you but which would be an omen of catastrophic proportions in a civilized country like Egypt.'

Tiro looked appalled. Cicero looked dyspeptic. 'An attack on your house – on the night you left Rome? But that can't possibly be connected to your work for me. How could anyone have known—'

'I can't answer that, but the message left in blood on my wall was explicit enough. "Be silent or die. Let Roman justice work its will." Probably good advice. Before I left Rome I had to cremate my cat, find lodgings for my slave, and arrange for a guard to watch my doorstep. As for the journey, I invite you to ride to Ameria and back in two days and see if it leaves you in a better humour. My backside is so sore I can hardly stand, let alone sit. My arms are sunburned, and my insides feel as if I'd been picked up by a Titan and thrown like a pair of dice.'

Cicero's jaw stiffened and quivered, his lips pursed. He was about to snap at me again.

I held up my hand to silence him. 'But no,

Cicero, don't thank me yet for all my pains on your behalf. First, let's sit calmly for a few moments while you have a servant fetch us something quenching to drink and bring a meal fit for a hungry man with an iron stomach who hasn't eaten since daybreak. Let me tell you what I discovered on my rounds with Tiro the other day, and what I found out in Ameria. Then you can thank me.'

Which, after I had finished my tale, Cicero did quite profusely. His indigestion seemed to vanish, and he even broke his regimen to share a cup of wine with us. I plunged into the murky matter of my finances and found him completely amenable. He agreed not only to pay for any additional expenses incurred by leaving Vespa for a few extra days in Ameria, but even volunteered to pay for an armed professional to guard my house until after the trial. 'Hire a gladiator from whomever you wish,' he said. 'Charge the debt to me.' When I produced the petition of the citizens of Ameria asking Sulla to reverse the proscription of old Roscius, I thought he might name me his heir.

As I told the tale I paid careful attention to Rufus's face. Sulla was his brother-in-law, after all. Rufus professed only disdain for the dictator, and in any event Titus Megarus's tale implicated not Sulla but Chrysogonus, his ex-slave and deputy. Nevertheless, I feared he would be offended. For an instant I considered that it might have been Rufus who betrayed me to the enemies of Sextus Roscius and set Mallius Glaucia invading my house, but I could see no guile in his brown eyes, and it was hard to imagine that those quizzical eyebrows and freckled nose belonged to a spy. (Red hair on a woman is a warning, the Alexandrians say, but put your trust in a redheaded man.) Indeed, when the tale turned to Sulla and cast him in a poor light, Rufus seemed quietly pleased.

When I was done with my tale and Cicero began plotting his strategy, Rufus was eager to be of help. Cicero wanted to send him down to the Forum, but I suggested that Rufus come with me instead and tend to legal errands later. Now that I had uncovered the truth I wanted to confront Sextus Roscius with it, to see if I couldn't break through his shell, and for propriety's sake I preferred to drop in on Caecilia Metella not as a lone inquisitor but as a humble visitor in the company of her dear young friend.

Tiro was busy completing his summary of my account. As soon as I mentioned visiting Caecilia, I saw him look up furtively. He bit his lip and furrowed his brow, trying to think of some legitimate excuse to come with us. He was thinking of the young Roscia, of course. As Rufus and I made ready to go, he became more and more agitated, but said nothing.

'And, Cicero,' I finally said, 'if you could possibly spare Tiro – that is, if you don't need him for something relating to the case – I'd appreciate your sending him along with us.' I watched Tiro's face light up.

'But I thought he and I might go over your

account. I may want to make some notes and observations of my own.'

'Yes, well, I only thought – that is, there were some details of my conversations when he went with me the other day, the interrogation at the House of Swans in particular, that I need to discuss with him – holes in my memory that need patching, that sort of thing. Of course it could wait for another day, but there aren't that many days left. Besides, I suspect I may need him to take down some new material from Roscius himself.'

'Very well,' Cicero said. 'I'm sure I can manage for the rest of the afternoon without him.' In his elation at the prospect of a stunning victory in the Rostra he went so far as to pour himself another cup of wine and to reach for a crust of bread.

Tiro looked so happy I thought he might weep.

I had lied to Cicero; I had nothing to ask Tiro. It was Rufus I talked to as we walked through the Forum and up the Palatine to Caecilia's house. Tiro trailed behind us, distracted and glassy-eyed.

I had taken little notice of Rufus when I first met him. Each of his qualities had been eclipsed by those around him. As a noble, Caecilia Metella exuded greater prestige, being more comfortable with her power and more conscious of it; Cicero outshone him as a scholar; and for the exuberance of youth, he could not compete with Tiro. Finally speaking to him alone, I was impressed by his reserve and his manner, and equally by his quick wits. Apparently Cicero had kept him busy in the Forum every day since he had taken the case, trusting Rufus to file the necessary papers and arrange court business in his name. As we walked through the Forum, he gave a nod or exchanged a few words with those he knew – deferentially to the older nobles, less so to those nearer his age or of a lower class. Despite the fact that he did not yet wear the toga of manhood, he was obviously known to important people and had earned their respect.

A man is known in the Forum for the size and impressiveness of his retinue. Crassus is legendary for strutting through with bodyguards, slaves, secretaries, sycophants, fortune-tellers, and gladiators in tow. We are a republic, after all, and the sheer mass of bodies surrounding a politician draws attention. The quantity rather than the quality of his supporters often lends a man prestige in the open Forum; some office seekers are said to purchase their retinues wholesale, and there are Romans who make a living off the crumbs they receive for showing up to follow a powerful man about the city. Midway through the Forum I realized that Tiro and I, however inadequate, were being looked upon as Rufus's retinue. The idea made me laugh.

Rufus seemed to read my thoughts. 'My brother-in-law,' he began, speaking the words in such a way that he could mean only Sulla, 'has fallen into the habit lately of walking through the Forum with no retinue at all, not even a bodyguard. In preparation for his retirement, he says, and his return to private life.'

'Can that be wise?'

'I suppose he's so great that he doesn't need a retinue to impress others. So brilliant that any companions would simply be invisible, obscured by his blinding light like candles beside the sun.'

'And whereas candles may be blown out on a whim, no man can extinguish the sun.'

Rufus nodded. 'Who thus needs no bodyguard. So Sulla seems to think. He's taken to calling himself Sulla, Beloved of Fortune – as if he were married to the goddess herself. He thinks he has a charmed life, and who would argue with that?'

Rufus had taken the first step, showing a willingness to speak frankly of his sister's husband. 'You have a sincere dislike for Sulla, don't you?' I said.

'I respect him greatly. I think he truly must be a great man. But I can hardly stand to be in the same room with him. What Valeria sees in him I can't imagine, though I know she truly loves him. How she wants to have his child! I hear her talking about it endlessly with the women of the household whenever she's home. Being the beloved of the Beloved of Fortune, I suppose she'll get what she wants.'

'You've come to know him well, then?'

'As well as I have to, being his wife's little brother.'

'And you've grown acquainted with his circle?'

'You want to ask me about Chrysogonus.'

'Yes.'

'All the stories are true. Of course there's nothing between them now except friendship. In matters of the flesh they say Sulla is very fickle, but at the same time faithful, because he never casts his lovers away; once he's given his affection he never withdraws it. Sulla is nothing if not steadfast, as a friend or an enemy. As for Chrysogonus, if you saw him I think you'd understand. It's true, he began as a mere slave, but sometimes the gods like to put the soul of a lion in the body of the lamb.'

'Chrysogonus is a ferocious lamb, then?'

'A lamb no longer. Sulla sheared his fleece, true enough, but the second growth was a mane of pure gold. Chrysogonus wears it well. He is very rich, very powerful, and completely ruthless. And as beautiful as a god. Sulla has an eye for that.'

'It sounds like you care for Sulla's favourite even less than Sulla.'

'I never said I disliked Sulla, did I? It's not as simple as that. It's hard to put into words. He's a great man. The attention he pays me is flattering, even if it is unseemly since he's married to my sister.' He glanced at me sidelong, looking far older than his sixteen years. 'I suppose you thought Caecilia was joking or off her head the other day when she suggested I charm Sulla on behalf of Sextus Roscius.' He grunted and wrinkled his nose. 'With Sulla? I can't imagine it.'

We passed a group of senators. Some of them, recognizing Rufus, paused to chat, asking after his studies and saying they had heard from his brother Hortensius that he was somehow involved in a case before the Rostra. With men of his own class Rufus displayed an exact approximation of perfect behaviour, at once charming and obsequious, self-effacing and at the same time self-promoting as all Romans are; but I could see that a part of him remained aloof and detached, the observer and critic of his own artificial decorum. I began to see why Cicero was so pleased to have him for a protégé, and I began to wonder if it was not Cicero who was the pupil, learning from Rufus how to rise above his own country-born anonymity to mimic that effortless self-assurance of a young noble born into one of Rome's great families.

The senators moved on, and Rufus resumed as if we had never been interrupted. 'In fact, I'm invited to a party tomorrow night, at Chrysogonus's house on the Palatine, quite near Caecilia's place. Sulla and his closest circle will be there; Valeria won't. I got a message from Sulla just this morning, saying I definitely should come. "You will soon be inducted into the toga of manhood," he writes. "It is time for your manly education to begin. What better place than in the company of the best people in Rome?" Can you imagine – he's talking about his friends from the stage, all actors and comedians and acrobats. Along with the slaves he's made into citizens to take the place of the ones he's beheaded. My parents are urging me to go. Hortensius says I'd be a fool not to. Even Valeria thinks I should.'

'So do I,' I said quietly, drawing a deep breath to begin the climb up the Palatine.

'And parry Sulla's advances all night long? For *that* I'd have to be an acrobat, actor, and comedian all in one.'

'Do it for Sextus Roscius and his case. Do it for Cicero.'

At the mention of Cicero his face became earnest. 'How do you mean?'

'I need access to Chrysogonus's household. I need to get inside, to see which of Sextus Roscius's slaves are still in his possession. I want to question them if I can. It would be easier if I had a friend inside his house. Do you think it's an accident that this party coincides with our need? The gods are smiling on us.'

'Fortune I hope, and not Venus.'

I laughed, even though it cost me a precious breath, and trudged up the hill.

'It's true, then?' I said, staring into Sextus Roscius's eyes and trying to make him blink before I did. 'Every word of the story Titus Megarus told me? But if that's so, why didn't you tell us in the first place?'

We were seated in the same stuffy, squalid room where we had met before. This time Caecilia Metella, having been told the tale in brief, came with us. The idea that her beloved Sextus had been proscribed as an enemy of Sulla was absurd, she said, obscene. She was eager to hear what his son had to say about it. Rufus sat close beside her, and one of her slave girls stood quietly in the corner fanning her with peacock plumes on a long handle, as if she were a Pharaoh's queen. Tiro stood at my right arm with his tablet and stylus, fidgeting.

Sextus stared back at me, unwilling to blink. The

effect became as unnerving as the heat. If he was hiding something he gave no sign of it. Most men, stalling for time to think up a lie or evasion, will glance away, shifting their gaze to something, anything, that doesn't stare back at them. Sextus Roscius stared me straight in the eye with no expression on his face at all, until finally I blinked. I thought he smiled then, but I may have only imagined it. I began to think he might truly be mad.

'Yes,' he finally said. 'True. Every word.'

Caecilia made a peculiar titter of distress. Rufus stroked her wrinkled hand.

'Then why didn't you tell Cicero? Did you tell Hortensius when he was your advocate?'

'No.'

'But how can you expect these men to defend you if you won't tell them what you know?'

'I never asked either of them to take my case. She did.' He rudely pointed at Caecilia Metella.

'Are you saying you don't want an advocate?' Rufus snapped. 'What chance do you think you'd have if you stood before the Rostra alone, against a prosecutor like Gaius Erucius?'

'What chance do I have now? Even if I somehow escape them in court, they'll find me afterwards and have their way with me, just as they did with my father.'

'Not necessarily,' Rufus argued. 'Not if Cicero is able to expose the lies of Capito and Magnus in court.'

'But to do that he'll have to drag in the name of Chrysogonus, won't he? Oh, yes, there's no way to

293

pick the fleas without wrestling the dog, and no way to do that without pulling at the master's leash. The dog may snap, and the master isn't going to like being publicly embarrassed by an upstart advocate. Even if he wins the case, your precious Master Chick-pea will only end up with his head on a stick. Don't tell me that there's an advocate in Rome who's willing to run the risk of spitting in Sulla's face. And if there is such a man, he's far too stupid to handle my case.'

Rufus and Tiro were both exasperated. How could Roscius say such a thing about Cicero, their Cicero? Roscius's fears meant nothing to them; their faith in Cicero was absolute.

But I feared that Sextus Roscius was right. The case was exactly as dangerous as he had described it. Someone had already made a threat on my life (a fact I intentionally had not mentioned under Caecilia's roof). If they had not done so to Cicero it was only because he was at that time still one step removed from the investigation, and a man with more powerful connections than my own.

Still, there was something disingenuous in Roscius's words. Yes, his case was a dangerous one and pursuing it could incur the wrath of the mighty. But what could that matter to him, if his only alternative was a hideous death? By fighting the case, by arming us with the truth that could prove his innocence and the guilt of his persecutors, he had everything to gain: his life, his sanity, perhaps even the reversal of his father's proscription and the return of his estates. Could he have sunk to such a level of hopelessness that he was paralysed? Can a man become so demoralized that he longs for defeat and death?

'Sextus Roscius,' I said, 'help me to understand. You learned of your father's death shortly after it occurred. His body was returned to Ameria and you began the funeral rites. Then soldiers came, announcing that he had been proscribed, that his death was an execution, not a murder, and that his property was forfeit to the state. You were forced from your home and stayed with friends in the village. There was an auction in Rome; Capito, or quite likely Chrysogonus, buys up the property. Did you know then who had killed your father?'

'No.'

'But you must have suspected.'

'Yes.'

'Very well. Once ensconced, Capito graciously invited you back to live on the estate, allowing your family to occupy a ramshackle house away from the villa. How did you bear this humiliation?'

'What could I do? The law is the law. Titus Megarus and the town council went off to petition Sulla himself on my behalf. I could only wait.'

'But finally Capito threw you off the estate altogether. Why was that?'

'I suppose he'd finally had enough of me. Maybe he started feeling guilty.'

'But by that time you must have realized without a doubt that Capito himself was involved in your father's murder. Did you threaten him?'

He looked away. 'We never came to blows, but

our arguments were fierce. I told him he was a fool to make himself so comfortable in the big house, that he'd never be allowed to keep it. He told me I was no better than a beggar, and I should kiss his foot for the charity he showed me.' He gripped the arms of his chair and his knuckles turned white. He ground his teeth in a sudden fury. 'He said I'd die before I got the land back. He said I was lucky not to be dead already. He kicked me out, at least that's what it looks like, but the truth is I was fleeing for my life. Even at Titus's house I wasn't safe; I could feel them watching the house after dark, like night-hawks biding their time. That's why I had to come to Rome. But even here I wouldn't be safe on the open streets. This room is the only place I'm safe. And they won't even leave me in peace here! I never thought it would come to this, that they'd drag me to the courts and tie me up in a sack. Can't you see, all the power is on their side? Who knows what sort of lies this Erucius will come up with? In the end it's only his word against Cicero's. Whom do you think the judges will side with if it comes down to offending the dictator? There's nothing you can do!' Suddenly he was weeping.

Caecilia Metella made a face as if she had eaten something disagreeable. Without a word she rose from her chair and strode out the door, with the slave girl and her peacock fan following behind. Rufus jumped up, but I motioned for him to stay.

Roscius sat with his face in his hands. 'You are a strange man,' I finally said. 'You are wretched, yet somehow I can't pity you. You stand close to a horrible death, in a place where most men would tell any lie to save themselves, and yet you omit telling the truth that alone could save you. Now that the truth is known you admit it and have no reason to lie, and yet . . . You make me doubt my own instincts, Sextus Roscius. I'm confounded, like a hound who scents a fox in a rabbit hole.'

He slowly lifted his head. His face was twisted with loathing, distrust, and the fear that lurked always in his eyes.

I shook my head. 'Talking to you exhausts me. You give me a headache. I only hope Cicero's head is stronger.' We rose to leave. I turned back. 'There was something else,' I said. 'A trifle, really. About a young whore named Elena. Do you know whom I mean?'

'Yes. Of course. For a while she lived in the house after Capito took it over.'

'And how did she come to be there?'

He stopped to think. At least the weeping had ended.

'Magnus and Glaucia found her in the city, I think. I suppose my father must have purchased her some time before, but had left her in the brothel owner's keeping. After the auctions Magnus claimed her as his property.'

'She was with child, I believe.'

He paused. 'Yes, you're right.'

'Whose child?'

'Who knows? She was a whore, after all.'

'Of course. And what became of her?'

'How should I know?'

'I mean, after she had the baby.'

'How should I know?' he said again, angrily. 'What would you do with a whore and a newborn slave child if you were a man like Capito? They've probably both been sold at market long ago.'

'No,' I said. 'Not both. At least one of them is dead, buried close by your father's grave in Ameria.'

I watched him carefully from the doorway and waited, but he made no response.

We walked back towards Caecilia's quarters in silence. From the corner of my eye I could see that Tiro dragged his feet, growing more anxious as we drew close to departing. My head was too full of Sextus Roscius to deal with him, but at last, as we returned to Caecilia's wing, I began to consider what flimsy excuse I might contrive to set him free to go in search of the girl.

But Tiro was ahead of me. He suddenly stopped and reached about himself with the air of a man who has lost something. 'By Hercules,' he said, 'I've left my stylus and tablet behind. It will only take a moment to fetch them – unless I didn't have them with me when you interviewed Roscius, and left them somewhere else altogether,' he added, grasping at some way to prolong his absence.

'You had them with you,' Rufus said with a faintly hostile edge in his voice. 'I remember seeing them in your hands.'

I shook my head. 'I'm not sure about that. At any rate, you'd better go back and see if you can find them, Tiro. Take your time. It's too late for Rufus to get anything done in the Forum today, and the sun is still too fierce to go hurrying back to Cicero's house. I think that Rufus and I may prevail on our hostess to entertain us in her garden for a while, so that we may take a respite from this heat.'

Caecilia, in fact, was unable to join us; the eunuch Ahausarus explained that the interview with Sextus Roscius had exhausted her. Though she was indisposed, she gave us the use of her servants, who scurried about the peristyle moving furniture out of the sun into the shade, fetching cool drinks, and doing their best to make us comfortable. Rufus was listless and on edge. I approached him again about the party to be held the following night at the house of Chrysogonus.

'If you're seriously uncomfortable about going,' I said, 'then don't. I only thought that you might be able to get me into the house, through the slaves' entrance perhaps. There are a few details I'm not sure I can discover otherwise. But of course I have no right to ask it of you—'

'No, no,' he murmured, as if I had caught him daydreaming. 'I'll go. I'll show you his house before we leave the Palatine; it's quite nearby. If only for the sake of Cicero, as you said.'

He called for one of the servants and asked for more wine. It seemed to me that he might already have had too much. When the wine came he drank it in a single draught and called for another. I cleared my throat and frowned. 'Surely the dictum reads, all things in moderation, Rufus. Or so I'm sure Cicero would insist.'

'Cicero,' he said, as if it were a curse; and then

said it again as if it were a joke. He moved from his backless chair to a plush divan and splayed himself among the pillows. A mild breeze moved through the garden, causing the dry leaves of the papyrus to rattle and the acanthus to sigh. Rufus shut his eyes, and from the sweet look on his face I was reminded that he really was still only a boy, despite his noble status and his manly ways, still dressed in a boy's gown with its long modest sleeves, the same way that Roscia was no doubt dressed at that very moment, unless Tiro had already pulled the garment from her body.

'What do you think they're doing right now?' Rufus suddenly asked, opening one eye to catch the startled look on my face.

I feigned confusion and shook my head.

'You know whom I mean,' Rufus groaned. 'Tiro is taking an awfully long time to fetch his stylus, isn't he? His stylus!' He laughed, as if he had just caught the joke. But the laugh was short and bitter.

'Then you know,' I said.

'Of course I know. It happened the first time he came here with Cicero. It's happened every time since. I was beginning to think you hadn't noticed. I was wondering what sort of finder you could be, not to notice something so obvious. It's ridiculous, how obvious they are.'

He sounded jealous and bitter. I nodded in sympathy. Roscia, after all, was a very desirable girl. I was a little jealous of Tiro myself.

I lowered my voice, trying to be gentle but not

300

patronizing. 'He's only a slave, after all, with so little to look forward to in life.'

'That's just it!' Rufus said. 'That a mere slave should be able to find satisfaction, and for me it's impossible. Chrysogonus was a slave, too, and he found what he wanted, just as Sulla found what he wanted in Chrysogonus, and in Valeria, and all the rest of his conquests and concubines and wives. Sometimes it seems to me that the whole world is made up of people finding one another while I stand alone outside it all. And who in all the world should want me but Sulla – it's a joke of the gods!' He shook his head but did not laugh. 'Sulla wants me and can't have me; I want another who doesn't even know I exist. How terrible it is, to want only one other in the whole world and to have your longing go unanswered! Have you ever loved another who didn't love you in return, Gordianus?'

'Of course. What man hasn't?'

A slave arrived with a fresh cup of wine. Rufus took a sip, then set it on the table and stared at it. It seemed to me that Roscia was hardly worth so much agony, but then I was not sixteen. 'So blatantly obvious,' he muttered. 'How long are they going to be at it?'

'Does Caecilia know?' I asked. 'Or Sextus Roscius?'

'About the lovebirds? I'm sure they don't. Caecilia lives in a fog, and who knows what goes on in Sextus's head? I suppose even he might feel obliged to muster a little outrage if he found out that his daughter is cavorting with another man's slave.'

I paused for a moment, not wanting to ply him with questions too quickly. I was thinking about Tiro and the danger he might be courting. Rufus was young and frustrated and highborn, after all, and Tiro was a slave committing the unthinkable in a grand woman's house. With a word Rufus could destroy his life forever. 'And what about Cicero – does Cicero know?'

Rufus looked me straight in the eye. The look on his face was so strange that I couldn't account for it. 'Cicero know?' he whispered. Then the spasm passed. He seemed very weary. 'About Tiro and Roscia, you mean. No, of course he doesn't know. He would never notice such a thing. Such passions are beneath his notice.'

Rufus slumped back against the pillows in utter despair.

'I understand,' I said. 'Though you may find it hard to believe, I do understand. Roscia is of course a fine girl, but consider her situation. There's no honourable way you could openly court her.'

'Roscia?' He looked baffled, then rolled his eyes. 'What do I care about Roscia?'

'I see,' I said, not seeing at all. 'Oh. Then it's Tiro whom you. . . .' I suddenly confronted a whole new set of complications.

Then I realized the truth. In an instant I understood, not by his words or even by his face, but by some inflexion just then remembered, some disconnected moment set next to another in memory, in that way that revelations sometimes come to us unprepared for and seemingly inexplicable.

302

How absurd, I thought, and yet how touching, for who could help being moved by the earnestness of his suffering? The laws of man strive for balance, but the laws of love are pure caprice. It seemed to me that Cicero – staid, fussy, dyspeptic Cicero – was probably the least likely man in Rome to reciprocate Rufus's desires; the boy could not have chosen a more hopeless object for his infatuation. No doubt Rufus, so young, so full of intense feeling, steeped in the Greek ideals of Cicero's circle, thought of himself as Alcibiades to Cicero's Socrates. No wonder it infuriated him to think of what Tiro and Roscia were enjoying at that very instant, while he burned with an unspoken passion and all the pent-up energy of youth.

I sat back, perplexed and without a word of advice to give him. I clapped and waved to the slave girl and told her to bring us more wine.

303

XXI

The stablemaster was not pleased when he saw the farm horse I came riding in place of his beloved Vespa. A handful of coins and assurances that he would be amply rewarded for any inconvenience satisfied him. As for Bethesda, he informed me that she had sulked throughout my absence, that she had broken three bowls in his kitchen, ruined the needlework she had been given and had driven both the head cook and the housekeeper to tears. His steward had begged for permission to beat her, but the stablemaster, true to my demands, had forbidden it. He shouted at one of his slaves to go and fetch her. 'And good riddance,' he added, though when she came striding imperiously out of his house and into the stables, I noticed that he couldn't take his eyes off her.

I pretended to be disinterested. She pretended to be cold. She insisted on stopping by the market on our way home so that we would have something to eat that night. While she shopped I wandered about the street, absorbing the squalid smells and sights of the Subura, happy to be home. Even the pile of fresh dung that we had to bypass on the climb up did not dampen my mood.

The stablemaster's slave Scaldus sat on the ground before the door, leaning against it with his legs outstretched. At first I thought he slept, but at our approach the colossus stirred and rose to its feet with alarming speed. Recognizing my face, he relaxed and grinned stupidly. He told me that he had taken turns with his brother so that the house had never gone unguarded, and that no one else had been there in my absence. I gave him a coin and told him to be off, and he obediently began loping down the hill.

Bethesda looked at me in alarm, but I assured her we would be safe. Cicero had promised to pay for protecting my house. I would find a professional in the Subura before we slept.

She began to speak, and from the way she curled her lips I knew she was about to say something sarcastic. Instead I covered them with a kiss. I walked her backwards into the house and closed the door with my foot. She dropped her armful of greens and bread and clutched at my shoulders and neck. She sank to the floor and pulled me with her.

She was overjoyed to see me again, and she showed me. She was angry at having been left in a strange household, and she showed that as well, clutching her nails against my shoulders and beating her fists against my back, nipping at my neck and earlobes. I devoured her like a man starved for days. It seemed impossible that I had been gone for only two nights.

She had bathed that morning. Her flesh had the taste of a different soap, and behind her ears and on her throat and in the secret places of her body she had anointed herself with an unfamiliar perfume – filched, she told me later, from the private cache of the stablemaster's wife while no one was looking. In the last rays of sunlight we lay exhausted and naked in the vestibule, our sweat leaving obscene imprints on the worn rug. That was when I chanced to look beyond the sleek planes of her body and noticed the message still scrawled in blood on the wall above us: 'Be silent or die. . . .'

A sudden breeze from the atrium chilled the sweat on my spine. Bethesda's shoulder turned to gooseflesh beneath my tongue. There was a strange moment in which it seemed that my heart ceased to beat, suspended between the fading light and heat of her body and the message above us. The world seemed suddenly a strange and unfamiliar place, and I imagined I heard those words whispered aloud in my ear. I might have read this as an omen. I might then have fled from the house, from Rome, from Roman justice. Instead I bit her shoulder, and Bethesda gasped, and the night continued to its desperate conclusion.

Together we lit the lamps – and though she showed a fearless face, again Bethesda insisted that every room be lit. I told her she should come with me down to the Subura to shop for a guard, but she insisted on staying behind to cook the meal. I felt a pang of dread at the idea of leaving her alone in the house even for a short while, but she was adamant and only asked me to be quick. I could see that she was choosing to be brave and that in her own way she wanted to reassert her power over the house; in my absence she would burn a stick of incense and perform some rite learned long ago from her mother. After the door closed behind me, I listened to make sure she bolted it securely from within.

The moon was rising and nearly full, casting a blue light over the quiet houses on the hillside, making the tile roofs look as if they had been scalloped from copper. The Subura was a vast pool of light and muted sound below me, that swallowed me up as I quickly descended the hill until I stepped onto the busiest nighttime street in Rome.

I could have found a gang member on any corner, but I didn't want a common thug. I wanted a professional fighter and bodyguard from a rich man's retinue, a slave of proven worth who could be trusted. I went to a little tavern tucked behind one of the more expensive brothels on the Subura and found Varus the Go-Between. He understood what I wanted immediately, and he knew my credit was good. After I had bought him a cup of wine he disappeared. Not too long after he returned with a giant in tow.

They made quite a contrast walking into the dim little room side by side. Varus was so short he came only to the giant's elbow; his bald pate and ringed fingers shone in the light while his doughy features seemed to soften and run together in the glow of the lamps. The beast beside him looked hardly tamed; there was a brooding red light in his eyes that didn't come from the lamps. He gave an impression of almost unnatural strength and solidity, as if he had been built out of granite blocks or tree trunks; even his face had the look of having been chiselled from stone, a rough model discarded by a sculptor who decided it was too brutal to finish. His hair and beard were long and shaggy but not unkempt, and his tunic was made of good cloth. Such grooming bespoke a responsible owner. He looked as well cared for as a fine horse. He also looked capable of killing a man with his bare hands.

He was exactly the man I wanted. His name was Zoticus.

'His master's favourite,' Varus assured me. 'The man never steps outside his house without Zoticus at his side. A proven killer – broke the neck of a burglar only last month. And strong as an ox, to be sure. Smell the garlic on his breath? His master feeds it to him like oats to a horse. A trick the gladiators use, gives a man strength. His master is wealthy, respectable, owner of three brothels, two taverns, and a gaming hall all located in the Subura; a pious man without an enemy in the world, I'm sure, but he likes to protect himself from the unforeseen. Who wouldn't? Never takes a step without his faithful Zoticus. But especially for me, because he owes a favour to Varus, the man will let me have this creature on loan – for the four days you requested, no more. To repay a long-standing debt he owes me. How very lucky you are, Gordianus, to be a friend of Varus the Go-Between.'

We haggled over the terms, and I let him have too sweet a deal, being anxious to return to Bethesda. But the slave was worth the price; stepping through the crowds of the Subura I watched strangers draw back and give way before us, and I saw the cowed looks in their eyes as they stared above my head at the monster behind me. Zoticus spoke little, which pleased me. As we ascended the deserted pathway to my house, leaving the noise of the Subura behind, he loomed behind me like a protective spirit, ceaselessly peering into the shadows around us.

As we stepped within sight of the house I heard his breath quicken and felt his hand like a brick on my shoulder. Another man stood before the door with crossed arms. He shouted at us to stop where we were, then pulled a long dagger from his sleeve. In the blink of an eye I found myself behind Zoticus instead of before him, and as the world whirled past I glimpsed a long steel blade in his fist.

The door rattled open and I heard Bethesda laughing, then explaining. It seemed that I had misunderstood Cicero. Not only had he offered to pay for a bodyguard, he had even gone to the trouble of sending the man over himself. Only minutes after I left Bethesda, there had been a banging on the door. She had ignored it at first, then finally peered through the grate. The man had asked for me; Bethesda pretended that I was in the house but indisposed. Then he gave her Cicero's name and his compliments and told her he had been sent by Cicero to guard the house, as her master would recall. He took up his place beside the door without another word.

'Two will be better than one, anyway,' Bethesda insisted, and I felt a pang of jealousy as she looked from one to the other; perhaps it was that tiny twinge of jealousy that blinded me to the obvious. I would have been hard-pressed to have said which of the two was uglier, or bigger, or more intimidating, or which Bethesda seemed to find more fascinating. Except for his red beard and ruddy face the other might have been Zoticus's brother; his breath even carried the same odour of garlic. They regarded each other as gladiators do, with locked jaws and basilisk eyes, as if the least twitch of a lip might mar the purity of their mutual contempt.

'Very well,' I told her, 'for tonight we'll use them both, and sort it out tomorrow. One to circle the house and patrol the pathway, another to stay in the vestibule, inside the door.'

Cicero had told me to make my own arrangements for a guard; I remembered that quite clearly. But perhaps, I thought, in the heat of his excitement over the news I had brought him, Cicero had forgotten his own instructions. All I could think of were the smells that came from Bethesda's kitchen and the long, careless night of sleep to come.

As I left the vestibule I glanced at the redbeard sent by Cicero. He sat in a chair against the wall, facing the closed door with his arms crossed. The naked dagger was still in his fist. Above his head was the message written in blood, and I could not help reading it again: 'Be silent or die.' I was sick of those words; in the morning I would tell Bethesda to scrub the wall clean. I glanced into Redbeard's unblinking eyes and gave him a smile. He did not smile back.

Often in comedies there are characters who do foolish things that are painfully, obviously foolish to everyone in the audience, to everyone in the universe except themselves. The audience squirm in their seats, laugh, even shout aloud: 'No, no! Can't you see, you fool?' The doomed man on the stage cannot hear, and the gods with great merriment go about engineering the destruction of yet another blind mortal.

But sometimes the gods lead us to the brink of destruction only to snatch us back from the abyss at the last moment, as richly amused by our inexplicable salvation as by our unforeseen death.

I woke all at once with no interval between sleep and waking, into that strange realm of consciousness that reigns between midnight and dawn. I was alone in my own bedchamber. Bethesda had led me there after a long meal of fish and wine, stripping off my tunic and covering me with a thin wool blanket despite the heat, kissing me on the forehead as if I were a child. I stood and let the blanket fall behind me; the night air was heavy with heat. The room was dark, lit only by a single beam of moonlight cast through a tiny window high in the wall. I walked by memory to the corner of the room, but in the darkness I couldn't find the chamber pot, or else Bethesda had emptied it and never put it back.

It did not matter. In the weirdness of that night a chamber pot might turn into a mushroom or disappear into thin air and it would have seemed a little thing. It was the same strangeness I had felt earlier, lying with Bethesda in the vestibule. I saw and sensed everything around me with absolute clarity, and yet it seemed mysterious and unfamiliar territory, as if the moon had changed her colour, as if the gods themselves drifted from the earth in heavy slumber and left existence to its own devices. Anything at all might happen.

I pushed aside the curtain and stepped into the atrium. Perhaps I wasn't awake after all and dreamed on my feet, for the house possessed that unreality of familiar places turned askew by the geography of the night. Blue moonlight flooded the garden and turned it into a jungle of bones casting shadows as sharp as knives. Here and there about the peristyle lamps burned low, like withered suns on the verge of extinction. The brightest of the lamps shone from behind the wall that hid the vestibule, casting a thin yellow light around the corner like the glow of campfires beyond a ridge.

I stepped to the edge of the garden and pulled up my tunic. I was as quiet as a schoolboy, aiming for the soft grass and making hardly a sound. I finished and let my tunic drop and stood gazing across the field of bones, transformed by the shadow of a passing cloud into the ashen ruins of Carthage on a moonless night.

Amid the smells of earth and urine and hyacinth, I caught the faint odour of garlic on the warm, dry air. The lamplight from the vestibule flickered and moved, and cast the wavering shadow of a man onto the wall that enclosed Bethesda's room.

Like a man in a dream I walked towards the vestibule; as in a dream, I seemed to be invisible. A bright lamp was set on the floor, casting weird shadows upward. Redbeard stood before the defaced wall with its threatening message, peering into it as if it were a pool and moving one hand over the surface. The hand that moved was wrapped in a red-stained cloth that dripped something dark and thick onto the floor. His other hand clutched his dagger. The glittering blade was smeared with blood.

The door to the house was wide open. Sprawled against it, as if to prop it open, was the massive body of Zoticus, his throat so severely slashed that his head was almost detached from his body. A great pool of blood had poured from his neck onto the stone floor. The rug was soaked with it. While I watched, Redbeard stepped back and stooped down to dip the cloth into the pool of blood, never taking his eyes from the wall, as if he were an artist and the wall a painting in progress. He stepped forwards and began to write again.

Then, very slowly, he turned his face and saw me.

He returned the smile I had given him earlier with a horrible, gaping grin.

He must have been upon me very quickly, but it seemed to me that he moved with a ponderous and impossible slowness. I had all the time in the world to watch him wield the dagger aloft, to note the sudden blast of garlic in my nostrils, to ponder the taut and quivering rictus of his face, and to wonder stupidly what possible reason he could have to dislike me so very much.

My body was wiser than my brain. Somehow I managed to grip his wrist and deflect the dagger. It barely grazed my cheek, slicing a thin red track that I felt only much later. Suddenly I was flat against the wall with the breath knocked out of me, so confused that I thought for an instant I was flat on the floor with the full weight of Redbeard's body on my chest.

With a great wrenching twist, as if we were acrobats out of step, we reeled to the floor. We grappled like drowning men pounded by surf, so that I never knew up from down. The tip of the dagger kept nipping at my throat, but each time I managed to push his arm off-course. He was absurdly strong, more like a storm or an avalanche than a man. I felt like a boy struggling against him. I had no hope of defeating him. It was all I could do to stay alive from one moment to the next.

I suddenly thought of Bethesda, and knew she must already be dead, along with Zoticus. Why had he saved me for last? That was when the truncheon came crashing down against Redbeard's skull.

While he swayed atop me, dazed, I caught a glimpse of Bethesda over his shoulder. In her hands she held the wooden slat for barring the door. It was so heavy she could barely wield it. She began to lift it again and then tripped beneath the weight and staggered backwards. Redbeard regained his senses. Blood ran downward from a cut in the back of his head, trickling into his beard and mouth, making him look like a crazed animal or a wolf-man gorged on blood. He rose to his knees and twisted around, raising his dagger. I struck at his chest, but I had no leverage.

Bethesda stood upright with the truncheon raised. Redbeard slashed with the dagger, but he only succeeded in slicing her gown. Quickly he spun around the other way and clutched a fistful of cloth with his free hand. He yanked hard and Bethesda fell backwards. The truncheon descended, powered by its own weight. By aim or accident it struck Redbeard square on the crown of his head, and as he toppled onto me I seized his stabbing arm and twisted it towards his chest.

The blade plunged hilt-deep into his heart. His face was above mine, his eyes rolled up, his mouth wide open. I reeled from the stench of garlic and rotten teeth as he sucked in a desperate, rattling breath. Then he jolted and pitched atop me as something exploded inside him. An instant later blood poured from his open mouth like the discharge from a sewer.

Somewhere far away Bethesda screamed. A great massive dead thing lay slick and heavy atop me, convulsing and belching venom, blinding me and flooding my nostrils and mouth, even clogging my ears with its blood. I struggled to escape and lay helpless until I felt Bethesda pushing alongside me. The great corpse rolled onto its back and stared slack-jawed at the ceiling.

I staggered to my knees. We clutched each other, both trembling so badly we could hardly connect. I spat blood and snorted and wiped my face on the bodice of her clean white gown. We stroked each other and babbled pointless words of comfort and assurance, like mutual survivors of a great devastation.

The lamp burned low and sputtered, casting lurid shadows and making the rigid corpses seem to twitch. The weird geography of the night reigned unbroken: we were lovers in a poem, one naked and the other half-dressed, hugging on our knees beside a vast, still lake. But the lake was made of blood — so much blood that I could see my own reflection in it. I stared into my eyes and with a shock I came to my senses, and finally knew that I was not in a nightmare but in the very heart of the great, slumbering city of Rome.

XXII

'Clearly,' I said, 'the message was meant as a warning to *you*, Cicero.'

'But if he intended to murder you and your slave, why didn't he get the bloodshed over with first? Why didn't he go ahead and kill you in your sleep and then write the message?'

I shrugged. 'Because he already had enough blood at hand, pouring out of Zoticus's slashed throat. Because the house was still, and he had no fear that I would wake. Because by having the message already written, in case there was some unforeseen complication or if we died screaming, he could flee the house immediately. Or perhaps he was waiting for another assassin to join him. I don't know, Cicero, I can't speak for a dead man. But he meant to kill me, of that I'm certain. And the warning was for you.'

The moon had fallen. The night was at its

darkest, though dawn could not be far off. Bethesda was somewhere in the slave quarters, fast asleep, I hoped. Rufus, Tiro, and I sat together in Cicero's study surrounded by sputtering braziers. Our host paced back and forth, grimacing and rubbing his chin.

His face was haggard and his jaw was covered with stubble, but his eyes were bright and glittering, far from sleepy – so he had looked when Bethesda and I had come rapping at his door after fleeing across half the city in the middle of the night. Remarkably, Cicero had still been awake and his house brightly lit. A puffy-eyed slave had led us to the study, where Cicero paced with a sheaf of parchment in his hands, reading aloud and drinking from a bowl of steaming leek soup – Hortensius's secret recipe for sweetening the voice.

With Tiro transcribing, he had almost finished his first provisional draft of his oration in defence of Sextus Roscius, having worked at it ceaselessly all night. He had been trying it out for Tiro and Rufus when we arrived, blood-soaked and shivering, at his door.

Bethesda had quickly disappeared, huddled against Cicero's chief housekeeper, who promised to take care of her. Cicero had insisted that I wash and put on a fresh tunic before I did anything else. I had done the best I could, but in the lamplight of his study I kept noticing tiny flecks of dried blood on my fingernails and bare feet.

'So now there are two dead bodies in your house,' Cicero said, rolling his eyes. 'Ah, well, I'll send someone over tomorrow to take care of the corpses. More expenses! No doubt the owner of this Zoticus won't be pleased at having a dead body returned to him; there'll have to be a settlement. You're like a bottomless well I keep pitching coins into, Gordianus.'

'This message,' Rufus interrupted, looking pensive, 'how did it read again, exactly?'

I shut my eyes and saw each word in vivid red, lit by a wavering lamp: ' "The fool disobeyed. Now he is dead. Let a wiser man take a holiday come the holy Ides of May." He also appeared to have been touching up the older message with fresh blood.'

'Quite meticulous,' said Cicero.

'Yes, and a better speller than Mallius Glaucia. His letters were well made, and he seems to have been working not from paper but from memory. A slave from a better class of master.'

'They say Chrysogonus keeps gladiators who can read and write,' said Rufus.

'Yes, too bad you had to kill this Redbeard,' Cicero said reproachfully. 'Otherwise we might have learned who sent him.'

'But he said he came from you, Cicero.'

'You needn't take that sarcastic tone, Gordianus. Of course I didn't send him. You were to hire a bodyguard on your own and I would pay, that was our agreement. To be quite honest, I forgot about the arrangement entirely once you were gone. I started working on my notes for the defence and didn't give it another thought.'

'And yet, when he came to my door, he distinctly

319

told my slave that he had been sent by you. It was a deliberate ruse, calculated to deceive me; that means whoever sent him *knew* of the arrangement we had made only hours before, that you would pay for a single guard to protect my house. How can that be, Cicero? The only people who knew of that discussion were the same ones who are in this room at this moment.'

I stared at Rufus. He blushed and lowered his eyes. Love frustrated may turn to hate, and thwarted desire may long for vengeance. All along he had been a viper, I thought, entrusted with the heart of Cicero's strategy and meanwhile plotting its perversion. You can never trust a noble, I thought, no matter how young and innocent he may appear. Somehow the enemies of Sextus Roscius had twisted his motives to their own ends. He had actually been willing to sacrifice my life and that of Sextus Roscius to see Cicero brought low – it seemed impossible, looking at his boyish face and freckled nose, but of such stuff are Romans made.

I was about to accuse him out loud and expose his secrets – his hidden passion for Cicero, his treachery – but at that instant whatever god had saved my life that night chose to save my honour as well, and I was spared from humiliating myself before a generous client and his highborn admirer.

Tiro made a stifled, choking noise, as if he tried to clear his throat and failed.

As one we turned to look at him. His face was the very image of guilt – blinking, blushing, gnawing his lip.

'Tiro?' Cicero's voice was high and hoarse, despite the leek soup. Yet his face betrayed only mild consternation, as if reserving judgment in expectation of a quite simple and satisfactory explanation.

Rufus glanced at me with fire in his eyes, as if to say: And how could you have doubted *me*? 'Yes, Tiro,' he said, folding his arms and looking down his freckled nose. 'Is there something you wish to explain to us?' He was more haughty than I could have imagined him. That cold, implacable gaze — is it a mask all nobles carry with them for use at a moment's notice, or is it the one true face they show when all their other masks have fallen away?

Tiro bit his knuckles and began to weep. Suddenly I knew the truth.

'The girl,' I whispered. 'Roscia.'

Tiro hid his face and sobbed aloud.

Cicero was furious. He paced the room like a wolf. There were times, as he passed by Tiro, who sat meekly wringing his hands and sniffling, when I thought he would actually strike the poor slave. Instead he threw his hands in the air and shouted at the top of his lungs until he was so hoarse he could hardly speak.

Occasionally Rufus tried to interpose himself, taking on the role of the all-comprehending, all-forgiving noble. He wore the part uneasily. 'But, Cicero, such things happen all the time. Besides, Caecilia need never know.' He reached up to take

Cicero by the hand, but Cicero angrily snatched his arm away, blind to Rufus's pained reaction.

'While her household laughs at her behind her back? No, no, Caecilia may have been fooled, just as I was fooled, but you don't think her slaves weren't onto it? There's nothing worse, nothing, than having a scandal take place beneath the very nose of a Roman matron while her slaves laugh behind her back. And to think that I brought such shame into her house! I can never face her again.'

Tiro sniffled and flinched as Cicero swept by. I scratched at the blood on my fingernails and winced at the first intimations of a headache. The light in the atrium showed the first faint blush of dawn.

'Whip him if you must, Cicero. Or have him strangled,' I said. 'It's your right, after all, and no man would object. But save your voice for the trial. By shouting you only punish Rufus and me.'

Cicero went rigid and scowled at me. At least I had put a stop to his constant pacing.

'Tiro may have acted stupidly and even immorally,' I went on. 'Or it may be that he simply acted like any young man eager for love. But there is no reason to believe that he betrayed you, betrayed us, at least knowingly. He was duped. It's a very old story.'

For a moment Cicero seemed to grow calm, drawing deep breaths and staring at the floor. Then he exploded again. 'How many times?' he demanded, throwing his hands in the air. 'How many?' We had already gone over this, but the number of times seemed particularly to irritate him.

'Five, I think. Maybe six,' Tiro answered meekly, just as he had answered every other time Cicero asked the same question.

'Beginning with the first time, the very first time I visited Caecilia Metella's house. How could you have done such a thing? And then, to have gone on doing it in secret, behind my back, behind the backs of her father and her father's patroness, in her very house! Had you no sense of decency? Of propriety? What if you had been discovered? I would have had no choice but to have given you the direst punishment on the spot! And I would have been held accountable. Her father could have brought suit against me, could have ruined me.' His voice had grown so hoarse and grating it made me wince to hear it.

'Hardly likely,' Rufus yawned, 'considering his circumstances.'

'That makes no difference! Really, Tiro, I see no way out of this. Every suitable punishment I can think of is so severe that it makes me shudder. And yet I see no alternative.'

'You could always forgive him,' I suggested, rubbing my sore eyes.

'No! No, no, no! If Tiro were some simple, ignorant labourer, a slave from the bottom rung, a man hardly better than a beast, then his behaviour might be excusable – he would still have to be punished, of course, but at least the crime would be comprehensible. But Tiro is an educated slave, more knowledgeable in the laws than many a citizen. What he did with the young Roscia was not the act of an ignorant creature of impulse, but the conscious choice of a well-taught slave whose master has clearly been much too lenient and much, much too trusting.'

'Oh, in the name of Jupiter, stop, Cicero!' Rufus had finally reached his limit. I closed my eyes and rendered a prayer of thanks to the unseen gods that it was Rufus who had finally spoken and not me, for I had been biting my tongue so hard it nearly bled. 'Can't you see this is useless? Whatever crime Tiro has committed, it's known only to those of us in this room, and to no one else who cares, at least so long as the girl keeps her mouth shut. It's a matter to be handled between you and your slave. Sleep on it and put it out of your mind until after the trial, and meanwhile simply see that he's kept away from the girl. As Gordianus says, save your voice and your anger for more important matters, such as saving Sextus Roscius. What matters now is discovering what Tiro told her and how the information got to our enemies.'

'And why the girl would betray her own father.' I looked wearily at Tiro. 'Perhaps you have some idea about that.'

Tiro looked meekly at Cicero, as if to see whether he had permission to speak or even breathe. For a moment Cicero seemed on the verge of another outburst. Instead he only cursed and turned towards the dimly glowing atrium, tightly hugging himself as if to contain his fury.

'Well, Tiro?'

'It still seems impossible,' he said softly, shaking

his head. 'Perhaps I'm mistaken. It's only, when you said it had to be someone in this room who betrayed you, I thought to myself, not me, I've told no one, and then I realized I had told Roscia . . .'

'Just as you told her all about me on the day I first interviewed Sextus Roscius,' I said.

'Yes.'

'And the very next day Mallius Glaucia and another of Magnus's thugs came to my house to frighten me off the case, killing my cat and leaving their message in its blood. Yes, it seems to me quite likely that your Roscia is the leak in our vessel.'

'But how? She loves her father. She would do anything to help him.'

'This is what she tells you?'

'Yes. That was why she was always pressing me with questions about the investigation, asking what Cicero was doing to help her father. Sextus Roscius always made her leave the room when he talked business and wouldn't tell her or her mother anything. She couldn't stand not knowing.'

'And so, in between, or during, or after your hurried little trysts, she plied you with detailed questions about her father's defence.'

'Yes. But you make it sound so sinister, so awkward and artificial.'

'Oh, no, I'm sure she's as smooth as burnished gold.'

'You make her sound like an actor.' He lowered his voice and glanced towards Cicero, who had turned his back and stepped into the atrium. 'Or like a whore.'

I laughed. 'Not like a whore, Tiro. You should know better than that.' I saw him blush and look again towards Cicero, as if he expected me to mention Electra now and destroy him even further in his master's eyes. 'No,' I said, 'the motivations of a whore are always transparent, comprehensible precisely because they are suspect, bewitching only to a genuine fool, or to a man who devoutly wishes to be fooled.' I rose from my chair, walked stiffly across the room, and laid my hand on his shoulder. 'But even the wise may be taken in by that which seems young and innocent and fair. Especially if they are young and innocent themselves.'

Tiro glanced towards the atrium, where Cicero had stepped out of earshot. 'Do you really think that's *all* she wanted from me, Gordianus? Just a way to find out what I knew?'

I thought of what I had seen that first day at Caecilia's, of the look on the girl's face and the yearning arch of her naked body against the wall. I thought of the little leer that had flashed in the eyes of young Lucius Megarus at the memory of her stay in his father's house in Ameria. 'No, not entirely. If you mean, did she feel nothing at all when she was with you, I doubt that very much. Trust is seldom entirely pure, and neither is deceit.'

'If she was collecting information,' Rufus said, 'perhaps she was passing it on in some innocent way herself. There might be a slave in the household she confides in, some spy placed there by Chrysogonus who plies her with questions the same way she plies Tiro.'

I shook my head. 'I don't think so. Tell me if I'm right, Tiro. So far you've only managed to see her whenever you could accompany one of us on an errand to Caecilia's house, correct?'

'Yes. . . .' He drew out the word tenuously, as if he anticipated the next question.

'But something tells me that Roscia made some proposal to meet you – tomorrow?'

'Yes.'

'But how did you know that?' asked Rufus.

'Because the trial draws very near. Whoever is gathering their information from Roscia would press her for more regular reports as the final day approaches. They can't rely on the haphazard chance of Tiro being able to see her every day. They would press her to plan for a tryst. True, Tiro?'

'Yes.'

'And tomorrow is here already,' I said, looking into the garden where Cicero was still composing himself. The light had changed from rose to ochre and was rapidly fading to white. Already the coolness of the night was receding. 'When and where, Tiro?'

He looked towards his master, who still gave no sign of hearing, then let out a deep sigh. 'On the Palatine. Near Caecilia Metella's house there's a patch of ground with trees and grass, an open park between two houses; I'm to meet her there at three hours after noon. I told her it might be impossible. She said that if I was with you or with Rufus I should tell you that I had an urgent errand to run for Cicero, or vice versa. She said she was sure I could think of something.'

'And now you won't have to. Because I'm going with you.'

'What?' It was Cicero, outraged, stepping into the room.

'Out of the question! Impossible! There will be no more contact between them.'

'Yes,' I said, 'there will be. Because I say so. Because every minute from now until the trial my life is at stake, and I will leave no path that might lead to the truth unexplored.'

'But we know the truth already.'

'Do we? Just as you knew the truth an hour ago, before Tiro made his confession? There is always more of the truth to discover, and more and more and more. Meanwhile I suggest we all try to get some sleep. We have a busy day ahead. Rufus has business in the Forum, Tiro and I have an appointment with the young Roscia. And tonight, while you, Cicero, work on your notes and polish your oration and drink leek soup, the three of us shall attend a little party given by the gracious Chrysogonus in his mansion on the Palatine. Now good morning, Cicero, and if you will show me to a place where I might sleep, good night.'

XXIII

How long my host slept or whether he slept at all I never knew; I only know that when Tiro came to wake me gently that afternoon in my tiny cubicle opposite the study, I heard Cicero declaiming in his harsh, reedy voice as he paced back and forth in the tiny garden.

'Consider, gentlemen, that story from not so long ago of a certain Titus Cloelius of Tarracina, a pleasant town you'll find sixty miles southeast of Rome on the Appian Way. One night he finished his dinner and then went to bed in the same room as his two grown sons. The next morning he was discovered with his throat slashed. Investigation uncovered no suspects or motives; the sons insisted they had both slept without hearing a thing. Yet they were charged with parricide – and indeed, the circumstances were certainly suspicious. How, the prosecution argued, could they have slept through such an event without waking? Why did they not rouse themselves and defend their father? And what sort of murderer would have dared to venture into that room with three sleeping men with the intent of killing one and then disappearing?

'And yet the good judges acquitted the sons and cleared them of all suspicion. And what was the conclusive bit of evidence? The sons were found the next morning *fast asleep*. How could this be so, it was argued, and the judges unanimously agreed, if they were guilty? For what man could first commit a crime unspeakable and repugnant before every law of god or man, and then afterwards fall blissfully asleep? Surely, it was argued, men who have perpetrated so outrageous an offence against heaven and earth could not possibly have slept soundly in the same room, snoring beside the still-warm corpse of their father. And so the two sons of Titus Cloelius were acquitted. . . .

'Yes, yes, that part's very good, very good, not a word needs changing.'

He loudly cleared his throat, then whispered rapidly to himself before raising his voice again. 'Legend tells us of sons who killed their mothers to avenge their fathers: Orestes who slew Clytemnestra to avenge Agamemnon, Alcmaeon who murdered Eriphyle to avenge Amphiaraus . . . or was it Amphiaraus who killed Eriphyle? No, no, that's right. . . . And yet even when these men are said to have acted in accordance with divine will, obeying oracles and the very voices of the gods, even so the Furies haunted them afterwards, ruthlessly depriving them of all rest, for such is the nature, even when justified by committing an act of filial duty on behalf of a murdered father, of the nature . . . No, no, wait, that won't do. No, it doesn't make sense at all. Too many words, too many words . . .'

'Shall I open the curtains?' Tiro asked. I sat on the divan, rubbing my eyes and licking my parched lips. The room was like an oven, oppressively hot and airless. The yellow curtains were suffused with a light as harsh as Cicero's voice.

'Absolutely not,' I said. 'Then I'd have to watch him as well as listen. Besides, I'm not sure I could stand the brightness. Is there anything to drink?'

He walked to a small table and poured me a cup of water from a silver ewer.

'What time is it, Tiro?'

'The ninth hour of the day – two hours past noon.'

'Ah, then we have an hour before our appointment. Is Rufus up?'

'Rufus Messalla has been down at the Forum for hours. Cicero gave him a whole list of errands.'

'And my slave?'

Tiro smiled demurely. What had Bethesda done – kissed him on the cheek, flattered him, teased him, or simply flashed her eyes? 'I'm not sure where she is now. Cicero gave orders that she needn't do anything except attend to your needs, but she volunteered to help in the kitchen this morning. Until the head cook insisted that she leave.'

'Screaming after her and tossing pots, I assume.'

'Something like that.'

331

'Ah, well, if you see the steward tell him he can confine her to my room if he wants. Let her sit here and listen to Cicero declaiming all day. That should be punishment enough for any broken bowls.'

Tiro frowned to show his disapproval of my sarcasm. A slight breeze wafted the yellow curtains and carried Cicero's voice with it: 'And it is because of the very enormity of the crime of parricide that it must be quite irrefutably proven before any reasonable man will believe it. For what madman, what utterly debauched wreckage of manhood would bring upon himself and his house such a curse, not only of the populace but of the heavens? You know, good Romans, that what I say is true: such is the power of the blood that binds a man to his own flesh that a single drop of it creates a stain that can never be washed away. It penetrates into the heart of a parricide and plants madness and fury in a soul that must already be utterly depraved. . . . Oh, yes, that's it, exactly. By Hercules, that's good!'

'In case you want to wash your face, I brought a bowl of water and a towel,' Tiro said, indicating the little table beside the divan. 'And since you didn't bring any clothes with you, I looked around the house and found a few things that I think will fit. They've been worn, of course, but they're clean.'

He gathered up the tunics and laid them on the divan beside me for my inspection. They could not have been Cicero's, whose torso was much longer and narrower than my own; I suspected they had been made for Tiro. Even the simplest tunic was better stitched and of finer material than my best toga. The night before, Cicero himself had given me a loose sleeveless gown to wear when he had shown me to my bed; apparently he was unaware that it was possible to sleep wearing nothing. As for the bloodstained tunic I had worn to his door, hastily thrown on as Bethesda and I made our escape, it had apparently been gathered from the floor of my room while I slept and thrown away.

While I washed and dressed, Tiro fetched bread and a bowl of fruit from the kitchen. I ate it all and sent him for more. I was famished, and neither the heat nor even Cicero's constant droning and repetitions and self-congratulations could spoil my appetite.

At last I stepped past the curtains with Tiro into the bright sunlight of the garden. Cicero looked up from his text, but before he could utter a word Rufus appeared behind him.

'Cicero, Gordianus, listen to this. You won't believe it. It's a positive scandal.' Cicero turned towards him and raised an eyebrow. 'Of course it's only hearsay, but surely somehow we can verify it. Do you know what the estates of Sextus Roscius, all combined, are worth?'

Cicero mildly shrugged and passed the question to me.

'A string of farms,' I calculated, 'some of them on prime land near the confluence of the Tiber and the Nar; an expensive villa on the main estate near Ameria; a bit of property in the city – at least four million sesterces.'

Rufus shook his head. 'Closer to six million. And

what do you think Chrysogonus – yes, it was the Golden-Born himself, not Capito or Magnus – what do you think he paid for the whole package at auction? Two thousand sesterces. *Two thousand!*'

Cicero was visibly shocked. 'Impossible,' he said. 'Even Crassus isn't that greedy.'

'Or that obvious,' I said. 'Where did you find this out?'

Rufus coloured. 'That's the problem. And the scandal! It was one of the official auctioneers who told me. He handled the bid himself.'

Cicero threw his hands up. 'The man would never testify!'

Rufus seemed hurt. 'Of course not. But at least he was willing to talk to me. And I'm certain he wasn't exaggerating.'

'It makes no difference. What we need is a record of the sale. And of course the name of Sextus Roscius on the proscription lists.'

Rufus shrugged. 'I've searched all day, and there's nothing. Of course the official records are a disaster. You can tell they've been rifled through, marked and remarked and, for all anyone knows, stolen altogether. Between the civil wars and the proscriptions, the state's records are an impossible mess.'

Cicero pensively stroked his lip. 'We know that if the name of Sextus Roscius was inserted into the proscription lists, it was a fraud. And yet if it's there it would acquit his son.'

'And if it's not, how can Capito and Chrysogonus justify keeping the property?' said Rufus.

'Which,' I interrupted, 'is no doubt why Chrysogonus and company want Sextus dead and out of the way entirely, and if possible by legal means. Once the family is wiped out there'll be no one to challenge them, and the question of proscription or murder will be moot. The scandal is self-evident to anyone who even casually inquires after the truth; that's why they've grown so desperate, and so crude. Their only strategy is to silence anyone who knows or cares.'

'And yet,' said Cicero, 'it strikes me more and more that they care nothing for the opinion of the populace, or even for the decisions of the court. Their chief objective is to hide the scandal from Sulla. By Hercules, I honestly believe he knows nothing of it, and they desperately want to keep it that way.'

'Perhaps,' I said. 'And no doubt they're counting on your own sense of self-preservation to keep you from opening an ugly scandal before the Rostra. You can't possibly cut your way to the truth without dragging in Sulla's name. You'll embarrass him at the least, implicate him at worst. There's no way to accuse the ex-slave without insulting his friend and former master.'

'Really, Gordianus, do you think so little of my oratorical skills? I shall be treading the dagger's blade, of course. But Diodotus taught me to appreciate tact as well as truth. In the hands of a wise and honest advocate, only the guilty need fear the weapons of rhetoric, and a truly wise orator never turns them against himself.' He gave me his most

335

self-confident smile, but I thought to myself that what I had heard of his speech so far only skirted the periphery of the scandal. Shocking the audience with inexplicable tales of corpses murdered in the night and lulling them with legends was one thing; dropping the name of Sulla, by Hercules, was quite another.

I glanced at the sundial. Half an hour remained before the young Roscia would begin to grow impatient. I took my leave of Rufus and Cicero and laid my hand on Tiro's shoulder as we departed. Behind me I heard Cicero launch immediately into his oration, regaling Rufus with his favourite parts: 'For what madman, what utterly debauched wreckage of manhood would bring upon himself and his house such a curse, not only of the populace but of the heavens? You know, good Romans, that what I say is true. . . .' I glanced over my shoulder and saw that Rufus was following every word and gesture with a gaze of rapt adoration.

I suddenly realized that Cicero had not said a word to Tiro before we departed, and had only registered a cold nod of dismissal when Tiro had turned to leave. Whatever further words had transpired between them concerning Tiro's conduct were never shared with me, and if there had been a formal punishment I was not told of it, either by Tiro or by Cicero; and not once, at least in my presence, did Cicero ever again make reference to the affair.

★   ★   ★

Tiro was silent as we crossed the Forum and ascended the Palatine. As we approached the trysting place, he grew increasingly agitated, and his face became as morose as an actor's mask. When we came within sight of the little park, he touched my sleeve and paused.

'Will you let me see her alone, only for a moment? Please?' he asked with his head bowed and his eyes lowered, as a slave begs permission.

I took a deep breath. 'Yes, of course. But only for a moment. Say nothing to send her running.' I stood beneath the shade of a willow tree and watched him step quickly into the passage between the high walls of neighbouring mansions. He disappeared into the foliage, hidden by yew trees and a great effusion of roses.

What he said to her in that green arbour, I never knew. When the time came that I might have asked him, I did not, and he never volunteered it. Perhaps Cicero interrogated him later and learned the details, but it seems unlikely. Sometimes even a slave may possess a secret, though the world allows him to possess nothing else.

I waited only a short while, and not as long as I intended; with each passing instant I imagined the girl fleeing through the park's farther exit, until I could no longer stand still. There would never be a good time to get the truth from her, but this was the best opportunity I could hope for.

The little park was shaded and cool, but choked with dust. Dust clung to the parched leaves of the roses and the ivy that crept up the walls. Dust rose underfoot where the grass had withered and worn thin. Twigs snapped and leaves crackled as I pushed my way through; they heard me coming, though I stepped as softly as I could. I glimpsed them through the tangle and in the next moment found them sitting together on a low stone bench. The girl stared up at me with the eyes of a frightened animal. She would have bolted were it not for Tiro's hand closed fast around her wrist.

'Who are you?' She glared at me and grimaced as she tried to pull her hand free. She looked at Tiro, but he would not look back, staring instead into the tangled leaves.

She sat absolutely still then, but I could see the panic and the furious calculation behind her eyes. 'I'll scream,' she said quietly. 'If no one else hears, the guards around Caecilia's house will. They'll come if they hear me screaming.'

'No,' I said, taking a step back and speaking softly to calm her. 'You're not going to scream. You're going to talk.'

'Who are you?'

'You know who I am.'

'Yes, I do. You're the one they call the Finder.'

'That's right. And you have been found, Roscia Majora.'

She chewed her lip and narrowed her eyes. For such a pretty girl it was remarkable how unpleasant she could make her face. 'I don't know what you mean. So you found me sitting with this slave – he's Cicero's slave, isn't he? He lured me here, he told me he had a message from his master about my father—'

338

She spoke not in the tentative tone of one fabricating a lie for later use, but as if it were the truth she spoke even as she invented it. I could see she had much experience in lying. Tiro still would not look at her. 'Please,' he whispered. 'Gordianus, can I go now?'

'Absolutely not. I'll need you here to tell me when she's lying. Besides, you're my witness. Leave me alone with her and she's likely to invent sordid stories about my conduct.'

'A slave can't be a witness,' she snapped.

'Of course he can. I suppose they don't teach Roman law to farmers' daughters in Ameria, do they? A slave is a perfectly reliable witness, so long as his testimony is obtained under torture. Indeed, the law requires that a slave bearing witness *must* be tortured. So I hope you won't scream and begin inventing trouble, Roscia Majora. Even if what you feel for Tiro is no more than contempt, I don't think you'd want to be responsible for having him racked and burned with irons.'

She glared at me. 'A monster, that's what you are. Just like the rest. I despise all of you.'

The answer came effortlessly to my lips, but I paused for a long moment before saying it, knowing that after it was spoken there would be no turning back. 'But your father most of all.'

'I don't know what you mean.' There was a catch in her breath, and the anger that shielded her face abruptly vanished to reveal the pain beneath. She was a child after all, despite her craftiness. She fumbled about, trying to cover herself with that bitter shield and only half succeeding, so that when she spoke again it was as if she were half-naked, brazenly hostile, but with her vulnerability painfully exposed.

'What is it that you want?' she whispered harshly. 'Why did you come here? Why can't you just leave us alone? Tell him, Tiro.' She reached for the arm that held her wrist and tenderly caressed it, glancing at Tiro and then casting her eyes demurely to the ground. The gesture seemed both calculating and sincere, manipulative and yet truly longing for tenderness in return. Tiro blushed to the roots of his hair. From the whiteness of his knuckles and the sudden grimace on Roscia's face, I saw that he was squeezing her wrist painfully tight, perhaps not even knowing it.

'Tell him, Tiro,' she gasped, and no man could have said for certain whether the tears in her voice were genuine or not.

'Tiro has already told me enough.' I looked straight at her but shut my eyes to the pain on her face. I made my voice cold and hard. 'Whom do you meet when you leave Caecilia's house – I mean, besides Tiro? Is it here on this spot that you give your father's secrets to the wolves who want to see him flayed alive? Tell me, you foolish child! What sort of bribe could convince you to betray your own flesh?'

'My own flesh!' she shrieked. 'Betray my own flesh? I have no flesh! This is my father's flesh, this!' she tore her hand from Tiro's grasp, pushed up her sleeve and pinched a handful of the flesh on her arm. 'This flesh, this is his flesh!' she said again, pulling up the hem of her gown to show me her bare white legs, pinching at the taut flesh as if she could tear it from the bone. 'And this, and this! Not mine, but his!' she shouted, tearing at herself, at her cheeks and hands and hair. When she pulled at the neck of her gown to bare her breasts, Tiro stopped her. He would have embraced her, but she slapped him away.

'Do you understand?' She shook as if she wept, but no tears came from her sparking, feverish eyes.

'Yes,' I said. Tiro sat beside her, shaking his head, still confused.

'Do you really understand?' A single tear sprang from one eye and threaded its way down her cheek.

I swallowed and slowly nodded. 'When did it begin?'

'When I was Minora's age. That's why –' Suddenly she sobbed and could not speak.

'Minora – the little one, your sister?'

She nodded. Tiro at last understood. His lips quivered. His eyes grew dark.

'So this is your revenge – to help his enemies however you can.'

'Liar! You said you understood! Not revenge – Minora . . .'

'To save your sister from him, then.'

She nodded, turning her face in shame. Tiro watched her with a look of utter helplessness, moving his hands as if to touch her but afraid to. I could not bear to watch them both at once and turned my face to the empty, endlessly burning sky above.

A breeze wafted through the park, causing the leaves to hiss and then subside. Somewhere far away a woman shouted, and then all was quiet. Deep within the silence one could still make out the distant murmur of the city below. A single bird flew high overhead and bisected the heavens.

'How did they come to you? How did they know?'

'A man . . . it was here . . . one day.' She no longer sobbed, but her voice was thin and broken. 'I've come here every afternoon since we came to the city. It's the only place that reminds me of home, of the country. One day a man came – they must have been watching Caecilia's house, they knew I was his daughter. He scared me at first. Then we talked. Gossip, he called it, trying to make it sound innocent when he started talking about my father, as if he were just a curious neighbour. He must have thought he was so subtle, or else he thought I was an idiot, the way he started asking questions. He offered me a stupid little necklace, the kind of thing Caecilia would throw out with the rubbish. I told him to put it away and stop insulting me. I told him I wasn't stupid and I knew just what he wanted. Oh, no, no, he says, and put on such a show I wanted to spit in his face. I told him to stop it, just to stop it! I knew what he wanted. I told him I knew he came from old Capito or Magnus, and he acted as if he'd never heard of them. I don't care, I told him. I know what you want. And I'll help you however I can. Finally he

342

got it through his head. You should have seen his face.'

I stared into the ivy above her head, into the dense, dust-choked darkness, the domain of wasps and snails and the myriad smaller forms of life devouring and redevouring one another. 'And you still come here every afternoon.'

'Yes.'

'And the same man always comes.'

'Yes. And then I send him away, so I can be alone.'

'And you tell him everything.'

'Everything. What my father ate for breakfast. What my father said to my mother in their bed last night while I listened at the door. Every time Cicero or Rufus visits and what they say.'

'And all the little secrets you can worm out of Tiro?'

She hesitated for just an instant. 'Yes, that too.'

'Such as my name, and the reasons Cicero hired me?'

'Yes.'

'Such as the fact that I asked Cicero to hire a guard for my house?'

'Oh, yes. That was just yesterday. He questioned me very closely about that. He wanted to know very precisely what Tiro had told me, the exact details.'

'And of course you're very good at getting the exact details and remembering them.'

She looked straight at me. Her face had grown hard again. 'Yes. Very good. I forget nothing. *Nothing.*'

I shook my head. 'But what can you gain from it? What about your own life? What future can you have without your father?'

'No worse than the past, no more horrible than all the years he made me . . . all the years I was his. . . .'

Tiro again tried to comfort her, and again she pushed him away.

'But even if you hate him with such a murderous hatred, what life will you have, you and your mother and little Minora, if this thing runs its course? With no one to turn to, reduced to beggars—'

'We're beggars now.'

'But your father may be acquitted. If that happens, there's a chance we can restore his estates.'

She looked at me hard, considering what I said, weighing it while her face showed no expression. Then she delivered her judgment. 'It makes no difference. If you offered me the choice of doing what I've done, or going back to the way things were before, then I'm still not sorry for it. I'd do it all again. I would betray him in every way I could. I would do anything to help his enemies put him to death. Already he's begun to move on her. I can see from the way he watches her when my mother leaves the room. The look in his eyes – sometimes he looks at Minora, and then at me, and he smiles. Can you imagine? He smiles to show me that he knows I understand. He smiles to remind me of all the times he's taken his pleasure with me. He smiles, thinking of all the pleasure over all the years that he could take from Minora. Even now, with his life almost over, he still thinks about it. Perhaps it's all he thinks about. So far I've kept her away from him – by guile, by lying; once I even threatened him with a knife. But do you know what I think? If they condemn him to death, it's the last thing he'll manage to do. Even if he has to do it in front of his executioners, he'll find some way to rip off her clothes and put himself inside her.'

She shivered and swayed as if she might faint. In her helplessness she allowed Tiro to embrace her shoulders gently. Her voice was distant and hollow, as if it came from the moon. 'He smiles because a part of him still believes they'll never kill him. He thinks he'll live forever, and if that's true then there's no way I can hope to stop him.'

I shook my head. 'You hate him so much you don't care whom your treachery hurts or how many innocent men you destroy. Twice now I might have been killed, because of you.'

She blanched, but only for an instant. 'No man who helps my father is innocent,' she said dully. Tiro's embrace began to loosen.

'And any man is worthy of your body if he can be of use to you?'

'Yes! Yes, and I have no shame for it! My father has every right to me, so the law says. I'm just a girl, I'm nothing, I'm the dirt beneath his fingernails, hardly better than a slave. What weapons do I have? What can I use to protect Minora? Only my body. Only my wits. So I use them.'

'Even if your treachery means my death?'

'Yes! If that's the price — if others have to die.'
She began to cry again, realizing what she had said.
'Though I never thought, I never knew. It's only
him I hate.'

'And whom do you love, Roscia Majora?'

She struggled to quiet her weeping. 'Minora,'
she whispered.

'And no one else?'

'No one.'

'What about the boy in Ameria, Lucius Megarus?'

'How do you know about him?'

'And Lucius's father, the good farmer Titus, your
father's best friend in the world?'

'That's a lie,' she snapped. 'Nothing happened
with him.'

'You mean you offered yourself, and he refused
you.' I was almost as surprised as Tiro when her
silence admitted the truth. He pulled away from her
entirely. She seemed not to notice.

'Who else has known your favours, Roscia
Majora? Other slaves in Caecilia's household, in
return for spying on your father? The spy who
meets you here, this creature of the enemy, what
about him? What happens after you give him the
information he wants?'

'Don't be stupid,' she said dully. She was no
longer weeping now, but sullen.

I sighed. 'Tiro means nothing to you, does he?'

'Nothing,' she said.

'He was only a tool that you used?'

She looked into my eyes. 'Yes,' she said. 'Nothing

346

more than that. A slave. A foolish boy. A tool.' She began to look at him, then turned away.

'Please—' Tiro began.

'Yes,' I said. 'You can go now, Tiro. We'll both go. There's nothing more to say.'

He did not attempt to touch her again, nor did he look at her. We stepped between the tangled leaves until we emerged into the slanting rays of the afternoon sun. Tiro shook his head, kicking at the dirt. 'Gordianus, forgive me,' he began, but I cut him short.

'Not now, Tiro,' I said, as gently as I could. 'Our little tryst is not quite over. I suspect we are being watched even now – no, don't look over your shoulder; look straight ahead and notice nothing. Every afternoon, she said. She would not have seen the man before your visit; she will see him after. He's only waiting for us to leave. Follow me to that willow tree that stands at the corner of Caecilia's house. If we stand behind it, I think we shall be able to watch the approach to Roscia's hiding place unobserved.'

We did not have long to wait. Only moments later a man in a black tunic stole across the open street and disappeared into the green defile. I motioned for Tiro to follow. We hurried back and made our way into the greenery until I began to hear their voices. I motioned for Tiro to stop. I strained my ears but caught only a few words before I glimpsed Roscia in a break between the yew trees. As luck would have it she saw me as well. For an instant I thought she would be silen⸍

347

but she was loyal to her father's enemies to the end.

'Go!' she shouted. 'Run! They've come back!'

There was a sound of crashing foliage as the man blundered towards us.

'No!' she screamed. 'Go the other way.' But the man was too panic-stricken to hear. He crashed headlong into my arms, butting his head against mine and knocking me to the ground. An instant later he was on his feet again, knocking Tiro aside. Tiro ran after him, but the pursuit was useless. I followed and met him in the open street, returning with a defeated look on his face and streaming sweat. He was holding his forearm, where a thorn on one of the rose bushes had scratched him.

'I tried, Gordianus, but I couldn't catch him.'

'Good; if you had you'd probably have got a knife in your ribs. It makes no difference. I got a close enough look at his face.'

'Yes?'

'A familiar face in the Subura, and in the Forum for that matter. A hireling of Gaius Erucius the prosecutor. I thought as much. Erucius stops at nothing to obtain his evidence.'

We made our way wearily down the slope of the Palatine, and though the way was downhill it nevertheless seemed long and hard. For interrogating the girl so harshly I felt a deep and bitter shame, but I had done it for Tiro's sake. He had loved her before; the revelation of her suffering made him love her even more – I had seen it blossom before my eyes. Such a hopeless passion could only bring him unending pain and regret. Only her own rejection could set him free, and so I had striven to stir up all her bitterness for him to see. But now I began to wonder if Roscia had conspired with me for Tiro's sake, for the final look she had given me before she spoke had told me she understood, and when she spoke of Tiro with such naked scorn it may have been the truth, or it may have been the last gift of tenderness she could give him.

XXIV

We returned to the house on the Capitoline to find Rufus gone. Cicero was resting, but had left word that I should be shown to him at once. While Tiro quietly busied himself in the study, Old Tiro, the doorkeeper, led me deeper into the house, into a region I had not seen before.

Cicero's bedchamber was as austere as the one he had given me. The only concession to luxury was the small private garden which opened onto the room, in which a tiny fountain sparkled and wept, reflecting in gentle waves the pensive face of the Minerva which stood over it. Cicero's idea of rest was apparently to work lying down rather than standing up. I found him lying flat on his back, poring over a sheaf of parchment in his hands. More bits of parchment lay scattered about the floor.

I told him in cold, simple language the facts of Roscia's treachery − her father's abuse, her bitterness, Gaius Erucius's wiliness in turning the girl's desperation to his own advantage. The news seemed to have no effect on Cicero at all. He asked a few questions for clarification, nodded to show that he understood, then resumed reading with a curt wave of dismissal.

I stood over him, puzzled and uncertain, wondering if the revelation of Roscius's character could have no effect on him at all. 'It means nothing to you?' I finally said.

'What?' He wrinkled his brow in irritation, but did not look up.

'Parricide or not, what kind of man is this Sextus Roscius?'

Cicero lowered the parchment to his chest and met my gaze for a long moment before he spoke. 'Gordianus, listen to me carefully. At this moment I have no interest in weighing the character of Sextus Roscius, or in assessing his moral peccadillos. The information you've brought me yields nothing that might be of help to me in my preparations; I have no use for it. I have no time for it – no time for anything that distracts from the simple, closed circle of logic I'm striving so earnestly to build in Sextus Roscius's defence. Your duty, Gordianus, is to help me build that edifice, not to go kicking at its foundation or pulling out bricks I've already mortared in place. Do you understand?'

He didn't bother to see whether I nodded or not. With a sigh and a wave he dismissed me and went back to studying his notes.

★ ★ ★

351

I found Bethesda in my bedchamber. She was busy staining her nails with a new henna compound she had discovered at a market near the Circus Flaminius, where she had spent most of the day strolling and gossiping. She was just finishing her big toe. She sat leaning forwards with her leg bent so that her gown folded back to bare her thigh. She smiled and wiggled her toes like a child.

I stepped close to her and stroked her hair with the back of my hand. She narrowed her eyes and raised her cheek, brushing the soft, smooth skin against my knuckles. I felt like an animal suddenly, weary of thoughts and craving only to sink into the body's sensations.

Instead I found myself beset by confusion. The image of Roscia kept flitting at the edges of my mind, inflaming me, making my face burn with a heat that was neither purely lust nor shame but both mixed together. I ran my hand over Bethesda's flesh, closed my eyes and saw the girl's naked, quivering body locked between the wall and Tiro's thrusting flanks. I put my lips to Bethesda's ear; she sighed and I shuddered because I imagined I heard her whisper the little girl's name, 'Minora, Minora.' Surely I had seen the child when I first interviewed Sextus Roscius, but I couldn't remember her face at all. I could only see Roscia's face contorted with anguish while I interrogated her, the same look she had worn when Tiro had his way with her.

Lust, shame; ecstasy, anguish; all things were one thing, and even my own body was no longer distinct as it melted into Bethesda's. She clamped

352

her cool thighs around my sex and squeezed, laughing softly. I remembered young Lucius on the road to Ameria, smirking and blushing; I pictured Roscia, her thighs still wet with Lucius's seed, offering herself to the boy's father. How had Titus Megarus refused her – with a sigh of regret, a shudder of loathing, a hard fatherly slap across her face? I saw the brutal, farm-hardened hands of Sextus Roscius slithering between the girl's cool thighs, his calluses rasping against her sleek flesh. I shut my eyes tight and saw his eyes staring back at me as hot as coals. Bethesda embraced me and cooed in my ear and asked why I shivered.

When the crisis came I pulled myself from her and spent myself between her legs, flooding the sheets already crumpled and moist from the steam of our bodies. A great void opened and then winked shut. My head lay between her breasts, which gently heaved like the deck of a ship far at sea. Slowly, slowly she withdrew her henna-stained nails from my back, like a cat retracting its claws. Above the sound of her heartbeat in my ear I heard a thin voice from the garden:

'Nature and the gods demand absolute obedience to the father. Wise men declare, to their credit, that even a mere facial gesture can be a breach of duty . . . no, no, I've been over that part enough. Where is it, the section where I . . . Tiro, come and help me! Ah, here: But let us now turn to the part played by this Chrysogonus – hardly born golden, as his foreign name suggests, but born rather of the basest metal, disguised and cheaply gilded by his own insidious efforts, like a tin vessel plated with pilfered gold. . . .'

The party at Chrysogonus's mansion did not begin until after sunset. By that time Cicero had already eaten and changed into his nightclothes. Most of the slaves were asleep, and the house was darkened except for the rooms where Cicero would work on his oration before retiring to bed. At my urging he had begrudgingly stationed some of his sturdier slaves to keep watch from the roof and to guard the foyer. It seemed unlikely that our enemies would dare to strike at Cicero directly, but they had already shown themselves capable of terror and bloodshed beyond my expectations.

I had originally thought that Tiro and I might accompany Rufus in the guise of his slaves, but that seemed out of the question now; there was every reason to think that someone among the guests might recognize one or both of us. Instead, Rufus was to attend the party on his own, leaving from his family's house and arriving with his own retinue. Tiro and I would wait in the shadows outside.

The house of Chrysogonus was only a short walk from Caecilia's mansion and very near Tiro's trysting place with Roscia. In the dying light I saw him glance furtively into the dense shadows as we passed, as if she might still be waiting for him there. He slowed his pace until he stopped entirely, staring into the darkness. I allowed it for a moment, then tugged at his sleeve. He gave a start, looked at me dumbly, then quickly followed.

The entrance to Chrysogonus's mansion was alive with sound and light. Torches surrounded the portico, some placed in sconces, others held by slaves. A group of slaves playing lyres, cymbals, and flutes stood nearby as a constant stream of guests arrived. Most of them were carried in litters by slaves left gasping from the climb up the hill. Some who lived on the Palatine were modest enough to come on foot, surrounded by hosts of fawning, superfluous attendants and slaves.

Litter bearers, having delivered their masters, were sent trotting around the corner to the back of the house. Attendant slaves were dispersed to whatever place slaves are sent to congregate and wait while their masters are entertained. The evening was warm; many of the guests lingered on the threshold to listen to the players. Their music seemed to float in the twilight sweeter than bird song. Chrysogonus could afford to purchase the best.

'Out of our way!' The voice was familiar and came from behind us. Tiro and I leaped aside as a lumbering litter swept by. It was an open sedan carried by ten slaves. The passengers were none other than Rufus chaperoned by his half-brother, Hortensius. It was Rufus who had called out; he seemed to be having a fine time, laughing and flashing a conspiratorial grin at us as he passed. From the flush in the cheeks I suspected he had already been drinking to fortify himself for the evening.

Hortensius, luckily, was looking the other way and did not see us. If he had, he would certainly have recognized me. I suddenly realized how conspicuous we were and pulled Tiro into the deep shadow beneath the overhanging branches of a fig tree. There we waited for some time, watching the revellers and their retinues arrive and disappear within the house. Chrysogonus, if he was greeting his guests in person, was doing so within the foyer; no handsome blond demigod showed himself on the steps.

At last the rush of guests slowed and dwindled until it seemed that everyone must have arrived, and yet the torch-bearers remained stiffly in place and the musicians continued to play. The scene became uncanny and slightly unreal and then eerie: on a deserted street bathed by moonlight, unattended slaves in opulent clothing made light and music for an invisible audience. The guest of honour had not yet arrived.

At last I heard the tramp of many feet. I looked back, to the way we had come, and saw a box of yellow gauze approaching in the darkness, bright and fluttering as if it were borne on invisible waves. It seemed to float without any means of propulsion or support, and for one brief moment the illusion was absolutely convincing, as if all had been contrived to fool my eyes at that very instant.

Then waves of motion took shape about the yellow box. For a confused moment the waves were only that, suggestions of something still unseen; then they abruptly became flesh. The litter bearers, to a man, were Nubians. Their skin was absolutely black and they were dressed in black loincloths and black sandals. In shadow they were very nearly invisible; when they stepped beneath the rising moon they seemed to swallow the light, giving back only a dull gleam to mark the width of their massive shoulders. There were twelve of them in all, six on either side, far more than needed to carry a private box with a single occupant. The strength of their numbers allowed them to move with uncanny smoothness. Behind them came a large retinue of slaves, attendants, secretaries, body-guards, and hangers-on. It might be true, as Rufus claimed, that Sulla had taken to crossing the Forum alone in broad daylight, but at night he still moved through the streets with all the pomp and precaution requisite to a dictator of the Republic.

At last Chrysogonus showed himself. As the retinue approached, one of the torchbearers on the portico dashed into the house. A moment later Chrysogonus, dressed all in yellow and gold, stepped out onto the portico. Somehow, in my various dealings, I had never seen him before, only heard of his reputation. He was indeed quite strikingly handsome, tall and strongly built, with golden hair, a broad jaw, and glittering blue eyes. In the wavering torchlight I read the shifting mask of his face: anxious and uncertain at first, like any host awaiting a tardy guest of honour, then suddenly harsh and intense, as if mustering his strength, and then suffused with a charm so abrupt and overpowering that it was difficult to imagine any other expression on his face. He made a slight motion with one hand. The musicians, whose playing had flagged, abruptly played louder and with more spirit.

The litter arrived and came to a halt. The Nubians lowered their burden. A man-at-arms cast back the yellow gauze that shielded the occupant of the box. Sulla arose, smiling, corpulent, his ruddy face shining in the torchlight. He wore an elaborate robe of Asiatic design, an affectation he had acquired during his campaigns against Mithridates; it was in shades of green embroidered with silver. His hair, once as fair as Chrysogonus's, was thick and faded, a pale yellow like millet porridge.

Chrysogonus stepped forwards to greet him, bowing slightly. They embraced. They spoke briefly, laughing and smiling. They put their arms around each other's shoulders and disappeared into the house.

The litter bearers were dismissed. The retinue, casually sorting themselves into ranks of importance, followed their master into the house. The musicians, still playing, followed them. The torch-bearers followed last, leaving behind two of their number to flank the door and cast a diminished light of welcome for any late arrivals. From within came a muted sound of clapping and cheering. The soul of the party had arrived.

Two days before, Rufus had shown me the exterior of Chrysogonus's mansion, pointing out each entrance and explaining as best he could remember the placement of the rooms within. On the north-ward side, around the corner from the portico and shielded by a stand of cypress trees from the grounds in the rear, there was a small wooden door recessed in the wall. It led, so Rufus thought, into a pantry adjoining the vast kitchens at the back of the house. We were to wait there until Rufus came, unless he managed on his own to find the slaves of Sextus Roscius, Felix and Chrestus, in which case he would send them to us. Darkness hid us from the street. The cypress trees concealed us from the litter bearers who idled in the open space between the house and the stables. The house itself had no windows at all on the northern side, only a deserted, unlit balcony on the upper storey.

I was afraid that Tiro would become agitated, unused as he was to sitting idle in the dark, but he seemed quite content to lean against the bole of a tree and stare into the night. He had said almost nothing to me since our tryst with Roscia. He was wounded more deeply than he showed. Occasionally he glanced at me and then quickly away, his dark eyes flashing.

It seemed that we waited a very long time. Music from within mingled with the sound of crickets, and at some point I heard voices declaiming, interrupted at regular intervals by bursts of laughter and applause. Finally the door flew open. I stiffened against the tree, ready to run, but it was only a slave girl lugging a pail of dirty water. She blindly flung it into the darkness, then spun around and slammed the door behind her. Tiro brushed his legs where the farthest-flung drops had spattered the hem of his tunic. I reached into my sleeve and felt the handle of my knife – the same knife the mute son of Polia had given me on the street of the House of Swans long ago, it seemed, and far away.

I was almost dozing when the door at last opened again. I clutched the knife and sat upright. The door creaked quietly on its hinges, swinging open with such conspicuous stealth that I knew it must be either Rufus or else assassins come to murder us.

'Gordianus?' A voice whispered.

'Step outside, Rufus. Close the door behind you.'

He closed it with the same exaggerated stealth and then stood blinking like a mole, unable yet to see in the darkness despite the bright moon.

'Have you found them yet?' I asked.

'They're in the house, yes. Or at least there are two slaves called Felix and Chrestus, both new to the household; so one of the serving girls tells me. But I've seen nothing of them. They don't serve guests. They have no contact with anyone outside the household. Chrysogonus uses them as personal drudges. The girl says they almost never leave the upper floors.'

'Perhaps she can take them a message.'

'I already asked. Useless, she says. Chrysogonus would be furious if they came down during the party. But she's willing to take you to them.'

'Where is this girl?'

'Waiting for me, in the pantry. She found an excuse to come and fetch something.'

'Or she might be running to Chrysogonus this very moment.'

Rufus looked worriedly at the door, then shook his head. 'I don't think so.'

'Why not?'

'You know how it is. You can tell when a slave is willing to do some dirty business behind her master's back. I don't think she cares for Master Golden-Born very much. You know what they say, slaves hate working for a freedman – it's a former slave who makes the cruellest master.'

I looked at the door, thinking how easily death could lurk behind it. I took a deep breath, then decided to trust Rufus's judgment. 'Lead the way.'

He nodded and stealthily opened the door. The lintel was so low I had to stoop. Tiro followed behind me. There was no reason for him to come, and I had meant to leave him outside, but when I looked over my shoulder I saw a look of such determination on his face that I acquiesced. With a faint creaking he closed the door behind us.

The girl was young and pretty with long black hair and creamy skin that glowed like honey in the soft light from the lamp in her hand. Had she been a courtesan, her looks would have been unremarkable; for a mere serving girl, her beauty seemed absurdly extravagant. Chrysogonus was famous for surrounding himself with pretty decorations and toys.

'These are the men,' Rufus explained. 'Can you take them upstairs quietly, so no one will notice?'

The girl nodded and smiled, as if he were foolish even to ask. Then her lips parted, she made a tiny gasp and spun around. The door behind her had begun to open.

The room was low and narrow, lined with shelves and crammed with bottles, urns, bowls, and sacks. Garlics hung from the ceiling, and the musty odour of flour was heavy in the air. I backed into one corner as deeply as I could, pushing Tiro behind me. At the same instant Rufus slid one arm around the girl's waist and pulled her close, pressing his mouth over hers.

The door opened. Rufus kissed the girl a moment longer and then they drew apart.

The man in the doorway was tall and broad, so large he almost filled the frame. Lit from behind, his hair made a shimmering golden halo around his darkened face. He chuckled softly and stepped closer. The girl's lamp, quivering in her hand, lit his face from below. I saw the blue of his eyes and the dimple in his broad jaw, the high cheekbones and the smooth, serene brow. He was only paces away and could surely have seen me between the clay pots and urns had it not been for the darkness. I realized the girl was intentionally blocking the light with her body, blinding him with the lamp and casting us into deeper shadow.

'Rufus,' he said at last, ending with a lingering hiss, as if it were not a name but a sigh. He said it again, slurring it and placing a strange accent on the vowels. His voice was deep and resonant, playful, showy, as intimate as a touch. 'Sulla is asking for you. Sorex is about to dance. A meditation on the death of Dido – have you seen it? Sulla would hate for you to miss it.'

There was a long pause. I imagined I could see the backs of Rufus's ears turn red, but perhaps it was only the lamplight shining through.

'Of course, if you're busy, I'll tell Sulla that you've gone out for a walk.' Chrysogonus spoke slowly, like a man with no reason to hurry. He turned his attention to the girl. He ran his eyes over her body and reached for her. He touched her; where, I couldn't see. She stiffened and gasped and the lamp shook in her hand. Tiro gave a jerk behind me. I blindly laid my hand over his and squeezed it hard.

Chrysogonus took the lamp from the girl's hand and set it on a shelf. He loosened her gown where it was clasped at her throat and slid it over her shoulders. It fluttered down her body like doves descending until she stood naked. Chrysogonus stepped back, pursing his broad, fleshy lips and looking from Rufus to the girl with a heavy-lidded stare. He laughed softly. 'If you want her, young Messalla, of course you can have her. I deny my guests nothing. Whatever pleasure you can find in my house is yours without asking. But you needn't do it like a schoolboy, cowering here in the pantry. There are plenty of comfortable rooms upstairs. Have the girl take you there. Parade her through the house naked if you want – ride her like a pony! It won't be the first time.' He touched her again, his arm moving as if he were tracing a mark across her naked breasts. The girl gasped and quivered, but stood absolutely still.

He turned and seemed about to go, then turned back. 'But don't take too long. Sulla will forgive me if you miss the dance, but later on Metrobius will be introducing a new song by . . . ah, well, by some sycophant or other – who can remember all their names? The poor fool's here tonight, trying to curry favour. I understand the song is a homage to the gods for sending a man to stop the civil strife: "Sulla, Rome's favourite, saviour of the Republic," I think it begins. I'm sure it goes on in the same nauseatingly pious vein – except. . . .' Chrysogonus smiled and laughed behind pursed lips, a low, gravelly laugh that he seemed to keep to himself, like a man rolling coins in his hand. 'Except that Metrobius tells me he's taken the liberty of adding a few ribald verses of his own; scandalous enough to get the young author's head chopped off. Imagine the look on the silly poet's face when he hears his homage turned into insults right in front of Sulla, who of course will grasp the jest at once and play along, stamping his feet and pretending to be outraged – just the sort of joke Sulla adores. It will be the evening's high point, Rufus; for some of us, anyway. Sulla will be very disappointed if you're not there to share it.' He made an insinuating smile, stared at them for a long moment, then retreated and shut the door behind him.

No one moved. I watched the flickering caress of the lamplight as it licked in silhouette about the sleek flesh of the girl's thighs and hips. Finally she stooped and gathered up her gown. Tiro, wide-eyed and resolute, pushed his way from behind me and helped her cover herself. Rufus studiously looked elsewhere.

'Well,' I finally said, 'I believe the master of the house himself has given us permission to go snooping upstairs. Shall we?'

XXV

The door through which Chrysogonus had vanished led into a short hallway. A narrow passage on the left opened onto the noise of a busy kitchen. The curtain which draped the opening on the right still swayed from Chrysogonus's passing. The girl led us through neither passage but instead to a door, at the end of the hall, that opened onto a winding flight of stone steps.

'There's another staircase in the room where the master entertains,' she whispered, 'very showy, very fine marble, with a statue of Venus in the centre. But this is the stair the slaves use. If we pass anyone, just ignore them, even if they look at us oddly. Or better yet, give me a pinch hard enough to make me squeal and pretend you're all drunk. They'll think the worst for sure, and then they'll leave us alone.'

But we met no one on the stairs, and the upstairs

hall was deserted. From somewhere below we could hear the muffled music of flutes and lyres, and an occasional burst of applause or laughter – presumably in appreciation of Sorex's dance – but the upper floor was dim and quiet. The hallway was quite broad and fabulously decorated, opening onto wide, high rooms even more sumptuously appointed. Every surface seemed to be carpeted, draped, inlaid, or painted. Everywhere the eye turned there was a riot of colours, textures, and shapes.

'Vulgar, isn't it?' said Rufus with a noble's disdain. Cicero would have agreed, but the furnishings were vulgar only for being so cramped and ostentatiously displayed. What impressed me most was the consistency of Chrysogonus's taste in acquiring only the best and most expensive handicraft and artwork – embossed silver, vessels of Delian and Corinthian bronze, embroidered coverlets, plush carpets from the East, finely carved tables and chairs with inlays of shell and lapis, intricate mosaics of richly coloured tiles, superb marble statues and fabulous paintings. That all these creations had been looted from the proscribed there could be no doubt; otherwise it would have taken a lifetime to accumulate so many things of such high quality and disparate origin. Yet no one could say that Chrysogonus had looted blindly. Let others take the chaff; for himself he had chosen only the best, with the trained eye for quality developed by slaves of the rich who dream of someday being free and rich themselves. I was glad that Cicero was not with us; to see Sulla's former slave living in stolen luxury on such a grandiose scale might have agitated his delicate bowels beyond endurance.

The hallway narrowed. The rooms became less resplendent. The girl lifted a heavy hanging, allowing us to pass beneath; she dropped it, and all sound from downstairs vanished. The world changed as well, and we were abruptly back in a house of plain plastered walls and smoke-stained ceilings. These were the rooms of necessity – storage chambers, slave quarters, work rooms – yet even here the booty was piled high. Crates of bronze vessels were stacked in the corners, rolled carpets drooped like sleepy watchmen against the walls, chairs and tables were wrapped in heavy cloth and piled to the ceiling.

The girl stole through the maze, glanced furtively about her, then motioned for us to follow. She drew back a curtain.

'What are you doing up here?' asked a petulant voice. 'Isn't there a party on tonight?'

'Oh, leave her alone,' said another, speaking through a mouthful of food. 'Just because Aufilia brings me extra portions and turns her nose up at your ugly face . . . but who's this?'

'No,' I said, 'don't get up. Stay where you are. Finish your meal.'

The two of them sat on the hard floor, eating cabbage and barley from cracked clay bowls by the light of a single lamp. The room was small and narrow with bare walls; the tiny flame carved their wrinkles into caverns and cast their stooped

367

shadows all the way to the ceiling. I stayed in the doorway. Tiro moved in close behind me, peering over my shoulder. Rufus hung behind.

The lean, petulant one snorted and scowled at his food. 'For what you want, Aufilia, this room's too small. Can't you find an empty room elsewhere with a couch big enough for the three of you?'

'Felix!' the other hissed, prodding his companion with his pudgy elbow and gesturing with the other. Felix glanced up and blanched as he noticed the ring on my finger. He had thought the three of us were all slaves, looking for a place to have a party of our own.

'Forgive me, Citizen,' he whispered, bowing his head. They fell silent, waiting for me to speak. Before, they had been human beings, one of them lean and irritable, the other fat and good-natured, their faces alive in the warm glow as they fed themselves and parried with the girl. In an instant I saw them turn grey and indistinguishable, wearing the identical blank face worn by every slave of every harsh master who ever breathed in Rome.

'Look at me,' I said. 'Look at me! And if you aren't going to finish eating, then put down your bowls and stand up, so that I can see you eye to eye. We don't have much time.'

'The knife was out before you could see it,' Felix was saying. 'In a flash.'

'Yes, literally in a flash!' Chrestus stood beside him, nervously rubbing his pudgy hands, looking from his friend's face to mine and back again.

368

Once I had explained who I was and what I wanted, they were amazingly willing, even eager, to speak to me. Tiro stood quietly beside me, his face pensive in the lamplight. I had posted Rufus at the nearest chamber along the main hallway so that he might turn back any wandering guests. I sent the girl with him; she was his excuse for loitering upstairs, and besides that, there was no reason to involve her any deeper, or to trust her with the full truth of what we had come for.

'We never had a chance to help the master. They threw us out of the way, onto the ground,' said Felix. 'Strong men, as big as horses.'

'And stinking of garlic,' Chrestus added. 'They'd have killed us, too, if Magnus hadn't stopped them.'

'Then you're sure it was Magnus?' I said.

'Oh, yes.' Felix shuddered. 'I didn't see his face, he was careful about that. But I heard his voice.'

'And the master called his name, remember, just before Magnus stabbed him the first time,' said Chrestus. ' "Magnus, Magnus, curse you!" in a thin little voice. I still hear it in my dreams.'

Felix pursed his thin lips. 'Ah, yes, you're right. I'd forgotten that.'

'And the other two assassins?' I asked.

They shrugged in unison. 'One of them might have been Mallius Glaucia, though I can't be certain,' said Felix. 'The other man had a beard, I remember.'

'A red beard?'

'Perhaps. Hard to tell in that light. Even bigger than Glaucia and he stank of garlic.'

'Redbeard,' I muttered. 'And how was it that Magnus stopped them from killing you?'

'He forbade it. "Stop, you fools!"' growled Chrestus, as if playing a role. ' "They're valuable slaves. Damage either one and it comes out of your wages!" Valuable, he called us – and look where we end up, oiling sandals and burnishing Master Golden-Born's chamber pots.'

'But of value nonetheless,' I said. 'As if Magnus planned to inherit you himself.'

'Oh, yes.' Felix nodded. 'That must have been part of the plan all along, that he and Capito would somehow get their hands on the master's goods. Who can imagine how they did it? And now we end up back in the city, except that we never see the city. The Golden One keeps us trapped in these stuffy rooms day and night. You'd think we were being punished. Or hidden away, the same as he hides half his loot away. What kind of coincidence is it, I ask you, that I can look around these very rooms and see so many things that came directly from the master's old house by the Circus? Those chairs you saw stacked out there, and the yellow vase in the hallway, and the Alexandrian tapestry rolled up there in the corner – they all belonged to the master before he was murdered. No, we're not the only property that ended up in Chrysogonus's hands.'

Chrestus nodded in agreement.

'The night of the murder,' I said, trying to draw them back. 'You were thrown aside, saved by a word from Magnus, and then you disappeared.

370

Vanished into the night without a shout or a scream for help – don't deny it, I have a witness who swears to it.'

Felix shook his head. 'I don't know what sort of witness you may have, but we didn't run away, not exactly. We ran down the street a way and then stopped. Chrestus would have kept running, but I held him back.'

Chrestus looked crestfallen. 'That's true,' he said.

'We stood in the dark and watched them do it. What a fine man he was! What a fine Roman! A slave couldn't ask for a better master. Never once in thirty years did he beat me, never once! How many slaves can say that?'

'A terrible sight!' Chrestus sighed, his fleshy shoulders shivering. 'I shall never forget how his body quaked while they plunged the daggers into him. How the blood spurted into the air like a fountain. I thought right then that I should run back and throw myself on the street beside him and tell them, "Take my life as well!" I as much as said so, didn't I, Felix?'

'Well . . .'

'Don't you remember? I said to you, "Now our lives are as good as over. Things will never be the same." Didn't I? And wasn't I right?' He began to weep softly.

Felix made a face and touched his friend's arm to comfort him, shrugging at me as if his own tenderness embarrassed him. 'That's true. I remember your saying that. Ah, it was a terrible thing, to see it done from start to finish. When it was over, when we knew the master was dead beyond all hope, we finally turned and ran all the way home. We sent a litter for his body, and the next morning I dispatched a messenger to Ameria.'

Suddenly he drew his eyebrows together. 'What is it?' I asked.

'Only something I just now remembered. Something strange. Strange then, and even stranger now that I recall it. When they were done – when there could be no doubt that the poor master was dead – the bearded one started to cut his head off.'

'What?'

'Grabbed him by the hair and pulled his head back sharp, then started slicing with a very long, very big blade. Like a butcher who'd spent a lifetime doing it. Magnus didn't see when he started, he was looking up at the windows, I think. But when he looked back, he shouted, told the man to stop it right away! Pushed him back and slapped him square across the face. Had to reach up high to do it.'

'Slapped Redbeard in the middle of cutting a man's head off? I think that may be too stupid for me to believe.'

Felix shook his head. 'You don't know Magnus if you think that would stop him. When he loses his temper he'd slap Pluto himself and spit in his eye. His hired friend knew him well enough that he didn't dare slap him back. But why do you think the man did that? Started to cut off the master's head, I mean?'

'Habit,' I said. 'It's what they did in the

proscriptions, isn't it? Cut off the head as proof to claim the state's reward. Redbeard was a professional, so used to cutting off the head as bounty that he automatically began to do the same to Sextus Roscius.'

'But why did Magnus stop him? What did he care?' It was Tiro, looking strangely wise in the lamplight. 'That was the story that they put out, wasn't it, that Sextus Roscius was proscribed? So why not have the head cut off?'

All three of them stared at me. 'Because – I don't know. Because Magnus wanted it to look like a murder, not a proscription? Wanted it to look as if it were done by thieves instead of assassins? Yes, because at that point they hadn't yet decided to use the false proscription story, nor were they yet planning to accuse Roscius *filius* of parricide. . . .' The words seemed to make sense as I uttered them, and for an instant I thought I glimpsed the truth. Then it flickered and vanished, just as if one of us had blown out the lamp with a puff of air. I shook my head. 'I don't know.'

'I don't understand the point of these questions, anyway,' Tiro said glumly. 'We knew all this before, from the mute boy.'

'Little Eco is hardly a competent witness. And his mother would never testify.'

'But what about Felix or Chrestus? Neither of them could give evidence, unless –' Tiro shut his mouth.

'Unless what?' Chrestus, ignorant of the law, actually looked hopeful. Until I had told them, they hadn't even known about the trial of Sextus Roscius. The novel idea of giving evidence to a court seemed to charm Chrestus. Tiro, the slave of an advocate, knew better.

'Unless,' I said, 'your new master allows it. And I think we all know that Chrysogonus will never allow it, so that is the end of that,' I said, knowing that it was hardly the end at all. In the morning I would ask Rufus to arrange for the court to send a formal request to Chrysogonus, asking that his slaves give evidence. It would be his right to refuse, but how would that refusal look? Cicero might just be able to pressure the man into allowing the court to question Felix and Chrestus. After all, they had never actually seen the killers' faces, and Chrysogonus might not realize how much they knew. And what excuse could Chrysogonus have to refuse evidence to the court, except to conceal his own complicity?

What if he did submit and handed them over? Roman law in its wisdom demanded that any slave giving evidence must be subjected to torture. Evidence given freely by a slave was inadmissible; only torture was an acceptable seal of good faith. How would it be done? I imagined the corpulent Chrestus hanging naked from chains, his buttocks seared by hot irons; gaunt, brittle Felix bound to a chair with his hand in a vice.

'And afterwards,' I said, to change the subject, 'you went to serve your master's son in Ameria?'

'Not immediately,' Felix explained. 'And we never served young Sextus Roscius. We stayed on at the house near the Circus Flaminius, managing things, taking care of outstanding affairs, helping the steward. We didn't go to Ameria, not even to assist the master's funeral rites. And then one day Magnus appeared at the door, claiming the house was his and so were we. It was all there in the papers he carried; what could we do?'

'That was when the cold weather began,' Chrestus said, 'but you'd think it was high summer, the way Magnus carried on. Oh, the old master lived well and enjoyed himself, make no mistake, but he knew that every vice has its place – drinking bouts belong in the tavern, pederasty in the baths, whoring in the brothel, not in the home, and every party has a beginning and an end. But with Magnus there was one vast, continual orgy interrupted by occasional brawls. The place stank of gladiators and gangs, and on some nights he even charged admission. It was harrowing, the people who passed in and out of that house desecrating the master's memory.'

'And then came the fire,' said Felix sourly. 'Well, what can you expect in a house so given over to drunkenness and neglect? It started in the kitchen and then leaped onto the roof. Magnus was so drunk he could hardly stand; he kept laughing at the flames – I actually saw him fall down from laughing. Which is not to say he was friendly. He kept making us go back into the house to bring out the valuables, threatening to beat us if we shrank back. Two of the slaves died that way, trapped inside when Magnus sent them to fetch his favourite slippers. That tells you how afraid of him we all were, that we were willing to face the flames rather than his wrath. I suppose living under Sextus Roscius had spoiled us all.'

'Next thing you know,' Chrestus said, edging forwards, 'we're loaded onto carts and trundled up to Ameria, the middle of nowhere, and we end up in the big house having to serve Capito and that wife of his. Out of the fire and into the flood, as they say. You could hardly sleep at night for the sound of them screaming at each other. The woman is mad, I tell you. Not eccentric – Caecilia Metella is eccentric – but stark, raving mad. In the middle of the night I'd find myself summoned to her room and told to count the number of hairs in her hairbrush, and then to separate the grey hairs from the black ones. She wanted an account book kept of every hair she lost! And no time would do for it except the middle of the night, while Capito was asleep in his own room and she sat before her mirror staring at her face. I thought she'd have me counting her wrinkles next.'

He paused for breath, and I thought he was done, but he had only started. 'And strangest of all, young Sextus Roscius kept appearing, the master's son. I'd thought he must be dead as well, or else we'd have ended up his slaves; but then I thought maybe he'd sold us and the land for some reason. But that hardly seemed right either, with him living practically like a prisoner or a pauper in a little cramped house on the estate. That was when we finally heard rumours about the proscription story from the other slaves, which made no sense at all. It seemed to me that the world had gone as crazy as Capito's wife.

'And strangest of all was the way Sextus Roscius would act. Now the man hardly knew us, granted, for he never spent more than moments in his father's house on the few occasions he came to Rome, and after all, we weren't his slaves. But you'd think he might have found some way to draw us aside, just as you've done, to ask about his father's death. We were there when it happened, after all; he must have known that. But whenever he saw us he looked the other way. If he was waiting to see Capito – come to beg him for money, usually – and one of us had some reason to be in the foyer, he'd wait outside instead, even in the cold. As if he were afraid of us! I began to think maybe they'd told him we'd been accomplices in his father's murder, as if anyone could believe such a thing about two harmless slaves!'

Again something like the truth flickered in the room, like a pale light beside the lamplight, too weak to cast shadows. I shook my head, confused. I felt a hand on my shoulder and gave a start.

'Gordianus!' It was Rufus, without the girl. Chrestus and Felix shrank back. 'Gordianus, I'm going to have to go back to the party. I've already sent the girl ahead. Chrysogonus sent a slave to look for us; Metrobius is about to sing. If I'm not there it will only attract their attention.'

'Yes, very well,' I said. 'Go on.'

'You'll be able to find your way out?'

'Of course.'

He looked around the room, uncomfortable amid the tawdry surroundings of the slave quarters. The role of spy didn't suit him; he was more at home playing the honest young noble in the sunlight of the open Forum. 'Are you almost done? I think you should try to leave as quickly as you can. Once Metrobius is finished, the entertainment will be over and there'll be all sorts of strange people wandering about the house. You won't be safe here.'

'We'll hurry,' I said, squeezing his shoulder and pushing him towards the doorway. 'Besides,' I said in a low voice, 'it can't have been so very awful, entertaining Aufilia for an hour.'

He twisted the corner of his mouth and shrugged my hand away.

'But I saw how you kissed her in the pantry.'

He spun around and glared at me, then looked askance at the others in the room and stepped back until they couldn't see him. He lowered his voice so that I could barely hear. 'Don't make a joke of it, Gordianus.'

I stepped into the hallway with him. 'It's not a joke,' I said. 'I only meant—'

'I know what you meant. But don't mistake me. I didn't kiss her for pleasure. I did it because I had to. I closed my eyes and thought of Cicero.' He tensed his face and then was suddenly serene again, sedated like all lovers by the act of speaking the beloved's name. He took a breath, smiled at me oddly, then turned to go. I watched him step

378

through the curtain into the formal hallway. What I saw next made my heart skip a beat.

'So there you are, young Messalla!' The voice was golden indeed, like honey, like pearls in amber. He was striding up the hallway towards Rufus, twenty paces away. For just an instant I saw his face and he saw mine. Then the curtain fell.

I heard him through the cloth. 'Come, Rufus, Aufilia is back at work and you must return to pleasure.' He laughed a deep, throaty laugh, muscular and ripe like heavy grapes tumbling on flesh. ' "Eros makes fools of the old and slaves of the young." So says sweet Sulla, who certainly should know. But I won't have you prowling about up here looking for more conquests while old Metrobius warbles his best.'

There was no suspicion in his voice, and to my relief I heard it fade into silence as they retreated down the hallway. But I knew what I had seen when our eyes met. A slight wrinkle had appeared across his smooth and eminently golden brow, and a look of puzzlement sparked in his blue eyes as if he wondered which of his many servants I might be, and if not his slave then whose, and what I was doing upstairs during the party. If my expression in that instant was as transparent as his – if I had looked a tenth as startled and fearful as I felt – Chrysogonus would be sending bodyguards up to investigate as quickly as he could.

I stepped back into the room. 'Rufus is right. We must hurry. There's only one other thing I wanted to ask you,' I said; in fact, it was the only real reason

I had for coming. 'There was a girl, a slave, a whore – young, blonde, pretty. From the House of Swans – Elena.'

I saw by their eyes that they knew her. They exchanged a conspiratorial glance, as if deciding who should speak. Felix cleared his slender throat.

'Yes, the girl Elena. The master was very fond of her.'

'How fond?'

There was a strained silence. I stood in the doorway, imagining sounds from the hall. 'Quickly!' I said.

It was Chrestus who spoke – Chrestus, the emotional one, the one who had wept before. But his voice was quite flat and dull, as if all passion had been burned from it. 'The House of Swans – you mentioned it, so you know where she came from. That was where the master found her. From the first she was different from the rest. At least the master thought so. We were only puzzled that he left her there so long. How he hesitated, as a man might hesitate in taking a bride. As if bringing her into the house would truly change his life, and such an old man wasn't sure he wanted such a change. He had finally made up his mind to buy her, but the brothel owner was a hard bargainer; he kept stalling and changing his price. The master was growing desperate. It was because of a note from Elena that he left Caecilia Metella's party that night.'

'Did he know that she was pregnant? Did you?'

They looked at one another thoughtfully. 'We

didn't know at the time,' said Chrestus, 'but that was simple enough to figure out later.'

'Later, when she was brought to Capito's house?'

'Ah, yes, so you know that as well. Then perhaps you know what they did to her on the night she arrived. They tried to break her body. They tried to kill the child inside her, though they wouldn't resort to outright abortion – for some reason Capito thought that would offend the gods. Imagine that, from a man with so much blood on his hands! Afraid of the unborn and the ghosts of the dead, but quite happy to strangle the living.'

'And Elena?'

'They couldn't break her will. She survived. They kept her shut away from the others, the way he keeps us shut away here, but I managed to speak with her a few times, enough that I finally won a bit of her trust. She swore she'd never sent the message that brought the master out into the streets that night. I don't know if I believed her or not. And she swore the child was his.'

Something rustled across the floor behind me. I grabbed the hilt of my knife and turned, just in time to glimpse the long tail of a rat slithering between two rolled carpets stacked against the wall. 'And then the child was born,' I said. 'And then what?'

'That was the end of them both.'

'What do you mean?'

'The end of Elena. The end of the child.'

'What happened?'

'It was the night she went into her labour. Everyone in the household knew her time had

381

come. The women seemed to know without being told; the male slaves were nervous and testy. That was the same night that the steward told Felix and me that Capito was sending us back to Rome. To Magnus, we thought; he was in the city then, along with Mallius Glaucia. But the steward said no, that we were being sent to a new master altogether.

'The next morning they herded us out bright and early and loaded us into an ox cart with a few other objects that were headed for Chrysogonus's house – furniture, crates, that sort of thing. And just before we were to leave, they brought out Elena.

'She could hardly stand, she was so weak. Thin and wasted, pasty, damp with sweat – she must have given birth only hours before. There was no place for her to lie in the cart; the best we could do was to make our clothes into padding and help her sit against the crates. She was groggy and feverish, she hardly knew where she was, but she kept asking for the baby.

'Finally the midwife came running out of the house. She was breathless, weeping, hysterical. "For the gods' sake," I whispered to her, "where is the child?" She stared at Elena, afraid to speak. But Elena hardly seemed conscious; she was lying against Felix's shoulder, muttering, shivering, her eyelids flickering. "A boy," the midwife whispered, "it was a boy."

' "Yes, yes," I said, "but where is it? We'll be going any minute!" You can imagine how confused and angry I was, wondering how we would ever manage to take care of a frail mother and a newborn infant. "Dead," the midwife whispered, so low that I could barely hear. "I tried to stop him, but I couldn't – he tore the boy away from me. I followed him all the way to the quarry and watched him throw the child onto the rocks."

'Then the driver came, with Capito behind him, yelling at him to start right away. Capito was as white as chalk. Oh, how strange! I remember it all in this very instant, as if I were there now! The crack of the driver's whip. The cart beginning to roll, the house receding. Everything loose and jostling. Elena suddenly awake, whimpering for her baby, too weak to cry out. Capito staring after us, as stiff as a pillar, ashen-faced, like a column of ash! And the midwife dropping to her knees, clutching Capito about the thighs, crying, "Master, mercy!" And just as we were driving onto the road, a man came running around the corner of the house, breathing hard, then stepping back into the shade of the trees – Sextus Roscius. The last I saw or heard was the midwife clutching at Capito and crying out louder and louder, "Master, mercy!"'

He took a shuddering breath and turned his face to the wall. Felix laid his hand on Chrestus's shoulder and continued the story. 'What a journey that was! Three days – no, four – in a jolting ox cart. Enough to splinter your bones and make your jaw come unhinged. We walked as much of the way as we could, but one of us had to stay in the cart with Elena. She could eat nothing. She never slept, but she never seemed awake, either. At least we were spared from having to tell her about the baby. On the third day she started bleeding between her legs. The driver wouldn't stop until sun-down. We found a midwife who could staunch the bleeding, but Elena was as hot as a coal. The next day she died in our arms, within sight of the Fontinal Gate.'

The lamp sputtered and the room became dim. Felix calmly stooped and picked up the lamp, took it to a bench in the corner of the room, and added more oil. In the flaring light I saw Tiro staring at the two slaves, his eyes wide and moist.

'Then it was Capito who killed the child?' I said, without conviction, like an actor speaking the wrong line.

Felix stood with his hands tightly laced, his knuckles bone white. Chrestus looked up at me, blinking like a man awakened from a dream. 'Capito?' he said quietly. 'Well, I suppose. I told you, Magnus and Glaucia were far away in Rome. Who else could it have been?'

XXVI

Chrysogonus's house was large, but not sprawling after the manner of Caecilia's mansion; yet somehow, without the girl Aufilia to guide us, Tiro and I took a wrong turn in search of the slaves' stairway. After a failed attempt to trace our steps backwards, we found ourselves in a narrow gallery that opened onto the empty balcony that overlooked our hiding place by the cypress trees outside the pantry door.

From somewhere within the house rose the sound of a warbling voice – a man singing unnaturally high, or else a woman singing very low. It grew louder as I pulled Tiro closer to the inner wall. The sound seemed to come from behind a thin tapestry. I pressed my ear next to a lecherous Priapus surrounded by equally lecherous wood nymphs, and could almost make out the words.

'Quietly, Tiro,' I whispered, gesturing for him to help me lift the tapestry's bottom edge and roll it upward, revealing a narrow, horizontal slit cut through the stone wall.

The aperture was wide enough so that two could comfortably stand abreast and share the view it afforded down onto Chrysogonus and his company. The lofty room in which he entertained rose from the marble floor to the domed roof without interruption. The window through which we peered was cut at a sharp downward angle, so that no edge obscured our view – a spy hole, plain and simple.

Like everything else in Chrysogonus's house, the dinner was sumptuous and overblown. Four low tables, each surrounded by a semicircle of nine couches, were gathered around an open space at the room's centre. Cicero or even Caecilia Metella would no doubt have balked at the idea of entertaining more than eight visitors at a time – few unwritten laws of Roman manners are more unyielding than that which holds that a host should never gather more visitors at his table than he can comfortably converse with at once. Chrysogonus had gathered four times that number at four tables piled high with delicacies – olives slitted and stuffed with fish eggs, bowls of noodles flecked with the first tender asparagus sprouts of the season, figs and pears suspended in a yellow syrup, the carcasses of tiny fowl. The mingled smells rose on the warm air. My stomach growled.

Most of the guests were men; the few women among them stood out on account of their obvious voluptuousness – not wives or lovers, but courtesans.

The younger men were uniformly slender and good-looking; the older men had that indolent, well-groomed look of the very rich at play. I looked from face to face, ready to dart from the window until I realized there was not much chance that any of them would look upward. All eyes were turned on the singer who stood in the centre of the room, or else cast fleeting, sly glances at Sulla or in the direction of a young man who sat fidgeting and chewing his fingers at the table of least distinction.

The singer was dressed in a flowing purple gown embroidered in red and grey. Masses of black hair streaked with white rose in great waves and ringlets in a coiffure so architecturally complex it was almost comic. When he turned in our direction I saw his painted face, made up in shades of chalk and umber to cover his wrinkled eyes and heavy jowls, and I recognized at once the famous female impersonator Metrobius. I had seen him a few times before, never in public and never performing, only in glimpses on the street and once at the house of Hortensius when the great lawyer had deigned to let me past his door. Sulla had taken a fancy to Metrobius long ago in their youth, when Sulla was a poor nobody and Metrobius was (so they say) a beautiful and bewitching entertainer. Despite the ravages of time and all the vagaries of Fortune, Sulla had never abandoned him. Indeed, after five marriages, dozens of love affairs, and countless liaisons, it was Sulla's relationship with Metrobius that had endured longer than any other.

If Metrobius had once been slender and

beautiful, I suppose at one time he must have been a fine singer, too. He was wise now to restrict his performances to private affairs among those who loved him, and to limit his repertoire to comic effects and parodies. Yet despite the hoarse voice and the strained notes, there was something in his florid mannerisms and the subtle gestures of his hands and eyebrows that made it impossible not to watch his every move. His performance was something between singing and orating, like a poem chanted to the accompaniment of a single lyre. Occasionally a drum joined in when the theme became martial. He pretended to take every word with utmost seriousness, which only enhanced the comic effect. He must have already begun changing the lyrics before we chanced on the scene, because the young poet and aspiring sycophant who had ostensibly authored the paean was suffering a visible agony of embarrassment.

Who recalls the days when Sulla was a lad,
Homeless and shoeless with not a coin to be had?
And how did he pull himself up from this hole?
How did he rise to his fate, to his role?
Through a hole! Through a hole!
Through the gaping cavern of well-worn size
That yawned between Nicopolis's thighs!

The audience howled with laughter. Sulla shook his head disdainfully and pretended to glower. On the couch next to him, Chrysogonus practically glowed with delight. At the same table Hortensius was whispering in the ear of the young dancer Sorex, while Rufus looked bored and disgusted. Across the room the rewritten poet blanched fish-belly white.

With each succeeding verse the song grew increasingly ribald and the crowd laughed more and more freely. Soon Sulla himself was laughing out loud. Meanwhile the poet chewed his lip and squirmed, changing colours like a coal in the wind, blanching white at each impiety and blushing scarlet at each tortured rhyme. Having finally caught the joke, he seemed at first relieved – no one would blame him for the travesty, after all, and even Sulla was amused. He managed a timid smile, but then he withdrew into a sulk, no doubt offended at the wreckage that had been made of his patriotic homage. The other young men at his table, having failed to tease him to laughter, turned their backs on him and laughed all the louder. Romans love the strong man who can laugh at himself, and despise the weak man who cannot.

The song continued.

It is not true that Lucius Cornelius Sulla was homeless as a boy. Neither, I imagine, was he ever without shoes, but in every account of his origins, his early poverty is stressed.

The patrician Cornelii were once a family of some influence and prestige, generations ago. One of them, a certain Rufinus, held the consulship, back in the days when the office actually denoted a man of integrity and character. His career ended in scandal – imagine those righteous days when it was illegal for a citizen to own more than ten pounds of silver plate! Rufinus was expelled from the Senate. The family declined and dwindled into obscurity.

Until Sulla. His own childhood was blighted by poverty. His father died young, leaving him nothing, and in his younger days Sulla lived in tenements among ex-slaves and widows. His enemies have charged that his rise to power and wealth, after such humble beginnings, was a sure sign of corruption and depravity. His allies and Sulla himself like to dwell on the mystique of what they call his good fortune, as if some divine will, rather than Sulla's own purpose and character, propelled him to so many triumphs and so much bloodshed.

His youth gave no sign of the great career to come. His education was haphazard. He moved among theatre people – acrobats, comedians, costumers, poets, dancers, actors, singers. Metrobius was among his first lovers, but far from the only one. It was among the vagabonds of the stage that his lifelong reputation for promiscuity began.

They say that young Sulla was quite charming. He was a big-boned, square-jawed lad with a stocky frame, his wide soft middle compensated by muscular shoulders. His golden hair made him stand out in a crowd. His eyes, so I have heard contemporaries recount, were as extraordinary then as now – piercing and pale blue, dominating all in their gaze and confounding those who gazed back, appearing merely mischievous while he perpetrated the most atrocious crimes, looking terrible and severe when he was merely intent on pleasure.

Among his first conquests was the wealthy widow Nicopolis. Her favours were notoriously accessible to virtually any young man who wanted them; it was said that she had resolved to give her body to all men but her heart to none. By all accounts, Sulla fell genuinely and deeply in love with her. At first she scoffed at his devotion, but ultimately his persistence and charm undid her resolve, and she found herself in love at the age of fifty with a youth less than half her age. When she died of a fever she left everything to Sulla. His good fortune had begun.

Another legacy came from his stepmother, his father's second wife, who in her widowhood had inherited a considerable sum from her own family. She died leaving Sulla her only heir, thus establishing him with a moderate fortune.

Having conquered the mysteries of flesh and gold, Sulla decided to enter politics through military service. Marius had just been elected to the first of his seven consulships; Sulla got himself appointed quaestor and became the great populist's protégé. In Africa to fight Jugurtha, Sulla engaged in marital derring-do, espionage, and the diplomacy of the perfectly timed double cross. The tortuously complicated details are all in his *Memoirs*, the first volumes of which are already circulating around Rome in purloined copies. The vanquished Jugurtha was brought to the city naked and chained and died shortly after in his dungeon cell, half-crazy from torture and humiliation. Marius had overseen the campaign, but it was Sulla, at the risk of his own life, who had persuaded the King of Numidia to betray his doomed son-in-law. Marius was afforded a triumphal parade, but many whispered that it was Sulla who deserved the credit.

Praise for Sulla rankled the old populist, and though Marius continued to use Sulla, elevating his rank with each campaign, soon the old man's jealousy drove Sulla to seek other patrons. Taking command of the troops of the consul Catulus, Sulla subdued the wild tribes of the Alps. When premature winter storms trapped the legions in the foothills without adequate food, Sulla did an expert job of rerouting and supplying fresh provisions – not only to his own troops, but also to those of Marius, who became livid with indignation. The long, withering rivalry between Sulla and Marius, which was ultimately to cause so much grief and chaos in Rome, began with such incidents of petty jealousy.

Sulla travelled east, where Fortune led him to further victories in Cappadocia. On diplomatic business he ventured as far as the Euphrates, and became the first Roman official ever to hold friendly discourse with that kingdom that owns the rest of the world, the Parthians. His charm (or else his blind arrogance) must have worked a wicked spell upon the Parthian ambassador, who actually allowed himself to be seated on a lower dais than Sulla, as if he were a suppliant of a Roman overlord. Afterwards the King of Parthia put the ambassador to death – having lost face, the man subsequently lost his head, a joke Sulla never tired of repeating.

Every powerful man must have omens of greatness attached to his legend – stars fell from the firmament at the birth of Alexander, Hercules strangled a snake in his cradle, eagles battled overhead when Romulus and Remus were torn from their mother's womb. It was while entertaining the Parthian retinue that Sulla's career begins to take on the patina of legend. Truth or fiction, only Sulla now knows for certain, but the story goes that a Chaldean savant attached to the Parthian retinue performed a study of Sulla's face, plumbing his character by using principles of science unknown in the West. Probably he was searching for weaknesses he could report to his Parthian masters, but instead the wise man drew back in astonishment. Sulla, never guilty of false modesty, recounts the old Chaldean's reaction word for word in his *Memoirs*: 'Can a man be so great and not be the greatest of all men on earth? It astounds me – not his greatness, but the fact that even now he abstains from taking his place as first in all things above his fellow men!'

When Sulla returned to Rome, Marius was not happy to see him.

The bone of contention snapped when a statue arrived from the friendly King of Numidia, commemorating the end of the African war and Jugurtha's downfall. Beneath the outstretched wings of Victory the gilded figures depicted the King handing over the chained Jugurtha to the King's

393

great friend, Sulla. Marius was nowhere depicted. Marius nearly went out of his mind in a jealous rage at the idea of Sulla stealing his glory, and threatened to destroy the statue with his own hands unless the Senate passed legislation to remove it from the Capitol. The rhetoric on either side escalated until the breach between the two men was irreparable. Violence would surely have followed, but at that moment all private feuds were abruptly postponed by the eruption of the Social War between Rome and her Italian allies.

The scale of the Social War was unprecedented on Italian soil, as was the suffering and disruption it caused. But finally compromises were reached, intransigent rebels were mercilessly punished, and Rome endured, but not all Roman politicians fared equally well. Marius, well over sixty, his military powers faded and his health erratic, accomplished practically nothing in the war. Sulla, in the prime of his manhood and riding the crest of good fortune, was everywhere at once, making his reputation as hero, saviour, destroyer, currying the favour of the legions and amassing political prestige.

When it was over, Sulla had his first consulship at the respectable age of fifty. Rome, like a patient in violent throes, having just survived one great spasm, was about to undergo another.

Marius's populist movement reached its peak. His right-hand man was the radical tribune and demagogue Sulpicius, the elected representative of the masses, whose every move mocked the power and prestige of the noble establishment. Under

Sulpicius, Roman citizenships were sold at auction to ex-slaves and aliens in the Forum, an act of impiety that drove the old nobility to apoplexy. More insidiously, Sulpicius gathered a private army of three thousand swordsmen from the equestrian class, ambitious and ruthless young men ready for anything. From these he culled an elite bodyguard of six hundred who milled constantly about the Forum. Sulpicius called them his Anti-Senate.

Abroad, Mithridates was ravaging Rome's eastern possessions, including Greece. The Senate voted to send Sulla to reclaim them, a duty which his previous service had earned and which should have fallen to him by right as consul. The command would be extraordinarily lucrative; there is nothing like a successful Eastern campaign to raise immense revenues through tributes, taxes, and outright looting. It would also give its commanding general immense power; in the old days Roman armies were loyal to the Senate, but now they follow the man who leads them. Sulpicius's Anti-Senate decided that the command should go to Marius. Chaos erupted in the Forum. The Senate was pressured into transferring the command from Sulla to Marius, and Sulla barely escaped being murdered in the streets.

Sulla fled Rome to take his appeal directly to the army. When the common soldiers heard what had happened, they pledged themselves to Sulla and stoned their staff officers (appointed by Marius) to death. Marius's followers reacted in Rome by attacking members of the Sullan party and looting their property. In a panic, people changed from one side to the other, fleeing from Rome to Sulla's camp or from the camp to Rome. The Senate capitulated to whatever Marius and Sulpicius demanded. Sulla marched on the capital.

The unthinkable came to pass. Rome was invaded by Romans.

On the night before, Sulla dreamed. Behind him stood Bellona, whose cult had been brought to Rome from the East, whose ancient temples Sulla himself had visited in Cappadocia. She placed thunderbolts in his hands. She named his enemies one by one, and as she named them they appeared through a mist like tiny figures seen from a hilltop. The goddess told Sulla to strike them. He cast the thunderbolts. His enemies were blasted asunder. He awoke, his *Memoirs* tell us, feeling invigorated and supremely confident.

What kind of man has such a dream? Is he mad? Or a genius? Or simply a child of Rome blessed by Fortune, sent a reassuring message of success by the power that guides his destiny?

Before dawn, as the army assembled, a lamb was sacrificed. By the smoky torchlight the soothsayer Postumius read the entrails. He rushed to Sulla and knelt, offering up his hands as if for shackles. He begged Sulla to keep him bound as a prisoner so that he might be summarily executed if his visions were false, so certain was he of Sulla's triumph. So the legend tells us. There is something about a man like Sulla that makes savants and soothsayers clamour to grovel at his feet.

Sulla attacked from the east with a force of 35,000. There are sections of the Esquiline Hill that still bear the blackened scars of his advance. The walls were breached. The unarmed populace resisted with a bombardment of tiles and rubble cast from rooftops. Sulla himself was the first to take a torch in hand and set fire to a building where the people had gathered to resist. Archers shot fire-arrows onto rooftops. Whole families were burned alive; others were left homeless and ruined. The flames made no distinction between the guilty and the innocent, friend and foe. All were consumed.

Marius was driven back to the Temple of Tellus. Here his radical populism reached its apex: in return for their support, he offered freedom to the slaves of Rome. It says something for the prescience of the slaves or for the decline of Marius's reputation that only three slaves came forward. Marius and his supporters fled the city and scattered. The tribune Sulpicius, master of the Anti-Senate, was betrayed by one of his own slaves and put to death. Sulla first rewarded the treacherous slave by granting him freedom, then punished him as a free man by having him hurled to his death from the Tarpeian Rock.

My thoughts, having wandered their own way on the wings of Metrobius's song, returned abruptly to the present. Echoing up from below us, Metrobius's voice affected a childish singsong with an atrociously crude Greek accent:

397

Sulla's face is a mulberry; Sulla's wife is a whore.
Sulla's face is red and purple; Sulla's wife is a bore.
Mottled and splotched with bumps that must itch—
Is it Sulla's face — or the breasts of his bitch?

The crowd gasped. A few in the room tittered nervously. Chrysogonus suppressed his golden smile. Sulla's face was a blank. Rufus looked disgusted. Hortensius had just put something into his mouth and was looking about the room, uncertain whether he should swallow. The ruined young poet looked nauseated — literally nauseated, pale and sweaty, as if something on the table had disagreed with him and he might vomit at any moment.

The lyre fell silent and Metrobius froze for a long moment. The lyre struck a twanging note. Metrobius cocked his head. 'Well,' he said archly, 'it may not be Sophocles, or even Aristophanes — but I like it!'

The tension broke. The room erupted in laughter; even Rufus smiled. Hortensius finally swallowed and reached for his goblet. The young poet staggered up from his couch and rushed from the room, clutching his belly.

The lyre player strummed and Metrobius took a deep breath. The song recommenced.

Sulla resumed his term as consul. Marius was outlawed. His enemies exiled, the Senate pacified, and the populace dazed, Sulla set out for Greece to win glory and drive back Mithridates. Afterwards, critics complained that his sweeping eastern campaign was the most expensive military expedition in the history of Rome.

For the Greeks the price was devastating. Always in the past the great Roman conquerors of Greece and Macedonia had paid homage to the local shrines and temples, endowing them with offerings of gold and silver – respecting, if not the present inhabitants, then at least the memories of Alexander and Pericles. Sulla treated the temples differently. He looted them. The statues at Epidaurus were stripped of their gilding. The sacred offerings at Olympia were melted for coin. Sulla wrote to the keepers of the Oracle at Delphi and requested their treasure, saying that in his hands it would be safer from the vagaries of war, and that if he did have occasion to spend it he would certainly replace it. Sulla's envoy, Caphis, arrived at Delphi, entered the inner shrine, heard the music of an invisible lyre, and burst into tears. Caphis sent word to Sulla, begging him to reconsider. Sulla wrote back, telling him that the sound of the lyre was surely a sign, not of Apollo's anger, but of approval. The portable treasures were carried away in sacks. The great silver urn was cut into pieces and carted off on a wagon. The Oracle fell silent. In a hundred generations the Greeks will not forget.

The Greeks, especially the Athenians, had welcomed Mithridates, happy to cast off the Roman yoke. Sulla punished them. If the Greeks could create another Euripides, a poet of agony and terror, he might find a theme in Sulla's devouring lust to vanquish Athens — except that in Sulla's life story there is no hubris, only the never-ending caress of Fortune, as steady as the waves of the sea. The siege was bitter and relentless. The populace, driven to starvation, kept up their spirits by composing crude ditties slandering Sulla. The tyrant Aristion railed at the Romans from the city walls, hurling down insults against Sulla and his wife (the fourth, Metella), accompanied by a broad and complicated vocabulary of obscene gestures, many of which the Romans had never seen before but which were subsequently imported and are now fashionable among the street gangs and idle youth of the city. Many of these gestures have facetious names, mostly on the theme of Sulla raping Athena, to the chagrin of his wife.

When the walls were scaled and the gates opened, the slaughter was appalling. It is said that the blood in the enclosed marketplace was literally ankle-deep. Once the fury had subsided, Sulla put a stop to the pillage, ascending to the Acropolis to say a few words of praise for the ancient Athenians, followed by his famous utterance. 'I forgive the few for the sake of the many, the living for the sake of the dead,' a quotation frequently cited as an example either of his profound wisdom or his very dry wit.

Meanwhile, civil war simmered and bubbled in Rome as if her walls were the rim of a cauldron. The Italian allies grumbled over the slow dispensation of citizenships promised at the end of the Social War; the conservatives in the Senate grumbled that the privileges of citizenship were being disastrously diluted; the exiled Marius wandered to Africa and back, like Ulysses pursued by harpies. The anti-Sullan consul Cinna, another radical demagogue, welcomed Marius back to Rome and outlawed Sulla instead. Amid chaos and bloodshed Marius attained his seventh consulship only to die seventeen days later.

Having driven Mithridates back to Pontus, Sulla summarily declared the Eastern campaign a total success and made his way back to Italy with all speed. Here the legends and *Memoirs* recount further encounters with fawning soothsayers and soaring dreams, but why repeat them? The goddess Bellona supplied fresh thunderbolts and Sulla dispensed them to his loyal generals, Pompey and Crassus foremost among them, who cast them all over Italy and Africa, turning Sulla's enemies to ash. Fortune never ceased to smile for an instant. At Signia, Sulla was engaged by the army of Marius the son of Marius. Twenty thousand of Marius's men were killed, eight thousand were taken prisoner; Sulla lost only twenty-three soldiers.

The second siege of Rome was not so easy. Sulla and Crassus approached from the north, Pompey from the south. The left wing under Sulla was annihilated, and he himself barely missed being killed by a spear; he later attributed his salvation to the tiny golden image of Apollo he had stolen from Delphi, which he always carried into battle, often holding it to his lips and murmuring prayers and whispered adorations like a lover. Rumours of

Sulla's death spread on both sides, even infecting Pompey's army with despair. Finally, after dark, word came to Sulla that the right wing under Crassus had destroyed the enemy.

Once in Rome, Sulla had the disarmed remnants of the defending army, six thousand Samnites and Lucanians, rounded up and herded like cattle into the Circus Maximus. Meanwhile, he called a meeting of the Senate, and even as he began his address the slaughter in the Circus commenced. The din of the massacred was audible all over the city; the noise echoed in the Senate chamber like the wailing of ghosts. The senators were dumbfounded. Sulla continued to speak in a perfectly even tone of voice, as if nothing unusual were happening. The senators grew distracted and began to mill about and murmur among themselves, until Sulla stamped his foot and shouted at them to listen to what he was saying. 'Ignore the noise from outside,' he told them. 'By my orders, some criminals are receiving correction.'

By consent of the Senate, Sulla proclaimed himself dictator, a constitutional seizure of authority that no one else had dared to attempt for more than a hundred years. As dictator, Sulla destroyed all opposition and rewarded his faithful generals. He was granted immunity for all his past actions. He reordered the constitution to strip the encroaching power of the populist tribunes and the masses and to restore the privileges of the nobles. When his original, legal term of one year as dictator expired, the Senate obliged him with an unprecedented and constitutionally questionable extension, 'to complete his vital work for the salvation of the state.'

For a time Sulla ruled with an even hand, and the city breathed a sigh of relief, as if spring had arrived after a long, hard winter. But Sulla was not satisfied with his almost total triumph. Perhaps a soothsayer warned him of danger. Perhaps in a dream Bellona issued him more thunderbolts.

The proscriptions began with the original List of Eighty. The next day a second list of more than two hundred names appeared. On the third day another list appeared, again with more than two hundred names.

Sulla was as witty as ever. On the fourth day he made a public speech defending the killings. When he was asked if a fourth list was yet to come, he explained that at his age his memory had begun to fail. 'So far we've posted the names of all the enemies of the state that I can remember. As more enemies occur to me, we'll post more names.' Eventually the lists numbered into the thousands.

The son of an emancipated slave was accused of having hidden one of the original Eighty. The penalty for concealing the proscribed was death. On his way to the Tarpeian Rock the wretch passed Sulla's retinue in the street and reminded him they had once lived in the same tenement. 'Don't you remember?' the man said. 'I lived upstairs and paid two thousand sesterces. You lived in the rooms under me and paid three thousand.' From the grin on his face no one could tell whether the man was joking or not. For once Sulla did not seem amused;

perhaps he was not in a mood to be reminded of his humble origins. 'Then you'll appreciate the Tarpeian Rock,' he told the man. 'The rent costs nothing and the view is unforgettable.' And with that he passed on, deaf to the man's pleas for mercy.

Some wags insinuated that men were proscribed simply so that the state and friends of the state could obtain their property. 'Did you hear,' the joke ran, 'So-and-So was killed by his big mansion on the Palatine, So-and-So by his gardens, and So-and-So by his new steam-bath installation.' There was the tale of one Quintus Aurelius, who went down to the Forum and discovered his name on the lists. A passing friend asked him to dinner. 'Impossible,' said Quintus. 'I haven't the time. I'm being hunted down by my Alban estate.' He rounded a corner and went no more than twenty paces before an assassin slit his throat.

But the proscriptions finally ended. Pompey went off to Africa to annihilate the last of his master's enemies. Crassus threw himself into real estate speculation. Young populists like Caesar fled to the ends of the earth. Sulla divorced his beloved Metella (whose breasts had been slandered by the Athenians) on the religious grounds that her fatal illness threatened to pollute his home, and the dictator found himself pursued by the beautiful young divorcee Valeria (yes, Rufus's sister); at a gladiator show she snatched a loose thread from the great man's toga to claim a bit of his good fortune, caught his eye, and became his bride. The doddering prestige of the nobility was shored up with

404

cracked plaster and straw, and rumours began to circulate that at any moment the newlywed Sulla would lay down his dictatorship and call for unfettered consular elections.

Down in Chrysogonus's banquet hall, surrounded by spoils of the Social War, the civil war, and the proscriptions, Metrobius stood with his head held high and his hands clasped, drawing a deep breath. His song was nearing its end, having reviewed in witheringly satirical detail the highlights of its subject's career. Even the humiliated poet, having emptied his belly of whatever ailed him and slunk back to his couch, had finally joined in the raucous laughter.

Tiro turned towards me, shaking his head. 'I don't understand these people at all,' he whispered. 'What sort of party is this?'

I had been wondering the same thing myself. 'I think the rumours may be true. I think our esteemed Dictator and Saviour of the Republic may be contemplating his imminent retirement. That will mean solemn occasions and ceremonies, hymns of praise, retrospective orations, the official publication of his *Memoirs*. All very stiff and formal, respectable, Roman. But here among his own, Sulla would rather drink and make a joke of it. What a strange man he is! But wait, the song isn't over.'

Metrobius was batting his eyes, shaping his hands in a demure, maidenly gesture, satirizing a shy virgin. He opened his painted mouth to sing:

405

They met, it is said, at a gladiatorial fest,
Where the living left living must be the best.
She plucked at his hem for a simple memento—
Or was it to glance at Sulla's pimiento?

The laughter was deafening. Sulla himself leaned forward, pounded his open palm against the table, and almost fell from his couch. Chrysogonus smiled and looked smug, leaving no doubt about the line's authorship. Hortensius playfully threw an asparagus spear in Metrobius's direction; it flew over his head and struck the poet square on the forehead. Rufus drew away from Sorex, who was smiling and trying to whisper something in his ear. He did not look amused.

Flesh was pierced that day; men writhed in the dust.
Sulla drew his sword to prove it hadn't gone to rust;
And the lady agreed, yes, the lady declared—

The song was interrupted by the clattering crash of an overturned table. Rufus was on his feet, his face quite red. Hortensius laid a restraining hand on his leg, but Rufus jerked away. 'Valeria may be only your half sister, Hortensius, but she's my flesh and blood,' he snapped, 'and I won't listen to this filth. And she's your wife!' he said, coming to a sudden halt before the couch of honour and openly glaring at Sulla. 'How can you stand for such insults?'

The room fell silent. For a long moment Sulla didn't move but remained as he was, leaning on one elbow with his legs outstretched. He stared into space and worked his jaw back and forth, as if a tooth bothered him. Finally he swung his legs to the floor and slowly sat upright, staring up at Rufus with a look on his face that was at once sardonic, rueful, and amused.

'You are a very proud young man,' he said. 'Very proud and very beautiful, like your sister.' He reached for his wine and took a sip. 'But unlike Valeria, you seem to lack a sense of humour. And if Hortensius is your half brother, perhaps that explains why you have only half his good sense, not to mention good manners.' He sipped more wine and sighed. 'When I was your age, many things about the world displeased me. Instead of complaining, I set about changing the world, and I did. If a song offends you, don't throw a tantrum. Write a better one.'

Rufus stared back at him, holding his arms stiffly at his sides, clenching his fists. I imagined all the insults running through his head and whispered a silent prayer to the gods that he would keep his mouth shut. He opened his mouth and seemed about to speak, then looked angrily about the room and stalked out.

Sulla settled back on his couch, looking rather disappointed to have had the last word. There was an awkward silence, broken by a quip from the would-be poet: 'There's a young man who's stunted his career!' It was an abysmally stupid remark, coming from a nobody and aimed at a young Messalla and brother-in-law of the dictator. The silence became even more awkward, broken only by scattered groans and a suppressed cough from Hortensius.

The host was undismayed. Chrysogonus smiled his golden smile and looked warmly at Metrobius. 'I believe there's at least one more verse – no doubt the best saved for last.'

'Indeed!' Sulla rose to his feet, his eyes twinkling, staggering just a bit from the wine. He walked to the centre of the room. 'What a gift you've all given me tonight! Even sweet little Rufus, acting so foolish and cocky – such a fiery head of hair, such a fiery temperament, as contrary as his sister. What a night! You've made me remember everything, whether I wanted to or not – good days and bad days alike. But the old days, those were the best, when I was a young man with nothing but hope, and faith in the gods, and the love of my friends. I was a sentimental fool even then!' With that he took Metrobius's face between his hands and kissed him full on the mouth, at which the audience spontaneously applauded. When Sulla broke the kiss, I saw tears on his cheeks. He smiled and staggered back, gesturing for the lyre player to resume as he fell back onto his couch.

The song began again:

And the lady agreed, yes, the lady declared—

but Tiro and I never heard the ending. Instead we turned our heads as one, distracted by the same unmistakable noise – the rasping slither of a steel blade drawn from its scabbard.

Chrysogonus had sent someone to check the upstairs after all, or else we had simply lingered too long in one place. A hulking figure emerged from the shadow of the doorway, limping slightly as he stepped into the pool of moonlight from the balcony. His wild hair was like a halo of blue flame and the look in his eyes turned my blood to ice. In his left hand he held a knife with a blade as long as a man's forearm – perhaps the same blade he had used to stab Sextus Roscius over and over again.

A heartbeat later Magnus was joined by his henchman, the blond giant, Mallius Glaucia. The scar rent across his face by Bast looked raised and ugly in the pale light. He held his blade at the same angle as his master, tilted up and forwards as if poised to gut an animal's belly.

'What are you doing here?' Magnus said, twisting the knife in his fingers so that the blade glimmered in the moonlight. His voice was higher than I had expected. His rural Latin was overlaid with the grating nasal accent of the street gangs.

I looked into both men's eyes; they had no idea who I was. Glaucia had been sent to my house to intimidate or murder me, no doubt at Magnus's order, but neither of them had actually seen me, except as a passing stranger on the road in front of Capito's house. I slowly withdrew my hand from my tunic. I had meant to reach for my knife; instead I slipped the iron ring from my finger. I threw my hands in the air.

'Please, forgive,' I said, surprised at how little effort it took to sound meek and humble in the face

409

of two giants bearing steel blades. 'We're the slaves of young Marcus Valerius Messalla Rufus. We were sent upstairs to fetch him, before the entertainment began. We lost our way – so stupid!'

'And is that why you're spying on the master of this house and his guests?' Magnus hissed. He and Glaucia separated and approached from two sides, like the flanks of an army.

'We paused here, just to have a look over the balcony and get some fresh air.' I shrugged, keeping my hands in sight and doing my best to appear pathetic and confused. I glanced at Tiro and saw that he was following my lead admirably, or else was simply frightened out of his wits. 'We heard the singing, found the little window – stupid and presumptuous of us, of course, and I'm sure the young master will see that we're beaten for such insolence. It's just that it's not often we have the chance to look down on a gathering of such splendour.'

Magnus grabbed me by the shoulder and shoved me onto the balcony, into the moonlight. Glaucia pushed Tiro against me so that I tripped backwards against the waist-high brick wall and had to grab the edge to steady myself. I looked over my shoulder. The yawning abyss below resolved into a grassy knoll dappled by the moon shadow of the cypress trees. From below, the balcony had not looked nearly so far from the ground.

Magnus pulled at my hair and poked the tip of his blade into the soft flesh below my chin, forcing me to turn and face him. 'I've seen you before,' he whispered. 'Glaucia, look here! Where do we know this dog from?'

The blond giant scrutinized me, pouted his lips, and wrinkled his forehead. He shook his head, baffled. 'Don't know,' he grunted. Then his face lit up. 'Ameria,' he said. 'Remember, Magnus? Just the other day, on the road, right before we got to Capito's villa. He was coming the other way, riding alone.'

Magnus snarled at me. 'Who are you? What are you doing here?' The knife pressed harder, until I felt the skin break. I imagined my blood trickling down the blade. *Never mind who I am*, I wanted to say. *I know who you are, both of you. You murdered your cousin in cold blood and stole his estates. And you broke into my home and left a bloody message on my wall. You would have murdered Bethesda if you'd had the chance. You'd probably have raped her first.*

I brought my knee up with a jerk, straight into Magnus's crotch. By reflex he reached downward. The blade ripped against my tunic, grazing my chest. No matter; I knew I was doomed anyway – Glaucia was right beside him with his dagger poised to strike. I braced myself for the blow to my heart. I even heard it, a sickening sound of ruptured flesh.

Except that no one had stabbed me, and Glaucia had tumbled to his knees, dropping his blade and grasping his head. Tiro stood over him holding a bloody brick in his hand. 'It came loose from the wall,' he explained, staring at it in amazement.

Neither of us thought to reach for Glaucia's

blade, but Magnus did. He snatched it up and retreated a few steps, then advanced with a blade in each hand, snorting like a Cretan bull.

I was over the wall before I even realized it, as if my body had leaped and left my head behind. I was falling through blackness, but not alone. To one side and a little above me, another body was dropping through space – Tiro. A little beyond him, plummeting like a burnt-out comet, was a fragment of brick, tumbling end over end and smeared with blood that glinted purple in the blue moonlight. Magnus was a furious face that peered over a wall high above, flanked by two upright daggers, growing smaller by the instant.

Part Three

Justice

XXVII

Something remarkably hard and immense rushed
up and struck me from below: packed, dry earth. As
if I'd been scooped up by a giant's hand, I felt myself
pitched forwards, rolling head over heels and then
abruptly coming to a complete stop. Beside me I
heard Tiro moaning. He was complaining about
something, but his words were slurred and indistinct. For a moment I forgot about Magnus entirely. All I could think of was how remarkably thin
the air is, and how extraordinarily dense the ground
seems by contrast. Then I came to my senses and
looked up.

Magnus's glowering face seemed incredibly far
away; how could I have possibly jumped such a
distance? There was no chance that he would
follow — no sane man would take such a leap
except to save his life. Nor would Magnus dare
to raise a general alarm, not with Sulla in the house

– that would risk raising too many questions and unpleasant complications. We were as good as free, I thought. In the time it would take Magnus to scurry through hallways and down stairs we would have long since disappeared into the night. Why then was he suddenly smiling?

The sound of a moan drew my eyes to Tiro, who shivered on his hands and knees beside me on the parched grass. He rose to his feet, or tried to, then fell helplessly forwards; tried again, and fell again. His face was twisted with pain. 'My ankle,' he whispered hoarsely, and then cursed. I looked up again at the balcony. Magnus was no longer there.

I scrambled to my feet and pulled Tiro upright. He clenched his teeth and made a strange gurgling noise – a howl of pain swallowed by sheer will.

'Can you walk?' I said.

'Of course.' Tiro pushed himself away from me and promptly collapsed to his knees. I pulled him upright again, clutched him against my shoulder, and began to walk as quickly as I could, then to trot. Somehow he managed to limp beside me, hopping and hissing with pain. We made our way a hundred feet or so before I heard a faint scuffling behind us and felt my heart sink.

I glanced over my shoulder to see Magnus dashing into the street, silhouetted by the blazing lamps of Chrysogonus's portico. Following him was another figure – the lumbering hulk of Mallius Glaucia. For an instant I saw the blond giant's face, lit by blue moonlight and framed by sputtering torches, streaked with blood and looking hardly human. They froze in the middle of the street, peering this way and that. I pulled Tiro into the shadow of the same tree from which we had watched Sulla's arrival, thinking the darkness might shield us, but the movement must have caught Magnus's eye. I heard a yell and then the slap of sandals against the paving stones.

'On my shoulders!' I hissed. Tiro understood immediately and hobbled to comply. I ducked between his legs, scooped him up, and started running, amazed at my own strength. I glided effortlessly over the smooth stones. I took a deep breath and laughed out loud, thinking I could run a mile and outdistance Magnus with every step. I heard them shouting behind me, but faintly; mostly I heard the pounding of blood in my ears.

Then, in an instant, with the drawing of a single breath that came up shorter than the others, the thrill of the moment subsided. Step by step the burst of energy dwindled. The level ground seemed to tilt uphill and then to melt, as if I were running through mud. Instead of laughing I was coughing, and suddenly I could hardly lift my feet; Tiro was as heavy as a bronze statue. I heard Magnus and Glaucia behind us, their footfalls drawing so near that the back of my neck began to twitch, flinching at the prospect of a knife between the shoulder blades.

We staggered along a high wall hung with ivy. The wall came to an end. That was when I saw Caecilia Metella's house to my left. The portico was lit with a single brazier, flanked by the two guardians stationed there for the safekeeping of Sextus Roscius.

A breathless citizen carrying a slave piggyback was probably the last thing the two bleary-eyed guards expected to come rushing at them out of the darkness. They fumbled for their swords and jumped to their feet, looking like startled cats.

'Help us!' I managed to gasp. 'Caecilia Metella knows me. Two men are running after us — street criminals — murderers!'

The soldiers drew apart and held their swords ready, but made no move to stop me when I bowed my head and let Tiro slip from my shoulders onto his feet. He took one limping step and then crumpled with a moan in front of the door. I stepped past him and began beating on the door, then looked over my shoulder to see Magnus and Glaucia come to a skittering halt just within reach of the brazier's light.

Even the armed guards stepped back at the sight of them — Magnus with his wild hair, scarred face, and flaring nostrils, Glaucia with blood streaming down his forehead, both clutching daggers in their fists. I banged on the door again.

Magnus turned shifty-eyed, lowered his blade, and gestured to Glaucia to do the same. 'These two are thieves,' he said, pointing at me. Despite his wild appearance, his voice was measured and even. He wasn't even winded. 'Burglars,' he declared. 'Housebreakers. We caught them forcing their way into the home of Lucius Cornelius Chrysogonus. Hand them over.'

The two soldiers exchanged confused glances. They had been ordered to keep a prisoner inside, not to keep anyone out or to keep peace in the street. They had no reason to help two wild-eyed men with knives. Nor did they have any reason to protect two unexpected callers in the night. Magnus should have told them we were escaped slaves; that would have obligated the soldiers, as fellow citizens, to hand us over. But it was too late to change his story now. Instead, when the guards made no response, Magnus reached into his tunic and pulled out a heavy-looking purse. The guards looked at the purse and then at each other, and then, without affection, at Tiro and me. I beat on the door with both fists.

Finally a slit opened and through it peered the calculating eyes of the eunuch Ahausarus. His gaze shifted from me down to Tiro and then beyond us to the assassins in the street. I was still breathing hard, fumbling for words to explain, when he opened the door, ushered us inside, and slammed it shut behind us.

Ahausarus refused to wake his mistress. Nor would he allow us to stay the night. ('Impossible,' he sniffed haughtily, as if hosting Sextus Roscius and his family were taint enough on the household.) Magnus might still be waiting in ambush outside the house; even worse, he might have sent Glaucia for reinforcements. The sooner we left the better. After some hurried negotiations (mostly I begged while the eunuch arched his eyebrows and stared at the ceiling), Ahausarus was quite happy to see us off with a team of yawning litter bearers to carry Tiro, along with some gladiators from his mistress's personal bodyguard.

'No more adventures!' said Cicero sternly. 'There's no point in it. When she hears of it in the morning, Caecilia will be scandalized. Tiro's injured himself. And there's no telling what sort of repercussions might have come of it – spying on Chrysogonus in his own house, with Sulla in the very room! My own slave and a disreputable henchman – forgive me, Gordianus, but it's true – caught wandering about a private home on the Palatine during a party to honour Sulla. It wouldn't be hard to make that out as some sort of threat to the security of the state, would it? What if they'd caught you and dragged you before Chrysogonus? They could have called you assassins as easily as thieves. Do you want to see *my* head on a spike? And all for nothing – you didn't learn anything new from the whole escapade, did you? Nothing of importance, as far as I can see. Your work is done, Gordianus. Give it up! Everything depends now on Rufus and me. Two more days – tomorrow, and the day after, and then the trial. Until then no more of these absurd adventures! Stay out of the way, and try to stay alive. In fact, I forbid you to leave this house.'

Some people are not at their best when roused from bed in the middle of the night. Cicero was snappish and rude from the moment he arrived in the vestibule, summoned by a slave to witness the bizarre nocturnal visitation of tramping bodyguards and a slave borne in a litter. His eyes were hollow with dark pockets beneath; I suppose in his dreams there was no friendly goddess handing out thunderbolts. Weary or not, Cicero talked constantly, mostly to deride me, while he hovered like a brooding hen near Tiro, who lay belly-down on a table as the household physician (who was also the head cook) examined his ankle, turning it this way and that. Tiro winced and bit his lip. The physician nodded gravely, his eyes red and puffy from interrupted sleep.

'Not broken,' he finally said, 'only sprained. He's lucky; otherwise he might have had a limp for the rest of his life. The best thing's to give him plenty of wine – thins the clotted blood inside and keeps the muscles loose. Soak his ankle in cool water tonight, the cooler the better – keeps down the swelling. If you wish, I can send someone after fresh spring water. Wrap it up tight tomorrow and see that he stays off it until the pain's completely gone. I'll have the carpenter carve him a crutch in the morning.'

Cicero nodded, relieved. Suddenly his jaw began to tremble. His mouth quivered. His chin dimpled. He opened his mouth in a gasping yawn, trying to keep it shut. He blinked, already falling asleep. He gave me one last disparaging glare through heavy-lidded eyes, shook his head disapprovingly at Tiro, and then returned to his bed.

I slunk wearily to my room. Bethesda was sitting wide-awake in bed, waiting for me. Listening through the door, she had been able to make out only the bare bones of the night's adventure. She asked question after question. I kept answering, long after my mumbled replies stopped making any sense at all.

At some point I began to dream.

In my dream I lay with my head in the lap of a goddess who stroked my brow. Her skin was like alabaster. Her lips were like cherries. Though my eyes were closed, I knew she smiled, because I could feel her smile like warm sunshine on my face.

A door opened and the room was filled with light. Apollo of Ephesus entered, like an actor stepping onto a stage, naked and golden and blindingly beautiful. He knelt beside me and put his mouth so close to my ear that his soft lips brushed my flesh. His breath was as warm as the goddess's smile, and smelled of honeysuckle. He whispered words of sweet comfort, like a murmuring brook.

Invisible hands played an invisible lyre, while an unseen chorus sang the most beautiful song I had ever heard – verse after verse of love and praise, all in my honour. At some point a wild giant with a knife ran blindly through the room, his eyes clotted with blood from a wound in his head; but nothing else occurred to spoil the absolute perfection of that dream.

A cock crowed. I gave a start and bolted upright, imagining I was back in my house on the Esquiline and thinking I heard strangers prowling in the grey dawn. But the noise I heard was only the sound of Cicero's slaves getting ready for the day ahead.

Beside me Bethesda slept like a stone, her black hair spread like tendrils about the pillow. I lay back beside her, thinking I couldn't possibly fall asleep again.

I was unconscious almost before I closed my eyes.

Sleep spread around me in all directions – featureless, dreamless, devoid of any landmarks. Such a sleep is like eternity; with nothing to measure the passage of time and no markings to show the volume of space, an instant is no different from an aeon and an atom is as large as the universe. All the diversity of life, pleasure and pain alike, dissolves into a primal oneness, absorbing even nothingness. Is this what death is like?

And then, all at once, I woke.

Bethesda sat in the corner of the room, stitching up the hem of the tunic I had worn the night before. At some point, perhaps when I jumped, I had ripped it. Beside her was a half-eaten piece of bread smeared with honey.

'What hour?' I said.

'Noon, or thereabouts.'

I stretched. My arms were stiff and sore. I noticed a large purple bruise on my right shoulder.

I stood. My legs were as sore as my arms. From the atrium I heard the buzzing of bees and the sound of Cicero declaiming.

'All done,' Bethesda announced. She held up the tunic, looking pleased with herself. 'I washed it this morning. Cicero's laundress showed me a new way. Even the grass stains came out. The air is so parched, it's already dry.' She stood behind me and lifted the tunic over my head to dress me. I raised my arms, groaning from the stiffness.

'Food, Master?'

I nodded. 'I'll take it in the peristyle at the back of the house,' I said. 'As far as possible from the sound of our host orating.'

The day was perfect for idleness. In the square of blue sky above the courtyard, puffy white clouds floated by one at a time, no more, no less, as if the gods had decreed a procession. The air was warm, but not as hot as on previous days. A cool, dry breeze rustled over the roof and wafted through the shaded porticoes. Cicero's slaves moved quietly about the household, wearing expressions of suppressed excitement and determination, infected by the gravity of the events transpiring in their master's study. Today and one day more, and then the trial.

Bethesda stayed close beside me, offering to fetch this or that, attending to whatever I desired – a scroll, a drink, a broad-brimmed hat. Her demeanour was uncharacteristically subdued. Though she said nothing about it, I could tell that the lingering signs of the night's danger – the torn tunic, the bruise on my shoulder – weighed on her spirit, and she was glad to have me safe and close at hand. When she brought me a cup of cool water, I set down the scroll I was reading, looked her in the eye, and let my fingers brush against hers. Instead of returning my smile she seemed to shudder, and I thought I saw her lips tremble, as slightly as the leaves of the willow trembled in the faint wind.

Then she withdrew her hand and stepped away as Old Tiro the doorkeeper came walking diagonally across the courtyard directly in front of me, oblivious of the rules of decorum that confined the slaves to pass quietly beneath the porticoes. He passed by and disappeared again into the house, all the while shaking his head and muttering to himself.

The old freedman was followed soon after by his grandson. Tiro came careening across the courtyard, leaning on a crude wooden crutch and holding his tightly wrapped ankle aloft, going faster than his skill allowed. He was smiling stupidly, as proud of his lameness as a soldier might be of his very first wound. Bethesda fetched a chair and helped him into it.

'The first scars and injuries of manhood are like a badge of initiation,' I said. 'But with repetition they become tedious and then depressing. Youth proudly gives up its suppleness, strength, and beauty, like sacrifices on the altar of manhood, and only later regrets.'

The sentiment left him unmoved. Tiro wrinkled his brow, still smiling, and glanced at the scroll I'd laid aside, thinking I was quoting epigrams. 'Who said that?'

'Someone who was once young. Yes, as young as you are now, and just as resilient. You seem to be in good spirits.'

'I suppose.'

'No pain?'

'Some, but why bother with it? Everything's too exciting.'

'Yes?'

'With Cicero, I mean. All the papers that have to be got ready, all the people dropping by – friends of the defence, good men like Marcus Metellus and Publius Scipio. Not to mention finishing his speech, trying to anticipate the prosecution's arguments – there's not enough time for everything, really. It's all a mad rush. Rufus says it's always like that, even with an advocate as experienced as Hortensius.'

'So you've seen Rufus today?'

'Earlier, while you slept. Cicero chided him for storming out on Sulla at the party, said Rufus was too rash and thin-skinned – the same way he chided you last night.'

'Except that I'm sure Cicero is secretly proud of what Rufus did, and they both know it. Whereas Cicero is genuinely disgusted with me. Where is Rufus now?'

'Down at the Forum. Cicero sent him to arrange for some sort of writ to be served on Chrysogonus, requesting that he bring forwards the two slaves, Felix and Chrestus, to make depositions. Of course Chrysogonus won't allow it, but that will look suspicious, you see, and Cicero can work that into his oration. That's the part we've been going over all morning. He's actually going to call Chrysogonus by name. It's what they least expect, because they think everyone is too frightened to speak the truth. He's even going to call Sulla to task. You should hear some of the things he wrote last night while we were out, about the free hand Sulla's given to criminals, the way he's encouraged corruption and outright murder. Of course Cicero can't use all of it; that would be suicide. He'll have to soften it into something milder, but even so, who else has the courage to stand up for truth in the Forum?'

He was smiling again, a different smile, not of boyish pride but in a kind of adoring rapture, giddy at the prospect of following Cicero into the Forum, flushed with excitement like a soldier in the train of a beloved general. Injury and danger only served to heighten the excitement and to make their cause more splendid. But just how far would Cicero really go to invoke Sulla's wrath? I snorted to myself and was on the verge of taunting Tiro with doubts. But I checked my tongue. After all, the danger he might face with Cicero was no less real than the danger he had faced with me. He had leaped into space beside me. He had raced across the moonlit Palatine in pain and fear without a word of complaint.

Now he was racing back to his master. He pulled himself up by his crutch and steadied himself on one leg. Bethesda moved to help him, and he blushingly allowed her. 'I have to go now. I can't stay. Cicero will be needing me again. He never stops, you know, not when he's in the thick of it. He'll send Rufus on a dozen errands to the Forum, and the three of us will be up all night.'

'While I catch up on my sleep. But why don't you stay longer? Rest; you'll need your strength tonight. Besides, who else is there for me to talk to?'

Tiro wobbled against his crutch. 'No, I really have to go back now.'

'I see. I suppose Cicero merely sent you to check up on me.'

Tiro shrugged as best he could, leaning against his crutch. He turned shifty-eyed, and his face coloured. 'Actually, Cicero sent me with a message.'

'A message? Why you, with a twisted ankle?'

'I suppose he thought the other slaves . . . that is, I'm sure he could have come himself, only – he told me to remind you of what he said last night. You do remember?'

'Remember what?' I was suddenly in a taunting mood again.

'He says you're to stay in the house and not to leave. Whatever comforts Cicero can offer, please feel free to take advantage of them. Or if you need anything from outside, feel free to send one of the household slaves.'

'I'm not accustomed to staying inside all day and night. Perhaps I'll make a trip down to the Forum with Rufus.'

Tiro reddened. 'Actually, Cicero gave certain instructions to the watchmen he hired to protect the house.'

'Instructions?'

'He told them not to allow you to leave. To keep you inside.'

I stared at him in quiet disbelief until Tiro lowered his eyes. 'To keep me inside? The way the guards at Caecilia's keep Sextus Roscius inside?'

'Well, I suppose.'

'I'm a Roman citizen, Tiro. How can Cicero dare to imprison another citizen in his house? What will these guards do if I leave?'

'Actually, Cicero told them to use force if they have to. I don't think they'd actually beat you. . . .'

I felt my face and ears turn as red as Tiro's. I glanced at Bethesda and saw that she was smiling very slightly, looking relieved. Tiro took a deep breath and backed away from me, as if he had drawn a line with his crutch and stepped behind it.

'You must understand, Gordianus. This matter belongs to Cicero now. It always did. You put yourself in danger in his service, and for that he's taken you under his protection. He asked you to find the truth, and you did. Now the truth must be judged by the law. That's Cicero's domain. The defence of Sextus Roscius is the most important event in his life. This could mean everything to him. He honestly believes you're more a danger than a help now. You mustn't confront him about this. You mustn't test him. Do as he asks. Obey his judgment.'

Tiro turned to go, giving me no time to answer and using his clumsiness with the crutch as an excuse not to look back or make any gesture of farewell. In the empty courtyard his presence lingered: eloquent, loyal, insistent, and self-assured – in every regard the slave of his master.

I picked up the history by Polybius I had been reading, but the words seemed to run together and slide off the parchment. I raised my eyes and looked

429

beyond the scroll, into the shadows of the portico. Nearby, Bethesda sat with her eyes closed, catlike and content in the warm sunlight. A ragged cloud crossed the sun, casting the courtyard into dappled shadow. The cloud departed; the sun returned. After a few minutes another cloud took its place. Bethesda seemed almost to be purring. I called her name.

'Take this scroll away,' I said. 'It bores me. Go back to the study. Beg our host's forgiveness for the interruption, and ask Tiro if he can find something by Plautus for me, or perhaps a decadent Greek comedy.'

Bethesda walked away, mouthing the unfamiliar name so that she wouldn't forget it. She clutched the scroll in that strange way that the illiterate handle all documents – carefully, knowing it to be precious, but not too carefully, since it would be hard to break, and without any affection at all, even with some distaste. When she had disappeared into the house, I turned around and scanned the peristyle. No one was about. The heat of the day had reached its peak. All were inside napping or otherwise taking refuge in the cool depths of the house.

Climbing onto the roof of the portico was easier than I had anticipated. I pulled myself up one of the slender columns, grabbed hold of the roof and scrambled up. The height seemed nothing to a man who had practically flown the night before. Evading the guard posted at the far corner of the roof loomed as a greater challenge, or so I thought until my foot loosened a cracked tile and sent a spray of tiny stones hissing on the paved court below. The guard stayed just as he was, his back to me, standing straight up and dozing against his spear. Perhaps he heard me when I leaped to the alley below and upset a clay pot, but by then it was too late. I made a clean escape. This time no one pursued.

XXVIII

There is a fine sense of freedom that comes from wandering about a familiar city with no particular destination in mind, with no one to meet, no duties, no obligations. My only concern was with certain men I wanted very much not to meet, Magnus chief among them. But I had a good notion of where a man like Magnus might or might not be found on such a fine afternoon, and as long as I stayed away from the familiar haunts to which those who knew my habits might direct a searching stranger, I felt relatively safe – almost a shadow, in fact. Or better, a man made of precious glass, as if the warm sunshine that beamed down on my shoulders and head passed straight through me, casting no shadow at all, and every citizen and slave I passed looked right through me. I was invisible. I was free. I had nothing to do and a thousand nameless, sun-drenched streets to do it in.

Cicero was right; my part in the investigation of the murder of Sextus Roscius was over. But until the trial was done, there was no way I could move on to other business, no way I could return with safety to my own home. Unused to having enemies himself (how soon that would change, with his ambitions!), Cicero expected me to hide myself away until all was clear, as if that were a simple thing. But in Rome one's path is never entirely clear of enemies. When even a perfect stranger could prove to be Nemesis, no man can protect himself completely. What point is there in cowering away in another man's house, behind the spear of another man's guard? Fortune is the only true protection against death; perhaps it was true that Sulla was followed everywhere by her protecting hand – how else to explain his longevity when so many others around him, far less culpable and certainly more virtuous, were long dead?

It would have been amusing to surprise Rufus in the Forum; I imagined stealing up behind him in some dusty corner of some dusty clerk's library, humming a snatch of Metrobius's ditty from the night before – 'and the lady agreed, yes, the lady declared' – but the Forum was probably the most dangerous place for me to loiter, except for the Subura. Without a plan, I wandered northward towards the Quirinal Hill, into a region where the houses were shabby and the streets littered. I came to the edge of the Quirinal, above the Servian Wall; the street dropped off in a steep descent and the houses on either side drew back from the road, leaving a wide plaza with a patch of unkempt grass and a single straggly tree.

Even in the city of one's birth there may be undiscovered streets that open onto unexpected vistas, and the goddess who guides aimless wanderers had guided me to such a spot. I paused for a long moment, looking out at the quadrant of Rome beyond the city walls, from the sweep of the Tiber on the left, sparkling beneath the sun as if it were on fire, to the straight, broad Flaminian Way on the right; from the jumble of buildings massed around the Circus Flaminius to the Field of Mars beyond, hazy with dust. The sound and the odour of the city rose on the warm air like a breath exhaled from the valley below. For all its danger and corruption, for all its meanness and squalor, Rome still pleases my eyes more than any other city on earth.

I made my way south again, following a narrow footpath that skirted the backyards of tenements, crossed alleys and wound through patches of green. Women called out to one another across the way; a child cried and his mother began to sing a lullaby; a man roared in a drunken, sleepy voice for everyone to be quiet. The city, languorous and good-natured from the warmth, seemed to swallow me up.

I passed through the Fontinal Gate and wandered aimlessly until I rounded a corner and saw looming ahead of me the charred mass of a burned-out tenement. Blackened windows opened onto blue sky above, and while I watched, a long section of one wall fell crashing to the ground, toppled by

434

slaves pulling long ropes. The ground all about was blackened with ash and tumbled with heaps of ruined clothing and what remained of household goods – a cheap pot melted by the heat, the black skeleton of a loom, a long jagged bone that might have been human or canine. Beggars picked through the sorry remains.

Because of the unfamiliar angle by which I had approached, a long, puzzled moment passed before I realized this was the same tenement that Tiro and I had watched go up in flames only a few days before. Another blackened wall came crashing down, and through the vacant space, standing in the street with his arms crossed and issuing orders to his foremen, I saw Crassus himself.

The wealthiest man in Rome looked quite cheerful, smiling and chatting with those among his large retinue privileged to stand within his earshot. I stepped carefully around the periphery of the ruins and placed myself at the edge of the group. A rat-faced sycophant, unable to insinuate himself farther into the throng, was willing to settle for a conversation with a passing stranger.

'Clever?' he said, following my lead and turning up his rat's nose. 'Hardly the word for Marcus Crassus. A brilliant individual. No other man in Rome is so economically astute. Say what you like about Pompey being a brilliant general, or even Sulla. There are other kinds of generals in this world. Silver denarii are the troops of Marcus Crassus.'

'And his battlefields?'

'Look in front of you. What more carnage could you desire?'

'And who won this battle?'

'You have only to look at Marcus Crassus's face to know that.'

'And who lost?'

'The poor beggars in the street, picking through what's left of their belongings and wishing they still had a roof over their heads!' The man laughed. 'And the wretched owner of this wreck. Previous owner, I should say. Off on holiday when it happened. Not a very good strategist. So saddled with debts that they say he killed himself when he got word of the fire. Crassus had to deal with the grieving son, and certainly got the better of him. They say he gave up the property for less than the cost of a trip to Baiae. And you think that's merely *clever*?' The man narrowed his rat's eyes and pursed his thin lips in an access of admiration.

'But he'll have to pay to have the tenement rebuilt,' I suggested.

The man arched one eyebrow. 'Not necessarily. Given the density of this neighbourhood, Crassus may leave the property undeveloped, at least for a while. That's so he can raise the rents on the tenement next door, and keep them up. He bought that property at the same time, off a panic-stricken fool who gave it up for a song.'

'You mean the building that barely escaped the flames? That one there, where people keep streaming out the door, assisted by those large men who look like brawlers from a street gang?'

'Those are employees of Marcus Crassus, evicting tenants unwilling or unable to pay the new rents.'

We watched together as a thin old man in a tattered tunic stepped cautiously out of the building next door with a large sack balanced on his back. One of the evictors intentionally stuck out his foot and tripped the man, causing the sack to slip from his shoulders and break open when it hit the street. A woman came running from an already loaded wagon, screaming at the enforcers while she helped the old man to his feet. The innocent guard turned red-faced and looked away in chagrin, but the culprit only began to laugh, so raucously that heads all around us turned to watch, including that of Crassus.

My new acquaintance seized the occasion of being in the great man's line of sight. 'It's nothing to bother you, Marcus Crassus,' he shouted, 'just an unruly ex-tenant blowing farts at one of your servants!' He let out a ratty little laugh. Crassus's eternal smile wavered a bit, and he stared at the man briefly with a perplexed expression, as if trying to remember who he might be. Then he turned away and resumed his business. The rat-faced man turned up his long nose in smug triumph. 'There,' he said, 'did you notice the way he laughed at my little joke? Marcus Crassus always laughs at my jokes.'

I turned my back on him in disgust, walking away so quickly I hardly noticed where I was going. I bumped into a half-naked slave covered with soot who had a rope slung over his shoulder. The rope went slack and he pushed me aside, shouting at me to look out. A section of wall fell crashing at my feet, shattering like bits of hardened clay. Had I missed bumping into the slave I might have walked right under it and probably died in an instant. Instead a cloud of soot billowed harmlessly about my knees, darkening the hem of my tunic. Feeling eyes on my back, I glanced over my shoulder and saw Crassus, alone of all those around him, staring straight at me. He did not smile, but very soberly gave a superstitious nod of his head in acknowledgment of a stranger's unaccountable good fortune. Then he turned away.

I walked on in the way that one walks when furious, or heart-broken, or lost in the inexplicability of existence – aimlessly, carelessly, with no more attention to my feet than a man pays to his heartbeat or breath. Yet it could hardly have been an accident that I found myself retracing exactly the route that Tiro and I had taken on the first day of my investigation. I found myself in the same square, watching as the same women drew water from the neighbourhood cistern and shooed away the same indolent children and dogs. I paused by the sundial and gave a start when the same citizen passed by me, the very man I had queried before about the way to the House of Swans, the quoter of plays and despiser of sundials. I raised my hand and opened my mouth, trying to think of some greeting. He looked up and stared at me strangely, then glowered as he leaned to one side, making it quite obvious that I was blocking his view of the sundial. He noted the time with a snort, glowered at me again and hurried on. It was not the same man at all, nor did he bear anything more than a passing resemblance.

I walked on, down the narrow winding street that led to the House of Swans, past blind walls mounted with sconces and the remnants of torches and scrawled with graffiti, political or obscene or sometimes both together. (P. CORNELIUS SCIPIO FOR QUAESTOR, A MAN YOU CAN TRUST, read one in an elegant hand, and next to it, hastily scrawled, P. CORNELIUS SCIPIO WOULD CHEAT A BLIND WHORE AND GIVE HER AN UGLY BABY.)

I passed the dead-end alley where Magnus and his two henchmen had lain in wait. I stepped around the dim bloodstain that marked the place where old Sextus Roscius had died. It was even duller than it had been on the day of my first visit, but not hard to locate, as the space all around it was markedly clean in contrast to the grimy cobblestones that filled the street. Someone had been out washing the very spot, scrubbing and scrubbing, trying to eliminate it once and for all. The job must have taken hours, and all for nothing – if anything, the spot was more conspicuous than before, and all the passing feet and soot-laden winds that had soiled it once would have to soil it again to make it disappear once more into the street. Who had worked here for hours on hands and knees (in the middle of the day? in the middle of the night?) with a scouring rag and a pail, desperately trying to wipe out the past? The shopkeeper's wife? The widowed mother of the mute boy? I imagined Magnus himself doing it, and almost laughed at the idea of the glowering assassin down on his hands and knees like a scrub maid.

I stooped down, brought my face near to the ground and stared into the flat stones and the tiny flecks of blackened red trapped in every fissure and pit. This was the very stuff that had given life to Sextus Roscius, the same blood that flowed in the veins of his sons, the same blood that heated the body of young Roscia, standing warm and naked against a dark wall in my memory; the same blood that must have run down her thighs when her father broke her maidenhead; the same blood that would burst from his own flesh when and if a Roman court saw fit to have him publicly scourged and then sewn up alive in a sack full of wild beasts. I stared into the stain until it grew so vast and deep that I could see nothing else, but even then it gave no answers, revealed nothing about either the living or the dead.

I unbent myself, groaning as my legs and back reminded me of last night's leap. I stepped forward just enough to peer into the gloomy shop. The old man sat behind the counter at the back, propping his head on his elbow, his eyes shut. The woman fussed about the sparsely stocked shelves and tables. The shop exhaled a dank, cool breath into the sunlit street, tinged with sweet rot and musk. I went into the tenement across the street. The downstairs watchman was nowhere in sight. His little partner at the top of the stairs was asleep with his drooling mouth wide open and a half-full cup of wine in his hand, tilted just enough so that he spilled a few drops with each snore.

Inside my tunic I fingered the hilt of the knife the boy had given me. I paused for a long moment, wondering what I could say to either of them. To the widow Polia that I knew the name of the men who had raped her? That one of them, Redbeard, was dead? To little Eco that he could take back his knife, because I had no intention of killing Magnus or Mallius Glaucia for him?

I walked down the long, dark hallway. Every board I stepped on creaked and groaned above the muffled voices from the cubicles. Who would huddle inside in the dark in the middle of such a day? The sick, the old, the infirm and crippled, the weak and starving, the lame. Ancients beyond any use, infants unable yet to walk. There was no reason that Polia and her son should be home at all, and yet my heart caught in my throat as I rapped on the door.

A young girl pulled the door wide open, giving me a view of the whole room. An ancient crone huddled amid blankets in one corner. A little boy knelt in the open window. He glanced over his shoulder at me, then went back to watching the street below. Except for its size and shape, everything about the room was different.

Two watery eyes looked out from the blankets. 'Who is it, child?'

'I don't know, Grandmother.' The little girl stared at me suspiciously.

'What do they want?'

The little girl made an exasperated face. 'My grandmother says, what do you want?'

'Polia,' I said.

'Not here,' said the boy in the window.

'I must have the wrong room.'

'No,' said the little girl crossly. 'Right room. But she's gone.'

'I mean the young widow and her son, the little mute boy.'

'I know that,' she said, looking at me as if I were an imbecile. 'But Polia and Eco aren't here any more. First she left, and then he left.'

'Gone,' added the old woman from the corner. 'That's how we finally got this room. Lived across the hall before, but this room is bigger. Big enough for all five of us – my son and his wife and the two little ones.'

'I like it better like this, when Mommy and Daddy are out and it's just us three,' said the boy.

'Shut up, Appius,' snapped the girl. 'One day Mommy and Daddy will go out and never come back, just like happened to Eco. They'll disappear, like Polia. You'll run them off because you're always crying. We'll see how you like that.'

The little boy started crying. The old woman clucked her tongue. 'What do you mean?' I said. 'Polia left without taking the boy?'

'Abandoned him,' said the old woman.

'I don't believe it.'

She shrugged. 'Couldn't pay the rent. The land-lord gave her two days to get out. The next morning she was gone. Took everything she could carry and left the boy all alone to fend for himself. Next day the landlord showed up, took what little was left of their things, and threw the boy into the street. Eco hung around here for a few days. People felt sorry for him, gave him scraps to eat. But the doorkeepers finally ran him off. Are you a relative?'

'No.'

'Well, if Polia owed you money, you'd best forget it.'

'We didn't like them, anyway,' said the little girl. 'Eco was stupid. Couldn't say a word, even when Appius would hold him down and sit on him and I'd tickle him till he turned blue. He'd just make a noise like a pig.'

'Like a pig getting poked,' said the little boy, suddenly laughing instead of crying. 'That's what Daddy said.'

The old woman scowled. 'Shut up, both of you.'

Business was brisk at the House of Swans, especially for so near to midday. The proprietor attributed the traffic to a slight change in the weather. 'The heat riles them all up, sets a man's blood boiling – but too much heat can cause even a vigorous man to wilt. Now that the weather is at least tolerable again, they're back in droves. All those pent-up fluids. You're certain you have no interest in the Nubian? She's new, you know. Ah!' He gave a sigh of relief as a tall, well-dressed man entered the vestibule from the inner corridor. The sigh meant that Electra was no longer occupied and would be able to see me, which meant that the tall stranger must have been her previous client. He was a handsome man of middle age with touches of grey at the temples. He made only a faint, compressed smile of satisfaction as he nodded to our mutual host. I felt a stupid twinge of jealousy and told myself that the reason he smiled with his mouth shut was because his teeth were bad.

In a perfect house of this sort we should never have seen one another, being consecutive customers of the same whore, but the perfect house of this sort does not exist. Our host at least had the decorum to step between us, nodding first to the stranger as he passed and then spinning back around to me. His wide body made a formidable screen. 'Just another moment,' he said softly, 'while the lady composes herself. Like a fine Falerian wine, one wouldn't want to open the bottle too quickly. Haste might spoil the bouquet with bits of cork.'

'Do you really imagine there's anything of Electra's cork left intact?' said one of the girls from the corner of her mouth as she passed behind me. My host made no sign that he heard, but his eyes flashed and his fingers twitched. I could see he was accustomed to using his hands on his whores, but not in front of a paying customer.

He left me for a moment and then returned, smiling unctuously. 'All ready,' he said, and waved me into the corridor.

444

Electra was as striking as I had remembered, but there was a weariness about her eyes and mouth that cast a shadow on her beauty. She reclined on her couch with one knee raised and her elbow balanced atop it, her head thrown back on the pillows amid the great mass of her dark hair. At first she failed to recognize me, and I felt a pang of disappointment. Then her eyes brightened a bit and she reached up self-consciously as if to compose her hair. I flattered myself that for another man she would not have cared how she looked, and in the next instant I wondered if she pulled the same subtle trick on every man who came to use her.

'You again,' she said, still acting, using a low, sultry voice that she might have used with anyone. And then, as if she suddenly, finally remembered exactly why I had come before and what I had sought, she unmasked her voice and gave me a look of such naked vulnerability that I trembled. 'This time you came alone?'

'Yes.'

'Without your bashful little slave?' A trace of wickedness, easy and lilting rather than studied, came back into her voice.

'Not only bashful, but naughty. Or so his master thinks. And too busy to come with me today.'

'But I thought he belonged to you.'

'He doesn't.'

Her face was suddenly naked again. 'Then you lied to me.'

'Did I? Only about that.'

She raised her other knee and clasped them both

against her breasts as if to hide herself from me. 'Why did you come here today?'

'To see you.'

She laughed and arched one eyebrow. 'And do you like what you see?' Her voice was sultry and false again. It seemed to change back and forth beyond her control, like the closing of a lizard's inner eyelid. She stayed just as she was, but her pose seemed suddenly coy rather than shielded. When I had first met her she had seemed so strong and genuinely lusty, almost indestructible. Today she seemed weak and broken, fragile, old, dreamless. A part of me had been excited at the prospect of seeing her again, alone and at my leisure; but now her beauty only caused me a kind of pain.

She shivered and looked away. The slight motion caused the gown to part across her thigh. Against the pale, sleek flesh there was a slender stripe, red at the edges and purple at the centre, like the mark of a cane or a stiff leather thong. Someone had struck her there, so recently that the bruise was still forming. I remembered the vaguely smiling noble who had left with his nose in the air.

'Did you find Elena?' Electra's voice had changed again. Now it was husky and thick, like smoke. She kept her face averted, but I could see it in the mirror.

'No.'

'But you found out who took her, and where.'

'Yes.'

'Is she all right? In Rome? And the child . . . ?' She saw me watching her in the mirror.

'The child died.'

'Ah.' She lowered her eyes.

'At birth. It was a hard birth.'

'I knew it would be. Only a child herself, such slender hips.' Electra shook her head. A tendril of hair fell across her face. Her image, captured just so in the mirror, was suddenly too beautiful to look at.

'Where was this?' she said.

'In a small town. A day or two from Rome.'

'The town where Sextus Roscius came from – Ameria, is that the name?'

'Yes, it was in Ameria.'

'She dreamed of going there. Ah, I think she must have liked that, the fresh air, the animals, and trees.'

I thought of the tale Felix and Chrestus had told me, and felt almost sick. 'Yes, quite a lovely little town.'

'And now? Where is she now?'

'Elena died. Not long after the birth. It was the birth that killed her.'

'Ah, well. She chose it then. She wanted to have his child so badly.' She turned her shoulder to me, making sure I couldn't see her in the mirror. How long had it been since Electra had allowed a man to see her weep? After a moment she turned back and laid her head against the pillows. Her cheeks were dry, but her eyes glistened. Her voice was hard. 'You might have lied to me. Did you consider that?'

'Yes.' Now it was I who lowered my eyes, not out of shame but because I was afraid she would see the whole truth.

447

'You lied to me before. You lied about the slave boy being yours. So why not this time?'

'Because you deserve the truth.'

'Do I? Am I that awful? Why not mercy instead? You might have told me Elena was happy and alive, with a healthy baby at her breast. How would I have known it was a lie? Instead you told me the truth. What good is truth to me? Truth is like a punishment. Do I really deserve it? Does it give you pleasure?' Tears streamed from her eyes.

'Forgive me,' I said. She turned away and said nothing.

I left the House of Swans, pushing past the grinning whores and tense-lipped, leering customers who lingered in the vestibule. The host veered by, smiling like a grotesque mask from a comedy. In the street I stopped to catch my breath. A moment later he came running after me, shouting and clenching his fists.

'What did you do to her? Why is she crying like that? Crying and refusing to stop. She's too old to cry and get away with it, even with her looks. Her eyes will puff up and she'll be useless for the rest of the day. What sort of man are you, anyway? There's something indecent about you, unnatural. Don't bother to come back. Go to another place. Find another man's girls to play your little games.' He stormed back into the house.

A little way down the road, close enough to have heard everything, stood the cool noble who had left before me, surrounded by a pair of bodyguards and a small retinue; he must have been at least a minor magistrate. The whole company guffawed and grinned as I passed by. Their master gave me a thin, condescending smile, the kind of look a powerful man gives to an inferior to acknowledge that despite the gulf between them the gods have given them the same appetites.

I stopped and stared at him, long and hard enough that he finally stopped smiling. I imagined him broken-jawed, bent over, and bleeding, shocked by an avalanche of pain. One of the guards growled at me like a hound sniffing invisible threats. I clenched my fists inside my tunic, bit my tongue so hard it bled, stared straight ahead, and forced myself to keep walking.

I walked until I longed to stop walking, through crowded squares where I felt a total stranger, past taverns I could not stand to enter. The illusion of invisibility descended on me again, but with it there was no sense of strength or freedom, only emptiness. Rome became a city of endless squalor, shrieking babies, the stench of raw onions and rotted meat, the grime of unwashed paving stones. I watched a legless beggar drag himself across the street while a pack of children followed behind, pelting him with pebbles and taunting him with insults.

The sun descended. I felt a gnawing in the pit of my stomach, but I could not stand to eat. The air became thin and cool in the gathering twilight. I found myself before the entrance to the Baths of Pallacina, that favoured haunt of the late Sextus Roscius.

'Busy day,' said the young attendant as he took my clothing. 'Hardly any business at all the past few days – too hot for it. No hurry this evening. We'll be staying open late to make up for the loss.' He returned with a drying cloth. I took it from him and said something to distract him while I draped the towel over my left arm, making sure it concealed my knife. Even naked I had no intention of going unarmed. I stepped into the caldarium, and he shut the door behind me.

The fading sunset cast a strange orange glow through the high window. An attendant with a burning taper lit a single lamp recessed in one wall, then was called away before he could light the others. The room was so dim and the steam on the water so thick that the score or so of men who lounged about the pool were as indistinct as shadows, like statues seen through a dull orange mist. I lowered myself into the water slowly, bit by bit, hardly able to tolerate the heat, until the swirling water lapped at my throat. Around me men groaned as if they were in pain or ecstasy. I groaned with them, merging into the obscurity of the warmth and vapour. The glow from the window failed by imperceptible degrees. The attendant never returned to ignite the lamps, but no one complained or shouted for light. The darkness and the heat were like lovers whom no one dared to separate.

The lamp sputtered. The flame leaped up and then grew small, leaving the room even darker than before. Water lapped quietly against tile, men breathed in sighs and soft groans. I looked about and saw nothing but vapour, featureless and infinite except for the single point of light cast by the lamp, like the glow of a lighthouse on a faraway hilltop. Shapes bobbed in the distance like floating islands or monsters of the deep prowling the surface.

I sank deeper in the water, until I could feel the breath from my nostrils swirl against the surface. I narrowed my eyes, stared across the gulf of mist at the flickering flame, and for a while I seemed almost to dream without shutting my eyes. I thought of no one and nothing. I was a dreaming man, a floating, moss-covered island in a humid sea, a boy playing at fantasy, a child in the womb.

Against the background of mist, one of the shapes drew nearer – a head floating on the water. It approached, and stopped; approached and stopped again, each time accompanied by the almost imperceptible sound of flesh parting water, followed by the advancing caress of tiny waves against my cheeks.

He drew so near that I could almost make out his face, outlined by long, dark hair. He rose a bit, just enough so that I glimpsed broad shoulders and a strong neck. He seemed to be smiling, but in that light I might have imagined anything.

Then he slowly sank beneath the water with a soft fuming of bubbles and a swirl of mist – Atlantis sinking into the sea. The surface of the pool closed over him and the water merged into the mist, undisturbed. He had vanished.

I felt something brush against the calf of my leg, like an eel slithering through the water.

My heart began to pound. My chest grew tight. I had wandered the city for hours, so blindly that the clumsiest assassin could have followed me and I never would have known it. I turned and reached for the towel on the edge of the pool, and the knife concealed beneath it. Just as my hand closed on the hilt, the water boiled and splashed behind me. He touched my shoulder.

I whirled about in the water, splashing, slipping against the floor of the pool. I reached out blindly and seized him by the hair, then brought the blade to his throat.

He cursed aloud. Behind me I heard the curious murmur of the crowd, like a blind beast stirred from its sleep.

'Hands!' I shouted. 'Out of the water!' The surrounding murmur turned to a commotion. On either side of me two hands leaped out of the water like snapping fish, empty and blame-less. I pulled my blade away from his throat. I must have cut him; a thin dark line marked the indent of the blade, and beneath it was a smeared trickle of blood. I was finally close enough to see his face – not Magnus at all, just a harmless young man with startled eyes and gritted teeth.

Before the chief attendant could come, before the lamps could be lit, exposing me for all to see as the fool I was, I let him go and pulled myself from the water. I dried myself as I hurried towards the door, taking care to conceal the knife before I stepped into the light and demanded my clothes. Cicero was right. I was unsettled and dangerous and unfit to be on the streets.

XXIX

It was Tiro who answered the door. He looked exhausted but exultant, so thoroughly pleased with himself and with existence in general that I could see it took him an effort to put on a disapproving face. In the background the voice of Cicero droned on, stopping and starting, an ambient noise like the sound of crickets on a summer night.

'Cicero is furious with you,' Tiro whispered. 'Where have you been all day?'

'Looking for bodies amid charred rubble,' I said. 'Chatting with friends of the great. Visiting ghosts and old acquaintances. Lying with whores; excuse me, lying *to* whores. Brandishing knives at amorous strangers . . .'

Tiro made a face. 'I don't have the least idea what you're talking about.'

'No? I thought Cicero had taught you

everything there is to know about words. And yet you can't follow me.'

'Are you drunk?'

'No, but you are. Yes, look at you – as giddy as a boy after his first cup of wine. Drunk on your master's rhetoric, I can tell. You've been going at it for eight hours straight, probably on an empty stomach. It's a wonder you could find your way to answer the door.'

'You're not making sense.'

'I'm making perfect sense. But you're so intoxicated with gibberish that a little common sense must seem as insipid to you as spring water to a hardened drunkard. Listen to him – like a knife against slate, if you ask me. Yet you act as if it were a siren's song.'

I had at last managed to eradicate the cheerfulness from Tiro's face and replace it with a frown of consternation. At that moment Rufus looked tentatively around the corner and then strode into the vestibule, flushed and smiling and batting his heavy-lidded eyes. He looked utterly exhausted, which at his age only served to make him look more charming, especially as he could not stop smiling.

'We've finished the second draft,' he announced. The constant droning from Cicero's study had abruptly stopped. On Rufus's face was the transported look of a child who might have seen a centaur in the woods and could not possibly hope to describe it. 'Brilliant,' he finally said. 'Of course, what do I know of rhetoric? Only what I've learned from teachers like Diodotus and Molo, and what

I've heard with my own ears, sitting in on the Senate and the courts since I was a child. But I swear to you, he'll bring tears to your eyes when you hear him at the trial. Men will come to their feet with clenched fists, demanding that Sextus Roscius be set free. There's no final version, of course; we have to contend with all sorts of possibilities, depending on whatever tricks Erucius comes up with. But Cicero's done what he can to foresee every contingency, and the core of his final argument is there, finished and perfect and ready, like pillars awaiting the dome of a temple. It's brilliant, there's no other word for it. I feel so humble simply to have been a witness to it.'

'You don't think it's too dangerous?' Tiro said in a low voice, stepping from behind me and drawing closer to Rufus, whispering so as to hide his doubts from Cicero in his study.

'In an unjust state, any act of decency is by its nature dangerous,' said Rufus. 'And also brave. A brave man will not fail to put himself into danger, if he has just cause.'

'Still, aren't you worried about what might happen after the trial? Such harsh words for Chrysogonus, and Sulla himself isn't spared.'

'Is there room in a Roman court for the truth, or not?' said Rufus. 'That's the question. Have we reached such a state that truth is a crime? Cicero is staking his future on the essential fairness and honesty of good Roman citizens. What else can a man of his integrity do?'

'Of course,' said Tiro soberly, nodding. 'It's his

nature to challenge hypocrisy and injustice, to act out of his own principles. Given his nature, what choice does he have?'

I stood by, forgotten and alone. While they conferred and debated, I quietly slipped away and joined Bethesda between the warm sheets of my bed. She purred like a half-asleep cat, then wrinkled her nose with a growl of suspicion when she smelled Electra's perfume on my flesh. I was too weary to explain or even to tease her. I did not hold her but instead turned my back to her and let her hold me, and so, just as the sound of Cicero's droning abruptly resumed from the atrium, I slipped into a restless sleep.

One might have thought the house had been deserted, or that someone was gravely ill, so supreme did quiet reign over Cicero's household the next morning. The strain and bustle of the previous day were replaced by a steady calm that had the appearance of lethargy. The slaves did not scurry back and forth but took their time, speaking always in hushed voices. Even the constant droning of Cicero's voice had stopped; not a sound came from his study. I ate a bowl of olives and bread that Bethesda brought me and passed the morning as I had the day before, resting and reading in the courtyard near the back of Cicero's house with Bethesda nearby.

The reproof I expected from Cicero never came. Instead he ignored me, though not in any pointed manner. I simply seemed to have slipped from his consciousness. I did notice, however, that the guard on the roof whom I had eluded the day before had changed his routine to include an occasional circuit of the colonnade surrounding the courtyard. From his sullen glances I could tell that he, at least, had not escaped Cicero's wrath.

At some point Tiro appeared. He asked if I was comfortable. I told him I had been reading Cato all morning, but except for that I had no complaints. 'And your master?' I said. 'I haven't heard a sound from him all day. Not a single epigram, not even the tiniest allusion, not one specimen of alliteration. Not even a metaphor. He's not ill, is he?'

Tiro bowed his head slightly and spoke with the hushed voice of one admitted to the inner circle of a great enterprise. His transgressions with Roscia forgiven (or at least momentarily forgotten), he had fallen more than ever under his master's spell. Now the climax approached, and his faith in Cicero had become almost mystical. 'Cicero is fasting and resting his voice today,' Tiro said, with all the gravity of a priest explaining the omens to be seen in a flying flock of geese. 'All his practising these past few days has worn his throat until he's hoarse. So today no solid foods, only liquids to soothe his throat and moisten his tongue. I've been recopying a fresh draft of his oration, while Rufus sorts through each of the legal references to make sure nothing has been overlooked or wrongly attributed. Meanwhile, the house is to be as still and quiet as possible. Cicero must have a day of rest and calm before the trial.'

458

'Or else – what?' I said. 'A crippling attack of gas before the Rostra?' Bethesda snickered. Tiro coloured, but quickly recovered. He was far too proud of Cicero to allow a mere insult to fluster him. His manner became haughty. 'I only bring it up so that you'll understand when I ask you to be as quiet as possible and to cause no disturbances.'

'Like the one I caused yesterday by escaping over the roof?'

'Exactly.' He held himself erect for a final haughty moment, then let his shoulders slump. 'Oh, Gordianus, why can't you simply do as he asks? I don't understand why you've become so . . . so unreasonable. If you only knew. Cicero understands things that we only guess at. You'll see what I mean tomorrow, at the trial. I only wish you trusted him as you should.'

He turned, and as he left he took a deep breath and shivered, the way dogs shiver to dry themselves, as if I had left a residue of ill will and disbelief on him and he did not wish to reenter his master's presence stained by my pollution.

'I don't understand you, either,' said Bethesda softly, looking up from her sewing. 'Why do you taunt the boy? It's obvious that he admires you. Why do you make him choose between his master and you? You know that's unfair.'

It was a rare thing for Bethesda to chide me in such open terms. Was my behaviour so blatantly inappropriate that even my slave felt free to criticize it? I had nothing to say in my defence. Bethesda saw that she had pricked me and made a further sally.

'If you have a quarrel with Cicero, it makes no sense to punish his slave for it. Why not go to Cicero directly? But I must confess, I don't understand your attitude any better than the boy. Cicero has been only fair and reasonable at every turn, at least so far as I can see; no, more than fair. Not like the other men you work for. He's taken you into his household for your own protection, along with your slave – imagine that! He's fed you, opened his library to you, even posted a guard to look after you from the roof. Try to imagine your good client Hortensius doing that! I wonder what the inside of Hortensius's house looks like, and how many slaves he owns? But I suppose I shall never know.'

Bethesda put down her handiwork. She shielded her eyes from the sun and looked about the courtyard, noting the decorations and flourishes as if they had been installed especially for her approval. I didn't bother to reprimand her for speaking out of hand. What did the opinions of a slave matter, after all – except that, as always, she had spoken the very doubts and questions that were spinning in my own head.

XXX

The Ides of May dawned with a pale blue light. I woke in slow stages, dislocated from my dreams and disoriented in a strange house – neither my house on the Esquiline nor any of the houses I had passed through in a lifetime of restless travel. Hushed, hurried voices penetrated the room from every quarter. Why should any house be so busy so very early in the morning? I kept thinking that someone must have died during the night, but in that case I would have been awakened by sobbing and lamentations.

Bethesda was pressed against my back with one arm slipped beneath my own, hugging my chest. I felt the soft, full cushion of her breasts against my back, pressing gently against me with each breath. Her exhalation was warm and sweet against the back of my ear. I began to wake and resisted it, in the way that men cling to even a troubled sleep when a dull despair hangs over them. I felt content with my own unhappy dreams and altogether apathetic about whatever hushed crisis was brewing in the strange house around me. I shut my eyes and turned the dawn back into darkest night.

I opened my eyes again. Bethesda, fully dressed, was standing over me and shaking my shoulder. The room was filled with yellow light.

'What's the matter with you?' she was saying. I sat up at once and shook my head. 'Are you sick? No? Then I think you'd better hurry. All the others have already gone.' She filled a cup with cool water and handed it to me. 'I had thought they must have forgotten you entirely, until Tiro came running back and asked me where you were. When I told him I'd tried to wake you twice already and you were still in bed, he just threw up his hands and went running after his master.'

'How long ago was this?'

She shrugged. 'Only a little while. But you won't be able to catch them, not if you take time to wash yourself and eat something. Tiro said not to worry, he'd save you a place beside him at the Rostra.' She took the empty cup from me and smiled. 'I had a look at the woman.'

'What woman?' The image of Electra flashed in my mind; it seemed I had dreamed about her, though I couldn't quite remember. 'And surely I have a clean tunic?'

She pointed to a chair in the corner where my best clothes had been laid out. One of Cicero's slaves must have fetched them from my house. The tunic was spotless. A rent corner in the hem of my toga had been newly restitched. Even my shoes had been freshly scrubbed and polished with oil.

'The woman,' Bethesda said again. 'The one they call Caecilia.'

'Caecilia Metella was here? This morning?'

'She arrived just after dawn in a very grand litter. There was such a commotion among the slaves that the noise got me out of bed. She's let you inside her house twice, hasn't she? It must be very grand.'

'It is. She came alone? I mean, with only her retinue?'

'No, the man came as well; Sextus Roscius. Flanked by six guards with their swords drawn.' She paused and looked remote, as if trying to recall important details. 'One of the guards was extremely handsome.'

I sat on the bed to fasten the leather straps of my shoes. 'I don't suppose you noticed Roscius himself?'

'I did.'

'And how did he look?'

'Very pale. Of course, the light was weak.'

'Not so weak that you couldn't see the guard well enough.'

'I could have seen the guard well enough in the dark.'

'I'm sure you could have. Now help me arrange my toga.'

The Forum had the unsettled feeling of a half-holiday. Since it was the Ides, both the people's

463

Comitia and the Curia of the Senate were closed. But a number of moneylenders and bankers had their offices open, and while the outlying pathways were empty, as I drew towards the centre of the Forum the streets became increasingly congested. Men of all classes, alone or in groups, were making their way towards the Rostra with an air of sombre excitement. The crowd that thronged the open square around the Rostra itself was so thick that I had to elbow my way through. There is nothing that thrills a Roman like a trial, especially when it promises to end in someone's ruin.

In the midst of the crowd I passed a sumptuous litter with its curtains drawn shut. As I stepped alongside, a hand shot through the hangings and gripped my forearm. I glanced down, amazed that so withered a limb could command such strength. The hand released me and withdrew, leaving behind the clear indentations of five sharp fingernails. The curtains parted and the same hand beckoned me to stick my head inside.

Caecilia Metella, reclined upon a bed of plush cushions, was wearing a loose purple gown and a necklace of pearls. Her high, coiled hair was held in place by a silver needle decorated at the head with a cluster of lapis. At her right shoulder, sitting cross-legged, was the eunuch Ahausarus.

'What do you think, young man?' she asked in a hoarse whisper. 'How will it go?'

'For whom? Cicero? Sulla? The assassins?'

She furrowed her brow and frowned. 'Don't be facetious. For young Sextus Roscius, of course.'

'Hard to say. Only augurs and oracles can read the future.'

'But with all Cicero's hard work, and with Rufus to help him, surely Roscius will receive the verdict he deserves.'

'How can I answer, when I don't know what that verdict should be?'

She looked at me darkly and touched her long, henna-stained nails to her lips. 'What are you saying? After all you've learned of the truth, you can't believe he's guilty. Can you?' Her voice trembled.

'Like every good citizen,' I said, 'I put my faith in Roman justice.' I pulled back my head and let the curtain drop.

Somewhere near the centre of the crowd I heard a voice call my name. At that particular moment it seemed very unlikely that anyone who knew me could wish me well; I pressed on, but a group of broad-shouldered labourers blocked my way. A hand gripped my shoulder. I took a deep breath and turned slowly around.

At first I didn't recognize him, having seen him only on his farm, weary from the day's work with dirt on his tunic, or else relaxed and full of wine. Titus Megarus of Ameria looked altogether different, wearing a fine toga, with his hair carefully oiled and combed. His son Lucius, not yet old enough for a toga, was dressed in modest long sleeves. His expression was one of rapturous excitement.

'Gordianus, what a piece of luck that I should find you in this crowd! You don't know how good it is for a country farmer to see a familiar face in the city—'

'It's fantastic!' Lucius interrupted. 'What a place – I could never have imagined it. So big, so beautiful. And all the people. Which part of the city do you live in? It must be wonderful to live in such a place, where so much is always happening.'

'You'll forgive his manners, I hope.' Titus fondly brushed an unruly forelock from his son's brow. 'At his age I'd never been to Rome either. Of course I've only been here three times in my life – no, four, but once it was only for a day. See over there, Lucius, just as I told you, the Rostra itself – that giant pedestal decorated with the prows of Carthaginian ships taken in battle. The speaker mounts it from stairs around the back, then addresses the audience from the platform on top, where everyone in the square can see him. I once heard the tribune Sulpicius himself speak from the Rostra, in the days before the civil wars.'

I stared at him blankly. On his farm in Ameria I had been struck by his graciousness and charm, by his air of wholesome refinement. Here in the Forum he was as out of his element as a fish out of water, pointing and yammering like any country bumpkin.

'How long have you been in the city?' I finally said.

'Only since last night. We rode from Ameria in two days.'

'Two very long and hard days.' Lucius laughed, pretending to massage his bottom.

'Then you haven't yet seen Cicero?'

Titus lowered his eyes. 'No, I'm afraid not. But I did manage to find the stables in the Subura and return Vespa to her owner.'

'But I thought you were going to arrive yesterday. You were going to come to Cicero's house, to let him interview you, to see if he could use you as a witness.'

'Yes, well . . .'

'It's too late now.'

'Yes, I suppose so.' Titus shrugged and looked away.

'I see.' I stepped back. Titus Megarus would not look me in the eye. 'But you decided to come to the trial anyway. Just to observe.'

His mouth tightened. 'Sextus Roscius is – was – my neighbour. I have more reason to be here than most of these people.'

'And more reason to help him.'

Titus lowered his voice. 'I've helped him already – the petition to Sulla, talking to you. But to speak out publicly, here in Rome – I'm a father, don't you understand? I have a family to consider.'

'And if they find him guilty and execute him, I suppose you'll stay for that as well.'

'I've never seen a monkey,' said Lucius happily. 'Do you suppose they'll really sew him up in a bag—'

'Yes,' I said to Titus, 'be sure to bring the boy to see it. A sight I'm sure he'll never forget.'

Titus gave me a pained, imploring look. Lucius meanwhile was gazing at something beyond my

467

shoulder, oblivious to everything but the excitement of the trial and the glories of the Forum. I turned quickly and slipped into the crowd. Behind me I heard Lucius cry out in his clear, boyish voice, 'Father, call him back – how will we ever find him again?' But Titus Megarus did not call my name.

The crowd suddenly compressed as an unseen dignitary arrived, preceded by a retinue of gladiators who cleared a path straight to the judges' tiers beyond the Rostra. I found myself trapped in an eddy of bodies, pushed back until my shoulders struck something as solid and unyielding as a wall – the pedestal of a statue that rose like an island from the sea of bodies.

I looked upwards over my shoulder, into the flaring nostrils of a gilded war horse. Seated on the back of the beast was the dictator himself, dressed as a general but with his head uncovered so that nothing obscured his jubilant face. The glittering, smiling warrior atop his steed was considerably younger than the man I had seen in the house of Chrysogonus, but the sculptor had done a credible job in capturing the strong jaw of the original, along with the imperturbable, terrible self-confidence of his eyes. Those eyes gazed out not over the Forum or down onto the crowd or into the judges' tiers, but directly at the speaker's stand atop the Rostra, putting whoever might dare to mount it eye to eye with the state's supreme protector. I stepped back and looked at the pedestal's inscription, which read simply: L. CORNELIUS SULLA, DICTATOR, EVER FORTUNATE.

A hand gripped my arm. I turned and saw Tiro leaning on his crutch. 'Good,' he said, 'you came after all. I was afraid – well, no matter. I saw you from across the way. Here, follow me.' He hobbled through the crowd, pulling me after him. An armed guard nodded at Tiro and let us pass beyond a cordon. We crossed an open space to the very foot of the Rostra itself. The copper-plated beak of an ancient warship loomed over our heads, fashioned in the shape of a nightmarish beast with a horned skull. The thing stared down at us, looking almost alive. Carthage had never lacked for nightmares; when we killed her, she passed them on to Rome.

The space before the Rostra was a small, open square. On one side stood the crowd of spectators from which the statue of Sulla rose like an island; they stood and peered over one another's shoulders, confined behind the cordon maintained by officers of the court. On the other side were rows of benches for friends of the litigants and for spectators too esteemed to stand. At the corner of the square, between the spectators and the Rostra, were the respective benches of the advocates for the prosecution and defence. Directly before the Rostra, in chairs set on a series of low tiers, sat the seventy-five judges chosen from the Senate.

I scanned the faces of the judges. Some dozed, some read. Some ate. Some argued among themselves. Some fidgeted nervously in their seats, clearly unhappy with the duty that had fallen on them. Others seemed to be conducting their regular business, dictating to slaves and ordering clerks about. All wore the senatorial toga that set them apart from the rabble that milled beyond the cordon. Once upon a time, courts were made up of senators and common citizens together. Sulla put an end to that.

I glanced at the accuser's bench where Magnus sat with his arms crossed, scowling and glaring at me with baleful eyes. Beside him, the prosecutor Gaius Erucius and his assistants were leafing through documents. Erucius was notorious for mounting vicious prosecutions, sometimes for hire and sometimes out of spite; he was equally notorious for winning. I had worked for him myself, but only when I was very hungry. He paid well. No doubt he had been promised a very handsome fee to obtain the death of Sextus Roscius.

Erucius glanced up as I passed, gave me a contemptuous snort of recognition, then turned about to wag his finger at a messenger who was awaiting instructions. Erucius had aged considerably since I had last seen him, and the changes were not for the better. The rolls of fat around his neck had become thicker and his eyebrows needed plucking. Because of the plumpness of his purple lips he seemed always to pout, and his eyes had a narrow, calculating appearance. He was the very image of the conniving advocate. Many in the courts despised him. The mob adored him. His blatant corruption, together with his suave voice and unctuous mannerisms, exerted a reptilian fascination over the mob against which homespun honesty and simple Roman virtue could not possibly compete. Given a strong case, he would skilfully whip up the mob's craving to see a guilty man punished. Given a weak case, he was a master at sowing corrosive doubts and suspicions. Given a case with political ramifications, he could be relied upon to remind the judges, subtly but surely, exactly where their own self-interest lay.

Hortensius would have been a match for him. But Cicero? Erucius was clearly not impressed with his competition. He yelled out loud for one of his slaves; he turned to exchange some joke with Magnus (they both laughed); he stretched and strolled about with his hands on his hips, not even bothering to glance at the bench of the accused. There Sextus Roscius sat hunched over with two guards at his back – the same two who had been posted at Caecilia's portal. He looked like a man already condemned – pale, silent, as inanimate as stone. Next to him, even Cicero looked robust as he stood and clutched my arm in greeting.

'Good, good! Tiro said he had spotted you in the crowd. I was afraid you'd be late, or stay away altogether.' He leaned towards me, smiling, still holding my arm, and spoke in a confidential voice as if I were his closest friend. Such intimacy after his coldness of late unnerved me. 'Look at the judges up there in the tiers, Gordianus. Half of them are bored to death; the other half are scared to death. To which half should I pitch my arguments?' He laughed – not in a forced way, but with genuine good humour. The ill-tempered Cicero who had fretted and snapped ever since my return from Ameria seemed to have vanished with the Ides.

Tiro sat on Cicero's right, next to Sextus Roscius, and carefully laid his crutch out of sight. Rufus sat on Cicero's left, along with the nobles who had been helping him in the Forum. I recognized Marcus Metellus, another of Caecilia's young relations, along with the esteemed nonentity and once-magistrate Publius Scipio.

'Of course you can't be seated with us at the bench,' Cicero said, 'but I want you nearby. Who knows? A name or a date might slip my mind at the last moment. Tiro posted a slave to warm a place for you.' He gestured to the gallery, where I recognized numerous senators and magistrates, among them the orator Hortensius and various Messalli and Metelli. I also recognized old Capito, looking wizened and small next to the giant Mallius Glaucia, who wore a bandage on his head. Chrysogonus was nowhere to be seen. Sulla was present only by virtue of his gilded statue.

At Cicero's gesture a slave rose from one of the benches. While I walked towards the gallery to take his place, Mallius Glaucia elbowed Capito and whispered in his ear. Both turned their heads and stared as I took my seat two rows behind them. Glaucia furrowed his brows and curled his upper lip in a snarl, looking remarkably like a wild beast in the midst of so many sedate and well-groomed Romans.

The Forum was bathed in long morning shadows. Just as the sun rose over the Basilica Fulvia, the praetor Marcus Fannius, chairman of the court, mounted the Rostra and cleared his throat. With due gravity he convened the court, invoked the gods, and read the charges.

I settled into that mental stupor that inevitably overtakes any reasonable man in a court of law, awash in an ocean of briny rhetoric pounding against weathered crags of metaphor. While Fannius droned on, I studied their faces – Magnus slowly burning like an ember, Erucius pompous and bored, Tiro struggling to suppress his eagerness, Rufus looking like a child amid so many grey jurists. Cicero, meanwhile, remained serenely and unaccountably calm, while Sextus Roscius himself nervously surveyed the crowd like a cornered, wounded animal too blood-spent to put up a fight.

Fannius finished at last and took his seat among the judges. Gaius Erucius rose from the accuser's bench and made a laborious show of carrying his portly fame up the steps to the Rostra. He blew through his cheeks and took a deep breath. The judges put aside their paperwork and conversations. The crowd grew quiet.

'Esteemed Judges, selected members of the Senate, I come here today with a most unpleasant task. For how can it ever be pleasant to accuse a man of murder? Yet this is one of the necessary duties that falls from time to time onto the shoulders of those who pursue the fulfilment of the law.'

Erucius cast his eyes downward to assume a countenance of abject sorrow. 'But, esteemed Judges, my task is not merely to bring a murderer to justice, but to see that a far older, far deeper principle than the laws of mortal men is upheld in

473

this court today. For the crime of which Sextus Roscius is guilty is not simply murder – and that is surely horrifying enough – but parricide.'

Abject sorrow became abject horror. Erucius furrowed the plump wrinkles of his face and stamped his foot. '*Parricide!*' he cried, so shrilly that even at the far edges of the crowd men gave a start. I imagined Caecilia Metella quivering in her litter and covering her ears.

'Imagine it, if you will – no, do not back away from the hideousness of this crime, but look straight into the jaws of the ravening beast. We are men, we are Romans, and we must not let our natural revulsion rob us of the strength to face even the foulest crime. We must swallow our gorge and see that justice is done.

'Look at that man who sits at the bench of the accused, with armed guards at his back. That man is a murderer. That man is a parricide! I call him "that man" because it pains me to speak his name: Sextus Roscius. It pains me because it was the same name that his father bore before him, the father *that man* put into his grave – a once-honourable name that now drips with blood, like the bloody tunic that was found on the old man's body, shredded to rags by his assassins' blades. *That man* has turned the fine name his father gave him into a curse!

'What can I tell you about . . . Sextus Roscius?' Erucius infused the name with all the considerable loathing his voice and countenance could muster. 'In Ameria, the town he comes from, they will tell you he is far from a pious man. Go to Ameria, as I have done, and ask the townsfolk when they last saw Sextus Roscius at a religious festival. They will hardly know of whom you speak. But then remind them of Sextus Roscius, the man accused of killing his own father, and they will give you a knowing look and a sigh and avert their eyes for fear of the gods' wrath.

'They will tell you that Sextus Roscius is in many ways a mystery – a solitary man, unsociable, irreligious, boorish, and curt in his few dealings with others. In the community of Ameria he is well known – or should I say notorious? – for one thing and one thing only: his lifelong feud with his father.

'A good man does not argue with his father. A good man honours and obeys his father, not only because it is the law, but because it is the will of heaven. When a bad man ignores that mandate and openly feuds with the man who gave him life, then he steps onto a path that leads to all manner of unspeakable crime – yes, even to the crime that we have assembled here to punish.

'What caused this feud between father and son? We do not really know, though the man who sits beside me at the accuser's bench, Titus Roscius Magnus, can attest to having seen many sordid examples of this feud at first hand; as can another witness I may call, after the defence has its say, the venerable Capito. Magnus and Capito are each cousins of the victim, and of *that man* as well. They are respected citizens of Ameria. They watched for years with dread and disgust as Sextus Roscius disobeyed his father and cursed him behind his back. They watched in dismay as the old man, to protect his own dignity, turned his back on the abomination that had sprung to manhood from his own seed.

'Turned his back, I say. Yes, Sextus Roscius *pater* turned his back on Sextus Roscius *filius*, no doubt to his ultimate regret – for a prudent man does not turn his back on a viper, nor on a man with the soul of an assassin, even his own son, not unless he wishes to receive a knife in the back!'

Erucius pounded his fist against the balcony of the Rostra and stared wide-eyed above the heads of the crowd, held the pose for a moment and then drew back to catch his breath. The square was strangely hushed after the thunder of his voice. He had by this point worked himself into a fine sweat. He clutched at the hem of his toga and dabbed it against his streaming jowls. He raised his eyes and looked to heaven, as if seeking relief from the gruelling ordeal of seeking justice. In a plaintive voice, pitched just loud enough for all to hear, he muttered, 'Jupiter, give me strength!' I saw Cicero cross his arms and roll his eyes. Meanwhile Erucius pulled himself together, stepped forward to the Rostra with bowed head and began again.

'*That man* – why bother to say his befouled name when he dares to show his face in public, where any decent man may see it and recoil in horror? – *that man* was not the only offspring of his father. There was a second son. His name was Gaius. How his father loved him, and why not? From all accounts he was the exemplar of what every young Roman

476

should be: pious towards the gods, obedient to his father, aspiring to every virtue, a young man in all ways agreeable, charming, and refined. How strange that a man could have two sons so different from each other! Ah, but then the sons had different mothers. Perhaps it was not the seed that was polluted, then, but the grounds in which it was planted. Consider: two seeds from the same grape are planted in different soil. One vine grows strong and lovely, bearing sweet fruit that yields a heady wine. The other is stunted and strange from the first, gnarled and pricked with thorns; its fruit is bitter and its wine is poison. I name the first vine Gaius, and the other Sextus!'

Erucius mopped his face, shuddered in revulsion, and went on. 'Sextus Roscius *pater* loved one son and not the other. Gaius he kept close to him always, proudly displaying him to the finest society, showering him in public with kindness and affection. Sextus *filius*, on the other hand, he kept as far from him as he could, relegating him to the family's farms in Ameria, keeping him from view as if he were a thing of shame not to be shown among decent folk. So deep did this division of affections run that Roscius *pater* thought long and hard about disinheriting his namesake completely and naming Gaius his sole heir, even though Gaius was the younger of his sons.

'Unfair, you may say. It is better when a man treats all his sons with equal respect. When he goes about choosing favourites he asks for nothing but trouble in his own generation and the next. True, but in this case I think we must trust the judgment of the elder Sextus Roscius. Why did he despise his firstborn so much? I think it must be that he, better than any other man, could see what wickedness lurked in the breast of young Sextus Roscius, and he recoiled from it. Perhaps he even had a presentiment of the violence that his son might one day wreak on him, and that was why he kept him at such a distance. Alas, the precaution was not enough!

'The tale of the Roscii ends in manifold tragedy – a series of tragedies that cannot be set right, but only avenged, and only by you, esteemed Judges. First, the untimely death of Gaius Roscius. With him vanished all his father's hopes for the future. Consider: is it not the greatest joy of existence to give life to a son, and to see in him an image of yourself? To rear and educate him so that you are renewed as he grows? I know, I speak as a father myself. And will it not be a blessing on departing this life to leave behind, as your successor and heir, a being sprung from yourself? To leave him not only your estate, but your accumulated wisdom, and the very flame of life passed from parent to child to pass on to his sons, so that when your mortal body fades away, you will live on in your descendents?

'With the death of Gaius, this hope for a kind of immortality died in his father, Sextus Roscius. But he had another son still living, you may protest. True, but in that son he saw not his own reflection, true and straight as one sees it in a pool of clear water. Instead he saw an image of himself like that

478

reflected from a crushed silver plate, distorted, twisted, and taunting. Even after the death of Gaius, Roscius *pater* still considered disinheriting his only surviving son. Certainly there were plenty of other, more worthy cousin candidates to be his heir within the family, not least his cousin Magnus – that same Magnus who sits beside me at the accuser's bench, who loved his cousin enough to see that his murder does not go unpunished.

'Young Sextus Roscius fiendishly plotted the death of his father. The exact details we do not know and cannot know. Only *that man* could tell us, if he dares to confess. What we know are the naked facts. On a night in September, leaving the home of his patroness, the much-esteemed Caecilia Metella, Sextus Roscius *pater* was accosted in the vicinity of the Baths of Pallacina and stabbed to death. By Sextus Roscius *filius* himself? Of course not! Think back to the turmoil of last year, esteemed Judges of the court. I need not dwell on the causes, for this is not a political court, but I must remind you of the violence that surged through the streets of this city. How very easy it must have been for a schemer like young Sextus Roscius to find the cut-throats to do his dirty work. And how clever, to try to stage the execution at a time of turmoil, hoping that his father's murder would be overlooked in the midst of so much upheaval.

'Thank the gods for a man like Magnus, who keeps his eyes and ears open and is not afraid to step forward and accuse the guilty! That very night his trusted freedman, Mallius Glaucia, came to him here in Rome with news of his dear cousin's murder. Magnus immediately dispatched Glaucia to carry the news to his good cousin Capito back home in Ameria.

'And now irony, bitter and yet strangely just, enters the tale alongside tragedy. For by a peculiar twist of fortune *that man* was not to inherit the fortune he had committed parricide to obtain. Now as I said before, this is not a political court, nor is this a political trial. We are not concerned here with the drastic measures forced upon the state in the recent years of upheaval and uncertainty. And so I will not try to explain the curious process by which it came about that Sextus Roscius *pater*, to most appearances a good man, was nevertheless found to be among those on the lists of the proscribed when certain conscientious officers of the state looked into the matter of his death. Somehow the old man had escaped with his life for months! What a fortunate man he must have been, or else how clever!

'And yet – what irony! *Filius* kills *pater* to secure his inheritance, only to discover that the inheritance has already been claimed by the state! Imagine his chagrin! His frustration and despair! The gods played an appalling joke on *that man*, but what man can deny either their infinite wisdom or their sense of humour?

'In due course the property of the late Sextus Roscius was sold at auction. The good cousins Magnus and Capito were among the first to bid, since they were intimate with the estates and knew their value, and thus they became what they should have been all along, the heirs of the late Sextus Roscius. So it is that sometimes Fortune rewards the just and punishes the wicked.

'And now – what of *that man*? Magnus and Capito suspected his guilt, indeed they were almost certain of it. But out of pity for his family they offered him shelter on their newly acquired estates. For a time there was an unsteady peace between the cousins – that is, until Sextus Roscius gave himself away. First it was discovered that he had held back various items of property that had been duly proscribed by the state – in other words, the man was no better than a common thief, stealing from the people of Rome what was duly theirs by right of law. (Ah, Judges, you yawn at an accusation of embezzlement, and rightly so – what is that, compared to his greater crime?) When Magnus and Capito demanded that he give these things up, he threatened their lives. Now, had he been sober, he probably would have held his tongue. But ever since the death of his father he had drunk excessively – as guilty men are known to do. Indeed, to all his other vices, Sextus Roscius had added drunkenness, and was hardly ever sober. He became intolerably abusive, to the point that he dared to threaten his hosts. To kill them, in fact – and in threatening their lives he inadvertently confessed to the murder of his father.

'Fearing for his own life, and because it was his duty, Magnus decided to bring charges against *that man*. Meanwhile Roscius slipped out of his grip and escaped to Rome, back to the very scene of his crime; but the eye of the law watches even the heart of Rome, and in a city of a million souls he could not hide himself.

'Sextus Roscius was located. Normally, even when accused of the most heinous crime, a Roman citizen is given the opportunity to renounce his citizenship and escape into exile rather than face trial, if that is his choice. But so severe was the crime committed by *that man* that he was placed under armed guard to await his trial and punishment. And why? Because the crime he has committed goes far beyond the mere offence of one mortal against the person of another. It is a blow against the very foundations of this republic and the principles that have made it great. It is an assault on the primacy of fatherhood. It is an insult to the very gods, and to Jupiter above all, father of the gods.

'No, the state cannot take even the slightest risk that such an odious criminal might escape, nor, esteemed Judges, can you take the risk of letting him go unpunished. For if you do, consider the divine punishments that are sure to be visited upon this city in retribution for its failure to wipe out such an abomination. Think of those cities whose streets have run with blood or whose people have withered from starvation and thirst when they foolishly sheltered an impious man from the gods. You cannot allow that to happen to Rome.'

Erucius paused to mop his brow. Everyone in the square was watching him with an almost dreamlike concentration. Cicero and his fellow advocates were no longer rolling their eyes and mocking Erucius behind their sleeves; they looked rather worried. Sextus Roscius had turned to stone.

Erucius resumed. 'I have spoken of the insult rendered to divine Jupiter by *that man* and his unspeakably vile crime. It is an insult as well, if I might digress only a little, to the Father of our restored Republic!' Here Erucius made quite a show of spreading his arms wide as if in supplication to the equestrian statue of Sulla, which seemed, from the angle at which I sat, to be granting him a condescending smile. 'I need not even speak his name, for his eye is on us all at this very moment. Yes, his watchful eye is on everything we do in this place, in our dutiful roles as citizens, judges, advocates, and accusers. Lucius Cornelius Sulla, Ever Fortunate, restored the courts, Sulla reignited the fire of justice in Rome after so many years of darkness; it is up to us to see that villains such as *that man* are withered to ashes by its flame. Or else I promise you, esteemed Judges, that retribution will fall on *all* our heads from above, like hail descending from an angry black sky.'

Erucius struck a pose and held it for a long moment. His finger pointed to heaven. His brows were drawn together, and he glowered like a bull at the gathered judges. He had spoken of Jupiter's retribution, but what we all had heard was that Sulla himself would be angered at a verdict of not guilty. The threat could not have been more explicit.

Erucius gathered the folds of his toga, threw back

his chin, and turned his back. As he descended the Rostra, there were no cheers or applause from the crowd, only a chilling silence.

He had proved nothing. In place of evidence he had offered innuendo. He had appealed not to justice, but to fear. His speech was a dreadful patchwork of outright lies and self-righteous bullying. And yet, what man who heard him from the Rostra that morning could doubt that Gaius Erucius had won his case?

XXXI

Cicero rose and walked resolutely to the Rostra, his toga billowing about his knees. I glanced at Tiro, who was gnawing on one of his thumbnails, and at Rufus, who sat with his hands folded in his lap and a barely suppressed smile of adoration on his face.

Cicero stepped forward to the podium, cleared his throat and coughed. A wave of scepticism ran through the crowd. No one had heard him orate before; a botched opening was a bad sign. At the accuser's bench Gaius Erucius made a great show of smacking his lips and staring up at the sky.

Cicero cleared his throat and began again. His voice was unsteady and slightly hoarse. 'Judges of the court: you must be wondering why, of all the distinguished citizens and eminent orators seated about you, it is I who have risen to address you. . . .'

'Indeed,' Erucius muttered under his breath. There was scattered laughter from the crowd.

Cicero pressed on. 'Certainly I cannot be compared to them in age or ability or authority. Certainly they believe, no less than I, that an unjust charge concocted by utmost villainy has been levelled at an innocent man and must be repelled. Thus they show themselves here in visible fulfilment of their duty to the truth, but they remain silent – due to the inclement conditions of the day.' Here he raised his hand as if to catch a raindrop from the clear blue sky – and at the same time seemed to be gesturing towards the equestrian statue of Sulla. Among the judges there was an uneasy shuffling of chairs. Erucius, who was inspecting his fingernails, did not see.

Cicero cleared his throat again. His voice returned, stronger and louder than before. The quavering vanished. 'Am I so much bolder than these silent men? Or more devoted to justice? I think not. Or so very eager to hear my own voice in the Forum, and to be praised for speaking out? No, not if a better orator could earn that praise by speaking better words. What, then, has impelled me, rather than a more important man, to undertake the defence of Sextus Roscius of Ameria?

'The reason is this: if any one of these fine orators had risen to speak in this court, and uttered words of a political nature – inevitable in a case such as this – then he would undoubtedly find people reading much more into his words than was actually there. Rumours would begin. Suspicions would be aroused. Such is the stature of these established men that nothing they say goes unremarked, and no implication in their speeches goes undebated. I, on the other hand, can say everything that demands to be said in this case, without fear of adverse attention or untoward controversy. That is because I have not yet begun a public career; no one knows me. If I should speak out of turn, if I should let slip some embarrassing indiscretion, no one will even notice, or if they do, they will pardon the lapse on the grounds of my youth and inexperience – though I use the word *pardon* rather loosely, since actual pardons and the free judicial inquiry they require have of late been abolished by the state.'

There was more rustling of chairs. Erucius looked up from his nails, wrinkled his nose, and gazed into the middle distance, as if he had just discerned an alarming plume of smoke on the air.

'So you see, I was not singled out and chosen because I was the most gifted orator.' Cicero smiled to ask the crowd's indulgence. 'No, I was simply the person left over when all others had stepped aside. I was the man who could plead with the least danger. No one can say that I was chosen so that Sextus Roscius would have the best possible defence. I was chosen simply so that he would have any defence at all.

'You may ask: what is this fear and terror that drives away the best of the advocates and leaves Sextus Roscius with only a rank beginner to defend his very life? To hear Erucius speak, you would never guess there was any peril at all, since he has deliberately avoided naming his true employer or mentioning that secret person's vicious motives for bringing my client to trial.

'What person? What motives? Let me explain.

'The estate of the late, murdered Sextus Roscius – which by any ordinary course of events should now be the property of his son and heir – embraces farms and properties exceeding six million sesterces in value. Six million sesterces! That is a considerable fortune, amassed over a long and productive lifetime. Yet this entire estate was purchased by a certain young man, presumably at public auction, for the astonishing sum of *two thousand* sesterces. Quite a bargain! The thrifty young buyer was Lucius Cornelius Chrysogonus – I see the very mention of his name causes a stir in this place, and why not? He is an exceptionally powerful man. The alleged seller of this property, representing the interests of the state, was the valiant and illustrious Lucius Sulla, whose name I mention with all due respect.'

At this point a soft hissing filled the square like a rain of mist on hot stones, as men turned to one another and whispered behind their hands. Capito clutched at Glaucia's shoulder and croaked into his ear. All about me nobles in the gallery crossed their arms and exchanged grim glances. Two elderly Metelli on my right nodded knowingly to each other. Gaius Erucius, whose plump jowls had abruptly turned scarlet at the mention of Chrysogonus, gripped a young slave by the neck, spat an order at him, and sent him fleeing from the square.

'Let me be frank. It is Chrysogonus who has

engineered these charges against my client. With no legal justification whatsoever, Chrysogonus has seized the property of an innocent man. Unable to enjoy his stolen goods to the fullest, since their rightful owner still lives and breathes, he asks you, the judges of this court, to alleviate his anxiety by doing away with my client. Only then can he squander the fortunes of the late Sextus Roscius with all the carefree dissipation he aspires to.

'Does this seem right to you, Judges? Is it decent? Is it just? In opposition let me put forward my own demands, which I think you will find more modest and more reasonable.

'First: let this villain Chrysogonus be satisfied with seizing our wealth and property. Let him refrain from demanding our lifeblood as well!'

Cicero had begun pacing back and forth across the podium, following his habit of pacing in his study. All uncertainty had left his voice, which had emerged more vibrant and stirring than I had ever heard it before.

'Second, good Judges, I beg this of you: turn your back on the wicked schemes of wicked men. Open your eyes and your hearts to the plea of an innocent victim. Save us all from a terrible danger, because the peril that hangs over Sextus Roscius in this trial hangs over every free citizen in Rome. If indeed, at the end of this inquiry, you feel convinced of Sextus Roscius's guilt – no, not even convinced, but merely suspicious; if one shred of evidence suggests that the horrendous accusations against him might possibly be justified; if you can honestly believe that his persecutors have brought him to trial for any other motive than to satisfy their own insatiable greed for loot – then find him guilty and I will not object. But if the only issue at hand is the rapacious avarice of his accusers and their lust to see their victim eliminated by a perversion of justice, then I ask you all to stand upon your integrity as senators and as judges, to refuse to allow your offices and your persons to become mere instruments in the hands of criminals.

'I urge you, Marcus Fannius, as chairman of this court, to look at the enormous crowd that has gathered for this trial. What has drawn them here? Ah, yes, the nature of the accusation is sensational in the extreme. A Roman court has not heard a case of murder in a very long time – though in the interim there have certainly been no lack of abominable murders! Those who have gathered here are sick of murder; they long for justice. They want to see criminals harshly punished. They want to see crime put down with frightful severity.

'That is what we ask for: harsh punishments and the full severity of the law. Usually it is the accusers who make such demands, but not today. Today it is we, the accused, who appeal to you, Fannius, and your fellow judges, to punish crime with all the vehemence you can muster. For if you do not – if you fail to seize this opportunity to show us where the judges and the courts of Rome stand – then we have clearly reached that point where all limits to human greed and outrage have been swept aside. The alternative is anarchy, absolute and unbounded. Capitulate to the accusers, fail to do your duty, and from this day forward the slaughter of the innocent will no longer be done in the shadows and hidden by legal subterfuge. No, such murders will be committed here in the very Forum itself, Fannius, before the very platform where you sit. For what is the aim of this trial, except that theft and murder can be committed with impunity?

'I see two camps before the Rostra. The accusers: those who have laid claim to the property of my client, who directly profited from the murder of my client's father, who now seek to goad the state into killing an innocent man. And the accused: Sextus Roscius, to whom his accusers have left nothing but ruin, to whom his father's death brought not only grief, but destitution, who now presents himself before this court with armed guards at his back – not for the protection of the court, as Erucius sneeringly implies, but for his own protection, for fear he may be murdered on the spot before your very eyes! Which of these parties is truly on trial here today? Which has invited the wrath of the law?

'No mere description of these bandits will suffice to acquaint you with the blackness of their characters. No simple catalogue of their crimes will make manifest their degree of high-handedness in daring to accuse Sextus Roscius of parricide. I must begin at the beginning and recount for you the whole course of events that have led to this moment. Then you will know the full degradation to which an innocent man has been subjected. Then you will understand completely the audacity of his accusers and the unspeakable horror of their crimes. And you will see as well, not fully but with frightening clarity, the calamitous state into which this republic has fallen.'

Cicero was like a man transformed. His gestures were strong and unequivocal. His voice was passionate and clear. Had I seen him from a distance I would not have recognized him. Had I heard him from another room I would not have known his voice.

I had witnessed such transformations before, but only in the theatre or on certain religious occasions, when one expects to be startled by the elasticity of the human vessel. To see it occur before my eyes in a man I thought I knew was startling. Had Cicero known all along that such a change would come upon him in his moment of need? Had Rufus and Tiro? Surely they must have known, for there was no other way to account for the serene confidence that had never left them. What had they all been able to see in Cicero that I could not?

Erucius had entertained the crowd with melodrama and bombast, and the mob had been well satisfied. He had threatened the judges to their faces, and they had suffered his abuse in silence. Cicero seemed determined to stir true passion in his listeners, and his hunger for justice was infectious. His decision to indict Chrysogonus from the beginning had been a bold gamble. At the very mention of the name, Erucius and Magnus were thrown into a visible panic. Clearly they had expected a meek opposition that would offer as rambling and circumstantial an oration as their own. Instead Cicero plunged into the tale up to his neck, omitting nothing.

He described the circumstances of the elder Sextus Roscius, his connections in Rome and his long-standing feud with the cousins Magnus and Capito. He described their notorious characters. (Capito he compared to a scarred and hoary gladiator, and Magnus to an old fighter's protégé who had already surpassed his master in wreaking havoc.) He specified the time and place of Sextus Roscius's murder, and noted the odd fact that Mallius Glaucia had ridden all night to take a bloody dagger and report the death to Capito in Ameria. He detailed the connection between the cousins and Chrysogonus; the illegal proscription of Sextus Roscius after his death and after all such proscriptions had ceased by law; the useless protestations of the town council of Ameria; the acquisition of the Roscius estate by Chrysogonus, Magnus, and Capito; their attempts to eliminate Sextus Roscius the younger and his flight to Caecilia Metella in Rome. He reminded the judges of the query applied to every crime by the great Lucius Cassius Longinus Ravilla: *who profits?*

When he approached the matter of the dictator, he did not flinch; he seemed almost to smirk. 'I remain convinced, good Judges, that all this took place without the knowledge, indeed beneath the notice, of the venerable Lucius Sulla. After all, his

493

sphere is vast and wide; national affairs of the utmost importance claim all his attention as he busily repairs the wounds of the past and forestalls the threats of the future. All eyes are on him; all power resides in his sure hands. To build peace or wage war – the choice, and the means to carry it out, are his and his alone. Imagine the host of petty miscreants who surround such a man, who watch and wait for those occasions when his attention is fully concentrated elsewhere so that they may rush in and take advantage of the moment. Sulla the Fortunate he truly is, but surely, by Hercules, there is no one so beloved by Fortune that there does not lurk within his vast household some dishonest slave or, worse still, a cunning and unscrupulous ex-slave.'

He consulted his notes and refuted every point of Erucius's oration, ridiculing its simplemindedness. He countered Erucius's argument that Sextus Roscius's obligations to remain in the country had been a sign of discord between father and son with a long digression on the value and honour of rural life – always a pleasing theme to citified Roman ears. He protested that the slaves who had witnessed the murder could not be called as witnesses, because their new owner – Magnus, who now kept them hidden away in the house of Chrysogonus – refused to allow it.

He meditated on the horrors of parricide, a crime so grave that a conviction demanded absolute proof. 'I would almost say that the judges must see the son's hands sprinkled with blood if they are

494

to believe a crime so monstrous, so foul, so unnatural!' He described the ancient punishment for parricide, to the crowd's mingled horror and fascination.

His oration was so exhaustive and lengthy that the judges began shifting in their seats, no longer from the alarm of hearing Sulla's name, but from restlessness. His voice began to grow hoarse, even though he occasionally took sips from a cup of water hidden behind the podium. I began to think he was stalling for time, though I couldn't imagine why.

For some while Tiro had been absent from the bench of the accused – relieving himself, I had assumed, since I felt a growing need to do the same thing myself. At that very moment Tiro came hobbling briskly along the gallery, leaning on his crutch, and took his place at the bench. From atop the Rostra Cicero looked down and raised an eyebrow. Some sort of signal passed between them, and they both smiled.

Cicero cleared his throat and took a long draught of water. He took a deep breath and for a brief moment closed his eyes. 'And now, Judges, we come to the matter of a certain scoundrel and ex-slave, Egyptian by birth, endlessly avaricious by nature – but look, here he comes now with a splendid retinue trailing behind, down from his fine mansion on the Palatine, where he dwells in opulence among senators and magistrates from the oldest families of the Republic.'

Alerted by Erucius, Chrysogonus had at last arrived.

His bodyguards made short work of clearing the last row of the gallery, where a few lucky members of the crowd at large had taken the only seats left over by the lesser nobles. Heads turned and a murmur passed through the square as Chrysogonus strode to the centre of the bench and sat. He was surrounded by so many retainers that some were left standing in the aisles.

I turned my head with the rest to catch a glimpse of the legendary golden locks, the lofty Alexander-like brow, the strong, broad jaw which today was set in a hard, grim line. I turned back to look at Cicero, who seemed to be physically girding himself for attack, drawing up his thin shoulders and lowering his forehead like a charging goat.

'I have been making inquiries about this ex-slave,' he said. 'I find he is very wealthy, and not ashamed to show it. Besides his mansion on the Palatine he has a fine country retreat, not to mention a host of farms, all of them on excellent soil and close to the city. His house is crammed with Delian and Corinthian vessels of gold, silver, and copper – among them a mechanical boiling urn which he recently bought at auction at so exorbitant a price that passersby, hearing his final bid, thought that a whole estate was being sold. The total value of his embossed silver, embroidered coverlets, paintings, and marble statues is beyond computation – unless one might compute the precise amount of plunder that could be looted from various illustrious families and heaped up in one house!

'But these are only his mute possessions. What of

his speaking possessions? They comprise a vast household of slaves with the most exquisite skills and natural endowments. I need hardly mention the common trades – cooks, bakers, garment makers, litter bearers, carpenters, upholsterers, dust maids, scrub maids, painters, floor polishers, dish washers, handymen, stableboys, roofers, and medical experts. To charm his ears and soothe his mind he owns such a host of musicians that the whole neighbourhood rings with the continual sound of voices, strings, drums, and flutes. At night he fills the air with the din of his debaucheries – acrobats perform and lewd poets declaim for his pleasure. When a man leads such a life, Judges, can you imagine his daily expenses? The cost of his wardrobe? His budget for lavish entertainments and sumptuous meals? One should hardly call his dwelling a house at all, but rather a factory of dissolution and vice, and a lodging house for every sort of criminal. The entire fortunes of a Sextus Roscius would hardly last him a month!

'Look at the man himself, Judges – turn your heads and look! With his hair so carefully curled and scented, how he struts about the Forum with his following of Roman-born citizens who disgrace their togas by appearing in the retinue of an ex-slave! See what contempt he has for all those about him, how he considers no one a human being compared with himself, how he puffs himself up with the illusion that he alone possesses all power and wealth.'

I glanced over my shoulder. Anyone who at that

moment might be seeing Chrysogonus for the first time would never have taken him for a handsome man. His face had turned so bloated and red that he appeared to be on the verge of apoplexy. His eyes bulged from their sockets. I had never seen so much fury pent up inside a body so rigid. If he had literally exploded I would hardly have been surprised.

Cicero, from the Rostra, could clearly see the effect his words were producing and yet went on without pausing. He, too, looked excited and flushed. He spoke more and more rapidly, and yet maintained complete control, never tripping over a syllable or searching for a word.

'I fear, from my attack on this creature, that some may misapprehend me, that you may assume that I mean to attack the aristocratic cause that has proven triumphant in our civil wars, and their champion, Sulla. Not so. Those who know me know that I longed for peace and reconciliation in the wars, but reconciliation having failed, victory went to the more righteous party. This was due to the will of the gods, the zeal of the Roman people, and of course the wisdom, power, and good fortune of Lucius Sulla. That the victors should have been rewarded and the vanquished punished is not for me to question. But I cannot believe that the aristocracy roused itself to arms only so that its slaves and ex-slaves should be made free to glut themselves on our goods and property.'

I could stand it no longer. My bladder felt as near to bursting as Chrysogonus's swollen cheeks.

I rose from my seat and sidestepped past nobles

who scowled at the distraction and fastidiously tugged up the hem of their togas, as if the mere touch of my foot might soil the cloth. While I escaped down the crowded aisle between the judges and the gallery, I glanced back into the square and felt that odd detachment of an anonymous spectator leaving the heart of the furore – Cicero passionately gesticulated, the crowd looked raptly on, Erucius and Magnus gritted their teeth. Tiro happened to glance towards me. He smiled, then looked suddenly alarmed. He gave me a cramped wave of summons. I smiled and gave him a wave of dismissal in return. He gestured more urgently and began to rise from his seat. I turned my back to him and hurried on. If there was some last, hushed conference he wanted with me, it would have to wait until I had tended to more pressing business. Only later did I realize that he was trying to warn me of the danger at my back.

At the end of the gallery I passed by Chrysogonus and his party. At that moment I imagined I could actually feel the heat that radiated from his blood-red face.

I pushed my way past the throng of retainers and slaves who filled the space behind the gallery. The street beyond was open and empty. Some spectators with no civic pride had already left a stench of urine in the nearest gutter, but my bladder wasn't so weak that I couldn't wait until I arrived at the public latrine. Behind the Shrine of Venus there was a small alcove specifically for the purpose, situated just above the Cloaca Maxima, with a slightly tilted floor and drains at the base of each wall.

An old man with a grizzled beard and a spotless white toga was just leaving as I stepped inside. He nodded as he passed. 'Quite a trial, is it not?' he wheezed.

'It is.'

'This Cicero is not a bad speaker.'

'A fine speaker,' I agreed hurriedly. The old man departed. I stood against the inmost wall, staring at the pitted limestone and holding my breath against the stench. Thanks to an acoustical curiosity I was able to hear Cicero from the Rostra. His voice was echoey but distinct: *'The ultimate aim of the accusers is as clear as it is reprehensible: nothing less than the complete elimination of the children of the proscribed, by any means at their disposal. Your sworn judgment and the execution of Sextus Roscius are to be the first steps in this campaign.'*

Cicero had reached his closing arguments. I tried to hurry my bladder. I closed my eyes and the floodgates opened. The sensation of relief was exquisite.

That was when I heard a low whistle behind me and stopped in midstream. I looked over my shoulder to see Mallius Glaucia standing ten paces behind me. He smoothed his hand down the front of his tunic until he closed it around the unmistakable shape of a dagger hidden within the folds at his waist. He fondled the hilt with an obscene grin, as if he were clutching his sex.

'Be vigilant, Judges; for otherwise you may on this very day and in this very place inaugurate a second wave of

proscriptions far more cruel and ruthless than the first. At least the first was directed against men who could defend themselves; the tragedy I foresee will be aimed at the children of the proscribed, at infant sons in their cradles! By the immortal gods, who knows where such an atrocity could lead this republic?'

'Go ahead,' Glaucia said. 'Finish what you were doing.'

I dropped the hem of my tunic and turned to face him.

Glaucia smiled. He slowly reached into his tunic, pulled out his knife, and toyed with it, dragging the sharp tip against the wall with a scraping noise that set my teeth on edge. 'I mean it,' he said, sounding very charitable. 'Do you think I'd stab a man in the back while he was pissing?'

'A reasonable point of honour,' I agreed, trying to keep my voice steady. 'What do you want?'

'To kill you.'

I sucked in a sharp breath, full of the smell of stale urine. 'Now? Still?'

'That's right.' He stopped scraping and touched the point of the blade to his fingertip. A bead of blood welled up from the flesh. Glaucia sucked it clean.

'*Judges, it behoves wise men, furnished with the authority you possess, to apply the surest remedies to the lingering ills of this republic. . . .*'

'But why? The trial is almost over.'

Instead of answering he continued to suck his thumb and recommenced scraping the blade against the wall. He stared at me like a demented child, monstrously overgrown. The knife in my tunic was a good match for his, but I judged his arm to be two hands longer. The odds were not good.

'Why kill me? No matter what happens now, nothing you do to me can change matters. My part in this affair was over days ago. It was the slave who struck your head the other night, if that's what you're angry about. You have no grudge against me, Mallius Glaucia. You have no reason to kill me. No reason at all.'

He quit scraping the blade. He stopped sucking his thumb. He looked at me very earnestly. 'But I've already told you: I *want* to kill you. Are you going to finish pissing or not?'

'There is not a man among you who does not know the reputation of the Roman people as merciful conquerors, lenient towards their foreign enemies; yet today Romans continue to turn on one another with shocking cruelty.'

Glaucia stepped towards me. I stepped back against the wall, directly over the drain. A powerful stench of excreta and urine rose into my nostrils.

He stepped closer. 'Well? You don't want them to find you with piss all over your toga, do you, along with all the blood?'

A figure appeared behind him – another spectator come to use the drains. I thought Glaucia might glance around for just an instant, long enough so that I could rush him, perhaps kick him between the legs – but Glaucia only smiled at me and held up his blade so that the newcomer could see it. The stranger vanished without so much as a gasp.

Glaucia shook his head. 'Now I can't give you a choice,' he said. 'Now I'll have to make it quick.'

He was big. He was also clumsy. He lunged and I was able to elude him with surprising ease. I pulled out my own blade, thinking I might not have to use it after all, not if I could simply slip past him. I dashed for open ground, slipped on the piss-covered floor, and fell face-first onto the hard stones.

The knife was jarred from my hand and went skidding away. I crawled desperately after it. It was still an arm's length away when something enormously powerful struck my shoulders and knocked me flat.

Glaucia kicked me in the ribs several times and then flipped me over. His grinning face, looming enormous as he descended on me, was the ugliest thing I had ever seen. So this is how it shall be, I thought: I shall die not as an old man with a toothless Bethesda crooning in my ear and the perfume of my garden in my nostrils, but choked by the stench of an unwashed latrine, with a hideous assassin drooling spittle on my face, and the echo of Cicero's voice droning in my ears.

There was a skittering sound, like a knife skipping over stones, and something sharp jabbed my side. I honestly believed, with the kind of faith reserved for the purist vestals, that my knife had somehow come skidding back to me, simply because I willed it to. I might have reached for it had I not been using both arms in a failing attempt to hold Glaucia off me. I stared into his eyes, fascinated by the sheer hatred I saw there. Suddenly he looked up, and in the next instant there was a stone the size of a bread loaf somehow attached to his bandaged forehead, as if it had popped out of his brain, like Minerva from Jupiter's brow. It stayed there, as if glued to the spot by the blood that abruptly oozed about the connection – no, the stone was held there by the two hands that had brought it crashing down. I rolled up my eyes and saw Tiro upside-down against a blue sky above.

He did not look happy to see me. He kept hissing something at me, over and over, until my hand (not my ear) finally apprehended the word *knife*. I somehow twisted my arm in an impossible back-wards bend, snatched my knife from where Tiro had kicked it and snapped it upright before my chest. There is no word in Latin, but there should be one, for the weird sensation of recognition I felt, as if I had done the exact thing once before. Tiro lifted the heavy stone and brought it down again on Glaucia's already smashed forehead, and the giant collapsed like a mountain on top of me, impaling his exploding heart upon the full length of Eco's blade.

'*Suffer this wickedness no longer to stalk abroad in the land,*' a distant voice was crying. '*Banish it! Deny it! Reject it! It has delivered many Romans to a terrible death. But worse than that, it has robbed our spirits. By besieging us with cruelty hour upon hour, day after day, it has benumbed us; it has stifled all pity in a people once known as the most merciful on earth. When at every moment in all directions we see and hear acts of violence; when we are lost in a relentless storm of cruelty and deceit;*

then even the kindest and gentlest among us may lose all semblance of human compassion.'

There was a pause, and then a great echoing thunder of applause. Confused and covered with blood, I thought for a moment that the cheering must be for me. The walls of the latrine did, after all, look something like the walls of an arena, and Glaucia was as dead as any dead gladiator. But gazing up I could see only Tiro, who was straightening his tunic with a look of exasperation and disgust.

'I wasn't there for the summation!' he snapped. 'Cicero will be furious. By Hercules! At least there's no blood on me.' With that he turned and disappeared, leaving me buried beneath a great quivering mass of dead flesh.

XXXII

Cicero won his case. An overwhelming majority of the seventy-five judges, including the praetor Marcus Fannius, voted to acquit Sextus Roscius of the charge of parricide. Only the most partisan Sullans, including a handful of new senators who had been appointed directly by the dictator, cast votes of guilty.

The crowd was equally impressed. Cicero's name, along with bits and pieces of his oration, was spread all over Rome. For days afterwards one might walk by the open windows of a tavern or a smithy and hear men who had not even been there repeat some of Cicero's choice jabs at Sulla or exclaim at his audacity in attacking Chrysogonus. His comments on farm and family life, his respect for filial duty and the gods were noted with approval. Overnight he gained a reputation as a brave and pious Roman, an upholder of justice and of truth.

That evening a small celebration was held in the home of Caecilia Metella. Rufus was there, glowing and triumphant and drinking a bit too much wine. So were those who had sat with Cicero at the bench of the accused, Marcus Metellus and Publius Scipio, along with a handful of others who had assisted the defence behind the scenes in some way. Sextus Roscius was given a couch at his hostess's right hand; his wife and eldest daughter sat demurely in chairs behind him. Tiro was allowed to sit behind his master so that he could take part in the celebration. Even I was invited and given my own couch to recline upon and assigned my own slave to fetch dainties from the table.

Roscius may have been the guest of honour, but all conversation revolved around Cicero. His fellow advocates cited the finer points of his oration with gushing praise; they picked at Erucius's performance with devastating sarcasm and laughed out loud recalling the look on his face when Cicero first dared to utter the name of the Golden-Born. Cicero accepted their praise with genial modesty. He consented to drink a modicum of wine; it took very little to bring a flush to his cheeks. Throwing aside his usual caution and no doubt famished from fasting and exertion, he ate like a horse. Caecilia praised his appetite and said it was a good thing he had made a victory party possible, or else all the delicacies she had ordered her staff to prepare in advance – sea nettles and scallops, thrushes on asparagus, purple fish in murex, figpeckers in fruit compote, stewed sow's udders, fattened fowls in pastry, duck, boar, and oysters *ad nauseam* – would have ended up being dumped in a Subura alley for the poor.

I began to wonder, as I sent my slave after a third helping of Bithynian mushrooms, if the celebration was not a little premature. Sextus Roscius had won his life, to be sure, but he still remained in limbo, his property in the hands of his enemies, his rights as a citizen cancelled by proscription, his father's murder unavenged. He had eluded destruction, but what were his chances of reclaiming a decent life? His advocates were in no mood to worry about the future. I kept my mouth shut, except to laugh at their jokes or to stuff it with more mushrooms.

All night Rufus gazed at Cicero with a passionate longing that seemed invisible to everyone but me; after witnessing Cicero's performance that day, how could I belittle Rufus's unrequited ardour? Tiro seemed quite content, laughing at every joke and even making bold to add a few of his own, but every now and then he glanced towards Roscia with pain in his eyes. Roscia steadfastly refused to look back. She sat in her chair, stiff and miserable, ate nothing, and finally begged her father and her hostess to excuse her. As she hurried from the room she began to weep. Her mother rose and ran after her.

Roscia's exit set off a peculiar contagion of weeping. First it struck Caecilia, who was drinking faster than anyone else. All night she had been vivacious and full of laughter. Roscia's exit plunged her into a sudden funk. 'I know,' she said, as we listened to Roscia sobbing from the hallway, 'I know why that girl weeps. Yes, I do.' She nodded tipsily. 'She misses her dear, dear old grandfather. Oh, my, what a sweet man he was. We must never forget what really brings us together here on this night – the untimely death of my dearest, dearest Sextus. Beloved Sextus. Who knows, had I not been barren all these years . . .' She reached up and blindly fussed with her hair, pricking her finger on the silver needle. A bead of blood welled up on her fingertip. She stared at the wound with a shudder and began to cry.

Rufus was instantly at her side, comforting her, keeping her from saying something that might embarrass her later.

Then Sextus Roscius began to weep. He struggled against it, biting his knuckles and contorting his face, but the tears would not be stopped. They ran down his face onto his chin and dripped onto the sea nettles on his plate. He sucked in a halting breath and expelled it in a long, shuddering moan. He covered his face with his hands and was convulsed with weeping. He knocked his plate to the floor; a slave retrieved it. His sobs were loud and choking, like a donkey's braying. It took many repetitions before I recognized the word he cried out again and again: 'Father, Father, Father . . .'

He had been his usual self for most of the night – quiet and glum, only occasionally consenting to smile when the rest of us roared at some clever joke against Erucius or Chrysogonus. Even when the verdict was announced, so Rufus told me, he had remained oddly impassive. Having lived so long in dread, he held his relief in check until it came bursting out. That was why he wept.

Or so I thought.

It seemed a good time to leave.

Publius Scipio and Marcus Metellus and their noble friends bade us good night and went their separate ways; Rufus stayed behind with Caecilia. I was anxious to sleep in my own bed, but Bethesda was still at Cicero's and the way to the Subura was long. In the good-natured flush of his success, Cicero insisted that I spend a final night beneath his roof.

Had I not gone with him, this story would have its ending here, amid half-truths and false surmises. Instead I walked beside Cicero, flanked by his torchbearers and bodyguards, through the moonlit Forum and up the spur of the Capitoline until we came to his house.

Thus I came face to face at last with the most fortunate man alive. Thus I learned the truth, which until then I had only dimly suspected.

Cicero and I were chatting amiably about nothing in particular – the long hot spell, the austere beauty of Rome beneath a full moon, the smells that filled the city at night. We rounded the corner and stepped into the street where he lived. It was Tiro who first noticed the retinue encamped like a small army about the entrance to Cicero's house. He clutched his master's toga and pointed open-mouthed.

We saw the company before they saw us – the empty litter and the litter bearers who leaned against it with folded arms, the torchbearers who slouched against the wall and held their flames at lazy angles. Beneath the flickering light some menials played trigon on the curb, while a few secretaries squinted and scribbled on parchments. There were also a number of armed guards. It was one of these who spotted us standing stock-still at the end of the street and nudged an expensively dressed slave who was busy wagering on the trigon players. The slave drew himself up and came striding haughtily towards us.

'You are the orator Cicero, the master of this house?'

'I am.'

'At last! You'll excuse the entourage camped on your doorstep – there seemed to be nowhere else to put everybody. And of course you'll excuse my master for paying a visit at such a late hour; actually we've been here a rather long time, since just after sunset, awaiting your return.'

'I see,' Cicero said dully. 'And where is your master?'

'He waits within. I convinced your doorkeeper that there was no point in keeping Lucius Sulla standing on the doorstep, even if his host was not home to greet him. Come, please.' The slave stepped back and gestured for us to follow. 'My master has been waiting for a long time. He is a very busy man. You can leave your torchbearers and bodyguards here,' he added sternly.

Beside me Cicero took deep, even breaths, like a man preparing to plunge into icy water. I imagined I could hear his heartbeat in the stillness of the night, until I realized it was my own. Tiro still clutched his master's toga. He bit his lip. 'You don't think, master – he wouldn't dare, not in your own home—'

Cicero silenced him by raising his forefinger to his lips. He stepped forward, motioning for the bodyguards to stay behind. Tiro and I followed.

As we made our way to the doorstep, the members of Sulla's retinue went about their business, giving us only quick, sullen glances, as if we were to blame for their boredom. Tiro stepped ahead to open the door. He peered inside as if he expected a thicket of drawn daggers.

But there was no one in the vestibule except Old Tiro, who came shuffling up to Cicero in a panic. 'Master—'

Cicero quieted him with a nod and a touch on the shoulder and walked on.

I had expected to see more of Sulla's retinue within – more bodyguards, more clerks, more flatterers and sycophants. But the house was populated only by Cicero's regular staff, all of whom were skirting the walls and trying to pretend invisibility.

We found him sitting alone in the study beneath a lit lamp, with a half-empty bowl of wheat pudding on the table beside him and a scroll in his lap. He looked up as we entered. He appeared neither impatient nor startled, only vaguely bored. He put the scroll aside and raised one eyebrow.

'You are a man of considerable erudition and passably good taste, Marcus Tullius Cicero. While I find far too many dull, dry works on grammar and rhetoric in this room, I am heartened to see such a fine collection of plays, especially by the Greeks. And while you appear to have intentionally collected the very worst of the Latin poets, that may be forgiven for your discernment in selecting this exceedingly fine copy of Euripides – from the workshop of Epicles in Athens, I see. When I was young I often entertained the fantasy of becoming an actor. I always thought I would have made a very poignant Pentheus. Or do you imagine I would have made a better Dionysus? Do you know *The Bacchae* well?'

Cicero swallowed hard. 'Lucius Cornelius Sulla, I am honoured that you should visit my home—'

'Enough of that nonsense!' Sulla snapped, pursing his lips. It was impossible to tell whether he was irritated or amused. 'There's no one else here. Don't waste your breath and my patience on meaningless formalities. The fact is that you're deeply distressed to find me here and you wish that I'd leave as quickly as possible.'

Cicero parted his lips and made half a nod, unsure whether to answer or not.

Sulla made the same face again – half-amused, half-irritated. He waved impatiently about the room. 'I think there are enough chairs for all. Sit.'

Tiro nervously fetched a chair for Cicero and another for me and then stood at his master's right hand, watching Sulla as if he were an exotic and very deadly reptile.

I had never seen Sulla from so close. The lamp-light from above cast stark shadows across his face, lining his mouth with wrinkles and making his eyes glitter. His great leonine mane, once famous for its lustre, had grown coarse and dull. His skin was splotched and discoloured, dotted with blemishes and etched all over with red veins as fine as bee's hair. His lips were dry and cracked. A tuft of dark hairs poked out of one nostril.

He was simply an old general, an aging debau-chee, a tired politician. His eyes had seen every-thing and feared nothing. They had witnessed every extreme of beauty and horror and could no longer be impressed. Yet there was still a hunger in them, something that seemed almost to leap out and grasp at my throat when he turned his gaze on me.

'You must be Gordianus, the one they call the Finder. Good, I'm glad you're here. I wanted to have a look at you as well.'

He looked lazily from Cicero to me and back again, laughing at us behind his eyes, testing our patience. 'You can guess why I've come,' he finally said. 'A certain trivial legal affair that came up earlier today at the Rostra. I was hardly aware of the matter until it was rather rudely brought to my attention while I was taking my lunch. A slave of my dear freedman Chrysogonus came running in all flustered and alarmed, raving about a catastrophe in the Forum. I was busy at the moment devouring a very spicy pheasant's breast; the news gave me a wicked case of indigestion. This porridge your kitchen maid brought me isn't bad – bland but soothing, just as my physicians recommend. Of course it might have been poisoned, but then you were hardly expecting me, were you? Anyway, I've always found it best to plunge into peril without giving it too much thought. I never called myself Sulla the Wise, only Sulla the Fortunate, which to my belief is much better.'

He dabbled his forefinger in the porridge for a moment, then suddenly swept his arm across the table and sent bowl and porridge crashing to the floor. A slave came running from the hallway. She saw Cicero's wide-eyed, blanching face and quickly disappeared.

Sulla popped his finger into his mouth and pulled it out clean, then went on in a calm, melodious voice. 'What a struggle it seems to have been for both of you, rooting and digging and sniffing for the truth about these disgustingly petty Roscii and their disgustingly petty crimes against one another. I'm told you've spent hour upon hour, day after day grappling for the facts; that you went all the way to godforsaken Ameria and back, Gordianus, that you put your very life in danger more than once, all for a few meagre scraps of the truth. And you still haven't got the full story – like a play with whole scenes missing. Isn't it funny? I had never even heard the name Sextus Roscius until today, and it took me only a matter of hours – minutes, really – to find out everything worth knowing about the case. I simply summoned certain parties before me

515

and demanded the full story. Sometimes I think justice must have been so much simpler and easier in the days of King Numa.'

Sulla paused for a moment and toyed with the scroll in his lap. He caressed the stitches that bound the sheets and dabbled his fingers over the smooth parchment, then suddenly seized it in a crushing grasp and sent it flying across the room. It landed atop a table of scrolls and knocked them to the floor. Sulla went on unperturbed.

'Tell me, Marcus Tullius Cicero, what was your intention when you took it upon yourself to plead this wretched man's case in court today? Were you the willing agent of my enemies, or did they dupe you into it? Are you cunningly clever, or absurdly stupid?'

Cicero's voice was as dry as parchment: 'I was asked to represent an innocent man against an outrageous accusation. If the law is not the last refuge of the innocent—'

'Innocent?' Sulla leaned forwards in his chair. His face was plunged into shadow. The lamp cast an aureole about his fire-coloured hair. 'Is that what they told you, my dear old friends, the Metelli? A very old and very great family, those Metelli. I've been waiting for them to stab me in the back ever since I divorced Delmaticus's daughter while she lay dying. What else could I do? It was the augurs and pontifices who insisted; I could not allow her to pollute my house with her illness. And this is how my former in-laws take their revenge – using an advocate with no family and a joke of a name to

516

embarrass me in the courts. What good is being a dictator when the very class of people you struggle so hard to please turn on you for such petty causes?

'What did they offer you, Cicero? Money? Promises of their patronage? Political support?'

I glanced at Cicero, whose face was set like stone. I could hardly trust my eyes in the flickering light, but it seemed that the corners of his mouth began to turn up in a very faint smile. Tiro must have noticed it as well; a strange look darkened his face, like a premonition of dismay.

'Which of them came to you, Cicero? Marcus Metellus, that idiot who dared to show his face at the bench with you today? Or his cousin Caecilia Metella, that mad old insomniac? Or not a Metellus at all, but one of their agents? Surely not my new brother-in-law Hortensius – he'll represent his worst enemy for money, Jupiter knows, but he was smart enough not to involve himself in this farce. A pity I can't say as much for Valeria's darling little brother, Rufus.'

Cicero still said nothing. Tiro wrinkled his brow impatiently and fidgeted.

Sulla sat back. The lamplight crept over his brow and into his eyes, which sparkled like glass beads. 'No matter. The Metelli recruited you against me, one way or another. So they told you this Sextus Roscius was innocent. And did you believe them?'

Tiro could stand it no more. 'Of course!' he blurted out. 'Because he is. That's why my master defended him – not to put himself into the pocket of a noble family—'

Cicero silenced him with a gentle touch on the wrist. Sulla looked at Tiro and raised an appraising eyebrow, as if noticing him for the first time. 'The slave is hardly handsome enough to be allowed to get away with that type of insolence. If you were any sort of Roman, Cicero, you'd have him beaten to within a knuckle of his life here on the spot.'

Cicero's smile wavered. 'Please, Lucius Sulla, forgive his impertinence.'

'Then answer the question instead of letting your slave answer it for you. When they told you Sextus Roscius was innocent, did you believe them?'

'Yes, I did,' Cicero sighed. He pressed his fingertips together and flexed the knuckles. He glanced at me briefly and then stared at his knuckles. 'At first.'

'Ah.' It was Sulla now who wore a faint, inscrutable smile. 'I thought you seemed too clever to have been fooled for long. When did you figure out the truth?'

Cicero shrugged. 'I suspected it almost from the beginning, not that it ever made a difference. There still is no proof that Sextus Roscius conspired with his cousins to have the old man murdered.'

'No proof.' Sulla laughed. 'You advocates! Always on one hand there is evidence and proof. And on the other there is truth.' He shook his head. 'These greedy fools, Capito and Magnus, thinking they could have their cousin Sextus convicted without confessing their own part in the crime. How could Chrysogonus ever have got himself mixed up with such trash?'

'I don't understand,' Tiro whispered. The look on his face might have been comic had it not been betrayed by such pain and confusion. I felt sorry for him. I felt sorry for myself. Until that moment I had been struggling to hold on to the same illusion that Tiro clung to so effortlessly – the belief that all our work for Sextus Roscius had a higher purpose than politics or ambition, that we had served something called justice. The belief that Sextus Roscius was innocent, after all.

Sulla raised an eyebrow and harrumphed. 'Your insolent slave does not understand, Cicero. Aren't you an enlightened Roman? Don't you see to the boy's education? Explain it for him.'

Cicero turned heavy-lidded and studied his fingers. 'I thought you knew the truth by now, Tiro. I thought you would have figured it out for yourself. Honestly, I did. Gordianus knows, I think. Don't you, Gordianus? Let him explain it. That's what he's paid for.'

Tiro looked at me so plaintively I found myself speaking against my will. 'It was all because of the whore,' I said. 'You remember, Tiro, the young girl called Elena who worked at the House of Swans.'

Sulla nodded sagely but raised a finger to interrupt. 'You've jumped ahead of the story. The younger brother . . .'

'Gaius Roscius, yes. Murdered by his brother in their home in Ameria. Perhaps the locals were fooled, but his symptoms were hardly caused by eating a pickled mushroom.'

'Colocynth,' Cicero suggested.

'Wild gourd? Possibly,' I said, 'especially in conjunction with some more palatable poison. I knew of an incident in Antioch once with very similar symptoms – the clear bile vomited up, followed by a surge of blood and immediate death. Perhaps Sextus was colluding with his cousin Magnus even then. A man with Magnus's connections can find just about any sort of poison in Rome, for a price.

'As for the motive, Sextus Roscius *pater* almost certainly intended to disinherit his elder son in favour of Gaius, or so at least Sextus *filius* was convinced. A commonplace crime for a commonplace motive. But that wasn't the end of it.

'Perhaps the old man suspected Sextus of killing Gaius. Perhaps he simply detested him so much he was looking for any excuse to disinherit him. At the same time he was becoming infatuated with the pretty young whore Elena. When she became pregnant, whether by Roscius or not, the old man hatched a scheme to buy her, liberate her, and adopt the freeborn child. Evidently he wasn't able to buy her right away; probably he bungled the purchase – the brothel owner sniffed his eagerness and drove the price absurdly high, thinking he could take advantage of an addled, lovesick old widower. This is only speculation—'

'More than speculation,' Sulla said. 'There is, or was, concrete evidence: a letter addressed to his son and dictated by the elder Roscius to his slave Felix, who thus knew the contents. According to Felix, the old man was in a drunken rage. In the letter he explicitly threatened to do what you have just described – disinherit Sextus Roscius in favour of a son as yet unborn. The document was subsequently destroyed, but the slave remembers.'

Sulla paused for me to continue. Tiro looked at Cicero, who did not look back, and then desperately at me. 'So Sextus Roscius decided to kill his father,' I said. 'Naturally he couldn't do it himself, and another poisoning would be far too suspicious; besides, the two were so estranged he had no easy access to the old man. So he called on his cousins Magnus and Capito. Perhaps they had assisted in Gaius's poisoning; perhaps they were already pressuring Sextus to do away with his father. The three of them formed a conspiracy. Sextus would inherit his father's estates and pay off his cousins later. There must have been assurances. . . .'

'Indeed,' said Sulla, 'there was a written contract of sorts. A statement of intent, if you will, to do away with old Roscius, signed by all three of them in triplicate. A copy for each, so they could all blackmail one another to a stalemate if things fell apart.'

'But things did fall apart,' I said.

'Yes.' Sulla curled his lip, as if the whole affair had a smell. 'After the murder Sextus Roscius tried to double-cross his cousins. He became sole owner of the estates by inheritance; how could they take what was his when the document they had all signed was equally incriminating to each? Sextus Roscius must have thought himself very clever; what a fool he was to try to break his bargain with the likes of those vultures.'

Sulla took a breath and continued. 'It seems it was Capito who came up with the false proscription ploy; Magnus knew Chrysogonus from some shady transaction or other and approached him with the scheme – how many times have I warned that boy not to let his avarice cloud his better judgment? Ah, well! The estates were proscribed and seized by the state; Chrysogonus bought them up himself and in turn shared them as agreed beforehand with Capito and Magnus. Sextus Roscius was left in the cold. What a fool he must have felt! What could he do? Run to the authorities waving a piece of paper that implicated himself along with the others in his father's murder?

'Of course there was always the possibility that in a fit of madness or guilt he might do just that, and so Capito allowed Sextus to stay on at the old family estate where he could keep an eye on him, living in poverty and humiliation. What grudges these country cousins all harboured for one another!'

Tiro, not daring to speak to Sulla, looked at me. 'But what about Elena?'

I opened my mouth to speak, but Sulla was too deep in the telling to pass the story to another. 'All the while Sextus Roscius was scheming to get back his estate somehow or other. That meant that the whore's child might still some day be his rival, or at least his enemy. Imagine him brooding day after day on the uselessness of his crime, the vileness of it; on the bitterness of Fortune, his own guilt, his ruined family. And it was all because of Elena and her child that he had first embroiled himself in the plot to kill his father! When the baby was born, Roscius killed it with his own hand.'

'And might as well have killed Elena,' I said.

'What was the shame of more blood on his hands after all his crimes?' Sulla asked, and I realized he had no sense at all of the irony of his words, spoken by one who was awash in the blood of others up to his chin. 'It was not too long afterwards that the cousins managed to get hold of Sextus's copy of the incriminating agreement. Without it he was defenceless; he had no check on them. No doubt they were turning over various ways to murder him and his family when he made his escape, first to a friend in Ameria, a certain Titus Megarus, and then to Caecilia Metella in Rome. Since he had slipped from their clutches, the cousins' only recourse was to destroy him via the law. Since he was in fact guilty of his father's murder, they naively thought they could reconstruct a narration of the events to leave themselves out of the picture. And of course they were counting on the intimidation of Chrysogonus's name to drive away any competent orators from mounting a defence — if the matter even came to trial. By this point the state of Sextus Roscius's mind was so disturbed that they hoped he might be driven to suicide, or perhaps to simply confess his own guilt and mount no defence at all.'

'They were obscenely self-confident,' Cicero said softly.

'Were they?' Sulla mused. His voice carried a dark, brooding edge. 'Not excessively so. If this trial had taken place six months ago, do you think an advocate for the defence would have dared to utter Chrysogonus's name? To mention me by name? To bring up the proscriptions? Do you think a majority of judges in one of the courts reconstructed *by me* would have dared to flaunt their independence? Capito and Magnus were simply six months out of step, that's all. Six months ago the Metelli would not have lifted a finger to save Sextus Roscius. But now they sense my power waning; now they decide to test the limits of my prestige and sting me with a defeat in the courts. How these powerful old families chafe beneath the steady hand of a dictator, even when I have always used my power to enrich their coffers and hold the jealous masses in check. They want it all for themselves – like Magnus and Capito. Are you really so proud to be their champion, Cicero, to have saved a bloody parricide just so you could kick me in the balls, all in the name of old-fashioned Roman virtue?'

For a long time Sulla and Cicero looked each other in the eye across the small space that separated them. Sulla suddenly looked to me very old and weary, and Cicero very young. But it was Cicero who dropped his gaze first.

'What becomes of Sextus Roscius now?' I said.

Sulla sat back and took a deep breath. 'He is a free man, exonerated by the law. A parricide, a fratricide twice over; does such a man deserve to live? But thanks to Cicero the wretch has become a sort of suffering hero, a petty little Prometheus chained to a rock. Peck at his entrails, as he

524

deserves, and the people will be outraged. So, to Sextus Roscius, Fortune will be merciful.

'His father's estates will not be returned to him. That's what my most radical enemies would like – to see a duly recorded proscription rescinded, to see the state admit such an embarrassing error. No! That will never happen, not while I live. The Roscius estates will remain disposed as they are, but—'

Sulla made a face and bit his tongue as if he tasted worm-wood. 'But Chrysogonus will voluntarily give to Sextus Roscius other estates equal in value to those that were taken from him, located as far from Ameria as possible. Let Sextus Roscius the parricide return to the life he knew, as best he can and away from those who know him and his past; but the proscription stands, and he is stripped of his family estates and his civil rights. Knowing what you know of the man, can you really say this is unjust, Cicero?'

Cicero stroked his upper lip. 'And what of my safety, and the safety of those who've helped me? Certain men are not above murder.'

'There will be no further bloodshed, no reprisals by Magnus or Capito. As for the mysterious death of a certain Mallius Glaucia, whose body was discovered earlier today, no doubt fittingly, in a public latrine – the incident is closed and forgotten. The creature never existed. I have been quite adamant with the Roscii on this point.'

Cicero narrowed his eyes. 'A bargain has two sides, Lucius Sulla.'

'Yes. Yes, indeed. I expect, Cicero, a certain restraint on your part. In return for my efforts on behalf of tranquillity and order, from you there will be no prosecution of Capito or Magnus for murder; no official complaint against the proscription of Sextus Roscius *pater*; no charge of malicious prosecution brought against Gaius Erucius. Neither you nor any of the Metelli or their agents will mount any sort of lawsuit against Chrysogonus. I tell you this explicitly, Cicero, so that you can pass it on to your friends among the Metelli. Do you understand?'

Cicero nodded.

Sulla rose. Age had weathered his face but had not stooped his shoulders. He seemed to fill the room. Next to him Cicero and Tiro looked like slender boys.

'You are a clever young man, Marcus Tullius Cicero, and by all accounts a splendid orator. You are either stupidly daring or madly ambitious, or perhaps both – just the kind of man my friends and I could use in the Forum. I would reach out my hand to recruit you, but you wouldn't take it, would you? Your young head is still too muddled with vague ideals – boldly defending republican virtue against cruel tyranny and that sort of thing. You have delusions of piety; delusions about your own nature. My other senses may be failing me, but I'm a wily old fox, and my nose is still keen, and in this room I smell another fox. Let me tell you this, Cicero: the path you've chosen in life leads to only one place in the end, and that is the place where I stand. Your path may not take you as far, but it will take you nowhere else. Look at me and see your mirror, Cicero.

'As for you, Finder . . .' Sulla looked at me shrewdly. 'Not another fox, no; a dog, I think, the kind that goes about digging up bones that other dogs have buried. Don't you ever get sick of all that mud in your snout, not to mention the occasional worm up your nose? I might consider hiring you myself, but I shall soon have no need ever again for covert agents or bribed judges or scheming advocates.

'Yes, citizens, sad news: in a matter of days I shall announce my retirement from public life. My health fails me; so does my patience. I've done what I can to shore up the old aristocracy and to keep the common rabble in their place; let someone else take on the job of saving the Republic. I can hardly wait to begin a new life in the countryside – strolling, gardening, playing with my grandchildren. Oh, and finishing my memoirs! I shall be sure to send a complete copy for your library, Cicero.'

Sulla flashed a sour smile and drew himself up to depart; then his smile abruptly sweetened. He was looking over our heads towards the hallway. He raised one eyebrow and cocked his head, radiating charm. 'Rufus, dear boy,' he crooned, 'what an unexpected delight!'

I looked over my shoulder to see Rufus standing in the doorway, dishevelled and out of breath. 'Lucius Sulla,' he muttered with a nod, averting his eyes; that formal acknowledgment dispensed with, he turned to Cicero. 'I'm sorry,' he said. 'I saw his retinue outside. Of course I knew who it must be. I would have waited, but the news . . . I ran all the way to tell you, Cicero.'

Cicero wrinkled his brow. 'Tell me what?'

Rufus looked at Sulla and bit his lip. Sulla laughed aloud. 'Dear Rufus, feel free to say anything you wish in this room. We were already engaged in a most frank discussion before you arrived. No one here has any secrets from me. No one in this Republic can keep a secret from Sulla. Not even your good friend Cicero.'

Rufus clamped his jaw shut and glared at his brother-in-law. Cicero stepped between them. 'Go on, Rufus. Say what you have to say.'

Rufus took a deep breath. 'Sextus Roscius . . .' he whispered.

'Yes?'

'Sextus Roscius is dead.'

XXXIII

All eyes abruptly turned to Sulla, who looked as startled as the rest of us.

'But how?' said Cicero.

'A fall.' Rufus shook his head in consternation. 'From a balcony at the back of Caecilia's house. It's a long drop. The hill falls away steeply from the ground floor below. There's a narrow stone stairway that winds down the slope. He apparently hit the steps and then tumbled quite a way. His body was terribly broken—'

'The fool!' Sulla's voice was like a thunderclap. 'The idiot! If he was so bent on exterminating himself—'

'Suicide?' Cicero said quietly. 'But we have no proof of that.' In his glance I saw that we shared the same suspicion. Without the guard on Caecilia's house, someone might have made his way into Sextus Roscius's quarters – an assassin sent by the

Roscii, or by Chrysogonus, or by Sulla himself. The dictator had declared a truce, but how far could be or his friends be trusted?

Yet Sulla's own indignation seemed proof of his innocence. 'Of course it was suicide,' he snapped. 'We all know the state of the man's mind over the last months. A parricide, slowly going mad! So justice prevails after all, and Sextus Roscius is his own executioner.' Sulla laughed without mirth, then turned ashen. 'But if he was determined to punish himself, why did he wait until *after* the trial? Why didn't he kill himself yesterday, or the day before, or last month, and save us all the trouble?' He shook his head.

'Acquitted – and yet he kills himself. His guilt catches up with him only after a court absolves him. It's absurd, ridiculous. The only result is my embarrassment before all Rome!' He made a fist and rolled his eyes heavenward, and in a low, accusing voice I heard him mutter, 'Fortune!'

I realized I saw a man engaged in a lovers' quarrel with his guiding genius. All his life Sulla had been blessed; glory, wealth, fame, and pleasures of the flesh had all been his for the merest effort, and not even the smallest setbacks had encumbered the pageant of his career. Now he was an old man, declining in body and influence, and Fortune, like a bored lover, had begun to turn fickle on him, flirting with his enemies, stinging him with petty defeats and trivial reverses that must have seemed perverse indeed to a man so spoiled by success.

He wrapped himself in his toga and proceeded

towards the doorway, his head lowered like the prow of a ramming ship. When Cicero and Rufus stepped aside, I stepped forward to block his path, keeping my head meekly bowed.

'Lucius Sulla – good Sulla – I assume this changes none of the conditions that were agreed upon here tonight?'

I was close enough to hear the sharp intake of his breath, and to feel its heat on my forehead when he expelled it. It seemed that he waited a long time to answer – long enough for me to contemplate the rapid beating of my heart and to wonder what mad impulse had driven me to bar his way. But his voice, however cold, was resolute and even. 'Nothing is changed.'

'Then Cicero and his allies are still immune from the Roscii's revenge—'

'Of course.'

'– and the family of Sextus Roscius, despite his death, will still receive recompense from Chrysogonus?'

Sulla paused. I kept my eyes averted. 'Of course,' he finally said. 'His wife and daughters shall be provided for, despite his suicide.'

'You are merciful and just, Lucius Sulla,' I said, stepping out of his way. He left without looking back, not even bothering to wait for a slave to show him out. A moment later we heard the sound of the door opening and slamming shut, and then the street was abruptly filled with the noise of his departing entourage. Then all was quiet again.

In the silence that followed, the slave girl

returned to clean up Sulla's debris. While she stacked the pieces of pottery, Cicero stared abstractedly at the mess of porridge Sulla had thrown against the wall. 'Leave the scrolls where they are, Athalena. They'll be all out of order. Tiro will pick them up later.' She nodded obediently and Cicero began to pace.

'What irony,' he said at last. 'So much effort on all sides, and in the end even Sulla is disappointed. *Who profits*, indeed?'

'You, for one, Cicero.'

He looked at me archly, but could not conceal the smile that trembled on his lips. Across the room, Tiro looked more confused and crestfallen than ever.

Rufus shook his head. 'Sextus Roscius, a suicide. What did Sulla mean, saying justice had been done, that Roscius had executed himself?'

'I'll explain everything to you on the way back to Caecilia's house,' I said. 'Unless Cicero would rather explain it to you himself.' I stared straight at Cicero, who clearly did not relish the prospect. 'He can also explain to me exactly how much of the truth he knew when he hired me. But in the meantime I see no reason to accept that Roscius's fall was a suicide, not until I see the evidence with my own eyes.'

Rufus shrugged. 'But how else to explain it? Unless it was simply an accident – the balcony is treacherous, and he'd been drinking all night; I suppose he could have tripped. Besides, who in the household would have wanted him dead?'

'Perhaps no one.' I exchanged a furtive glance with Tiro. How could either of us forget the bitterness and desperation of Roscia Majora? Her father's acquittal had dashed all her hopes for revenge, and for the protection of her beloved sister. I cleared my throat and rubbed my weary eyes. 'Rufus, if you will, come back with me now to Caecilia's house. Show me how and where Roscius died.'

'Tonight?' He was tired and confused, and had the look of a young man who had drunk too much wine too early in the evening.

'Tomorrow may be too late. Caecilia's slaves may disturb the evidence.'

Rufus acquiesced with a weary nod.

'And Tiro,' I said, answering the plea in his eyes. 'May he come as well, Cicero?'

'In the middle of the night?' Cicero pursed his lips in disapproval. 'Oh, I suppose he may.'

'And you, too, of course.'

Cicero shook his head. The look he gave me was part pity, part disdain. 'This game is ended, Gordianus. The time has come for all men with a clear conscience to take their well-earned rest. Sextus Roscius is dead, and what of it? He died by his own choice; Sulla-from-whom-there-are-no-secrets himself says so. Give it up, Gordianus. Follow my example and go to bed. The trial is done with, the case is over. It's finished, my friend.'

'Perhaps it is, Cicero,' I said, walking towards the vestibule and gesturing for Rufus and Tiro to follow. 'And perhaps it is not.'

★   ★   ★

'It must have been here, from this very spot,' Rufus whispered.

The full moon shone down brightly on the flagstones of the balcony and the knee-high stone railing that bordered it. Peering over the edge, I saw the stairway Rufus had mentioned, thirty or more feet directly below; the smooth, well-worn edges of the steps gleamed dully in the moonlight. The stairway twisted down into darkness, surrounded by tall weeds and overgrown shrubbery, and obscured here and there by overhanging branches of oaks and willows. From deep within the house the sound of wailing carried across the warm night air; the body of Sextus Roscius had been placed in the sanctum of Caecilia's goddess, and her slave girls were mourning with ceremonial wails and screams.

'This railing seems woefully short,' said Tiro, kicking at one of the squat pillars from a safe distance. 'Hardly high enough to keep a child safe on the balcony.' He backed away with a shiver.

'Yes.' Rufus nodded. 'I made the same remark to Caecilia. It seems there used to be a second railing atop it, a wooden one. You can see the metal brackets for it here and there. The wood got all rotten and dangerous, and someone had it torn away. Caecilia says she meant to replace it but never got around to it; the back wing of the house hadn't been used for a long time until Sextus and his family arrived.' He stepped beside me and peered cautiously over the edge. 'That stairway down there is steeper than it looks from here. Very steep and worn, slippery and hard. Dangerous enough to walk down; for a man who'd fallen or tripped . . .' He shuddered. 'He tumbled halfway down the hill before his body came to rest. There, you can see the place, through that opening in the oak tree, where the stairway takes a sharp bend. You can see the very spot – where the blood catches the moonlight, like a pool of black oil.'

'Who found him?' I said.

'I did. That is, I was the first actually to go down and turn his body over.'

'And how did that come about?'

'Because I heard the scream.'

'Whose scream? Roscius, as he fell?'

'Why, no. Roscia, his daughter. Her bedchamber, the one she shares with her little sister – it's just within the house, the first doorway down the corridor.'

'Explain, please.'

Rufus took a deep breath. It was clearly a struggle to keep his muddled thoughts straight. 'I had already gone to my own bedchamber – the one I always sleep in when I stay over. It's near the centre of the house, about midway between Caecilia's chambers and these. I heard a scream, a girl's scream, followed by loud weeping. I ran from my room and followed it. I found her here on the balcony, shaking and weeping in the moonlight – Roscia Majora. Of course she'd been crying all night, but that hardly explained the scream. When I asked her what was wrong, she shuddered so violently she couldn't speak. Instead she pointed there, to the spot where Roscius's body had come

535

to rest.' He frowned. 'So I suppose it was actually Roscia who first discovered the body, but I was the one who ran down to have a look.'

I glanced over my shoulder at Tiro, who shook his head sadly. His worst suspicions seemed confirmed. 'And just how did Roscia happen to be standing here on the very balcony from which her father had fallen?' I said.

'I asked her that myself,' Rufus said, 'once she was finally able to stop trembling. It seems that she'd just awakened from a bad dream, and she decided to step out onto the balcony for some fresh air. She stood here for a short while, just looking at the full moon, she said, and then she chanced to look down—'

'And just happened to see her father's body, fifty feet or more away, amid all the jumble of leaves and grass and stonework?'

'It wasn't so unlikely,' said Rufus defensively. 'The moon was shining right on the spot, I saw it myself right away when she pointed. And the sight wasn't pretty, the way his limbs and neck were twisted so unnaturally. . . .' He stopped and sucked in a breath, suddenly understanding. 'Oh, Gordianus, you don't think the girl . . .'

'Of course she did,' said Tiro dully from the shadows behind us. 'The only question is how she managed to lure Sextus out here onto the balcony, though I'm sure that was no challenge to her.'

'That is not the only question,' I objected, though it seemed merely pedantic to consider all the possibilities. 'For example, why did she scream after she pushed him, if indeed she did push him, and especially if it was a premeditated murder? Why did she stay on the balcony until someone could find her?'

Tiro gave a disinterested shrug; his mind was already made up. 'Because she was shocked at the reality of what she'd done. She's only a girl, after all, Gordianus, not a hardened assassin. That's why she was weeping, too, when Rufus came to her; the horror of having actually done it, the relief, the sight of his broken body. . . . Oh, these Roscii! Cousins and brothers and sons and even daughters all desperate to exterminate their own line. I'm sick of them all! Is it a poison in their blood? Some foul imbalance in their humours?' Tiro shook his head in despair, but when he looked up and I saw his face, half in moonlight, half in shadow, what I read were not thoughts of foulness or horror, but the memory of something irretrievably lost and too painfully sweet to bear.

I turned back to face the abyss, the deep pit of moonlight and shadow into which Sextus Roscius had finally fallen, whether by his own will or by someone else's. I knelt on one knee before the rail and placed my hands on it. I ran my palms aimlessly over the bevelled surface, almost perfectly smooth except for a few tiny grains of stone that stuck to my hands. A thought struck me.

'Tiro, bring one of the lamps. Here, hold it just above the railing, where I can have a closer look.' The light quavered and I looked up to see Tiro blenching at standing so near the edge. 'If you can't

hold it steady, then hand it to Rufus.' Tiro sur-
rendered the lamp without hesitation. 'Here, Rufus,' I said, 'follow me and keep the light directly
over the railing.'

'Don't scrape your nose,' Rufus said, feeling my
excitement and reacting with a joke. 'What are you
looking for, anyway?'

We traversed the full length of the rail twice,
without success. I stood up and shrugged. 'It was
only an idea. If Sextus Roscius actually did jump by
his own choice, it only makes sense that he might
first have stepped onto the railing and jumped from
there. I thought perhaps there might be some ghost
of a footprint in the fine dust. But no.'

I turned my hands over in the lamplight and
looked at the powdery dust on the heels of my
palms, flecked here and there with a few grains of
gravel that adhered to the flesh. I was about to clap
my hands clean when I noticed that one speck of
debris was quite different from any of the others. It
was larger and glossier, with smooth, sharp edges;
instead of a bleached grey, it shone dull red in the
lamplight. I turned it over with one finger and saw
that it was not a piece of stone at all.

'What is it?' whispered Rufus, squinting beside
me. 'Is there blood on it?'

'No,' I said, 'but something the colour of dried
blood.'

'But *this* is blood!' said Tiro. While Rufus and I
examined the railing, he had taken his own lamp
and surveyed the flagstones of the balcony at a safer
distance from the edge. At his feet, so insignificant

that we had not noticed them before, were a few scattered drops of dark liquid. I knelt and touched them. The beaded drops of blood were dry at the edges but still moist at the centre.

I stepped back and indicated a straight line with my hand.

'There, on the floor of the balcony, are the drops of blood. There, just before them, is the place on the railing where I found this object.' I held the red fragment carefully between my finger and thumb. 'And directly before that, down below, is the spot where Sextus Roscius struck the stairway.'

'What does it mean?' asked Rufus.

'First tell me this: who else has been on this balcony tonight?'

'Only Roscia and myself, so far as I know. And of course Sextus Roscius.'

'None of the slaves? Or Roscius's wife?'

'I don't think so.'

'Not even Caecilia?'

Rufus shook his head. 'That I'm sure of. When I brought her the news, she said she wouldn't even come near this wing of the house. She ordered the slaves to bring Sextus's body to her sanctum for purification.'

'I see. Take me to see his body now.'

'But, Gordianus,' Tiro pleaded, 'what have you learned?'

'That Roscia did not murder her father.'

His brow smoothed with relief, then clouded with sudden doubt. 'But if he jumped, how can you explain the blood?'

I placed my finger to my lips. Tiro obediently fell silent, but I wasn't gesturing for him to hush; I was superstitiously kissing the tiny shred of evidence I held between my finger and thumb, and praying that I was not mistaken.

The doors to the sanctum of Caecilia's goddess were tightly shut, but the odour of incense and the wailing of her slave girls penetrated to the corridor without. Ahausarus the eunuch stood guard and sombrely shook his head when we tried to enter. Rufus gripped my arm and pulled me back.

'Stop, Gordianus. You know the rules of Caecilia's household. No men are admitted to the goddess's sanctum.'

'Unless they're dead?' I snapped.

'Sextus Roscius the son of Sextus Roscius has been claimed by the Goddess,' crooned Caecilia, who suddenly stood behind us. 'She has summoned him to her bosom.'

I turned to see a woman transformed. Caecilia stood very straight, with her head thrown proudly back. In place of a stola she wore a loose, flowing gown dyed deepest black. Her hair had been undone for the night and hung over her shoulders in long, crinkled tresses. The various layers of makeup had been washed from her face. Wrinkled and dishevelled, she nevertheless displayed a vigour and a determination that I had not seen in her before. She looked neither angry nor pleased to see us, as if our presence were of no significance.

'The goddess may have summoned Sextus

Roscius,' I said, 'but if I may, Caecilia Metella, I should appreciate the opportunity to examine his remains.'

'Of what possible interest could his body be to you?'

'There is a mark I wish to search for. For all I know, it's the mark of the goddess, calling him home.'

'His body is twisted and broken inside and out,' Caecilia said, 'too mangled for the eye to discern any single wound.'

'But my eye is very keen,' I said, fixing it on her and refusing to look away.

Caecilia drew herself up, looked at me sidelong, and at last gave her assent with a nod. 'Ahausarus! Tell the girls to bring Sextus Roscius's body here into the corridor.' The eunuch opened the doors and slipped within.

'Are they strong enough?' I asked.

'They were strong enough to bear him up the stairway and through the corridors to this room. The moon is full, Gordianus. The power of the goddess invests them with a strength greater than any man's.'

A moment later the doors to the sanctum swung open. Six slave girls bore a litter into the corridor and lowered it to the floor.

Tiro hissed and drew back. Even Rufus, who had seen it already, drew in a sharp breath at the sight of what remained of Sextus Roscius. His clothing had been cut away, leaving him naked. The sheet beneath him was soaked with blood. He was covered all over with bruises and gashes. Numerous bones had been broken; in some places they speared through the torn flesh. Some attempt had been made to straighten his limbs, but nothing could be done to disguise the ruin of his skull. He had apparently landed headfirst. His face was a wreckage, and the top of his head was a confusion of blood and phlegm held together by shards of bones. Unable to look at him, Tiro turned his back and Rufus lowered his eyes. Caecilia gazed down steadily at the body with no expression at all.

I knelt and pushed the broken chin aside; cartilage and bone grated beneath my touch. I ran my fingers down the throat, past mottled bruises and clumps of blood, and found what I sought by touch. 'Rufus, look here, and you too, Tiro. See, where my finger is pointing, the hole in the soft flesh just below the larynx?'

'It looks like a puncture wound,' ventured Rufus.

'Yes,' I said, 'such as might be made by a very sharp, slender object. And if we turn him on his side – here, Rufus, push with me – I believe we'll find the exact twin of this wound in the back of Roscius's neck. Yes, there, see it – just to one side of the spine.'

I stood and wiped my bloodied hands on a cloth offered by one of the slave girls. I choked back an abrupt surge of nausea and caught my breath. 'A strange wound, wouldn't you agree, Caecilia Metella? Not at all consistent with a plummeting headfirst collision and a tumble down stone stairs.

Nor is it the type of wound that might be made by a knife. It seems to have gone straight through his neck – in the front and out the back, or the other way around, I wonder? Such a sharp, slender object, made of such strong metal that it plunged all the way through and then was pulled free. Such a clean wound that only a few drops of blood fell from the instrument onto the floor of the balcony. Tell me, Caecilia, was your hair already down when you encountered Sextus Roscius on the balcony? Or was it still up in a coil, held in place by one of those long silver pins you wear?'

Rufus gripped my arm. 'Hush, Gordianus! I told you already, Caecilia was never on the balcony tonight.'

'Caecilia was never on the balcony *after* Sextus Roscius fell. But before that – while you made ready to go to bed, Rufus, and Roscia Majora slept? Did he confess his guilt to you freely there on the balcony, Caecilia, or did you happen to overhear him babbling in his drunken stupor?'

Rufus tightened his grip until it began to hurt me. 'Shut up, Gordianus! Caecilia was never on that balcony tonight!'

I pulled my arm free and stepped towards Caecilia, whose basilisk composure never wavered. 'But if she was never on that balcony, how is it that I came to find this curious object there, lying on the railing?' I held up the tiny thing I clutched between my thumb and forefinger. 'Caecilia, may I see your hand?'

She raised one eyebrow, curious but not much

concerned, and extended her right hand to me, palm down. I took it in mine and gently spread her fingers apart. Rufus and Tiro moved in beside me, keeping a respectful distance and peering over my shoulders.

What I sought was not there.

If I was wrong, I had gone too far to cover myself with excuses. An outrageous affront to a Metella was a spectacular way, at least, to destroy one's reputation and livelihood. I swallowed nervously and looked up into Caecilia's eyes.

No glint of comprehension sparkled there, no quiver of amusement, but a smile as cold as frost crossed her lips. 'I think,' she said in a low, earnest voice, 'that it must be this hand you wish to examine, Gordianus.'

She placed her left hand in my palm. I sighed with relief.

At the tips of her withered fingers I saw five perfect red-stained nails – perfect except for the nail of her forefinger, which was chipped on one side, leaving a broken gap near the tip. I took the bit of red fingernail I had found on the balcony and placed it into the gap, where it fit as neatly as a nut in a shell.

'Then you *were* on the balcony tonight!' said Rufus.

'I never told you otherwise.'

'But – then I think you should explain, Caecilia. I insist!'

It was now I who restrained Rufus, laying my arm gently across his shoulder. 'No further

544

explanation is called for. Beneath her own roof, Caecilia Metella is hardly obligated to explain her movements. Or her motives, for that matter. Or her methods.' I looked down at the ruined corpse. 'Sextus Roscius is dead, claimed by the goddess of this house to satisfy her own vengeance. No further explication is wanted. Unless, of course' – I cocked my head – 'the mistress of the house would condescend to explain the facts to three unworthy supplicants who have made a very long and tireless journey in search of the truth.'

Caecilia paused for a long moment. Gazing down at the corpse of Sextus Roscius, she at last allowed her disgust for him to show on her face. 'Take him away,' she ordered with a wave of her hand. The slave girls came running to bear the litter back into the sanctum. Clouds of incense roiled from between the doors as they opened and shut. 'And you, Ahausarus – round up the garden slaves and have them start scrubbing the rear stairway. I want every trace of that man's blood cleaned away by daybreak. Oversee the work yourself!'

'But, Mistress—'

'Go on!' Caecilia clapped her hands and the eunuch sullenly departed. She then turned a disdainful eye on Tiro. Clearly she wanted no superfluous witnesses to her confession.

'Please,' I said, 'let the slave stay.'

She scowled, but acquiesced. 'A few moments ago, Gordianus, you asked me whether Sextus *filius* confessed to his father's murder, or whether I overheard him. Neither is quite true. It was the

Goddess who revealed the truth to me. Not in words and not in a vision. But it was her hand – I'm sure of it – that lifted me tonight from where I had prostrated myself in the sanctum, and led me down the corridors into the quarter of the house where the Roscii are lodged.'

She narrowed her eyes and clasped her hands together. Her voice became low and dreamlike. 'I came upon Sextus *filius* in one of the hallways, staggering about in a stupor, too drunk even to notice me in the darkness. He was babbling to himself, alternately weeping and laughing. Laughing because he was acquitted and free. Weeping because of the shame and uselessness of his crime. His thoughts were rambling and disconnected; he would start to say a thing and then stop short, but there was no mistaking the meaning of his ravings. "I killed the old man, killed him as surely as if I'd struck the blows myself," he kept saying, "arranged for the whole thing and counted the hours until he was dead. Murdered him, murdered my own father! Justice had me in the palm of her hand and I slipped away!"

'To hear him speak that way made the blood burn in my ears. Imagine what I felt, standing hidden in that dark corridor, listening to Sextus *filius* confess to his crime with no one but myself to witness it – no one but myself and the Goddess. I felt her within me. I knew what I had to do.

'It seemed that Sextus was on his way to his daughters' bedchamber – why, I can't imagine; he was so drunk I suppose he must have lost his way.

He started to step inside, but that would have been no good to me, having him wake the girls. I hissed at him, and he gave a terrible start. I stepped closer and he began to cringe. I told him to step outside onto the balcony.

'The moonlight was fierce, like the very eye of Diana. She is a huntress indeed this night, and Sextus was her prey. Moonlight captured him like a net. I demanded that he tell me the truth. He stared back at me; I could see that he was judging his chances of lying to me, just as he had lied to everyone else. But the moonlight was too strong. He laughed. He sobbed. He looked into my eyes and said to me: "Yes! Yes, I murdered your old lover! Forgive me!"

'He turned his back to me. He was still several paces from the edge of the balcony. I knew I could never force him to the rail and over, even as drunk as he was and as strong as the moonlight had made me. I prayed to the Goddess to guide him closer to the rail. But the Goddess had led me so far, and I knew I would have to finish the matter on my own.'

'So you reached up,' I said, 'and pulled the pin from your hair.'

'Yes, the same one I had worn to the trial, decorated with lapis.'

'And you drove it clear through his neck, from spine to throat.'

The muscles of her face went slack. Her shoulders slumped. 'Yes, I suppose I did. He never screamed, only made a strange, gurgling, choking sound. I pulled the pin free; there was hardly any blood on it at all. He reached up to his throat and staggered forwards. He struck the rail, and I thought he would surely fall. But instead he stopped. So I pushed him, with all my strength. He never made a noise. The next thing I heard was the sound of his body striking the stairway below.'

'And then you fell to your knees,' I said.

'Yes, I remember kneeling. . . .'

'You peered over the edge and clutched the rail – clutched it so hard that you broke a fingernail against the stone.'

'Perhaps. I don't remember that.'

'And what became of the pin?'

She shook her head, confused. 'I think I must have cast it into the darkness. I suppose it's lost among the weeds.' Having told her tale she was suddenly emptied of all her vigour. Her eyes flickered and she drooped like a withered flower. Rufus was instantly at her side. 'Dear boy,' she whispered, 'would you see me to my chambers?'

Tiro and I took our leave without ceremony, to the smell of incense and the muffled wailing of the slaves within the sanctum.

'What a day!' Tiro sighed as we stepped inside his master's house. 'What a night!'

I wearily nodded. 'And now, if we're lucky, we might get an hour of sleep before the sun comes up.'

'Sleep? I can't possibly sleep. My head is

spinning. To think, this morning Sextus Roscius was still alive . . . and Sulla had never heard of Cicero . . . and I honestly believed—'

'Yes?'

In answer he only shook his head. Cicero had disappointed him terribly, but Tiro would not say a word against him. I followed him into his master's study, where a lamp had been lit awaiting his return. He glanced about the room and walked to the pile of scrolls that Sulla had knocked from their table.

'I might as well straighten these now,' he sighed, kneeling down. 'Something to do.'

I smiled at his energy. I turned towards the atrium and studied the play of moonlight on the sand. I breathed deep and let out a great yawn.

'I'll be leaving with Bethesda tomorrow,' I said. 'I suppose I'll see you then; or perhaps not, if Cicero has some errand for you. It seems long ago that you came to my door, doesn't it, Tiro, though it's been only a few days. I can't remember a case with so many twists and turns. Perhaps Cicero will use me again, or perhaps he won't. Rome is a small place, in a way, but I might not see you again.' I suddenly had to clear my throat. It was the moonlight, I thought, making me sentimental. 'I suppose I should tell you now, Tiro – yes, here and now, while it's quiet and the two of us are alone – I should tell you that I think you're an exceedingly fine young man, Tiro. I speak from the heart, and I think Cicero would agree. You're fortunate to have a master who values you highly. Oh, I know,

Cicero may sometimes seem brusque, but – Tiro?'

I turned about to see him lying on his side among the scattered scrolls on the floor, quietly snoring. I smiled and stepped softly towards him. In sleep, beneath the mingled lamplight and moonlight, he looked truly childlike. I knelt and touched the smooth skin of his brow and the shock of soft curls above. I took the scroll that lay in his hand. It was the crumpled copy of Euripides that Sulla had been reading and had thrown across the room. My eyes fell upon the chorus's summation:

> *The gods have many guises.*
> *The gods bring crises to climax*
> *while man surmises.*
> *The end anticipated*
> *has not been consummated.*
> *But god has found a way*
> *for what no man expected.*
> *So ends the play.*

XXXIV

I was up by mid-morning, despite my late hour to bed. Bethesda was already long awake and had my few things gathered together. She hurried me into my clothes and watched me like a cat while I ate a few bites of bread and cheese; she was ready to be home.

While Bethesda waited impatiently in morning sunlight in the peristyle, Cicero called me into his study. Tiro was asleep in his room, he said, and so Cicero himself took down a box of silver and a bag of loose coins, and counted out my fee, exact to the last sesterce. 'Hortensius tells me it's customary to deduct for the meals and lodging I've given you,' he sighed, 'but I wouldn't think of it. Instead—' He smiled and added ten denarii to the pile.

It is not easy to put unpleasant questions to a man who has just paid you a handsome fee, and a substantial bonus as well. I modestly lowered my eyes as I gathered up the coins and said, as offhandedly as I could, 'There are still a few points, Cicero, that puzzle me. Perhaps you could enlighten me.'

'Yes?' His bland smile was infuriating.

'Am I correct in assuming that you knew much more about this case than you told me when you hired me? That perhaps you even knew about the proscription of Sextus Roscius *pater*? That you knew Sulla was in some way tied to it all, and that there would be grave and immediate danger to any man investigating the whole squalid affair?'

He shrugged his narrow shoulders. 'Yes. No. Perhaps. Really, Gordianus, all I had to go on were whispers and fragments; no one would tell me all they knew, just as I didn't tell you everything I knew. The Metelli thought they could use me. To some extent they did.'

'Just as you used me – as bait? To see if a stray dog sticking his nose in the Roscius affair would be threatened, attacked, killed? As I very nearly was, more than once.'

Cicero's eyes flashed, but his smile was indestructible.

'You've emerged unscathed, Gordianus.'

'Thanks to my wits.'

'Thanks to *my* protection.'

'And does it really not disturb you, Cicero, that the man you defended so successfully was guilty all along?'

'There is no dishonour in defending a guilty client – ask any advocate. And there is some honour in embarrassing a tyrant.'

'Murder means nothing to you?'

'Crime is common. Honour is rare. And now, Gordianus, I really must bid you farewell. You know the way out.' Cicero turned and walked from the room.

The day was warm but not unpleasant. At first Bethesda seemed skittish back in the house on the Esquiline, but soon she was busy going from room to room, restoring the place to her liking. In the afternoon I accompanied her down to the market-place. The bustle of the Subura swept about me – the cry of the vendors, the odour of fresh meat, the rush of half-familiar faces through the street. I was happy to be home again.

Later, while Bethesda prepared my supper, I took a long, aimless stroll through the neighbourhood, feeling the warm breeze on my face and turning my eyes to the pale golden clouds above. My thoughts drifted to the rooftop of Titus Megarus's house beneath the stars; to the hot sunlight flooding Cicero's atrium; to the House of Swans and the depths of Electra's eyes; to a glimpse of young Roscia's naked thigh as Tiro desperately clutched her and moaned against her throat; to the broken body of Sextus Roscius, who had brought together all these disparate things and cemented them with his own blood and that of his father.

I felt a pang of hunger and was ready to be home again. I looked around, not recognizing my sur-roundings for a moment, and then realized I had somehow ended up at the distant mouth of the

Narrows. I had not meant to walk so far or to come anywhere near the place. Perhaps there is a god whose guiding hand can fall so lightly on a man's shoulder that he never knows it.

I turned towards home and began to walk.

I passed no one on the path, but every now and again I heard from windows above the sound of women calling their families to supper. The world seemed peaceful and content, until I heard the stamping of feet behind me.

Many feet, pounding against the paving stones, together with high-pitched shouts that echoed down the Narrows and the clatter of sticks being dragged against the uneven walls. For a moment I couldn't tell whether the noise came from behind or before me, so strange was the echo. It seemed to draw closer and closer, now from the front, now from the back, as if I had been surrounded on both sides by a shrieking mob.

Sulla lied, I thought. *My house on the hill is in flames. Bethesda has been raped and murdered. Now his hired rabble have trapped me in the Narrows. They will beat me with sticks. They will tear my body apart. Gordianus the Finder will vanish from the earth and no one will know or care except his enemies, who will soon forget.*

The noise became shrill and deafening. It came from behind me. The voices I heard were not the voices of men, but of boys. At that moment they appeared around a bend in the Narrows, smiling, screaming, laughing, and waving sticks, tripping over one another as they careened against the walls.

They were chasing another boy, smaller than the rest and dressed in a blur of filthy rags, who ran headlong against me and burrowed into my tunic as if I were a tower where he might hide himself.

His pursuers skittered to a halt, tripping against one another, still screaming and laughing and beating their sticks against the walls. 'He's ours!' one of them yelled at me in a shrill voice. 'Hasn't got a family hasn't got a tongue!'

'His own mother left him,' yelled another. 'He's no better than a slave. Give him back! We were just having some fun with him.'

'Fun!' cried the first. 'Especially the noises he makes! Hit him hard until he tries to cry "stop," and only a croak comes out!'

I looked down at the squirming mass of rags and sinew in my arms. The child looked up at me, fearful, doubting, suddenly jubilant when he recognized me. It was the mute boy, Eco, abandoned by the widow Polia.

I looked up at the shrill, screaming gang of boys. Something monstrous must have passed across my face; the nearest of them backed away and blanched as I gently thrust Eco aside. Some of the boys looked frightened. Others looked surly and ready for a fight.

I reached into my tunic, where I had never ceased to carry his knife, day by day, since the hour he had given it to me. *He thinks we bring justice, Tiro.* I pulled it out. The boys opened their eyes wide and tripped over one another in a rush to escape. I heard them for a long time, laughing, screaming, and raking their sticks against the walls as they retreated.

Eco reached up, grasping for the handle. I let him take it. There were still a few flecks of Mallius Glaucia's blood on the blade. Eco saw them and squealed with satisfaction.

He looked up at me inquiringly with a grimace on his dirty face as he pantomimed stabbing the air. I nodded my head.

'Yes,' I whispered, 'your revenge. With your dagger and my own hand I avenged you.' He stared at the blade and parted his lips in a thrill of rapture.

Mallius Glaucia had been one of the men who raped his mother; now Glaucia was dead by the mute boy's blade. What matter that I would never have killed Glaucia had I any other choice, not even for the boy's sake? What matter that Glaucia – giant, lumbering, blood-mad Glaucia – was only a dwarf among giants compared to the Roscii? Or that the Roscii were only children in the lap of a man like Chrysogonus? Or that Chrysogonus was but a toy for Lucius Sulla? Or that Sulla was only an unravelled thread in the gold and blood-red scheme that had been woven for centuries by families like the Metelli, who by their tireless plotting could rightfully claim to have made Rome everything it was today? In their Republic even a tongueless beggar boy could have pretensions to Roman dignity, and the sight of a petty criminal's blood on his very own blade made him squeal with excitement. Had I delivered the head of Sulla on a platter, the child could not have been more pleased.

I reached into my purse and offered him a coin, but he ignored it, clasping his knife with both hands and dancing in a circle around it. I slipped the coin back into my purse and turned away.

I had walked only a few steps before I stopped and looked back. The boy stood as still as a statue, clutching his dagger and looking after me with solemn eyes. We stared at each other for a long moment. Finally I extended my hand, and Eco came running.

We walked through the Narrows hand in hand, down the crowded Subura Way and up the narrow path. When I stepped into my house, I shouted to Bethesda that there would be another mouth to feed.

AUTHOR'S NOTE

Readers of historical novels who habitually read the afterword ahead of the text should know that *Roman Blood* is also a mystery; certain matters germane to its solution are discussed here, if only obliquely. *Caveat lector.*

Our chief sources for the life of Sulla are Plutarch's biography, which is typically full of gossip, scandal, and hocus pocus – in other words, a good read – and Sallust's *Bellum Iugurthinum* (Jugurthine War), which recounts Sulla's African exploits with Kiplingesque verve. There are also numerous references in the works of contemporary Republican writers, especially Cicero, who seems never to have tired of holding up Sulla as a symbol of vice against whom the standard-bearer of virtue (Cicero) could be compared. Sulla's own autobiography is lost, a cause for some regret. Given what we know of his character, it seems unlikely that his memoirs could have been as spellbinding as those of Caesar or as unconsciously revealing as those of Cicero, but they must surely have been more lively and more literate than those of our own political leaders.

For the trial of Sextus Roscius, we have the text of Cicero's defence. It is a long document, and to the extent that I have compressed and adapted it, I do not feel I have taken any undue liberties. Historians agree that Cicero's original, spoken orations by no means corresponded exactly to the published versions handed down to us, which Cicero (and Tiro) revised and embellished after the fact, often for political purposes. There is considerable doubt, for example, that certain satirical jabs at Sulla found in the written text of the *Pro Sexto Roscio Amerino* would actually have been spoken from the Rostra while the dictator was still alive. However, certain of Cicero's rhetorical flourishes, as reproduced here, are absolutely authentic; I would never have dared to invent the melodramatic 'by Hercules!' to which Cicero resorted more frequently in his own writings than I have allowed him to do in *Roman Blood*.

The known details of the murder case are all supplied by Cicero; the prosecutor's speech has not survived and its main points can only be inferred from Cicero's rebuttals. In drawing certain conclusions about innocence and guilt that go beyond the judgment of the original court, I have gone out on a limb, but not, I think, unreasonably far. Cicero was not above defending a guilty client; he could take considerable pride in doing so and could boast, as he did after the trial of Cluentius, of having thrown dust in the judges' eyes. Curiously, he speaks on the issue of defending guilty men in his treatise *De Officiis* (On Duties), and almost immediately (consciously or unconsciously) brings up the matter of Sextus Roscius.

But there is no need, on the other hand, to have any scruples about defending a person who is guilty – provided that he is not really a depraved or wicked character. For popular sentiment requires this; it is sanctioned by custom and conforms with human decency. The judges' business, in every trial, is to discover the truth. As for the counsel, however, he may on occasion have to base his advocacy on points which *look like* the truth, even if they do not correspond with it exactly. But I confess I should not have the nerve to be saying such things, especially in a philosophical treatise, unless Panaetius, the most authoritative of Stoics, had spoken to the same effect. The greatest renown, the profoundest gratitude, is won by speeches defending people. These considerations particularly apply when, as sometimes happens, the defendant is evidently the victim of oppression and persecution at the hands of some powerful and formidable personage. That is the sort of case I have often taken on. For example, when I was young, I spoke up for Sextus Roscius of

Ameria against the tyrannical might of the dictator Sulla.

Cicero is best read between the lines, especially when he hammers hardest upon his own boldness and sincerity.

As for the high-level intrigue behind the trial, I have taken some cues from ideas in Arthur D. Kahn's monumentally detailed *The Education of Julius Caesar* (Schocken Books, 1986), a radically revisionist view of political wheeling and dealing in the late Roman Republic as seen from the perspective of a citizen-survivor of the Republic of McCarthy, Nixon, Reagan, *et alia*. I should also mention the prolific Michal Grant, whose translation of Cicero's *Murder Trials* (Penguin Books, 1975) first set me on the trail of Sextus Roscius.

Metrobius's song in chapter 26 is original. The anonymous ditty about sundials (chapter 9) and the passage from Euripides (chapter 33) are my own adaptations.

'Every detective story writer makes mistakes, of course, and none will ever know so much as he should.' Raymond Chandler's dictum is doubly true when the setting is historical. I want to thank all those who helped to eliminate anachronisms from the original manuscript, including my brother Ronald Saylor, an expert on ancient glassware; a certain classicist who prefers to be anonymous; and the attentive copy editors at St Martin's Press. My thanks also to Pat Urquhart, who gave technical advice on the map; Scott Winnett, for his practical advice on publishing in the mystery genre; John Preston, who appeared like a *deus ex machina* when the manuscript was finished and literally whisked it into the right hands; Terri Odom, who helped batten the hatches on the *Roman* galleys; and my erudite editor, Michael Denneny.

A final acknowledgment: to my friend Penni Kimmel, a perceptive student of mysteries modern, not ancient, who meticulously studied my first draft and delivered invaluable oracles in the form of yellow Post-its. Without her sybilline interventions, a wretched girl might have needlessly suffered, a wicked man might have gone unpunished, and a lost boy might have wandered silent and lonely forever in the dark, dingy alleys of the Subura. *Culpam poena premit comes*; but also, *miseris succurrere disco*. Or in plain English: punishment follows hard on crime, yet I learn to comfort the wretched.

ABOUT THE AUTHOR

Steven Saylor's fascination with Ancient Rome began at the age of eight, when he saw a censored print of *Cleopatra* at a drive-in theatre outside Goldthwaite, Texas. He studied history at the University of Texas at Austin before becoming a newspaper and magazine editor in San Francisco. His stories and essays have appeared in *The Threepenny Review*, the *San Francisco Bay Guardian*, and *The Magazine of Fantasy & Science Fiction*. *Roman Blood* is his first novel.

Steven Saylor Roma sub Rosa Series

No. of copies	Title	Price (incl. p&p)	Total
	Roman Blood	£6.99	
	The House of Vestals	£6.99	
	The Gladiator Only Dies Once	£6.99	
	Arms of Nemesis	£6.99	
	Catilina's Riddle	£6.99	
	The Venus Throw	£6.99	
	The Murder on the Appian Way	£6.99	
	Rubicon	£6.99	
	Last Seen in Massilia	£6.99	
	A Mist of Prophecies	£6.99	
	The Judgement of Caesar		
	Grand Total		£.

Name: _____

Address: _____

_____ Postcode: _____

Daytime Tel. No. / Email _____
(in case of query)

Three ways to pay:

1. **For express service telephone the TBS order line on 01206 255 800 and quote 'SAY'. Order lines are open Monday – Friday 8:30am – 5:30pm**

2. I enclose a cheque made payable to **TBS Ltd** for £_____

3. Please charge my ☐ Visa ☐ Mastercard ☐ Amex ☐ Switch (switch issue no._____) £_____

   Card number: _____

   Expiry date: _____ Signature _____
   (your signature is essential when paying by credit card)

Please return forms *(no stamp required)* to, FREEPOST RLUL–SJGC–SGKJ, Cash Sales/Direct Mail Dept, The Book Service, Colchester Road, Frating, Colchester CO7 7DW.

Enquiries to readers@constablerobinson.com.
www.constablerobinson.com

Constable and Robinson Ltd (directly or via its agents) may mail, email or phone you about promotions or products. ☐ Tick box if you do not want these from us ☐ or our subsidiaries.